Faces in the Fire

14 Intriguing Short Stories
and
Thou Shalt Be Mine

Steven Hagy

WingSpan Press

Published in the United States and the United Kingdom by WingSpan Press, Livermore, CA

The WingSpan name, logo and colophon are the trademarks of WingSpan Publishing.

ISBN 978-1-59594-559-4 (pbk.)
ISBN 978-1-59594-894-6 (ebk.)

First edition 2015

Printed in the United States of America

www.wingspanpress.com

Library of Congress Control Number 2015936303

Cover Design: David Mellish designinc45@yahoo.com
Story Consultant: Craig Barnett
Doce Robles Winery (Paso Robles, Ca.): Wonderful friends, great wines, a heavenly vineyard, and an inspiring place to write.

CONTENTS

The fires of life consume a man,
leaving bare his soul.
A verdict, indeed, must follow;
righteous or wicked?

TO MY SONS,
GARY, KEVIN, AND JEFFREY

Stoke the fire
of your spirit
to burn hot
so that others
in their darkest
and coldest hour
may see a
flame of hope
and feel the
warmth of your
compassion.

THE DISAPPEARANCE OF CHESTER RAY

Larlene's husband, Chester Ray, disappeared. Speaking in an Ozarkian accent soft as summer rain, she told the two police officers standing on her front porch, "Last time I seen Chester Ray, he was sittin' over there on his filthy side of the sofa. All he had on were them tacky, orange gym trunks layin' right there on the couch where he left 'em. His stinky, dirty feet were propped up on the coffee table and he knows how I hate that 'cause, we eat supper off that table. He was watchin' football and ever'time them Titans made a good play, his whoohoohollerin' or, if they made a bad play, his cussin' rattled this house, givin' me the most god-awfullest headache. I was doin' the warsh like I do every Sunday afternoon, yankin' his work clothes out of the warsher and hangin' 'em up on the clothes line 'cause the dang dryer's been broke for six months. I could call out a repairman, but don't, 'cause if I did, Chester Ray would get all butt-hurt, then furious, feelin' like less of a man. I'd say it was quarter past three when I was done with the warsh. I started out the door to take my seven-year-old boy, Michael Jay and my baby girl, Trista Jo, she's five, down to the Wal-Mart to do some shoppin' for

1

school clothes when Chester Ray, on his twelfth beer and last cigarette, hollered at me to pick up another twelve pack and a carton of smokes. Just before I shut the door, he hollered again, 'and dammit, Larlene, make it quick!' He gets all irate when he loses his buzz. Anyway, I drove that eyesore of an El Camino parked there under the carport. As always, it took a few dozen cranks to start and lordy how that fan belt squealed all the way to the store and back. It's flat-out embarassin'. I done ask 'im a hunnerd times to fix it, but he won't; he wants me to suffer right along with 'im. I went dreckly to the store and bought clothes for both kids, but didn't have 'em try 'em on, on account I had to rush home to keep Chester Ray in a good mood. If the clothes didn't fit, I'd return 'em later. On the way back, I swung by Boozie's liquor store down on the corner."

The police officers, officer Daughtry, a womanly man with delicate features, short and thin in a tight fitting uniform and sergeant Raff, a manly woman with a paunchy gut, rugged looks, a no-nonsense fem-mullet, and no make-up, also taller and twenty-years older than Daughtry, were listening patiently to Larlene; yet, all the while she rattled on, Daughtry, a high school classmate of Larlene's was thinking, how different she looked now, compared to seven years ago.

Back then, when Ricky Dee Daughtry wore a MacGyver mullet instead of his current buzz cut and he had a heart-hammering crush on Larlene, she was as cute as a kindergarten cupcake with lively make-up, playful blue eyes, a Tinkerbelle nose, and a Disney smile. Closer-to-God-than-you bangs and peek-a-boo ears flaunting big hoop earrings accented her teased, mile-high, sandy-blonde hair. Though she was bit shorter than average, she was thickset with wide hips and muscular thighs making her one of two rah-rahs who flipped another in the air to catch. In her senior year, before her teen pregnancy, she dressed fashionably, mostly wearing *Fer-Sure* off-the-shoulder tops, tight stonewashed jeans, and white, high top, *LA Gears* with purple laces. Spunky, she sparkled with school spirit, shared a generous smile, and chattered with anyone who would listen.

Now, at twenty-five, after birthing two kids, her hips and thighs were bigger with a bigger butt riding shotgun, so she wore way-big, pink sweatpants, a roomy, yellow *American Idol* T-shirt, and purple flip-flops matching purple toenails. She pulled her shoulder-length hair back into a messy ponytail, exposing her ears looking like side mirrors on a Winnebago. Standing there without make-up and chattering like she was, she was still cute as a cupcake, though one with very little icing and no candy sprinkles. She just looked and sounded so horribly downtrodden from a duty-bound marriage to an alcoholic felon who had years ago extinguished her smile, sparkle, and spunk.

When Daughtry heard that had she swung by Boozie's with her kids, he snapped out of his thoughts and asked, "So you stopped by the liquor store with your youngsters?"

"Yes, I did," replied Larlene soberly, "and I'll say this about that. I don't like buyin' liquor and cigarettes in front of my young'uns. It bothers me to the core and I ain't no bad mother, but bad as I hate to, if I came home without no beer and smokes, the fight with Chester Ray would be worse on us than me teachin' 'em bad habits. I wish he'd drive his own dang self to the liquor store, but as you two officers know, his license got revoked and with another DUI, he'll go straight back to prison. Not only that, I know how he gets when he's been drinkin'. Ever' little thang riles 'im, 'specially no beer and no cigarettes. The man has a burr in his butt, 'cause he didn't amount to much after high school and frankly, he never will. He knows it and he knows I know it; heck, ever'body knows it. Sure, back in high school, he was cool with all his drinkin' buddies, but that was it—cool with all his drinkin' buddies. Nothin' else. Course, he still drinks, but he ain't cool no more. The bad thang is, is when he gets all tore up from too many beers, his eyes get all red and wild, and then he gets all out threatenin', pickin' on me and the kids. Officer Raff, you know. You've been out here 'nuff times. It's the same ever'time, ain't it? Chester Ray might be short as a fireplug and skinny as a cue stick, but he's as mean as a constipated Pit bull. More than that, he's scary with that shaved head of his and all them brotherhood tats he got doin' time. Course, I call ya'll to come out and I know I should press charges, but I don't, 'cause either way, I'll most likely wind up with a black eye, a split lip, and traumatized kids; and if I threaten to leave 'im, he threatens to hurt my babies. God knows there are many times, I wish he'd just get gone, but don't get no wrong ideas, I didn't have nothin' to do with him disappearin'. Anyway, when me and the kids got home, I come in through the carport and into the kitchen. The kids ran to their room to try on their new clothes, while I popped open a beer for Chester Ray and put the rest of 'em in the fridge, then brung him that beer and a pack of cigarettes. He wasn't on the couch, but like I already told ya, his disgustin' gym trunks were. It sure was odd his drawers just layin' there where he'd been sittin' and it sure ain't no good thang if he's poop-faced and runnin' 'round butt-nekkid. I figured maybe he was drivin' the porcelain bus, you know, on the toilet, so I checked the bathroom. Not there. He weren't in the kid's room neither. When he gets hammered, he likes to take, as he says, 'a big dog leak' outside, so I checked the back yard. Weren't there, so I went out front and looked everwhichaways. Nope, weren't there and not passed out on the lawn neither. I thought, well, he's got to be somewheres; he must be down the street at Dwayne's, one of his co-workers. When he's there, all they do is smoke one fat bowl after another while listen' to Kid Rock."

Officer Raff interrupted, "Whoa, Larlene, if Chester Ray's smokin' marijuana, then, we've got a parole violation here."

Daughtry added, "Yea, we sure do, so we're gonna need to

find Chester Ray for a drug test. We'll drop in on this Dwayne character too, to see what he's up to and how much he's up to it."

"Well, y'all go ahead," said Larlene, "and do what y'all gotta do. So anyway, I told my young'uns, I'd be right back and footed it down to Dwayne's. Chester Ray wasn't there neither, but that idiot Dwayne, who's flat-out disgustin' was. I seen 'im peepin' out the winda blinds, then, before I could blink, he yanked open the door, scaring the bejeebers outta me. I'm beside myself still wonderin' how he got from the winda to the door so lightnin' fast. He stood there, stick skinny, wearing no shirt and no shoes in only his Budweiser boxers, and his stupid whacky-tabacky smile sportin' all of his five teeth. 'Fore I could say a word, he exhaled a big bong hit right in my face and then, the de-generate asks me in to do the humpty-bumpty. I told 'im, 'Sure Dwayne, when a frog grows wings so it don't bump its butt when it hops or when your skanky girlfriend, Candy quits crack. Neither never gonna happen.' Then, I left. When I got back home, I called all of Chester Ray's kin, well only the few he still speaks to, and no one seen 'im. I waited a little while and then called the police."

The two officers checked the premises from front to back without finding any clues to the whereabouts of Chester Ray. Ready to leave, standing out on the front lawn, officer Daughtry said in his effeminate, yet commanding voice, "Larlene, if you'll recall, I went to high school with you and Chester Ray. He's the reason why I'm in law enforcement. There never wasn't a day when Chester Ray didn't tease me, beat me up, and stuff me in a trashcan. I got this badge and a weapon now, and just so you know, if he ever tries it again, I'll shoot 'im."

"Yeah, sure, Ricky Dee, I 'member you. You were a nice boy and I'm sure sorry he bullied you like that. The truth is, I wouldn't blame you if you did shoot 'im and just so you know, a lot of folks have a mind to if they get the chance."

Officer Raff, speaking in a surly voice loaded with

aggravation, said, "Larlene, I've had many encounters with Chester Ray Rascoe, not just here at your house and 'round town over the years, but way back when I first got my badge. When Chester Ray was just a kid at Ledford Elementary, I arrested him three times. Once, when he burned down ol' man Traxton's shed, the second time when he was shopliftin' cigarettes down at Boozie's, and again for shootin' out Mayor Branson's car windows with a BB gun. Chester Ray is down right no good. We'd all be lucky if he did just disappear. Well, we gotta get to another call. Your husband will most likely show up in the mornin'. In the meanwhile, we'll keep an eye out for 'im. Now if he comes home all crazy drunk and starts raisin' hell, you call us and we'll be here right quick."

The officers sped away in their cruiser. The nosey neighbors dawdling around the front yard left disappointed. They were hoping for something scandalous to happen so they could be an eyewitness on the eleven-o-clock news.

Larlene cleaned up after Chester Ray, throwing away his empty beer cans and dumping the ashtray. She checked on Michael Jay and Trista Jo. Their new clothes looked good and fit fine. With Chester Ray gone, all the tension in the house was gone, so the kids got along and didn't fight. To keep her mind off her husband and wondering what kind of trouble he was getting into, she took the kids to Bucky's Burgers for supper.

She told them, "Kids, your daddy's done disappeared."

They asked, "How?"

She said, "Don't know."

They wondered out loud, "Mama, when's he comin' back?"

She replied, "Don't know that neither."

It didn't bother them much, because they smiled a lot and seemed thrilled with every bite of their Bucky's Big Dawg Bacon Burger and every Curlicue Fun Fry they dipped in ketchup swirled with chipotle mustard. Still sipping milkshakes, they returned home. They watched a few shows on TV, programs that Chester Ray dubbed 'ignorant' and never let them watch, then Larlene tucked the youngsters into bed. For a second time, she went out front and peered up and down the street: no Chester Ray staggering home. The night air felt good; still humid, but a bit cooler. Even the full moon acting as a giant search light couldn't find him. She sat in a plastic lawn chair and waited. After ten minutes of watching fireflies and hearing crickets, she went back inside, washed her face, brushed her teeth, changed into her pajamas, and climbed into bed.

She couldn't fall asleep. Where was Chester Ray and would he ever come home? If and when he did, no doubt he'd be falling down drunk and reeking of beer, cigarettes, and weed. Would he be bad-tempered or pretend sweet? She never knew. It all depended on whether his buzz was on or gone. Either way, he'd demand sex. No kind words, romance, or gentle touches; just sex. The only good thing about sex with Chester Ray—it didn't last more than half a minute.

She lay on her back in the dark with the moon peeping in her open window. Two buzzing June bugs clung to the window screen. A Dixie-sized daddy-longlegs tiptoed across the windowsill. Wide awake, she stared up at the clicking, wobbling ceiling fan. Her mind whirred along with it, asking herself: how in the world did I wind up with such a deadbeat like Chester Ray? Back in high school I was pretty, well mannered, and on the cheerleadin' squad. In our yearbook, my classmates voted me, 'Best Smile'. I earned good grades with dreams of being a dental hygienist. That fateful night, ohhh that awful fateful night when I met Chester Ray at that after game party. He was sort-a cute and kind-a cool, bein' reckless; dangerous. I should've heeded mama's warnin's. Ever' time mama spotted him, she told me, 'You see that boy, that no-good Chester Ray Rascoe hangin' out in front of Boozie's, hopin' someone'll buy him beer? Well, do ya? You keep a good distance from the likes of him. You hear? If'n you see 'im, you skedaddle right then and there.' Why didn't I listen to mama? Of course, I ignored her, thinkin' that chattin' with Chester Ray at that party was no big thang. Weren't long, with all his swagger, he had introduced me to rum'n cokes and smokin' pot. I barely 'member, or maybe I'm tryin' to forget, but we wound up in a sleepin' bag on top of an old mattress in the bed of his El Camino. I told him 'no' a hunnerd times; nonetheless, he finally had his way with me. He said he'd 'pull out' but of course, he didn't. Next thing I know'd, four months before graduation, I'm expectin' a baby. We graduated; him just barely, 'cause I did all his homework. We got married two months before Michael Jay was born. No wedding, just a quick trip to the courthouse. Chester Ray's Uncle Wade got him a job at the waste treatment plant. From that point on, his drinkin' and takin' drugs, the arguments, verbal and physical abuse, and cussin' in front of the children got worse. I wound up with a never-ending headache and on-going stomach cramps. Despite him tellin' me for the seven-and-a-half years of our marriage that, I'm 'fat, ugly, and stupid,' I still believe in myself. I can survive without that jerk. Yes, I can, and with a better life too. If he never comes home, I'll find a job, pay the bills, and take care of my children. In fact, raisin' 'em would be easier without all his bad habits and awful attitude.

"I hate my life," she whispered, afraid that Chester Ray might be lurking nearby to hear her, "and I hope you stay gone, Chester Ray—gone forever."

With her mind reeling, there was no way she could fall asleep, so she climbed out of bed, put on her pink terrycloth robe and white fluffy slippers, and went into the kitchen for a bowl of Froot Loops. She flipped on the light, then gasped, jumping back startled to see a huge cockroach scurrying across the yellow linoleum countertop. Though quick as roaches are, she saw it hide behind the coffee maker. She pulled off a slipper and gripped it in her hand with the intention of quickly sliding the coffee maker away from the wall and squashing the surprised bug. She took a step toward the appliance when the grotesque insect dashed out from behind it, stopped, stared up at her, and twitched its antennae. Like most cockroaches, it was shiny reddish brown with a yellowish margin on its body region behind its head, yet this roach was a bit bigger than most. She took another step closer to smash it, but to her shock and horror, the roach stood up on its bristly hind legs and sounding exactly like Chester Ray, the big, ugly bug shouted, "Larlene, where's my beer and smokes?"

Larlene put her hand over her mouth, trembled a bit, and stuttered, "Chester Ray, is—is that you?—a—a cockroach?"

"Duhhh, Larleeeene, you think any other cockroach could speak to you. You're so damn dumb."

"I'm just in—in shock. You're—you're a—a bug. What—what happened?"

"I don't know what happened, but I do know it's too dang bright in here. Out that damn kitchen light and turn on that little light over the stove. Come on, Larlene—make it quick! Now, I was kickin' back on the sofa watchin' football and wonderin' what in the hell was takin' you so dang long when the next thang I know'd, I'm crawlin' 'round down by the skid marks in my gym trunks. I have no idea why. It just happened. I made my way out of 'em, off the couch, across the floor, and into the kitchen. When I finally got in here, I climbed up the cabinet to be on this here countertop. While up here, I heard you badmouthin' me to the cops. I'm still pissed-off about it, but before I learn you on how things really are, I cain't believe that whimpy-ass Daughtry is a cop and that old she-he Raff ain't retired yet. I sure miss kickin' his ass and out runnin' her. Okay, now, to tell you like it is—I drink and cain't get nowheres 'cause you and 'em kids ruint my life. Another thang, I heard you say that Dwayne was hittin' on you, so he's got an ass-whoopin' comin'. As for you callin' 'round lookin' for me—it ain't none of your damn bus'ness what the hell I do and where the hell I go. You got that? Do you? Somethin' else, I seen you and the kids come home from the store, leave again, and come back sippin' Bucky shakes. Now, Larlene, did it ever cross your itty-bitty mind that I might be home and that I might be hungry too? Did it? I mean, maybe you should have brung me a #5 combo—you know, like I always order—a Backfire Jalapeño Burger, a basket of Fun Fries, and a forty-four ounce Orangy drink. You think maybe you could've 'membered your husband? Ohhh, hell nooo! 'Cause, I ain't important; and then, to make me more madder, you, like sprayin' lighter fluid on a fire, turned on them ignorant TV shows that I told you, you ain't allowed to watch in my house. Dammit Larlene! You're worthless! Anyway, stop standin' there gawkin' at me like you're brain damaged and pour me some beer in a saucer, bring the ashtray over and light me a cigarette, and cook me one of them frozen pizzas—and dammit, Larlene, make it quick! I done lost my buzz!"

Still in a state of shock, Larlene just stood there staring at him while he scratched his bug butt with a bristly leg.

"Larlene, you ain't doin' what I told you, so why don't you go look in the mirror at that scar on your lip and see if you 'member the last time you didn't do what I told you to do."

"But Chester Ray—you cain't be no cockroach. You got work in the mornin'. We got bills to pay."

"To hell with work and bills! I ain't slavin' no more around all the crap that spews out of people's toilets and drains. The way I see it, that stinky sewage is most likely what turned me into a roach. Anyhow, you're goin' to have to step up and getta job. Another thang, I'm gettin' horny, so later on you're gonna let me have a little fun crawlin' all over your body. You hearin' me? We're goin' to get nasty! No way you're gonna deny me. You been a nothin' wife and a nothin' mother and while we're talkin' here, you're fat, ugly, and stupid! Don't you ever forget that! And don't forget neither—I might be a cockroach, but I'm still the man of this here house."

Larlene shuttered at the thought of his hairy spindly legs touching her skin, put the thought out of her mind, and said, "Please, Chester Ray, what about your son and daughter?"

"Them kids are spoilt brats! I ain't got no use for 'em. Oh, and just so ya'know, durin' the few hours I've been here, I made me a whole bunch of friends. They think I'm cool, 'cause I know where all the eats are and I got you to fetch 'em for me, which reminds me, right now, it's party time!" He let out a loud hiss and as he did, hundreds of cockroaches scurried out of cracks in the walls, dropped out of cupboards, and climbed out from under the sink. Every cockroach in the neighborhood gathered on the countertop and surrounded their cool party host. Some of the insects were afraid of Larlene and hissed.

Chester Ray hissed back at them and then said to Larlene, "I told 'em you ain't nothin' to fear. You're so weak and pathetic you couldn't even kill a bug. Now, brang us beer! Light us a cigarette! Get to cookin' that pizza! And dammit, Larlene, make it quick!"

Larlene turned like always, to do as Chester Ray ordered, but stopped as awful feelings welled up inside her. She felt angry for not standing up to Chester Ray, depressed for giving up her dreams for him, and regretful that she put up with his abuse for so long and now—now she was taking orders from Chester Ray, the cockroach. Her head throbbed, her stomach churned, and she felt nauseous. She began to tremble, like everything she held tightly inside was shaking loose. She turned to face Chester Ray, gripped her slipper so tight her knuckles turned white, and after a flash of utmost exasperation, she screamed; a shrieking, fed-up scream which started at the soles of her feet and picked up volume all the way up through her gut until it burst out her mouth, "Chester Ray, you're a horrible husband, a mean father, and a total failure as a man! It's no wonder you're a cockroach! It fits you! I don't want to live like this no more! I won't live like this no more!" She lunged at Chester Ray, raised her slipper, and swung it down hard with a loud whack! All the roaches except the one under her slipper scattered. She swept Chester Ray into the sink, flipped on the garbage disposal, and washed all of his pieces down the drain.

Still breathing heavy from her fit of rage and struggling to grasp what had just happened, she watched the water swirl and swirl until her heartbeat, breathing, and emotions returned to normal. Calm now, yet now in a daze, she turned off the water, slipped on her slipper, left the sink, opened a cabinet for a bowl, and slid out a drawer for a spoon. There was not a cockroach in sight. She poured Froot Loops in the bowl along with milk, sat at the kitchen table, and ate her cereal, taking slow, crunchy bites. When she ate the last floating green loop and slurped down the milk, she put the bowl and spoon in the sink. One more time, she peered at the drain, fearful she would see creepy bug legs climbing out of the disposal's rubber splashguard. Seeing nothing, she shrugged her shoulders followed by a smirk that flashed into a smile, which burst into giggles. After shutting off the stove light, she peeked in on her sleeping children, and then went to bed where she fell fast asleep.

That next day, she called the pest man to come out and he exterminated every ant, bedbug, earwig, flea, silverfish, spider, termite, tick, weevil, and of course every single cockroach in, around, and within a hundred feet of her house.

That afternoon, she met her youngsters at the bus stop and while walking home, she told them, "Kids, I'm gonna tell you again, so listen up. You're daddy's lost and most likely, ain't gonna be found."

They didn't shed a tear or say a word about it, but, hearing the ice cream truck blaring, Pop Goes the Weasel and seeing the vehicle turn up their street, they both asked excitedly, "Please mama, can we get an ice cream?"

Larlene enjoyed a Fudgsicle. The youngsters each ate a choclitty, peanuty Drumstick.

That next week, she got a job at the Wal-Mart. The next month, she had the dryer and the El Camino fixed. The month after that, she filed for divorce. Three months passed and she started school to be a dental hygienist. Six months had gone by and the divorce was final. During that time, she slimmed down and bought herself a makeover. Right around then, on her way home from work, she saw a flashing police car in front of Dwayne's house. Driving by slowly, she watched as officers Raff and Daughtry shoved Dwayne, handcuffed and still wearing only his boxers, into the back seat of the police car. His tweaker-thin, girlfriend Candy, also handcuffed, followed in right behind him. Daughtry grinned and waved at Larlene. Not long after that, she started dating officer, Ricky Dee Daughtry. He had loved her since high school and loved her still. She fell fast in love with him. Though short with delicate features, he was ten times the man of Chester Ray. He was wonderful with Michael Jay and Trista Jo, and they were happy with him. Larlene and her kids had never felt so loved and so safe. After another six months, he asked her to marry him and she eagerly accepted. A few months later, they were married. They held the wedding at the church they had recently joined and all their family and friends attended. Her delighted mother babysitted the kids while Larlene and Ricky Dee honeymooned in Hawaii.

Chester Ray, as far as anyone knew, just disappeared.

BEAN

My name is Joey; Joey Garbonzo. Yeah, like the bean. My family—they call me Joey; the regulars comin' in—they call me, "Bean." I don't mind it. When folks call you a nickname, they like you. Am I right? I wanna tell you somethin' crazy and I'm gonna tell you like I'm talkin' to the Pope, like I'm kneelin' down kissin' his ring, you know, I'm gonna tell you the truth.

I've worked at Carpelli's bar down here on the northeast corner of 10th and 42nd for thirty years. It's hard to believe, three freakin' decades. Started at twenty-five. Where'd my life go? Huh? Where the hell did it go? Look at me. The customers, they razz me, sayin' I'm a Nicky Newark, you know, 'cause I dress fashionably. Just because my salt and pepper hair is slicked back and I wear a polyester shirt unbuttoned halfway so's to show off my gold chain, that don't mean I'm some wise-guy from Jersey. The way I see it, at my age, I'm a good-lookin' link of sausage even though I smell like Brasso and gotta dicky-do—a dicky-do? You know, a dicky-do, 'cause I eat a lotta pasta, my stomach sticks out farther than my dicky do. Hey, whatever. I am what I am. It is what it is. Kay-say-rah-say-rah.

Back in my younger days, I used to box; I was in good shape; could've been a contender; could've been somebody.

14

Right? Nah—got my brains knocked out. I got out of the ring before I got punched ugly. Only scar I got is right here over my left eye when in the fifth round, Jimmy 'Knuckles' Baroni sucker punched me after his 3-2 combination had my manager throwin' in the towel. Hey, I did my best, but my best was like Knuckles snackin' on a bocconotto cream puff.

All these years mixin' drinks; that's what I do; pour a little of this, pour a little that; a shot of this; a shot of that; toss in an olive, a cherry, a lemon wedge or a lime twist, then, badda bing badda boom serve it on the rocks. I don't think there's a concoction out there I haven't mixed. I even invented one. Yeah, you got it, it's called, The Bean. What's in it? Rum. What else is in it? Not tellin'. It's sweet, sour, and little salty, and will punch you in the face, knock you off your bar stool, kick you out to the curb, and stuff you into the backseat of a cab. That's all you need to know.

This dump here; this dump used to be a nice place; real nice with high class customers. We had celebrations, you know, like birthdays, anniversaries, or some shmuck gets a promotion, but now, look at it; it's a dive. The place is old and out of style, yet it's clean 'cause I keep it that way. It wouldn't be so bad, if the boss, Tony 'Big Shoes' Carpelli, would spend a freakin' dime or two on paint, upholstery, and a few new bathroom fixtures. If'n he did, maybe we would be happenin' again; however, I got no beef with Tony. He's mostly a good guy.

Years ago, the customers were real people; people with faces. There was a time when I knew their names; though not anymore; yet, I still know what they drink and what they smoke, except now, I sort of see everyone as a gullet, you know, like everyone is just a throat, drinkin', slammin', chuggin', dumpin' booze down as if their throat was a sink drain. These people, these gullets, they drink to be someone different, you know, to come out of their shell from shy to bold; from scared to brave; from small to big; from seemin' righteous to bein' profane.

They drink to remember the good times or to forget the bad, to laugh when they can't laugh or cry when they can't cry, to, you know, to feel good when they feel rotten. I've heard all their sob stories. Somebody loves somebody who loves somebody who loves somebody else. Follow me? You're lookin' like the lights are on, but nobody's home, so just nod your head. Good. Okay, so I try to help them, you know, make them a strong drink, then listen to them gripe or whine. Then, I'll impart a few words of wisdom, but who am I? I'm just a bartender; got it?

So like I was sayin', I see 'gullets' who are mostly lonely guys drinkin', drownin' in their mistakes and misfortunes, but, this guy, this guy who came in that night—around eleven—this guy was no gullet. The last two throats had left so the place was empty when he shoves open the door and steps in escorted by an icy gust from the river. I glances up from washin' glasses and shiver. He was tall, maybe six-foot-two and dressed in black: black shirt, black tie, black suit coat and pants, black socks and black shoes and I'd wager ten to one, black boxers too. On his head and tilted down to shade his face, he wore a black fedora hat made of felt, you know like he was Sammie 'The Hat' Turatelli who bought a new hat every three years. A couple of days after Sammie disappeared, his last hat was found floatin' in the Hudson where he's most likely at the bottom, with his Salvatore Ferragamo loafers encased in concrete. I'll say this, dressin' in black ain't so strange, 'cause I do it all the time, you know, a lot of us goombahs do. How can I put it? Our Mediterranean features go good with it. I appreciate style, although, with him wearin' all black it seemed kind an odd that he wore gray gloves. So he sort of shuffles like his shoes are heavy over to the end of the bar where it's the darkest in an already dark place and he sits on a stool facin' the door. The red vinyl upholstery has a crack that pinches, so he grimaces, stands up, and moves over a stool. After he gets comfortable, he takes off his hat and sets it on the bar. I see that his wavy hair is jet black and slicked back which is okay too 'cause it's a sort of a neighborhood hair style. Without the shadow of his hat's brim, the neon light from the Jimmy Walker sign on the wall lights up his face and I got to tell you, the sight of it scared the Hell out of me, makin' me drop the beer mug I was washin' into the sink. It don't break; only bounces around a little.

Anyway, this guy, he looks to be in his mid-thirties and is almost good lookin', except his face is gray and drawn like my dead cousin Jimmi's face when he was layin' on a table at the morgue. The coroner yanked back the sheet and I had to identify his body. It was Jimmi. You see, Jimmi like a jamook got in with a couple of very tough cafones who ended their partnership with him by stickin' a sharp knife in his a-orta. *Che peccato.* What a pity. Jimmi was a good fella.

So this bizarro at the bar has the same skin color as cold, dead Jimmi after all his blood drained out. He doesn't have any wrinkles neither, so his face is not only gray, but also as smooth as putty. When he places his hands on the bar, I realize his gloves aren't gray; his hands are gray; gray like Uncle Dino's before Razzo 'The Mortician' Rossi, like an artist, touched them up beautifully and folded them nice like across my deceased uncle's chest. I notice that this guy's index finger on his right hand is encased in this long shiny thimble, lookin' to be silver with strange words and symbols engraved on it. At the time, I didn't know why he wore it. However, I found out later.

So I says to this strange person at my bar, I says, 'How you doin'?'

He doesn't say a word, just stares at me with his dark eyes which I glances away from 'cause they remind me of the eyes of ol' man Torello's dog. I'll elaborate. You see, the ol' man owned a drug store a few blocks down and around the corner. He leashed his dog, a black pit-bull named, Bruno to the cash register. If punk kids or seedy types tried to shop lift or start a hassle, ol' man Torello with a swipe of his hand would unleash

Bruno. If you even glanced at that dog when he was lookin' at
you, the crazy beast would attack, barkin', growlin', and barin'
it's teeth chompin' at the space between you and his sharp teeth.
I always carried exact change so's to get out quick. The only
way to rob ol' man Torello was to shoot the dog first—of course,
that's what happened—badda boom, boom, the dog's dead, ol'
man Torello's dead, and badda bing—the cash is gone.

I'm thinkin' that this peculiar individual sittin' at my bar
would appreciate a stiff shot of bourbon with a splash of soda
on the rocks, so I make it for him, place it front of him, and say,
'Hey, here's a drink—it's on the house.'

You see, I do what I do because it's best to get on the good
side of anybody lookin' as bad as him. There's somethin' I
know—a sayin' that 'Good Cop' Manfredi always says. He
says, 'anyone can die 'cause anyone can kill you anywhere,
anytime, for any reason'. I believe him.

So this weirdo looks down at his on-the-house drink, glances
up at me, which of course, I looks away, 'cause, like I said, his
eyes reminds me of ol' man Torello's dog, however, I see out
the corner of my eye that he pulls out a round gold watch from
his breast pocket and glances at it. This fine watch is so bright
and so shiny it's like he's peerin' into a spotlight and it not only
illuminates his face, it lights up the dark corner of the bar where
he's sittin'. His gray skin takes on a sort of golden glow.

So I says to him, 'Nice watch,' and then I asks him, 'You
waitin' on somebody?'

He don't say a word, so I try to be funny, which is not
smart unless you know for sure you'll getta laugh, and I says
to him, 'So you waitin' to do a certain job to a certain someone
at a certain time or maybe you're clockin' your pal robbin' the
liquor store across the street?'

He don't answer me. He drops the watch back in his breast
pocket so that his face turns back to gray and the corner goes
back to dark. His eyes, I swear, go black in their sockets and his

putty smooth forehead creases like my ol' man's did back when I was a teenager and he'd slap me around for stayin' out too late. Next, this pissed off guy grabs his drink, shoots it down, slams the glass on the bar, and stands up from his bar stool, then yanks off the silver thimble and thrusts this long naked index finger across the bar to stop about a half inch away from right between by eyes. You hearin' me? It's not a piece. It's a freakin' finger; and it's a half inch away from my face. I stare sort-a cross-eyed at his finger twitchin' in front of my forehead. If it had been a gun—I would've crapped myself; however, it's only a finger. His furious face is a bit scary; however, I ain't scared of no finger. You with me here? Good. Only later did I find out just how close I came to joinin' cousin Jimmi and ol' man Torello and his dog. I should'a been terrified of that finger with no thimble.

This guy, I'm thinkin' is *u pazzu*, you know crazy, so I says, whilst I back up a step, 'Hey, whoa, whoa, wait a minute fella. Sit down; let me pour you another drink. It's on the house too. You seem edgy. Come on, sit back down, and tell me what's got you wound so tight.'

He doesn't say nothin' as he slowly sits back on his stool and slides the thimble back on his finger. He places both his hands on the bar to steady himself and takes a few deep breaths to calm down.

I'm thinkin' he's got an anger problem like my Cousin Gino who's still doin' time over a lost game of pool, a broken cue stick, and a comatose pool player. Get the picture? So while I'm mixin' him the Bean, my signature drink, I hear him speak. I didn't expect it. Sort of startles me. His voice is monotone and dead serious remindin' me of a G-man out of a 1930s gangster movie and he fires his words like bullets out of a Tommy gun. You know, like rat-tat-tat-tat-tat. Anyway, I put the drink in front of him and he says, 'Thanks-for-the-drinks. Just-so-you-know, I-don't-have-a-cent.'

I think he's feelin' sort a bad for actin' psycho. Too, I'm thinkin', what's he doin' sittin' at my bar when he's got no dough? Whatever. I says to him, 'Hey, like I said, it's on the house. Fuhgeddaboutit.'

He clams up for a few seconds to where I can hear the Crown Royal clock tickin' on the wall behind me—and then, he shakes his head mumblin', 'I-can't-do-it. I-just-can't-do-it.'

Hey, I ain't no G-Man so enough of me talkin' all serious and fast like him. You got it? Rat-tat-tat. That's how he talks.

Okay, so I says to him, 'Hey, fella, people call me, Bean. So now, you know me. Tell me what it is—you can't do.'

Whilst he's thinkin' whether to tell me or not, I'm thinkin', his trouble involves a woman. Ninety-nine out of hundred times it's a girl who's the pain in the ass. The one time out of hundred when it's not—it's hemorrhoids. I try to help get his words rollin' so I ask him, 'You gotta name? He says to me, 'No' and I says, 'Okay, if you ain't tellin'—I doh wanna know. Just tell me pal, what it is—you can't do?'

He fidgets for a moment like a get-away driver parked in front of a heist or maybe like he did have hemorrhoids, then he says, 'You see—there's this girl.'

I knew it. It was a girl; a greedy ex-wife or a psycho girlfriend. Maybe, the love of his life—which really means: the best sex he ever had—dumped him.

So I say, 'What about her, this girl? Tell me. I'm listenin'.'

He says, 'You see, there's this girl. She's beautiful. Her face glows like an angel's.'

I'm thinkin' all girls glow when you first meet 'em; however, it don't take long for a guy to piss 'em off—and then there ain't no more glow—just overcast with a chance of snow.

So he continues strummin' his heart mandolin, tellin' me about her olive green eyes, delicate features, and heavenly smile. Stuff like that. I'm wonderin' how he's sittin' on the bar stool with cupid's arrow stickin' out his butt cheek.

He keeps blubberin' soundin' like some lovesick poet from the village sayin' somethin' like, 'ohhh, her long black hair flows over her shoulders like a waterfall at night reflectin' the radiance of the moon. And that she's a goddess of beauty and her scent is like the mornin' dew in a spring garden.' I'm askin' myself—is this weirdo for real? He's tough! He's scary! He's mushy? It don't add up. His sugary words are flarin' up my type-2 diabetes like I'm snackin' on Rocky 'The Baker' Marichini's sweet cannoli.

Next, he says he watches her when he's not workin'. He spies on her day and night, checkin' her out while she eats and sleeps, when she's at work or home, and while she dresses and undresses and … . I says, 'Whoa, hold on. Back it up. You peepin' in her window or what? Cause, that ain't cool.'

He ignores me and keeps rattlin' on as if I've got all night, which I don't. It's Tuesday; on Tuesdays, I close the joint at midnight. He keeps blabbin' how she's such a kind soul who works hard seven days a week to pay the bills for her mother and her little brother and how she rushes home every night to cook dinner, clean up the kitchen, and help her brother with his homework. When she ain't workin', cookin' or sleepin' she's paintin' beautiful portraits. He loves to watch her paint. It makes him feel good.

So I asks him, 'Does this gal, painter of portraits, gotta name?'

'Yes,' he tells me, 'her name is Angelica.'

I says, 'That's a beautiful name. My mother's name is Angelica. Go figure.' Then, I asks, 'Does Angelica know you watch her?'

He replies, 'Oh, nooo, she doesn't know I exist.' Then he tells me, that he stands in the shadows. He's a shadow in a shadow. No one knows he exists.

I says to him, thinkin' I'm smart, 'I'm seein' you.'

His comeback is, is that I see him only because he lets me

see him, because he needs my advice. 'Okay,' I says, 'So talk to me. The Royal Crown clock is tickin'. What can't you do? And, how can I help?'

So this black-suited strange-o rattles on to tell me and it goes somethin' like this. He met Angelica two years ago when she took her sick father to the park for sunshine and fresh air. The ol' man throws a few breadcrumbs to the quackin' ducks then has a killer stroke. My new acquaintance blabs on about how he has this job of dealin' with death. His work zone is the neighborhood around Carpelli's bar all the way down to the river. He calls it his 'Zone of Death', which makes me, think he's some sort of goon workin' for Don Maurizio Moretti. He knows what I'm thinkin', so he tells me that I gotta understand somethin', understand that he don't take lives, 'he *extracts* lives, lives *already taken.*' Just like Dino 'Stiletto' Salzano who used to come in for a couple of drinks after he did what he did. This brute was no fugazi; he was the real deal. I knew he did what he did, because the next day, the newspaper reported somebody went missin'. I overheard Dino talkin' one night to another made guy. He said that he never chose who got whacked—he just followed orders. The order came first and at that very moment when it did—they were already dead. You follow me? Dino just made sure they didn't walk, talk, and breath no more. Same sort of situation for 'no name' at my bar.

So this shadowy man of death tells me what he does is just a job. There are lots of guys like him all over the place. He used to work up in Buffalo; however, the Bronx needs a worker of his experience and caliber because us New Yorkers cause trouble. He explains, which I found very interestin' that there is an appointed time for each of us to die, but we fight it, so he has to help us or our stubborn souls will try to stay in this world. You still with me? Good. I thought you were dosin'. So anyway, he's coverin' his zone of death like Pablo Prigioni of the Knicks covers the basketball court and he shows up at the park standin' next to Angelica's dyin' father.

I got to tell you, by now the two drinks he slammed down are takin' effect and he props both elbows on the bar and he's leanin' toward me. He's speakin' freely now, tellin' me his story. He says while he's holdin' up his long index finger encased with the silver thimble, he says, 'See this finger right here?' and he slides off the thimble.

I says, 'Yeah, I'm lookin' at it,' and I takes a step back.

He explains to me that with that finger out of the thimble, he touches the forehead of someone whose time is at hand and who is usually sick, hurt, or very old, and then, when he pulls away his finger, the living soul pops out of its dead body. The spirit sees him as he's pointin' that finger of his at a bright light. The spirit is expected to go to the light without screwin' around, then, step into the light, and badda boom badda zoom float up and up and into another place he calls, 'Life beyond Life.'

That's when I realizes, just how close I came earlier to takin' a permanent vacation to Life beyond Life when he tried to poke me between the eyes with his finger of death.

When he was out at the park standin' next to Angelica's father and he touched the ol' man's forehead. Her father's good soul stepped out of his sick body and went directly to the light.

My man from Life beyond Life tells me that, usually, after a withdrawal of a soul, he leaves right away so as to not hang around for all the panic and grief that death brings the livin'. However, because of Angelica's beauty, he didn't leave immediately; he stayed and watched her. He witnessed her go from shock to grief to tears to sobs and he said, and I quote, 'Her tears were like tiny diamonds tricklin' down her rosy cheeks.'

Then, like it hurt him too much to think of Angelica's tears, he slams down his drink and changes the subject, sayin' that since ages ago when he began this work of extractin' souls he has never delayed or missed one. Then, he asks me if I remembered, 'elderly Mrs. Parducci, teenager Bobbi Giordini, and hairdresser Louisa Marinara?'

I says, 'Yeah, I do.' Feelin' sorta bristly, 'cause I attended two out of the three funerals. Now—he's hittin' close to home. I'm gettin' irritated. Next, he tells me that he was there when all three died. He knew their circumstances: Mrs. Parducci broke a hip. Bobbi Giordini overdosed on cocaine, and Louisa Marinara died in an auto accident crossin' the Brooklyn Bridge on a very cold day. Then, he says he could name a whole lot more, but mainly, he wanted me to know that he was there with me at the hospital when my dear Rosetta died along with Michael our newborn son. Though it was just the night doctor and myself in the room that night, this wise guy tells me all the details like how it was stormin' outside when the doctor tells me the double whammy about how my son didn't make it and neither will my wife. This no name at my bar tells me the exact time when she died and how I fell to my knees and sobbed while pressin' my face into her lifeless hand. Not only that, he heard her last words tellin' me and he quotes them word for word, 'Joey, I love you. You're a good man. Don't be angry. Please, find a nice lady. I don't want you to be alone.'

First of all, I never got over bein' angry that my wife and son died. Second, I never met no nice lady who rocked my world. Third, this crazy jerk bringin' up my anguish is pissin' me off, so I yell at him, 'Hey, the deaths of my wife and son are my business!' He snaps back, 'No, the deaths of your wife and son are my business!'

I wanted to kill him; however, I knew that would be impossible, so I don't argue, I just says, 'Okay, okay, so you were there. Whadda you want from me?'

He tells me that he wants me to believe who he is so that I will do what he asks. I say, 'Sure, I believe who you are, but I'm tellin' you, don't ever talk again about my wife and son.'

He agrees, no problem, he even apologizes, and then

continues with his story. So, day and night, he's busy with the dyin'; however, every chance he gets, he watches Angelica. I remember him sayin', 'she's my vacation of life—from a job of death' and that when he's in her apartment—he's a shadow standin' in the shadow behind her bedroom door.'

The thought of him watchin' her creeps me out. Though, I'm thinkin' as long as he ain't hurtin' nobody by watchin' and as long as he ain't touchin' and extractin' when he ain't supposed to, and since I can't do anything about it, I guess, I'll leave it alone.

So I make him another drink, stiffer this time. He swallows down half of it and then continues sayin' that his dear sweet Angelica has some sort a blood disease. It's her time to die and has been for a long time, like months ago. She's stubborn with a lot of reasons to live, along with he can't do it and he says it again, 'I just can't do it. I just can't do it.' He gets all emotional, picks up the glass, slams down the booze, and throws the glass across the room where it smashes against the bathroom door.

I say, 'Whoa, settle down. No more drinks for you! Thanks, I'll be hangin' out after closin' to clean up the mess.'

Right at that moment, the front door blows open and a middle-aged businessman in a wrinkled suit stumbles in the door thinkin' maybe he ain't drunk enough 'cause he can still think about his messed up life, knowin' all along it was the alcohol that messed it up. He spots the gray man with no name dressed in black and thinkin' maybe he can cry on his shoulder about his sorry life, lost job, bitter wife, and out of control kids, he staggers over to the stool next to him and sits down. Sportin' a silly grin on his face, this bozo looks at the somber stranger, extends out his hand, and says, 'Hi, I'm Dumbshmuck.' Of course, that's not what he says; I just can't remember his name.

Before Dumbshmuck can sit down on the stool, the stranger begins to remove the thimble from his finger, but before he does,

I tell the drunken gullet that we're closed. Besides, I wouldn't serve him anyway; he was too inebriated.

Ready to fight for more booze, the drunk's eyes pop open and he reels backward slurrin' words that would send Father Benidetto into cardiac arrest. He falls backward over a table, rolls onto a chair, and hits the floor, then picks himself up and staggers back out the door into the cold night.

Like nothin' just happened, the strange somebody at the end of the bar asks me, "So what am I do to?"

So I says, 'First, don't throw no more glasses. Let's sort this out. So what happens if you let her live?'

He says, 'She will suffer horribly.'

I asks, 'So what if she dies?'

And he says, 'I will suffer horribly.'

I asks, 'Will she be in a better place; a place without pain and sorrow?'

He says, 'Absolutely.'

So I ask him, 'So fella—you in love with Angelica?'

He takes the fifth whilst thinkin' about it, then says, 'I've always had compassion for people in a way that I am always on time and that I execute my job quick and thorough. I never linger to look into anyone's eyes or even notice those around me; nevertheless, I could not ignore Angelica. The more I watched her the more I wanted to watch her. I felt feelings. Feelings I've never felt before.'

So again, I asks him, 'So fella—you in love with Angelica?'

He looks straight at me with those mean dog eyes of his, but I don't see the eyes of Ol' Man Torello's dog no more, I see eyes of pain and sorrow, and the shine of a tear. Speakin' without his rat-tat-tat, he says quiet and slow, 'Yes—I love her.'

So I says to him, 'It's okay to love somebody, no matter who you are or what you do. You follow me?'

He nods and I says, 'However, you fella, gotta a very

important job to do and you're no loser who takes his job lightly. Am I right?'

He nods his head again, then I tell him, 'You love Angelica and when a man loves a woman, he wants the very best for her. You can't think about what you want. Her needs come before your needs. Love ain't selfish. You got to sacrifice for love. You gettin' what I'm sayin'? You gotta do your job with integrity and you gotta do what is right for Angelica. You're a good guy with a tough job to do and you're a tough guy who will do what's good. Think only of Angelica—and do what's right by her.'

For a moment, whilst starin' up at the Crown Royal clock, he goes introspective. Hey, don't look so surprised. I know a few big words. Then, he sighs, his shoulders droop, and he rests his forehead on the bar. After fifteen seconds of agonizing, he sits up straight on the barstool and proclaims, 'I'll do it! I'll do what's right by her!'

He then locks eyes with me to where I can't look away while he makes me an offer I cannot refuse. He says that he will help me, if I help him, by helpin' Angelica's mother and brother. He wants me to keep an eye on them; to pop in once in a while to make sure her little brother is on the straight and narrow and to make sure her mother has a little cash now and then.

He asks me, 'Will you do it?'

I says, 'Sure, I'll do it.'

'Solemn oath?' he asks.

'Solemn oath,' I answer.

He asks me while he's twirlin' the thimble on his finger, if I break my oath, do I know what'll happen to me?

I reply, 'I'll get the finger—am I right?'

He answers, 'Yes. By your next breath, I'll be in your shadow.' He then says, 'I'm not supposed to do what I'm about to do, but, you know that little vial of nitro-glycerin you carry in the left pocket of your pants?

I says, 'Yeah, of course I do. How'd you know about it?'

He answers, sayin', 'I know about it, because, I've stood in your shadow before. Lucky for you, you have those pills. The last time you took one, it gave you just enough time to see a doctor. He saved your life. It was a closer call than you think.'

He again reaches in his breast pocket and takes out that glow watch. Like the first time, it lights up his face and that dark corner of the bar.

He glances at it and says, 'Right here and right now, I want you to take out two pills and slip them under your tongue. Then, you go see your doctor first thing in the mornin'. Trust me,' he says, 'this time they'll make sure you live for many more years.' Then, he surprises the hell out of me by saying, 'You know Bean, you were next on my list tonight. My finger was twitchin' for you.'

That's why he was checkin' his shiny watch. There was an X on me and he was clockin' the time; it was my appointed time to go. Right in the middle of washin' glasses, heart attack, badda bing badda dead, however, since I was helpin' Angelica's mother and brother, I gets to live. I get it. You get it? Good. I reach into my left pocket, take out the vial, twist off the cap, shake out two pills into the palm of my hand, and like the man ordered, I place them under my tongue.

So he stands up off his barstool and puts on his hat, pulls it down tight so his face is hidden in the shadow of its brim and then he tells me since he's got a tough job to do, he'd better go do it. He thanks me for the drinks and for the advice, steps over to the door, yanks it open, and no kiddin', the truth here as if I'm talkin to the Pope, before this man of death and love steps outside, he becomes a shadow and departs in an icy gust of wind.

So I clean up the bar includin' sweepin' up the broken glass and close the joint down. I couldn't think about anything except that shadow man. The thought of him made me twitch a little.

I walk home the four blocks to my place. My apartment ain't much, but it's home. Even though I wore a heavy overcoat with the collar turned up and a newsboy wool cap, a cold wind chilled me to my bones. After steppin' around every night shadow the streetlights ignored, I made it home safely. I didn't sleep much with my eyes open peerin' into the shadow behind my bedroom door.

The next day after that crazy night, I saw my doctor, Dr. Giappanano who scheduled me right in for a cardio-look-see and I wound up badda bing badda thump thump with a few stints in my heart. A few days after that, I show up at Angelica's funeral. A photo of Angelica was next to her coffin. She was beautiful with the sweetest smile I'd ever seen. I felt like I already knew her. I felt all emotional about her. Don't ask me to elaborate. However, I did pull out my handkerchief in case I needed it. I briefly met her mother Rosa and brother Dominic. Rosa is a few years younger than me and a lovely woman. Her grief overwhelmed me so I turned away for a few seconds and dabbed my eyes with my handkerchief. Dominic's a good kid. Respectful. Not a punk like most kids. I told Rosa a little fib about how I met Angelica while she was paintin' a portrait at the park, and then I asked Rosa, 'How can I help?' Between sniffs and sobs, she tells me, that only time would heal her grief, but for now, Angelica's car was broken and she needed it for errands. I told her it would be my pleasure to help her. Just let me get my hands on it for a half a day and I'll fix it. I ain't no wrench jockey, so I took it to Micki the Mechanic and badda boom badda zing, he fixes it. I pay for the repairs and drop off the car to Rosa. While I'm there, I ask her and Dominic out to dinner. I was very nervous whilst askin' and even more so whilst waitin' for her answer.

That next Monday night, my night off, they picked me up in her smooth runnin' car and we went to my pal, Luigi's place. We got a special table lookin' out at the river. Of course, I had meatballs and spaghetti. She had Lasagna. The kid had a large pepperoni pizza and ate the whole pie. We had a wonderful time. After that first date, 'cause a date is what it felt like, Rosa and me, we spent a lotta time together, takin' walks in the park, cookin' dinners together, and runnin' errands with each other. She knows a lotta people I know, which is cool. They're happy for us. I wanna take care of her and her son. Dominic shows me respect and I love him as if he was my own flesh and blood. Rosa loves me and I love her. We get along. Soon, we'll be married. I gotta tell you, I ain't been so happy for a long, long time; however, I'm always checkin' the shadows, if you know what I mean.

NAMELESS

Two orderly lines of spirits, one going, the other returning, both floating precisely at the center of creation amidst a celestial setting of twinkling stars. In the line going, a multitude of spirits, nameless, vaporous forms, golden like misty sunbeams, migrated away from their genesis, a human-sized sun; a blazing sphere, flashing, flaring, creating each new being in its own image. One creation after another swelled, separated from the divine sphere, then drifted away as an identical orb of brightness. As each orb joined the line going, it burst like a kernel of popcorn, transforming into a hazy, human form, a distinct individual, full of life, manifesting the five senses, thinking, feeling, and humming. Yes, humming. For each new self instinctively hummed, hummed along with the concourse of spirits, humming an eternal song melodic and joyful, celebrating life. In patient rhythm, no shoving, step by weightless step, all humming, the golden spirits waited, imagining who and just how incredible they might be, all the while drawing closer to the dazzling doorway, to a new beginning with flesh and bone, as man or woman, forgetful of purpose, unaware of destiny, and bestowed with free will.

Now, in the middle of this advancing line, there was a particular popped kernel of life that was more curious, more eager to go, and a great deal more talkative. While humming, not missing a note, and stretching, looking all around, it saw in front, a multitude of glowing spirits seemingly shrinking in size, growing distant all the way to the far-off door of departure. Behind the spirit waited another multitude of beings steadily progressing, as this eager spirit was, away from the distant sphere of creation. To the left of the spirit, two wispy arm lengths away moved another line of souls, returning, trudging along in the opposite direction of the line going. They appeared one by one from the radiant re-entry door next to the faraway exit door. These returning souls, still sustaining the shape of their abandoned human shell, were not so golden, but having been tempered by life, were smooth and gray like burnished steel. Furthermore, they did not hum, but were silent, reflecting on all that was and all that could have been, all that was uttered and all that went unspoken, all of their choices and all of the outcomes, and all that defined life: pleasure and pain, joy and grief, hope and despair, fleeting days and bodily death. Returning whence they began, they plodded along, waiting, contemplating, ending up at a magnificent heraldry of brightness where each knelt for a moment, arose again golden, and now knowing their purpose, their destiny, and all mysteries, each stepped through the veil, entering into yet another realm, a place of eternal life, abiding in love, living in peace, and filled with joy.

After looking all around, the eager spirit withdrew into its plain, wispy shape, peered across the aisle at a returning soul, stopped humming, and asked in a homogeneous voice, "Hey, what was life like?"

The gray being, the shape of a very old man, snapped out of its contemplation and replied in a manful voice, "Who me?"

"Yes, you. What was life like?"

Both of them drifted forward a step in opposite directions as the old soul said, "Well, I've just been thinking, life was easy—difficult too, especially those years away at war. The fear, the blood, the death—horrible, meaningless. To think that we are here, humming harmoniously, and then we are there, hating, killing each other. It didn't make any sense. Though I lived to a ripe old age, life there was much too short. All in all, now that I reflect upon it, life was good."

They both took a wafty step forward in their respective lines. The aged soul resumed reflecting, while the chatty spirit, feeling restless, joined in humming louder than the rest, thinking that the louder it hummed, the quicker the line might move. A few annoyed spirits shushed it.

Two-thirds of the way to the brilliant entrance, the fidgety spirit again stopped humming and said to another returning soul, "Pssssst, hey you. What was life like?"

The contemplating soul in the form of a middle-aged woman looked up and in a feminine voice answered, "My, my, my, I was just thinking about it. It was ohhh such happiness, the joy of loving and being loved, but ohhh, such heartbreak, the grief of losing a loved one. I lost my mother and father when I was young, my husband when he was young, and then my family lost me. Funny, we all start here in the same place, never knowing when it all will end, and then one day, it does, and we return here. We have that in common, wondering when, where, and how we'll die, yet there, we mostly see our differences. All in all, hmmm, life was good."

They moved forward a step as the womanly soul again became quiet while contemplating her life. The impatient spirit, hearing twice how life was good, now tried humming faster, hoping to pick up the pace. Spirits within hearing range hummed even louder drowning out the offbeat spirit.

With the radiant door looming just ahead, the excited spirit again stopped humming and asked another returning soul, "What was life like?"

The small being, not as gray and with a bit of its original gleam, replied in a boy's voice, "My life was short with lots of doctors, and surgeries, and medicines, and stuff. I felt lots of pain, but there were lots of nice people with lots of love, and I got to make a wish. My family, all of us, went for free to the beach for a whole week. The sun really shined though it was kind-a windy. I played in the ocean and picked up seashells. I flew a kite too. We had lots of fun. Now that I'm back here, I see how all of us start here happy and perfect, but once we get there, bad things happen to good people and good things happen to bad people. What really matters is how you live your life. All in all, I'd say, life was good."

The young soul resumed reflecting as the eager spirit danced with anticipation and hummed so loud as to rouse frowns and glares from both lines.

When the zealous spirit arrived at the glorious entrance, with only a few spirits ahead of it, it saw that a glowing being, a pudgy puff of vapor with a round face of cheerful features, hovered between the going and returning doors. A huge, timeless book opened with gilded pages and a cover of silver inlaid with sparkling diamonds levitated in front of the being. As each spirit gravitated over to the threshold, stopped humming, and stepped in to go, the bright being spoke to them. To one, it said, "Seek and you will find," and to the next, "Ask and you will receive," and to another, "Knock and the door will open." To all it would say, "Have a good life!" and with a flash of blinding light, the going spirits vanished.

When a soul appeared into the blazing brightness of the returning door and stepped out, the chubby spirit exclaimed, "Welcome home," and then asked, "your name please?" The returning souls stated their birth name and moved along in line. At, which point, the rotund being replied, "Thank you," and wrote their names, using a shiny pen with shimmering ink in the age-old book, a testament to their life's journey.

Finally, it was the fervent spirit's turn to go. Anticipating greatness, it stopped humming and burst out saying to the glimmering being between the doors, "You know, I will be someone great! Maybe a doctor curing the sick, a missionary sharing faith, a police officer rescuing a victim, or a firefighter saving a life; or perhaps a sculptor, painter, author, or musician creating, expressing, and sharing the beauty of life. Indeed, my life will be amazing! There will be few before or after me so full of love and striving so hard to help humanity. I will leave my life-stamp, a mark to be remembered." The fiery spirit filled with visions of virtue and trembling with excitement stepped up to the luminous entrance.

The gleeful gold being, grinned, nodded its head with approval, and for the first time ever, gave two vapory thumbs up and said, "My dear eager spirit, seek and you will find. Have a good life!"

The enthusiastic spirit sporting a wide smile, leapt through the door, and bathed in brilliancy, disappeared.

A very short time had passed when the same aspiring spirit arrived in a flash of light at the returning door and stepped out into the line of contemplating gray spirits.

"Welcome home," said the golden spirit with a double take. "I remember you. You were so excited to go, but my goodness, you are back so terribly soon, and you still shine bright and have very little life shape at all."

"Yes," replied the once elated but now greatly disappointed spirit hanging its hazy head, "I am back so soon."

"So very sorry that you are, but your name please?"

The grieving spirit wafted forward a step in line. On the verge of sobbing and as a glimmering tear drifted away from its sad, misty face, it groaned, "I don't have a name."

"No name! Oh my! Again, I am so sorry." The usually cheery, plump spirit, now somber, wrote a long number in the old book and asked, "What happened my dear spirit?"

A spirit at the front of the going line stopped humming and rudely interrupted, "Hey, it's my turn to go now."

The tubby host stated respectively with great authority,

"Please, just a second, my impatient spirit. Indeed—hold up the lines!"

Never in all of time had the confluence of going or returning spirits stopped, but never had there been such a zealous goer who had returned so soon. The going spirits at the front of the line, upon hearing the command, halted, interrupting the advancing cadence of spirits, compressing the line like a squeezed accordion, jumbling up the humming with gasps, grunts, and grumbles. The souls returning, who were close enough to hear the resounding order, also stopped. Startled out of their quiet reflection, they spun and peered with curiosity while those out of earshot kept their stride, creating a growing gap in the line.

The compassionate spirit between the doors, expressing deep sympathy, again asked the despairing spirit, "Please, tell me. What happened my dear spirit?"

As another soul, this one gray and smooth from a long, fulfilling life emerged smiling from the returning door, the despondent spirit floated a half-step forward out of its way, turned, peered at the gleaming spirit with the book, and in a voice cracking with despair and ending with an outpouring of grief, replied, "Before my teenage mother, a runaway, even thought to give me a name, she overdosed, and this is her poor soul in front of me."

THE LITTLE BRAT

The little brat looked to be about four-years-old. He had red hair buzzed into a hurried crew-cut no doubt by a fraught mother and he had a ruddy face with a gang of freckles aiding and abetting a suspicious expression of, *I didn't do it.*

I had just ordered lunch and was sitting gingerly in a booth at the Denny's across the street from the Southside Medical Center. I say gingerly, because a few minutes earlier I had left my urologist's office where I endured an in-depth prostate exam. After my doctor noodled up my yahoo as if he was hand fishing for catfish and squeezed my swollen prostate like it was a rubber ducky, I could barely sit. Not only that, I had to have blood tests, so I hadn't eaten for twelve hours. A menu full of fried, grilled, and roasted aromas made my stomach rumble and the racket of plates crashing into bus trays, glasses filling with ice, and people chattering gave me a headache. Besides all that, with me being an old guy at sixty-eight, I have a predisposition for being grumpy, so believe me, I was grumpy.

Two seconds after a wrinkled waitress, slinging routine friendliness and wearing a *Ronnet* nametag slid my Bourbon Bacon Burger and fries in front of me, the little monster showed up. He stood rigid like a bad little boy in a corner, except he faced me and he was so close, maybe two-feet away, I could count every 3-D freckle on his face. Like an after school cartoon, his mischievous brown eyes were too big for his feisty face and his big round head was too big for his scrawny body trying to catch up. He wore a light-blue T-shirt and tan shorts, both soiled with splotches of filth and if his shoes hadn't had shoestrings, I would have swore they were shoe-shaped dirt clods. *I wondered, where were his socks? Who dressed this kid?*

Only as tall as my table, he stared directly eye to fry at my food. As old as I am, the pintsized food stalker could have been my great-grandson, but he wasn't, so he was annoying. Then—then, as I gripped my juicy burger in both hands, the runt, brandishing this perfect pitiful pose, lifted ever so slowly his hungry-puppy-dog eyes from ogling my food to locking eyes with me. I peered into the kid's eyes, big twinkling saucers glowing like two suns in a galaxy of space freckles. I'll give it to him; the kid bested my childhood pet, a beagle named Regal that used that same persuading look sitting on the floor next to me at the dinner table. Re-living happy memories of Regal, I felt compelled to give the lad all of my food, however, I resisted—and took a big bite out of my burger. Without blinking, he watched me. His eyes, my god, his hypnotic Svengali eyes, were trying to control my mind. My headache pounded like a beatnik on bongos. I wiped sweet bourbon sauce from my chin. He watched me. I took another bite. He edged closer. I squirmed and slid back in my seat. He watched me. *How long would this standoff last?*

His eyes grew even larger, then blinked and with a quick movement of his skinny arm, slight of his small hand, and an upward cramming of his Vienna sausage sized index finger, he picked his nose like an anteater digging for ants. I looked away, closing my eyes. I could barely chew my mouthful of burger without gagging. *Good grief, what did he dig out and where did he put it? Why wasn't his mother minding him?*

I glared over the top of his fiery stubble to the corner booth. There she sat, oblivious to it all, holding her cup of coffee with both hands and staring down into it. *What was she looking at? This wasn't Starbucks and her coffee wasn't a latte so there wasn't any foam with a little heart swirled in it. She probably had stayed up all night partying and now had a massive hangover.* Her reddish-brown hair was pulled back in a tight ponytail exposing her thin haggard face and I could see that her trouble-making son had inherited his big brown eyes from her. She didn't wear any make-up and dressed in a wrinkled yellow top, old blue jeans, and worn sandals as if she had rolled out of bed and put on yesterday's clothes. *She didn't care about herself, so how could she care for three kids?*

She sat at one entrance to the horseshoe shaped booth and to her right sat her daughter who'd I guess to be six. The girl's stringy brown hair unwashed and uncombed draped in front of her face like that creepy girl from that movie, *The Ring*. Her purple top didn't match her lime-green shorts that didn't match her pink flip-flops. *Shouldn't a mother take pride in dressing her daughter pretty?*

The girl banged her feet on a hollow spot under her seat sounding like a bass drum while chanting, "I wanna go home. I wanna go home. I wanna go home."

Her mother mumbled, "Please, Michelle, be good," then returned to staring into her coffee. Next to the daughter sat a tow-headed little imp of about two in a booster seat. He wore Huggies and a too tight T-shirt, which probably fit him perfectly three months ago. He too had big brown eyes like his trouble-making brother and coffee-staring mom. He became restless and began squirming so his sister tried to entertain him by dancing the salt and pepper shakers in front of him. He thought it boring, shoved them away, and threw a tantrum thrashing back and forth in his seat, beating the top of the table and kicking the table underneath. For his fit finale, he reached out a tiny plump hand, grabbed all the pink and blue packets of sugar at the center of the table, and threw them at his sister who immediately retaliated by leaning across the table, snatching his hand and smacking it, causing the little stinker to wail at the top of his lungs followed by green snot bubbling out of his nose.

I felt sick. Wipe the kid's nose and make him stop crying or as my father used to growl at me when I was a tyke, 'Stop that crying or I'll give you something to cry about!' *Now that I think about it, where was their father? In prison? Or he couldn't take all the stress of three bratty kids and ran off?*

The mother snapped out of her stupor and pleaded, "Please, Joey! Michelle! Both of you—stop it! Please—just, stop it. Michelle, please wipe your brother's nose." She finally noticed her middle child loitering at my table and said, "Rusty, please, honey, come over here and sit down."

The holy-terror shuffled reluctantly back to his table, sat down, guzzled down a glass of water, then whined, "I have to go peepee!" He jumped out of the booth, held his peepee thing in his balled up fist and started what I would call a Kickapoo Peepee Dance.

His mother said, "Go ahead, go, but don't run."

He ran as fast as he could right under Ronnet balancing a tray of food. She sidestepped him and almost lost the tray, but only spilt a splash of iced tea. The mother resumed gazing into her coffee. Tyranno-toddler rex stopped his fit, grabbed a squirt bottle of ketchup, squeezed a glob out on the table, and began finger painting in it. I guess as long as he was quiet, she was happy. I know, I was, and so were all the other diners. He wasn't happy for long though before he started fussing, yelling, "Hungy, Mama! Hungy!" *Didn't she feed her kids any breakfast?*

The other diners in our section, which was the side with all the windows looking out across the street at the emergency entrance to the medical center, all glared at the mother and kids, then at me like I was supposed to do something about the nuisance; me, with the grandfatherly gray hair of wisdom, squinting eyes of discernment, thick glasses of vision, creases of experience, and grumpy face of old age. *What could I do? Get grumpier? Yell at them? Gripe at the manager?*

Two skinny old biddies, I mean, elderly ladies, much, much older than me, most likely widows, both with silver hair, thick glasses, pursed lips holding in their dentures, and dried up wrinkles within wrinkles like a topographical map of Afghanistan, muttered, "Well, I never. Somebody should say something. How dare they ruin our lunch?"

I decided I would ignore everyone and just enjoy *my* lunch. I picked up my plastic bottle of ketchup, flipped it upside down, and squirted it on my fries. I picked up a fry and ate it. It tasted good, mmm: hot, salty, crunchy, and ketchuppy. I felt a little better. Within a minute, really, about thirty-five seconds, Rusty raced back through the restaurant, tripped over a woman's bulky purse on the floor, and fell headlong. Watching him tumble, the nearby diners gasped, muttering, "Is he hurt? He shouldn't run in the restaurant. Where are his parents?"

The spirited lad skidded a few feet, scrambled to his feet, hustled past his table, and straight to mine where he reached out both of his small hands and placed them on my table. As I have said before, there was no way he had been gone long enough to wash his hands, plus the condemning evidence: two grimy, gropey, booger picking, microbe infested little hands were exhibited right in front of me.

I said firmly and as nicely as I could to the kid, "Go back to your table," of course, I'm thinking, *you little brat*, but didn't say it.

Though still breathing hard from his dash and drop through the restaurant, he didn't say a word or make a move. He just kept staring at my food, then up at me, then at my food. For a moment, I thought he might be hard of hearing, so I asked him, "Did you hear me?" He nodded. I picked up another fry, dipped it in the ketchup, and ate it. He snatched a fry, dipped in my ketchup, and ate it. *You're kidding me! Did he really just do that?*

While he reached for another one and before I could say anything, his mother had seen him steal the first fry and pleaded again, "Pleeease, Rusty, come back to our table."

If I was his mother and he was my child, I would spank his bottom and teach him a few manners. Spare the rod; spoil the child. Some parents have no clue. People reproduce themselves then unleash the little devils for the rest of the world to deal with. Just thinking about it makes me all the grumpier.

Thank heavens, Ronnet, the food angel arrived and served their hot steamy food at his table enticing him to make a beeline back to it. I saw Michelle take a napkin and wipe the ketchup paint off the hands of little Vincent Van Gerber. All three hungry kids began wolfing down their food as if it was feeding time at the Roeding Park Zoo.

My cell phone rang. It was my wife, Susan.

I answered, saying rather gruffly, "Hi, hun!"

She said, "Hi, John," and then asked me, "What's the matter?"

I snapped, "Nothing, except, I'm irritated."

She probed, "About what?"

I started to tell her, but sitting within earshot of the mother and kids, I turned away from them, cupped my hand around my mouth, and whispered, "I'm annoyed by a bunch of bratty kids and their drugged out mother who won't discipline them."

She wanted to know where I was, so I told her, "I'm at the Denny's across from the hospital." Then I explained, "You know I haven't eaten anything for over twelve hours because of blood tests and of course the doctor visit wasn't any fun; squeezing my prostate like he was checking the ripeness of a piece of fruit. He said it's enlarged, but normal for a man my age."

She said, "Well, that's good to hear."

I looked down at my lunch getting cold and said, "Ok, well, thanks for checking up on me. I want to finish my lunch. I'll see you when I get home."

She said, "Okay, dear. Hang in there and John—please, don't be grumpy with people. I love you."

I told her, "I love you too. See you in a little while."

We said goodbye and I again started eating my cold burger and fries. I ate while the mother and her kids ate their hot food, though the mom didn't seem to eat much. She lifted a long fry, looked at it, and dropped it back on her plate. I finished most of my meal, left money on the table to cover the check, threw down a couple of bucks for a tip, then stood to leave. I stomped past the mother and her children in the booth, giving my best cranky frown to the carrot-topped menace. He gazed up at me with that look of, *I didn't do it.*

Even though I heard my wife's voice in my head saying, 'Please, don't be grumpy with people,' I had to. It's just not right that parents let their kids run all over the place and ruin the lives of people around them, especially in restaurants, movie theatres, and Wal-Mart. Naw, forget about Wal-Mart, bratty kids will always rule there. Kids should be taught to respect others. *Shouldn't parents step up?*

I stopped, turned around, and headed back to her booth. I cleared my throat, getting the mother's attention, and said politely, "Excuse me, I don't mean to tell you how to raise your kids, but you really need to discipline them a little better. Especially that one." I pointed at the red-on-the-head mischief-maker. The two eighty-something old ladies watched me and nodded their wrinkles with approval.

The mother looked up at me with this drugged-out dazed look as if she hadn't heard me.

I said, "You know, your kids have been disrupting everyone in the restaurant."

She glanced around at her little angels as if to say, *Who? My kids?*

They all sheepishly smiled at her with the same angelic look of, *I didn't do it.* Even the diaper squirt had the look dialed in. He could have modeled that look and tight T-shirts in a J.C. Penney's ad.

She slid out of the booth, stood up, and said to her kids, "Please, sit there and eat your lunch. Rusty, don't leave this booth or you'll be in big trouble." She motioned me down to an unoccupied table away from her booth. I followed her. She leaned in toward me and said softly, "I'm so, so sorry. You see—." She hesitated, her eyes tearing up as if she was about to cry, but reeled in her emotions, and continued, "We've just moved out here from Ohio. My husband, Bobby—." She sniffed as her eyes welled with tears with one glistening tear running down her cheek. "He's an electrician; got a better paying job out here. This morning—right after he went to work—I got a call from the hospital—we threw on some clothes and rushed down to emergency. I still can't believe it, but, Bobby was … ."

Her voice cracked as she started sobbing, leaned over, and rested her head on my shoulder.

Her daughter whined, "Mommy? What's the matter?"

Feeling awkward, I gently patted the woman on her back. All the diners around us were gawking and listening. The two ancient women leaning toward us nearly fell out of their booth. I reached down for a napkin so she could dab her tears. Her kids stopped eating and were now peering over at us: Michelle standing next to the booth, Rusty standing up on his seat, and Joey on his knees in the booster seat. All three kids looked horrified, knowing something was horribly wrong. Michelle started crying, wiped her hair from her face revealing bright blue eyes, and whimpered, "Where's daddy?"

Her mother replied lovingly, "Just a minute sweetie."

The young mother lifted her head off my shoulder, placed

her mouth close to my ear, and while trembling, her words breaking, whispered barely audible so that her kids wouldn't hear her, "I don't know how to tell my kids—before we could get to the hospital—their daddy died."

She broke out sobbing as the two not-so-hard-of-hearing elderly women came over and wrapped their arms around her. All three kids scooted out of the booth and raced over.

The manager, passing by, asked sternly, "What's going on?"

I walked with him between the tables far enough away so the kids couldn't hear me and said softly, "There was an accident—her husband has just died."

My heart dropped into my stomach as her grief twisted my soul. I felt horrible for thinking the thoughts I had thought; to think one way instead of another; to be grumpy; to be unloving. *Why hadn't I put the pieces of the puzzle together?* They were all there: the emergency sign out the window and across the street looming directly behind the mother's booth and the distraught mother with the hungry, unruly kids. My eyes saw, my mind processed, and my heart cast judgment. *How could I see so clearly, but be so blind? How could I be so clever, yet be so thoughtless?* I was focused on me, on my selfish needs, me, irritated, hungry, annoyed, and grumpy, rather than seeing the needs of those around me. I wish I would have asked that red-on-the-head little rascal to plop down in the seat across from me, then pointed at my fries, and said, "Help yourself." *How could an old guy like me still have lessons to learn?*

The elderly ladies walked with the grief-stricken mother back to her booth. The kids, afraid and crying, followed in a cluster holding on to each other. The manager and I trailed behind the kids.

I said to the mother, "I'm so sorry. Please, let my wife and I help you. Our pastor and his wife can help too. How about if we box up this food to go? Also, I'd like to pay for it."

The manager heard me and said, "Please, I've got it

covered." He turned, walked over to Ronnet serving a couple their check, and whispered his intentions to her.

The mother looked silently up at me with big tears in her eyes and streams of them running down her cheeks.

I asked, "What's your name?"

She replied, "Theresa."

I said, "Theresa, my name is John. Would you and your kids like to come home with me and meet my wife, Susan? We'll come back later to pick up your car. I'll invite our pastor and his wife over. You can talk with them. They are wonderful, caring people. My wife and I will watch your children. We'll help you through this."

She glanced around at her frightened kids, then back up at me and said, "We don't have any family out here so—sure, I would appreciate your help since I have arrangements to make. Thank you so much."

I said, "Okay. Good. Please—give me a minute to call my wife." I stepped away from the booth, called Susan, and said, "Hi, honey. Hey, I confronted the lady and kids and ... ."

Disappointed with me, she moaned, "Oh, John, I reminded you not to be grumpy."

I explained to her, "I know, yet I was grumpy and now I know, I was wrong. Come to find out her husband has just passed away. He was an electrician. Bad accident. I feel horrible for her. They recently moved from Ohio and don't have any family out here. I'd like to bring her and her three kids home with me. They need our help. What do you think?"

She said, "Sure, dear, bring them home. I would love to help."

I said, "Good," and then asked her, "Will you call Pastor Bill and ask him if he and his wife will come over? Oh, and will you plan some sort of dinner for all of us? Something simple is okay."

She replied, "I can do that. I'll be waiting."

I told her, "Thanks," and that I would see her shortly.

As soon as I was off the phone, one of the elderly ladies said, "I'm Grace and this is Gladys. We would like to help too. Counting her family and mine, we have seven children, fifteen grandchildren, twenty-three great-grandchildren, and two great-great-grand babies. Can we come over? We'll watch these young'uns."

I said, "We would love your help. I'm John. Please, follow me."

After Ronnet boxed up the food, we left the restaurant. The grieving mom and her confused kids climbed into my car. I buckled up the children in their seatbelts and then drove a block down to Theresa's car where she retrieved a huge diaper bag and Joey's car seat. She tossed the diaper bag in my car's trunk and strapped Joey in his car seat. We then drove to my house followed by Grace and Gladys in Grace's clean, sea-foam green, 1978 Buick Regal. She swerved quite a bit, but stayed up with me. Pastor Bill and his wife Joyce arrived at my home a few minutes after we did. We all introduced each other, then, as the rest of us stood listening in the living room, Theresa sat in one of our kitchen chairs and gathered Michelle and Rusty to her side. Joey sat in her lap while her arms wrapped around all three of them. In her restrained grief, she said, "Kids—I'm really, really sorry, so sorry—but your daddy—your daddy was in an accident at work this morning. He was badly hurt and—and—he—he died."

Michelle didn't understand and asked, "But when's daddy coming home?"

Theresa, bravely holding back her tears, replied sweetly, "Honey—he's not coming home. He's in Heaven now. "

Michelle then asked, "He went to Heaven without saying goodbye?"

Rusty, not comprehending and feeling scared whined, "I want my daddy."

Joey muttered, "Dadda," then stuck his bottom lip out as if he was about to cry.

Theresa said, "I want daddy to be home too. I know that if he could have, he would have told us goodbye and he would have given each of us a big hug. He loved us all very, very much. I want to tell you, that in a few days, we are all going to fly on an airplane back to Ohio. We are going to stay with Grandpa Russell and Grandma Jean. You're going to see Grandpa Joe and Grandma Sarah too. "

The faces of all three kids lit up at the thought of riding in an airplane and seeing their grandparents.

Theresa continued, "All the family, your uncles, aunts, and cousins are going to meet us at our little church where you used to go to Sunday School and we're all going to say goodbye to your daddy. Something else I want you to know. Mommy will be crying a lot because she misses daddy and anytime you miss him, you can cry too. We'll hug each other and cry together."

Theresa could no longer hold in her grief and sobbed. Michelle cried too. Rusty and Joey didn't truly comprehend, yet sobbed because their mother and sister sobbed.

Their loss, their sadness was heartbreaking. Tears welled up in the eyes of the rest of us and we wept. I have to say, I have never seen such motherly love except in my wife with our three children.

While Theresa went into one of our guest bedrooms and called her family out in Ohio, Grace and Gladys bathed each child and helped them brush their teeth with the extra toothbrushes we have from years of dental check-ups. After that, they dressed the kids in the clothes we keep around for grandkids.

I put on a Disney movie on the TV out in the living room. Grace held Michelle in her lap while Gladys cradled Joey. Pastor Bill and Judy consoled Theresa in the back bedroom. I turned the volume up on the TV so the kids couldn't hear their mother weeping. Susan busied herself planning dinner. I sat in my rocking lounge chair: the same chair I rocked my kids and the same chair I now rock my grandkids. Rusty, that redheaded little rascal parked himself in front of me and stood rigid like a bad little boy in a corner, except facing me, and he was close enough, maybe two-feet away to count every 3-D freckle on his face. I smiled and held out both my arms inviting him in. He scrambled onto my lap. I looked down into those big brown eyes of his while he gazed up at me as if I was his long lost great-grandfather. *How could I have missed the sweetness in this little boy?* I thought my heart would explode from all the love I felt for him. I held him close and rocked him to sleep.

Only One of Us

Marcus awoke from a short, afternoon nap, saw his twin brother Matthew pressing a 9mm pistol to his head and shouted, "Stop! Matt, don't do it! Please—take the gun away from your head!"

"No, Marc! I won't! I'm killing myself!"

"Matt, come on! Put the gun down!"

"I said, NO! I can't take it anymore and I'm warning you— if you even reach for this gun—I'll blow my brains out; blow them out right now! I will!—You know I will!"

"Okay, Matt, okay, I believe you. Please, just calm down and give me the gun."

"No! I won't calm down and NO!—You can't have the gun! I told you, I'm going to put a bullet in my head."

"Tell me why, Matt—before you kill yourself. I want to know and of course, the police will want to know too. In fact— I'm going to call them right now."

"Here, I'll hand you your phone. Go ahead; call them. I promise you—they'll be too late."

"Hello. Yes, I have an emergency. My name is Marcus Olsen. My brother, Matthew has a loaded gun to his head. He's going to kill himself. Yes, he's very serious. My address is 221 Bunker Street, apartment B. There's a blue van parked out front.

Ok, sure, I'll keep the line open.—So Matt, why do you want to kill yourself?"

"Hmmm. Let's see. Like you don't already know. Come on, Marc! You know! The family knows! The entire town knows! And of course now with the police listening in, they'll know."

"What do I know, Matt? Tell me! What does everybody know?"

"That you—and how many times have I heard people say it—that you, Marc, you're 'the stronger one, the smarter one, and the better looking one,' while me, your helpless brother Matt, I'm the, 'weaker one, the dumber one, and the uglier one.'"

"Oh, come on Matt, we're identical twins: we look alike, sound alike, dress alike, and think alike. For twenty-five years, we've been inseparable. We've shared our lives together: schooldays, workdays, Saturdays at the movies, and Sundays at church; you and me, together, we celebrated every birthday, holiday, and vacation."

"Yes, Marc, we've spent our lives together and yes, we're *supposed* to be identical, but, compared to you, I've always been weak and getting weaker, while you've always been strong and growing stronger. Next to you, I look sickly; thin and pale. I'm a burden to you and as time passes, I'm becoming a greater burden. Even now, there are times when I can hardly walk and need to lean on you. I hate ruining your life. I always have. Think of where you'd be today if you didn't have to take care of me."

"Matt, you're not a burden. I wouldn't know how to act without you in my life. We are who we are and it is what it is. Most importantly, we are brothers and brothers help each other. So, please, let me help you. Put the gun down."

"No! Today we part. Today there will be only one of us. You hear me? Only one of us! How blessed does that sound? Just one; survival of the fittest and that my brother is you."

"Stop all this crazy talk and tell me how you got my gun?"

"It was easy. I waited for you to fall asleep, then, I quietly slid open the top drawer of your nightstand and took the gun. You woke when you heard me load the magazine."

"You know that gun is for home defense only! We both attended those gun safety classes, so stop screwing around. Give me the gun!"

"No! I want to die!"

"Damn it, Matthew! Give me the gun!"

"No, Marcus! I'm squeezing the trigger. See, I'm squeezing it."

"Okay, okay. Settle down. So, you were going to kill yourself while I was asleep?"

"Yes, because I knew if you were awake, you'd try to stop me."

"So did you even consider that I would jolt awake to a loud gunshot to see your blood and brains splattered all over the bedroom? Do you think that's the way I want to remember you: the gunshot; the blood; the horror of your death forever in my mind?"

"I don't want to hurt you, Marc. Really, I don't. I'm doing this for me and I'm doing this for you and Amy; for your marriage, so you two can live happily ever after; consider my death a wedding present."

"That's absurd! You think I want to begin my new life with Amy while I'm traumatized over your suicide? Do you? Besides, you have no reason to kill yourself over her. She's okay with you being a part of our lives."

"No, she's not!"

"Yes, she is!"

"She's NOT! Come on Marc, I'm a third wheel! She doesn't want me around. She *acts* as if she's okay with me just to make you happy. She'll change after you two are married."

"No, she won't."

"Yes, she will."

"Listen to me, Matt, she genuinely likes you and tries really hard to show it."

"I'll say it again, Marc, she's only nice to me because *you* want her to be nice to me. When she's here, she ignores me by pretending I don't exist. Plus, what really makes me angry is while I'm sitting there trying to watch TV or read, you two are making out and doing the touchy-feely. It's horrible! I don't want to live like this anymore! I just can't ignore your relationship with her. It's in my face all the time. You, her, and frankly me will be better off with *me* gone. Then, you two can romance each other all day and night without worrying about me."

"Oh come on, Matt, Amy and I, we're in love."

"Oh Matt, we're in love. Whaaateveeer!"

"Stop mocking me! We're in love and we do what lovers do. I'm sorry we make you feel uncomfortable. Hear me on this—I would not be better off if you were gone—who would I talk to?"

"Amy."

"Who would play video games with me?"

"Amy."

"Who would watch football with me on Sunday afternoons?"

"Amy, Amy, AMY! For God's sake, Marc, you'll be married to Amy. You'll do everything with Amy. With Amy! Got it? She'll be your wife. As for me, well, I'm just your 'in the way' brother."

"You're not in the way. I promise you. Wait a minute—I know what's really bothering you. *You* don't like Amy, do you?"

"Not true. It's just that I've heard her whispering to you. She's all for you and me going our separate ways. She's right you know. It's said that 'a man shall leave his father and mother,' including his twin brother I might add, 'and he shall cleave to his wife and *they* shall become one flesh.' Deep down I agree with her. You and me should part. With all your body and soul,

53

you should embrace her. So lately, I've just kept to myself and kept my mouth shut. I've tried to stay apart from you and her. However, I can't take it anymore."

"Ohhh, now I know what it is. I can tell Matt. It's obvious. You're really not happy for *us*."

"Oh, I'm very happy for the two of you. I want the both of you to live a normal life without fretting over me. I want you two to focus on each other and start a family."

"Thank you. We hope to start a family soon and someday, so will you. I believe that you'll meet the love of your life and be as happy as I am with Amy."

"How can you say that when you know I've never found a girl to love me and now that I'm so sick all the time, I never will? Don't even go there! It's obvious that I'm in the way of your blessed happiness. Once I'm gone, you'll live a fulfilling life. Think of the freedom! No more sickly brother to support. Don't forget when Dad's life insurance helped us to go to college. You excelled; I failed. I was too exhausted to study and too stupid to do well on tests. You earned your degree in engineering and then got a good job; a good job making good money and working from home. No grueling commute. No demanding boss breathing down your neck. Nevertheless, when you're working, all I do is sleep. I'm too sick to work. All these years, I've mooched off you. I'm a parasite: a leech sucking the life out of you. After I'm gone, you'll get my share of the inheritance from mom and I'll finally give back to you. The money will help you newlyweds buy a house."

"I don't want your money, Matt. I'd rather have you."

"Once I'm gone, you'll think differently. Besides, the doctors have always told me that with all the complications I suffered at birth, I should be dead already. I've lived on borrowed time. I could die at anytime and still feel lucky to have lived this long. The way I figure it, if I die today, you'll have six months before your wedding to adjust to your new life without me."

"I want you at my wedding; you're my brother; my best man. I need you by my side, supporting me. I'm strong because I had to be for you. If you're not with me, I'll lose my strength."

"You'll do just fine without me and you'll be stronger than ever before."

"No, no, NO! If you die, I'll die!"

"No, you won't. You'll survive. As for me, I believe in an afterlife: a place where there is no sorrow or pain; no doctors, no surgeries, and no pills: no rude people staring at me. I'm ready to go to that place. I want to end this sad life with this sick body and exchange it for a happy life with a new body. Please understand and don't judge me harshly when I'm gone. I want you happy. I want me happy. For any happiness at all—I have to die. There is no other way."

"Matthew, listen to me. Please—I beg you—hand me the gun."

"No, Marcus, I've made up my mind. Listen to me. If you even twitch, I'll pull the trigger. Let me say this before I go, I'm sorry for depending on you so much; for holding you back; for the times I got sick and made you sick; for whenever I embarrassed you with the stupid things I said; for making you late for school; for jacking up your love life; and one last thing, I want a clear conscious before I go, I apologize for being so jealous."

"You? Jealous?"

"Yes. I was extremely jealous. When Amy first started hanging out with you, I didn't want her stealing you away from me. I was jealous of her having you. It was always only the two of us. Then, all of a sudden, it was three of us. I hated her, but over time, I'm sorry to confess and please forgive me, I fell in love with her too. She's so beautiful and her scent, ohhh her scent: the lotions, perfumes, and shampoos; she drives me crazy. Not only all that, she is very loving and affectionate. Then, I became jealous of you having her. I love her. I do, Marcus. How could I not? I'm lonely and have needs too. Yes, dear brother, I long to kiss her as you do and to caress her as you do. I pray to be you and make Amy *my* wife, however, as much as I desire her, she desires you—and rightly so, for you are hers and she is yours. I can't live life like this anymore; losing my brother to a girl he loves and I love who doesn't love me and only loves him."

"Matthew, I've always suspected that you had feelings for her and I am so sorry for your anguish. She's beautiful, she's loving, and she's easy to fall in love with. I forgive you. Although, like you said, she's mine and frankly, you can't have her, but I promise you—we'll be sensitive to your feelings. We'll include you in our lives when and where we can."

"Thank you, but it will never be enough. I'll always want more; more time with you without her and more time with her without you. It can never be, so please lay back down and close your eyes. Let me do what I need to do."

"Isn't your arm tired from holding the gun to your head? Why don't you stop this craziness and give me the gun."

"My arm is fine and I haven't changed my mind."

"Matt, listen to me. I know you'll meet someone; a lovely girl who you will cherish and who will adore you as well."

"I doubt that, Marc. Who would love a freak like me?"

"Don't say that! You know how much I hate that word! I found love and so will you. Pleeease—hand over my gun. I'm getting very angry."

"I'm sorry, Marc. I won't. I need it to set me free."

"Listen Matt, I hear the police out front. Please put the gun down and talk to them."

"Yeah, I hear them too and no, I won't put the gun down and talk to them. They're too late. I apologize before hand for the gory mess I'll make. Aside from that, my death is best for all of us; you, me, and Amy. I love you Marcus and tell Amy, I love her too."

"Don't do it! Matthew, pleeease—*we* love *you*; we'll get you help; help to feel better; help to be happy."

"Oh, Marcus, Marcus, Marcus, no more doctors, no more drugs, no more surgeries, and no more hospitals. No more of any of this. I'm done. So done. Goodbye."

"Matt, just give me the gun!"

A police officer rapped on the front door and called out. Marcus lunged for the pistol. Matthew only had to squeeze the trigger. The bullet went through his head, ricocheted off the bedpost, and struck Marcus in the shoulder. Matthew died. Paramedics raced Marcus to the hospital where doctors mended the gunshot wound to his shoulder and after another twelve hours of surgery, Matthew and Marcus Olsen, conjoined twins, attached mid-torso sharing a liver and a kidney, were separated.

Second Chance

TEXAS DEPARTMENT OF CRIMINAL JUSTICE
Alan B. Polunsky Unit (Death Row)
3872 FM 350 South, Livingston, Texas 77351

Name: Ronald Lane Wilky
Death Row Number: 999278
Cell Number: 266
Race: Caucasian
Hair: Brown
Eyes: Blue
Height: 5'10"
Weight: 190 lbs.
DOB: 05-13-1977
Crime: First Degree Murder
Date of Crime: 07-10-1997
Sentence: Execution by lethal injection.
Scheduled Date of Execution: 07-10-2012
Scheduled Time of Execution: 7:00 a.m.
Appeals: Denied. None pending.

On July 10th, one hour before his scheduled execution, waiting on death row in the isolation of a six by ten foot concrete cell, Ronald Lane Wilky knelt on his knees praying, beseeching God for mercy, a miracle, and a second chance.

Like all the men sentenced to death housed in building 12 at the Allan B. Polunsky Unit, he wore a white jump suit with his name and number patch ironed on the front, big black letters "DR" printed across his back, and white slip-on canvas sneakers; slip-on so that a despairing man facing execution could not hang himself with shoe laces. He possessed as well, the same defiance as those condemned, rarely following any rules or obeying any laws his entire life, though at this moment, with his execution imminent, he prayed exactly as his mama had taught him to pray: on his knees with his head bowed, eyes squeezed shut, hands tightly clasped, and his elbows perfectly propped up on his bed; ironically, the thin, soiled mattress on a cement prison bed. Imploring his maker all through the muggy night and the sweltering day before, he had waived his one hour per day recreation in a roomier cage outside of the windowless cell and had refused the meals that the guards had slid through the "bean slot" in the solid cell door. Though he prayed without ceasing, sadly, he begged God for mercy not from a repentant heart, but from holy terror that his soul would suffer the fiery torment of eternal damnation.

With his knees raw from kneeling on the hard concrete and his clothes soaked in sweat from feverish pleading, he opened his eyes, staggered to his feet, leaned the back of his head against a wall and peered up at the dim nightlight on the ceiling. Believing he was gazing directly into Heaven and hoping that if God peered down and saw his anguished face glimmering with tears, then, maybe, just maybe, he would receive greater compassion, he cried out in desperation, "Please, please, please, God! I don't wanna die. I don't wanna burn in Hell. Pleeease— show me mercy, make a miracle, and give me a second chance!"

Wilky's sobbing plea resonated so loudly that a restless, soon to be executed killer in the next cell heard him through the concrete wall and shouted in a gravelly voice, "Shut up, and take what's comin' to you! In here—there ain't no mercy, there ain't no miracles, and there sure as hell ain't no second chances!"

Wilky heard the murderer's remarks, ignored him, and now hysterical, wailed even louder, "God, please! I never planned on killin' that old man. You know that! I was just a dumb kid. Neither did I want to break my mama's heart. She's a good woman, never missin' a church service, prayer meetin', or potluck. Out of every one of her measly paychecks and out of her tip money too, she puts her tithe in the offerin' basket, and then drops in a little bit more for the missionaries. She's a genuine saint, prayin' non-stop for me. Answer her prayers. Do what she asks. Please, please, God, give me a second chance! Give me a second chance! Give me a second chance!"

"Shut your mouth," yelled the agitated convict from the other side of the wall. "I'll say it again. No one in this place gets a second chance! No one! Your mama's prayers can't help you now!"

Wilky paid him no mind. While resuming his noisy lamentations, he heard a loud clank, shut his mouth, and listened. Barely breathing, he leaned down. Peeking out the meal slot in his door, he saw the guards changing shifts at the end of the corridor; they would come for him soon. He envisioned plodding down the dim corridor, his knees weak and buckling; the guards holding him up as they drag him to the death chamber. The execution team forces him up on a table and strap down his arms, legs, and head. He can't move. His eyes dart around the room. No smiles; no chitchat; everyone is efficiently doing their job. A chaplain; a prayer; any last words? The warden gives the proceed order. IVs stick into his arm, drip, drip, dripping death into his veins; his mind and body go numb; then, no breath; no heartbeat; a quick trip to Hell—Fire! Fire!

Souls afire! The damned are writhing, screaming, engulfed in hot flames, burning, burning, burning on their torment though never consuming their souls. Scorching heat; blistering skin; feet aflame; hair ablaze!

"Ahhhhhh! I'm on fire! I'm on fire! Forever on fire!" Enveloped in make-believe flames, Wilky grabbed his bed sheet, wrapped it around his body, and dropped to the floor of his cell. He rolled back and forth between his concrete bed and stainless steel toilet, screaming, "God, put out the fire! Put out the fire! Don't let them kill me! Please, please, answer my mama's prayers! Do it for her! I beg you! Do it for my mama!" Exasperated and out of breath, he stopped rolling and yelling, returning to his right mind. He slowly stood, dropped the bed sheet, gazed up again into the glow of the divine nightlight, and whispered, "Please God—show me mercy, make a miracle, and give me a second chance!"

While Wilky prayed, so did his mama, Gloria Grace praying on her knees at the foot of her bed in a perfect prayer position just as she had taught her son Ronnie Lane to do. Due to the sticky humidity and her ailing swamp cooler, she wore a pink cotton tank top, white baggy shorts, and was barefoot. A wild party life before she met Jesus, as well as the hardships of being a single mom aged her to look much older than fifty-three. Despite wrinkles and gray hair, and being small and thin, she had a big faith accompanied by twinkling blue eyes attesting to it. On the inside of her skinny right wrist was a tattoo of praying hands, a reminder to pray, and inked up the inside of her bony left arm were the words, *Ask and You Shall Receive*, a promise to the power of prayer. Every time she knelt to pray, she prayed first for her incarcerated son, then her pot smoking sister Jolene up in Dallas, and then for other family members experiencing any sort of life difficulties. After them, she lifted up to the Lord any suffering soul on her church's prayer chain and then anybody the Lord laid upon her heart. Lastly, she spoke of her own needs.

Countless years of kneeling in the same spot the first thing after climbing out of bed and the last thing before climbing into bed had worn two ruts in her green shag carpet. She'd been on her knees praying all the day before except for taking a few breaks to eat and visit the restroom and all the night before except for falling asleep for a few hours on the floor next to her prayer spot. Upon hearing the cooing of morning doves, she abruptly awoke. Feeling guilty, thinking she'd failed her son by sleeping on the job, she quickly resumed praying. Loquacious with a Texan drawl, she chatted with God as though she had just bumped into Him at a church potluck scooping potato salad onto a paper plate.

"Goodmornin' Lord. My boy, Ronnie Lane needs You. Always has. Most especially at this final hour before the State of Texas sends him before your throne of judgment. Me bein' a good mama, I wanted to be up at Polunsky for him, but yesterday mornin' when me and my boy were talkin' on the phone, he told me not to come up there. He said there was no time for good-byes and tears; just to stay home and pray; pray all day and night if I could, askin' You to give him a second chance or at the very least, not to cast him into the fires of Hell. You know, God, how Ronnie Lane has a powerful fear of fire ever since his daddy, Jesse burned to death in that car crash. Lord, like I've said to You a million times, 'Thank You for pluckin' my little seven-year-old out that shattered car window.' It's a miracle that after that car rolled three times, explodin' into a ball of fire, all my young'un got was scrapes and bruises. Unfortunately, the poor child seen his daddy trapped inside screamin' and burnin; screamin' and burnin' 'till the demons of Hell dragged the man's hateful soul down to everlastin' torment. My boy still shudders at the sight of fire. Shakes even when he lights a cigarette. Poor boy. That itty-bitty match reminds him of his screamin', burnin' daddy. Jesse done brung it on himself though; all that drinkin' and drivin' like he did. My goodness that man was evil. Never holdin' down a job and puttin' me to work waitressin' down at the IHOP. Please forgive me, for back then, I couldn't tithe a nickel with him takin' all my tip money to get drunk or high. Mean-spirited man too, always slappin' me around and beatin' on Ronnie Lane. Jesse didn't deserve no mercy and got his come-uppins. That's why, once he was gone, I cried not one tear for 'im. He was always talkin' that when he died, he'd ride a Harley straight to Hell and party-hearty with the Devil. I'll wager he's in Hell alright and I'm a bettin' too—it ain't no party. Anyway, Hell ain't no place for my boy, Ronnie Lane. I believe You saved his life, 'cause You have a greater purpose for him. Besides, I've got two reasons to ask You for mercy on account of my only son. One: 'cause seein' his daddy fry like that traumatized him to the point where the youngster was never again right in his mind and two: it was his daddy's fault that the boy got into so much trouble. Jesse brung him up to be an outlaw; to smoke, to drink, and to fight; to steal, to sell drugs, and to rebel against all authority. I know—and I know that You know, Lord—that Ronnie Lane never paid You or Your Good Book no mind, nevertheless, You're in his heart, 'cause back when he was in first grade, on Easter Sunday, he darted from our pew for preacher Ed's alter call. The tyke asked Jesus into his heart and that very day was baptized receiving the Holy Ghost. I understand there's no way I can talk You into helpin' my boy unless it's Thy will. If it is, then, I believe that You can do anything, anyhow, anywhere, at anytime, 'cause You're everywhere, all knowin', and almighty. Besides, You say in Your Word that if I have the faith the size of a tiny mustard seed that I can move a mountain. Well, I'm not askin' You to move a mountain; I'm just askin' that You save my only child. Forgive the transgressions of a wayward boy. Show Ronnie Lane mercy. Do it for me, Lord. Yes, I'm a sinner, yet I'm forgiven, for the Cross is my salvation. So, please give my son a second ... ."

Suddenly, while Gloria Grace pleaded with God on her knees at the foot of her bed, and as her only son Ronald Lane Wilky stood in his holding cell gazing up at Heaven, a thin band of blinding light scanned over him from head to toe making his whole body sparkle. He frantically tried to brush it off, then wiggle it off, and then kick it off. As soon as the first band reached his feet, another band of light encircled his head. This second band of light, wider than the first and descending much slower and merely glowing, scanned down his body too, filling him with a peace he had never known.

At the foot of her bed, Gloria Grace felt the blessed assurance of an answered prayer and praised God, "Thank You. Thank You, Lord. I know your workin' a miracle for my boy." She exclaimed, "Hallelujah!" Then burst out singing, "Amaaa-zing graaace, how sweeet the sound ... ."

Though there had never been a successful escape from the ironfisted prison, Wilky levitated between floor and ceiling, launched forward, and miraculously passed through the concrete outer wall of his cell. He zipped across the exercise yard, shot through two rows of razor wire fences without suffering cuts, and slipped quietly past the guards in the gun towers without triggering alarms. With only a pallid hint of the rising sun, he rocketed across the fleeting twilight beyond the prison lights, above streetlamps, car beams, and house lights; soaring over Farm to Market Rd 350, the placid waters of Lake Livingston, and the verdant hills of Livingston State park; zooming on, the rush of air cooling his sweat soaked clothes, he sailed above the small towns of Shephard, Cleveland, and Atascocita. Gliding over Lake Houston, he flew just above the flocks of waterfowl paddling on its surface. Finally, descending into the city of Houston, he set foot on the ground and abruptly stopped—

though the momentum of riding in the hand of God caused him to stumble forward a few steps.

Feeling dizzy as if he just stepped off an airport peoplemover, he thrust out his hands to regain his balance. Glancing around, he saw that he stood out of his cell and seventy-five miles away on a corroded sidewalk in the fifth ward, a high crime district northeast of downtown Houston. He grew up living with his mother in a small home just a few blocks away and two streets over. Across the street, the sunrise stabbed a dagger of light between a horribly neglected home and a boarded-up house defaced with graffiti. He blinked, having not seen a sunup for fifteen years. Sweat trickled down his brow. Even daybreak during the summer months in Texas is hot and humid.

Wilky couldn't believe he had returned to his old neighborhood. Behind him was the old man's small, run-down house, gray with peeling paint, a leaning front porch, and security bars covering its windows. On one side of the house was a vacant lot with overgrown weeds and on the other side, a fire damaged house with its roof covered in green plastic sheets. At one end of the block stood the grim little grocery store and at the other end sat the cheerless liquor store. Across the street from the liquor store, stood the old Baptist church, mama's church, white with clapboard siding, its cross at the top of the steeple beckoning repentance to all the sinners coming out of the liquor store. Looking at the neighborhood closer, he realized nothing had changed. He had traveled back fifteen years earlier to the place and to the time just before he had committed the murder.

The street lamp hummed then shut off glowing for another few seconds. A mockingbird chirped from on top of a nearby power pole while a dog barked far off down the street. In the dim light of dawn, Wilky peered at the old man's car parked in the driveway. Though the car was an older model, an '83, four door, Chrysler Fifth Avenue, its old paint shined and its tires still had tread. Without a killswitch, steering wheel lock, or an alarm, the car would be easy to steal. Back when Wilky shot the old man, he didn't even know the old guy's name. All he knew when he had determined to steal the car, was that the man lived alone, worked maintenance on the graveyard shift at Mim's Meat Packing Company, and that his daily routine was to arrive home at 6:15 am, going directly to bed. Back then, while stealing the car, Wilky had discovered that the old man owned a cat—and a shotgun. Only after his arrest had he learned that the dead man's name was Roy Matson.

Wilky glanced up and down the street. A few houses had lights on. The rest were dark and quiet. Not a soul out except a man in boxers a few houses down reached out his screen door to grab his newspaper. Wilky focused on old man Matson's car, noticing a dark figure in the driver's seat. He crept over to the Chrysler, yanked open its passenger door, and jumped inside. On the console between the seats lay a Slim Jim, a dead blow hammer, and a 9mm pistol. A screwdriver stuck out of the ignition.

Startled, the young man leaning under the smashed steering column sat up, grabbed his gun, jammed it in Wilky's face, and yelled, "What the hell? Get out!"

"Hold on," said Wilky, holding up his hands. "I just want to talk to you."

"Talk to me? Right now? Get out, or I swear, I'll blow your head off!"

"Listen! We don't have much time."

"GET OUT!"

"Listen to me," said Wilky. "Don't do what you're about to do!"

The kid looked young with a head full of curly brown hair, a skinny torso with boney arms and hands, and a narrow face dotted with zits.

The young man noticed Wilky's white jump suit and asked, "You from prison? You escaped?"

"It looks that way don't it," snapped Wilky. "Now listen. I know what you're doin' and why. Who you're seein' and when. What'll happen and how you'll go down for it."

"You don't know sh... ."

"Hear me out punk! I know your plans. You'll jack this car, thinkin' the sleepin' ol' man will never miss it until you're done with it. Then, you'll pick up Darryl. You always do what he says 'cause he's older than you, even though he don't have a lick of brains. In fact, he's as dumb as you."

"Shut up! I'm warnin' you. Get out of the car!"

"Then you guys will drive over to Joey's trashy apartment where you'll hang out for a few hours until the bank opens. Since it's payday for all the factories around here, the bank will have lots of cash."

"Who told you?"

"No one. I just know. I know this too. You're nervous about robbin' the bank. Armed robbery is a whole hell of a lot worse than the crimes you've committed before. You know if you get caught, you'll go down for a long time. You'll do it anyway though, thinkin' about all that cash buyin' you a fast car, cool clothes, hot chicks, and all the killer weed you can smoke."

The teenager's eyes grew big and his hand holding the gun to Wilky's head trembled as he said, "How do you know anything? Huh? How?"

Wilky persisted, "What you don't know is, you ain't goin' no where in this car. Before the ol' man went to bed, he forgot to put his stupid cat out. Any moment now, that cat wakes him up. He opens the front door to toss it out and sees you stealin' his car. He grabs his shotgun leanin' in the corner behind his front door and comes runnin' over here, screamin' 'Help!' for the entire neighborhood to hear. You start the car and slam it into reverse. The engine dies. The old man yanks open the car door, points his shotgun at you, and shouts, 'Get out of my car or I'll blow your head off!' You keep tryin' to start it. You smell the gas. It's flooded. He yells again, 'Get out of my car!' then hesitates, lowers his gun to get a better look at you and says, 'You're from around here. I know who you are.' You panic, grab your pistol, and plug him in the chest with two bullets. That fast. Boom! Boom! He stumbles backward and drops flat on his back on the driveway. You try to start the car again. It cranks over and over, but won't start. You hear police sirens. Scared, you jump out of the car and flee down the street. Every person on this block who heard those shots, rush out of their home and see you runnin' down the street with the gun in your hand. The old man dies on the way to the hospital, but before he does—he tells the cops who you are. Within the hour, the cops arrest you hidin' under your mom's front porch. With so much evidence and so many witnesses, you're found guilty and sentenced to death by lethal injection. Fifteen years from now, on this day, in just a few minutes, the Texas Department of Criminal Justice carries out that judgment and put you to death. You hear me? You die!"

The young man in the car yells at Wilky, "You're crazy! How could you know all that? What do you mean, I die?"

"You're gonna die 'cause I'm gonna die. As insane as it sounds—I'm you!"

"What? What are you talkin' about? That's impossible!"

"Listen to me. Fifteen years ago, I tried to steal this car so me and my buddies could rob a bank. I shot the old man and now I'm goin' to die for it. You're going to die for it. Then, you as me are going to burn in Hell."

The young man seeing that Wilky was thirty pounds heavier than he was, had a considerable receding hairline, and a steeled face of a hard life doin' time, yelled, "You can't be me! You're too old and you look like Hell!"

"Death Row *is* Hell. There's no hope. Your body ages, your mind dulls, and your soul shrivels to the size of a cigarette butt. You don't have to spend your life locked up. You don't have to die. You've got a second chance here. I can't explain it. All I know is mama has always prayed, prayin' for you since you were born, prayin' for you right now, and prayin' for you all the way up to your execution. She's worn out the carpet prayin' for you, Ronnie Lane. "

"You know my name," asked Ronnie Lane, "and you've been in my house?"

"Of course. I'm tellin' you, I'm you. I grew up there. I remember falling out of the tree out back by the alley. I remember hiding under the front porch when Jesse and mama fought, and I still miss Rocket."

"How could you know that stuff? How could you know about my dog?"

"I know. That was a tough day when Rocket got sick and died. Just try to understand! Mama's prayers brought me here to talk sense into you. Listen, fifteen years from this day, the State of Texas will execute you. Mama prayed and God answered her prayer giving me—giving you—a second chance. Just get out of this car! Get out before it's too late! Get out before you— me—burn in Hell. All that fire; burnin' like Jesse burned. You saw him screamin' and burnin'! Same thing's goin' happen to you, screamin' and burnin' forever in Hell!"

"Shut-up about fire! Shut-up about Hell!"

"You can't even light a match without shakin'!"

"Shut up! I'm warnin' you. Shut up!"

"Run away from here! Right now, before it's too late! Stay away from those loser friends and take your mama to church. You got that! Take her to church!"

Ronnie Lane sucked in a few deep breaths, regained his coolness, sneered at Wilky, and said, "Get out or on the count of three, I'm gonna shoot. One, two, … ." He stopped counting when he saw the old man's front door swing open. A white cat flew out the door and landed on all four paws. The indignant feline snapped its long tail and then scampered across the yard.

As always, whenever the old man tossed the cat out, he leaned out the door and glanced around. Seeing the two men inside his car, he grabbed his shotgun from behind the door. Chubby, bald, and with a full gray beard, he charged out barefoot, wearing only his striped boxers and a white undershirt. He ran toward his car and shouted, "Help! Help!" A few neighbors heard him and called the police.

Wilky yelled at Ronnie Lane, "Get out! Run!"

The old man pointed his shotgun at the passenger window and hollered, "If you make a move, I'll shoot."

Ronnie Lane and Wilky froze.

The old man slowly sidestepped around to stand by the trunk of his car, never taking his gun off the two car thieves. He growled, "Get out! Don't try to run. I swear, I'll shoot!"

Ronnie Lane and Wilky slowly opened their car doors. Wilky shouted, "We're comin' out, Mr. Matson. Don't shoot."

Ronnie Lane snatched up his 9mm, gripped it in his right hand, and hid it behind his back. Wilky saw him do it. Both men stepped out of the car. Their eyes met. Wilky inconspicuously shook his head warning Ronnie Lane not to use the gun. Matson jerked his gun left and right, back and forth, covering both men stepping toward him to stand by the taillights of the car. Police sirens wailed in the distance. Matson, seeing Wilky in what looked to be prison garb and assuming Wilky was much more dangerous than Ronnie Lane, pointed his gun at Wilky.

Ronnie Lane, thinking once the shotgun was on the ground, he could run away, slowly wiped the sweat from his forehead, quickly drew out his pistol, and said, "Put the gun down, mister."

Matson swung his shotgun toward Ronnie Lane.

Time seemed to stop. Birds stopped chirping. Dogs ceased barking. Sweat beaded on the foreheads of all three men. Silent seconds ticked off while each man's stone face concealed his squirming mind playing out multiple scenarios of, what will he do? What will the other do? What will I do?

A little white butterfly wandered in between the men and fluttered in erratic circles. Ronnie Lane panicked. So did Matson. Wilky saw their bodies stiffen and their jaws clench as both men tightly gripped their guns. He lunged at the old man knocking the barrel of his shotgun up and away. As he did, both guns blasted. The shotgun blast grazed Ronnie Lane's right shoulder, but mostly trimmed a hedge next to him. The bullet Ronnie Lane fired plugged Wilky in the back between the letter D and R and exited out his chest, dropping him to his knees. In shock, his face frozen in horror, he collapsed, and then rolled over on his back to lock eyes with Ronnie Lane.

Horrified and shaking, Ronnie Lane pointed his pistol at Matson and yelled, "Put the gun down ol' man!"

Matson hesitated.

"Do it now! I mean it! Don't make me shoot you!"

"Settle down, young man, I'm doing it" said Matson, bending over and setting down his shotgun on the driveway.

"Now move away from it," ordered Ronnie Lane.

"Okay. Okay. Don't shoot."

Wilky lay in a brilliant patch of sunrise. He raised a hand to Ronnie Lane and muttered, "Please, stop this now. Hand your gun to Matson and give yourself up. Just do it!"

Ronnie Lane peered down at Wilky's face. In the bright sunshine, he noticed Wilky's same blue eyes as his, the same chipped front tooth as his, the same round chicken pox scar on his forehead as his, and for the first time, he read Wilky's nametag, Ronald Lane Wilky.

Wilky closed his eyes and vanished from the driveway, leaving behind a small pool of glistening blood.

Neither Matson nor Ronnie Lane could believe their eyes. Wilky was gone.

The old man asked, "Where'd he go?"

Ronnie Lane stammered, "I—I don't know, but, I'm

thinkin'—if I give you this gun, will you promise not to shoot me?"

"I promise," replied the old man.

"When the police get here, will you tell them what I'm about to tell you right now?"

"Sure son, I will. You have my word. Tell me."

Wilky opened his eyes expecting to see Ronnie Lane hovering over him pointing his gun at Matson. Unfortunately, he found himself back in the present time with his legs, arms, and head strapped to the table in the execution chamber at Polunsky. His eyes darted around the room. He saw bags of saline hanging on hooks, a cardiac monitor, and IV tubes. Next to him was a tray with three syringes, one each of sodium pentothal, pancuronium, and potassium chloride. Somber faces stared down at him. Solemn witnesses watched through a window. The warden, ending his phone call with the Governor, stated, "No stay of execution. Begin the sodium pentothal." The prison chaplain bowed his head whispering a prayer. A physician stood by waiting to declare death.

Wilky felt hot, as if on fire. Horror filled his eyes, reflecting the inferno of Hell all around him. Eager flames of damnation licked at his soul. A large fiery hand reached out to snatch him. He fought his restraints, screaming, "Fire! I'm on Fire!"

The execution team scrambled to control him. Someone gasped, "Oh my god! He's bleeding! His chest is bleeding!"

At that moment, time shifted. The past and present occurred at the same time, both becoming an expression of Wilky's repentant heart.

In the old neighborhood, fifteen years in the past, Ronnie Lane told the old man, "I'm gonna tell you what I want you to tell the cops and then I'll hand over the gun to you. Okay?"

"Sure kid. What is it you want me to tell them?"

Neighbors were rushing toward the old man's house. Police sirens were a block away.

"I want you to tell them," said Ronnie Lane, "that I gave myself up to you. Tell them that I'm sorry and that I don't want to end up on death row."

As he spoke to the old man, his mama, Gloria Grace, living a few blocks over, heard police sirens, jumped out of bed, and knelt directly into her prayer spot, praying, "Dear, Lord, wherever my boy is right now, help him do the right thing. Help him to see the error of his ways. Talk to him so he can hear Your voice. Change his heart, oh, Lord and please forgive him."

While his mama prayed, Ronnie Lane continued speaking to the old man, "Tell them that I want to change my life. No more hurtin' my mama. No more hurtin' anybody. I want to do what is right."

In present time, on the execution table, Wilky, horrified at the sight of Hell and covered in his own blood, yelled, "God, please forgive me!"

On the driveway, Ronnie Lane stepped forward and handed the pistol to the old man and as he did, he whispered, "God, please forgive me."

Two police cars screeched to a halt in front of the old man's house. Ronnie Lane lay down next to Wilky's pool of blood and as he placed his hands behind his back ready to be handcuffed, his shoulder wound dropped blood into the blood of Wilky's.

When the blood of the past and of the younger mixed with that of the future and of the older, the two time-lines merged, becoming one life; the life of a young man set upon a new course.

Instantly, in the death chamber, the fiery hand of Hell withdrew from Wilky, the vision left him, and he disappeared. So did his records and his presence at the Alan B. Polunsky unit. For Ronald Lane Wilky, the murder of Roy Matson, fifteen years in prison, and death row had never happened.

Roy Matson and Ronnie Lane found it difficult to explain to the police the disappearance of Wilky. Since there was no body, there was no murder. DNA tests on the blood in the driveway proved to be from Ronnie Lane's shoulder injury. The judge considered the fact that Mr. Matson testified on behalf of Ronnie Lane and that the young man had given himself up. Ronnie Lane received a reduced sentence of two years. After serving twelve months, the Texas Department of Criminal Justice released him on parole.

Once out of prison, Ronnie Lane took his mama to church every Sunday. He learned about God's grace and forgiveness and never feared Hell or fire again.

After a church service one Sunday morning, Pastor Ed asked Ronnie Lane to reach out into their community to help troubled teens. Ronnie Lane accepted the call to serve the Lord and over the years, the ministry grew, providing thousands of wayward kids with not only a second chance, but a first chance.

To fulfill a greater purpose, God altered time, thus transforming a man's heart, his life, and his eternity. Ronald Lane Wilky received mercy, a miracle, and a second chance.

TEXAS DEPARTMENT OF CRIMINAL JUSTICE
Huntsville Unit
815 12th Street, Huntsville, Texas 77342

Name: Ronald Lane Wilky
Inmate Number: 444235
Cell Number: 256
Race: Caucasian
Hair: Brown
Eyes: Blue
Height: 5'10"

Weight: 160 lbs.
DOB: 05-13-1977
Crime: Assault/Attempted Grand Theft
Date of Crime: 07-10-1997
Sentence: 2 years.
Time served: 1 year
Released on Parole: 7-10-1998

In-Flew-Enza

The muffled voices of young girls singing a jump rope rhyme drifted in through the slightly open window, "I had a little bird. Its name was Enza. I opened a window. And in-flew-Enza."

A late autumn breeze, feeble though chilly, stirred the drab curtains bordering the window frame. Gracie Everett, a seventeen-year-old nurse's aid drew close to the window and peered outside. The bright fall days blessing the small township of Emporia, Kansas had changed to overcast skies and the advent of winter had chased away nature's cheerful colors. Just outside the window, two dark-haired girls, the Nicoletti sisters, seven-year-old Zita and nine-year-old Aletta, each held an end of the rope, twirling, singing, while a small red-haired girl, eight year-old Margaret Kelly skipped in perfect rhythm to the rope slapping the sidewalk. It was mid-morning, a school day, but health officials had suspended all classes since the outbreak of influenza. The girls wore sweaters over their play clothes and a white gauze mask covered the nose and mouth of each girl. Naïve of the lyrics, they repeatedly chanted the disturbing rhyme, "I had a little bird. Its name was Enza. I opened a window. And in-flew-Enza."

Gracie listened, staring out the window, lost in her thoughts, wondering if the sickness and death would ever end. She sighed, remembering last March, the spring of 1918. The season had started like every glorious spring; sunshine and showers, buds and flowers, new life, happy days picnicking on the banks of the Neosho River, shopping trips to Topeka, and then, the virulent, highly contagious virus arrived. Everyone lost family members. Many were deathly ill. No one could have fathomed that by June of 1920, when the cases of influenza mercifully subsided, the virus would have spread around the world, including the Arctic and remote Pacific islands. With more than 500 million infected and between 50 and 100 million deaths, the Spanish Flu became one of the deadliest natural disasters in human history. Even if Gracie had foreseen the forthcoming human toll and known the extreme peril to her own life, she would have remained helping; the sick needed care and compassion; they needed her.

The girls outside stopped jumping rope while Zita and Margaret traded places. Gracie turned away from the window and looked at all the afflicted lying in metal foldout beds, evenly spaced, filling the assembly hall at Emporia High School. Red Cross doctors, nurses, and volunteers all wearing gauze masks moved from one sick person to the next. Not far from Gracie, six beds away, two older men in masks, Frank and Earl wrapped the decimated body of twenty-nine-year-old Anna Nicoletti in her thin bed sheet, carried her out the back door, and laid her in a wooden wagon with five other bodies. Her husband, Rinaldo Nicoletti, sobbing with his masked face in his hands, still sat in the chair next to her empty bed. After a few minutes, he stood, composed himself, and stepped outside to tell his daughters skipping rope of the passing of their mother.

A few beds over lay thirteen-year-old Tommy Kelly moaning in agony. Not wearing a mask, a blood-tinged froth trickled out of his nose and mouth. His skin appeared blue from respiratory failure. He wore a small bag of camphor around his neck and his breath smelled of onions, both home remedies with little effect against the virus. His mother, Myrna, wearing a mask, knelt by his bed and whispered prayers.

Gracie left the window, walked over to the lad's mother, and said, "Don't worry Mrs. Kelly, I'll watch over your son."

The woman didn't hear her, but prayed faster and louder, "God, please save my boy. Please, please, please, save my boy," until she broke out wailing. Influenza had taken her husband, Shawn Kelly three days before.

Gracie heard a man violently coughing and then moan through his mask, "Water. Please, someone, I need a drink of water." She spun and saw the middle-aged man rise up off his pillow, cry out again, but louder, "Water, please, I need water!" In his grave condition, she barely recognized Mr. Sanders, her math teacher. The instructor, utterly fatigued, looked past her with glazed eyes and then collapsed on his pillow.

Just as she took a step to give the suffering man a cup of cool water, one of the other young nurse's aids, Ellen, brought it to him. Ellen, wearing a mask, cradled his head, raised him up, lowered his mask, and held the cup to his lips while Mr. Sanders drank. He groaned with meager relief and fell unconscious. Ellen laid his head down, adjusted his mask, and moved on to other patients.

Gracie felt strange; there, in the moment, but somewhat removed. Maybe she couldn't take it anymore; all the moaning and groaning, the coughing and wheezing, the blood, sweat, and vomit, the toil, the long hours, and the pungent smell of human misery. She beheld all of the sick laid out before her and grimaced at the terror in their eyes, knowing they had little chance to live. Perhaps, she had witnessed far too many deaths, seeing her cousins, aunts, and uncles, neighbors, classmates, and town's people die. It was horrifying that the masses of rotting corpses were stacking up like cordwood all over town due to the lack of coffins and gravediggers. All seemed hopeless. She felt helpless. However, in the middle of it all, there was one blessing amidst the curse of the flu. Her parents and little sister seemed healthy—for now. Nevertheless, she still grieved over Doris Fuller, her best friend since grade school. Not long ago, in September, they had attended an ice cream social at their church. The entire evening, the two girls giggled over meeting a handsome, new boy. Afterwards, the girls had shared secret dreams of romantic dates and first kisses. Doris died two weeks later. The nice, good-looking boy passed a week after Doris.

Gracie had volunteered at the makeshift hospital against her parent's wishes. She had to help. As a child, she had nursed sick kittens, runt puppies, and fuzzy baby birds. How could she not help a human being in such dire need? Her heart was big, her compassion great, and the agony of those suffering cried out to her, hailing her to be brave, to pray, to love, and to sacrifice, if she must, her very life to serve those who so desperately needed her. She would not leave until the flu left and every sick soul recovered.

Hazel Schmidt, a Red Cross nurse wearing a bonnet, mask, and woolen uniform, checked the forehead and the pulse of a teenage girl in a bed across the aisle. The stout, older woman peered down at the once vibrant girl, pretty, with big green eyes and long brown hair. Now, the poor girl, consumed by the high fever and pneumonia, was dead, her eyes closed and her sweat soaked hair sticking to her ashen face. Hazel, overwhelmed with sorrow, sighed, whispered under her breath, "Such a nice girl," and somberly shook her head while summoning Frank and Earl returning through the back door.

Gracie walked over to the nurse, stood next to her, and asked, "Hazel, may I help you?"

Before Hazel could respond, a wheezing young man, yelled in a panic, and the busy nurse scrambled to help him.

Gracie glanced down at the dead girl and gasped, reeling a step back in horror, covering her mouth with her hand. Gracie didn't wear a mask, strange as it might be; she didn't need a mask. In shock, she watched as Frank and Earl, obviously saddened by the young girl's death, covered her body in her bed sheet, lifted her gently, and carried her out to the wagon. An elderly woman, a volunteer by the name of Mildred, quickly changed the pillowcase and covered the bed with a new sheet. Before the bed grew cold, another victim lay on it.

Still dazed by the sight of the dead girl, Gracie heard a familiar voice call out, "Gracie! Gracie!"

She spun, peered at the double entrance doors, and saw her best friend, Doris Fuller, standing there smiling, bathed in brilliant light.

Doris said, "Gracie, it's time to go. Please, come with me!"

Gracie stepped back bewildered, but then, filled with joy, ran to Doris. They hugged as Gracie asked, "Doris, what are you doing here? I was at your bedside when you—you died."

"I've come to walk with you home, just like we did everyday after school."

"I can't leave," said Gracie sternly. "The sick need me."

"Oh, but you must leave. It's your time. Others will help them."

"I can't. I must stay and help."

Doris gazed into Gracie's big green eyes, brushed back her long brown hair, and softly said, "Gracie, you and I are best friends, so please listen to me. You have helped many suffering people, but you must realize that you've made the supreme sacrifice—your life."

"No, no, no, I must help those who ... ." Gracie became silent, turned, and gazed at all the sick. Suddenly, the veil of denial lifted and she recalled the agony of the flu, the struggle to breathe, the burning fever, and the weariness. She had simply closed her eyes to rest, if only for a moment.

Her parents, Ted and Ruth, both wearing masks, rushed in through the doors and hastened past her straight to Hazel

Schmidt. Hazel spoke softly and shook her head. Gracie's mom and dad wept.

Gracie faced the truth. No one had seen or heard her. Frank and Earl were carrying her lifeless body out to the wagon.

Doris took Gracie's hand and led her outside. A scant breeze rustled fallen leaves across the sidewalk as the sun reached down between the clouds and gave Emporia, Kansas a warm embrace. The best friends strolled hand in hand while Gracie, with her other hand, held the hand of Tommy Kelly. Anna Nicoletti and many others followed behind them. Free of the flu and filled with peace, all of them were smiling as they walked past the three girls jumping rope.

The Nicoletti sisters had left sobbing with their grieving father, while little redheaded Margaret Kelly had made friends with two other girls, one of them Gracie's little sister, Judy. Unaware of the glowing spirits stepping into a blazing light and vanishing just beyond them, the young girls wearing masks skipped rope, chanting, "I had a little bird. Its name was Enza. I opened a window. And in-flew-Enza. I had a little bird. Its name was Enza. I opened a window. And in-flew-Enza. I had a little bird. Its name was Enza. I opened a window. And in-flew-Enza."

HAIRPIN CURVE

Tom and Betty Elders, married for forty-eight years and both in their early seventies rode in their 2011 Buick LaCrosse up to their mountain cabin to celebrate Christmas. The time was around 7 p.m., Christmas Eve. Darkness and heavy snowfall made for poor visibility on the winding two-lane highway. The wipers slapped back and forth while the defroster blasted to keep the windshield clear. The car stereo played a CD of Christmas songs, though neither Tom nor Betty sang along. He gripped the steering wheel with both hands while she clasped her hands in her lap. They traveled at a safe distance behind a two-tone, colonial white and steel blue 1959 Ford Fairlane. As the classic car navigated the curves, its large red taillamps would appear and disappear along with its headlights illuminating pine trees and the granite faces of the hewn mountainside. Patches of ice covered the road. A road sign warned of a hairpin turn. The Fairlane disappeared.

Tom turned off the Christmas music and said, "Hey, Betty, where'd that old Ford go in front of us? I don't see it anymore."

"I don't see it either, Tom. Did it speed up?"

"With so much ice on the road, I would hope not."

"Did we pass any driveways or side roads for it to turn onto?"

"Not that I saw. I'm thinking it slid off the road back at that hairpin curve."

"We'd better turn around and go see."

At the next turnout, Tom maneuvered the car around and drove the half-mile back to the tight curve. He parked as far onto the shoulder as possible, climbed out of his car, stood on the edge of the embankment, and peered down. He hurried back to the car, opened the door, leaned in, and said with a shiver, "Yep, that old car is down in the ravine and its headlights are still on. I think it's upside down. The embankment is steep and the car must have rolled five or six times. It's pretty far down. I can't get to it."

"Well, hurry back in the car Tom. Warm up while I call emergency.—Oh nooo, there's no signal."

"Okay, we'll drive up to the cabin as fast as we can and call 9-1-1 on the land line."

"Okay, but let's not slide off the road too."

"Don't worry, I'll drive careful. You watch for a road marker."

Fifteen minutes later up at the Elder's cabin, Tom called emergency, reported the accident, and told them the closest road marker to it. Emergency dispatched an officer with a 4-wheel drive vehicle to the scene.

The next morning the sun shone bright making the freshly fallen snow sparkle like diamonds. The phone rang. Tom answered."

"Hello."

"Hello, Mr. Tom Elders?"

"Yes."

"This is Officer Samuels with the California Highway Patrol. We found the car you called us about last night."

"Good, good. Was everyone okay?"

"There wasn't anybody in the car."

"No one in the car?"

"Nope. Nobody. All we found down in that ravine was the rusted, vandalized shell of that '59 Ford."

"But—but, Officer Samuels, we saw it on the highway. I saw its headlights in the ravine."

"I believe you. Same situation as nine times before. If a motorist is on that highway at around seven-o-clock on Christmas Eve, we receive a call about an old car careening off the road, rolling, and landing upside down with headlights blazing. We investigate it, but like always—all we find down in that ravine is that old junker."

"I still don't understand."

"Sorry, Mr. Elders—can't explain it."

"Wow. That's weird."

"For sure. Well, Mr. Elders, you and your wife have a Merry Christmas."

The day before Christmas, 1961, at about 10 in the morning, John Franklin called his six-year-old daughter, Natalie. He had just checked out of a run down motor inn and made the call from a phone booth at the filling station next door."

"Hi, Nat. How are you, honey?"

"Hi, Daddy. I had a bad tummy ache all day."

"Ohhh, sweetie, I'm so sorry. Did you eat too many Christmas cookies?"

"No, only the two that mommy gave me."

"You didn't sneak a few more?"

"No, Daddy, I didn't. I promise. Anyway, I feel better now."

"Good. I'm glad you're feeling better. Are you excited about Christmas?"

"Yes, but I just want it to hurry up. I've been waiting sooo long."

"Christmas is in the morning and you can open presents."

"Yaaay! I hope Santa remembers my wish."

"Oh, sugar, how could he forget a good little girl like you?"

"He'd better not. I've been very, very, very, very, very, very good!"

"Yes, you have. In fact, I'll bet, you're the sweetest little first-grader in the whole world. There's no doubt that Natalie Franklin is on Santa's nice list. Besides, he knows exactly what you wished for. I promise, you'll get your Christmas wish."

"Okay, Daddy. Where are you?"

"I'm way up in Redding closing a few sales."

"When are you coming to see me?"

"Well, it's a long drive back to you in San Jose and there's a bad storm coming, but nothing is going to keep me from my little girl on Christmas. No snowstorm, hailstorm, or rainstorm. No earthquake, hurricane, or tornado. No flood, no fire, and definitely no herd of huge elephants, no flock of pink flamingos, and no band of silly monkeys. Ooo, ooo, eee, eee, ahh, ahh!"

"You're funny, Daddy! I miss you a whole bunch."

"I miss you too, but I'll be there early in the morning."

"Okay, Daddy."

"Don't forget, you're my special little girl. I love you, Natti-bug!"

"Okay, Daddy," giggled Natalie. "I'm your Natti-bug and you're my Daddy-bug!"

"That's right. Okay, honey, please, put mommy on the phone and you go watch *Lassie* on TV."

"Okay Daddy. I love you. Here's mommy. Bye, bye."

"Bye, bye, Nat."

"Hello, John. Did you mail out the child support check yet?"

"Woah! Straight to business, huh, Joan? How about, how's your trip? Or, drive careful, there's a blizzard heading your way."

"It's Christmas, John. I bought a few extra gifts for my family. I need the money to pay bills."

"You mean extra gifts for Chad. Why doesn't he start paying a few of your bills? He practically lives with you?"

"Please, John, don't start about Chad. Just tell me if you mailed the check or not."

"No, I didn't. I'll drop it off in the morning."

"That makes you late again. You'd better bring it or I'll take you back to court. You know I will. Did you pick up what we discussed a couple of weeks ago?"

"No, not yet. I'm stopping to buy it at a toy store here in Redding."

"Are you kidding me? You'll be lucky if they still have one. Last week, the news reported that stores everywhere were running out."

"I've been so busy. Don't worry, I'll get it."

"That's so typical of you. Work, work, work, that's all you think about."

"All I think about is making sales to make commission to pay child support so I can make damn sure my daughter doesn't go without! That's why I'm working the day before Christmas. I'm doing it for Natalie. You know how December is always a tough month for me."

"I ask you to pick up the most important Christmas gift for your daughter and you wait until the last minute. I can't depend on you. Never could. That's why we're getting divorced."

"No, we're getting divorced because you fell in love with your boss."

"Enough, John! Be a good father and pick up the present that Natalie told Santa she wanted."

"Shhhh, she can probably hear you."

"No, she's watching, *Lassie*. Just make sure your daughter gets her gift and has a wonderful Christmas."

"Okay, listen, right after we hang up, I'm seeing a few customers and then stopping by a toy store. Right after that, I'm leaving Redding. I'm hoping I can beat the bad storm that's blowing in. I'll stop by in the morning at around eight-o-clock with Natalie's present. It'll be store wrapped with a big red bow. I'll write out your check when I'm there. When

I get home, I mean to *your* place, I'll leave the gift on the porch. Then, I'll distract Natalie while you sneak her present under the tree. I'll only stay long enough to watch her open her presents."

"Okay, but you'd better have my check or we'll be back in court. Got it? What's more, you'd better have that doll or your daughter will hate you forever."

"Don't threaten me and don't worry, I'll have your check and her present."

"Okay, and just because it's Christmas Eve and you're alone at home tonight, don't start drinking again. Goodbye, John."

"I haven't had a drop of alcohol in three months! Moreover, if not for Chad, I wouldn't be alone. Goodbye, Joan. Oh, and tell that cocky boyfriend of yours to be cool tomorrow. I don't want any trouble."

"Goodbye, John."

"Hey, one more thing, tell Natalie how much I love her."

"You can tell her in the morning. Goodbye."

Christmas day, 2011. Fifty years had passed since Natalie spoke that day on the telephone with her father. She has been married for thirty years to her husband, Brian Vale. They have a daughter, Karen, twenty-seven and an eight-year-old granddaughter, Becky. Since Karen's divorce, she and her daughter lived with Natalie and Brian in Sacramento, California. Natalie's mother, Joan, never remarried and still resided in San Jose. She was on her way driving to Natalie's for Christmas dinner. Brian heard a knock at the front door and called out to Natalie.

"Hey, Natalie. Someone's at the door. Can you get it?"

"Come on Brian, I'm busy in the kitchen. Why can't you get it?"

"I'm waiting to watch the instant replay on a 49er touchdown. Besides, it's probably your mother."

"Ohhh, Brian, I can never depend on you for anything. Karen, get the door, please?"

"I can't mom. I just stepped out of the shower and I'm getting dressed."

"Becky, honey, can you get the door?"

"Sorry, grandma, I'm on the phone with my friend Jenny."

"Okay, fine. I'll get it!——Oh, hello, officer. Oh my god! What's the matter? What's wrong?"

"Hello, I'm Officer Dixon with the Sacramento Police Department. I'm so sorry to interrupt your Christmas. Are you Natalie Vale, maiden name, Franklin?"

"Yes, I am. My eighty-year-old mother, Joan Franklin is driving over from San Jose to celebrate Christmas with us. Is she okay?"

"Mrs. Vale, I'm not here about your mother. I'm here about your father."

"My father?"

"Yes, Mr. John William Franklin. He is your father, correct?"

"Yes. Yes, he is, but—but he hasn't been around for a long time."

"The California Highway Patrol up in Lake County contacted the authorities in San Jose. They've been unable to talk with your mother so they requested my department to contact you."

"Sooo, you finally found that dead-beat dad of mine? Didn't you?"

"Yes, but … ."

"Ohhh, you did! Isn't that nice? Fifty years ago, and I remember as if it were yesterday, he was supposed to come visit me on Christmas. Since he owed my mother a child support payment and he was too busy to buy me a Christmas present, he never showed up."

"Yes, we did locate him, however … ."

"Good! Now that I'm fifty-six with a daughter who's

twenty-seven and a granddaughter who's eight. What kind of a father would miss out on his daughter's birthdays, graduations, and wedding! Huh? And what kind of man would never see his granddaughter and great granddaughter?"

"Hello officer, I'm Brian Vale, Natalie's husband. What's going on?"

"Well you see … ."

"The officer said they found my father. I'll never forget what he did or shall I say it, didn't do. He was supposed to bring me a present from Santa. I know it's silly now, but when I was a little girl, it was all I truly wanted for Christmas. My mother told me that he put off buying it until all the stores had sold out. Plus, he owed her child support that he didn't have, so, he made up his mind, to run away from us. As mom always says, 'we could never depend on him for anything.' If not for my mother's boyfriend at the time, we would have been hurting for food the next month."

"Officer, my wife acts like she doesn't care, nevertheless, over our thirty years of marriage, she's told the story a thousand times."

"Well, Brian, I'm telling the story again."

"Please, Mrs. Vale," interjected the officer, "I read the accident and missing person reports filed back in 1961. As you probably know, his '59 Ford Fairlane was found on Christmas, the morning after his crash on Christmas Eve."

"Yes, my mother told me all about the accident. She said that he had been drinking a lot since their separation. He was most likely drunk when he crashed his car. She always suspected that he fled the scene to avoid going to jail. He just hiked away from the crash, changed his name, and hid somewhere far away. He's probably remarried and has a family of his own. Right?"

"Hold on now, Mrs. Vale. Let me tell you why I'm here. From the missing person report filed by your mother at that time, your father had checked out of his motel up in Redding around 10 am. He made a few sales calls on customers, stopped to do a little Christmas shopping, and then headed south on Interstate 5. The blizzard blew in causing a sixteen-car pile up just south of the small town of Williams. Motorists were directed to take a frontage road north back to Williams while road crews worked all night clearing the highway. Schools, churches, and civic-centers were opened to shelter the stranded travelers. Your father must have searched a map and decided to head west across the mountains on highway 20 to the 53 around Clear Lake and then south on the 29 to Santa Rosa. From Santa Rosa, it's a straight shot down the 101 to San Jose. To risk it, a mountain road at night in a blizzard, he must have really wanted to get home by Christmas. The route begins easy enough, but on highway 53 near the lake, it becomes treacherous with steep grades and hairpin turns. To say the least, it's dangerous in the summer and life threatening in winter. With hazardous conditions: snow, ice, and poor visibility, he missed a turn and slid off the road. His vehicle rolled numerous times and landed upside down a few hundred feet down in a ravine. The next morning, Christmas day, 1961, the storm diminished to snow flurries. A man driving down the highway pulled his car over to take off his snow chains when he spotted something glinting in the ravine. He saw that it was an overturned car and reported it to CHP who responded to the scene. They conducted a thorough search of the area, but never found your father."

"Like my mother said at the time they informed her of the accident and what she says to this day, 'bad things happen when you drink and drive.'"

"Natalie, please, let the officer tell us what happened."

"Stay out of this Brian. It's none of your business."

"First of all, it is my business! Every Christmas season you become depressed over your missing father, then, you turn angry and take it out on me."

"I do not!"

"Yes, you do!"

"Please, Mr. and Mrs. Vale, let me say what I need to say. So fifty years ago, on Christmas Eve, your father took a detour through the mountains, crashed, and disappeared. It's weird to say and you've never been contacted about it, but every Christmas Eve right up there on that mountain road something bizarre happens. Folks going to and from their cabins to spend Christmas report seeing an old model car careen off the road. Last night, there was another report by a Mr. and Mrs. Elders. Just like the Elders and in all the other cases, people stop, see headlights shining below, and call 9-1-1. Every time authorities arrive and investigate the reports, they find only your dad's stripped '59 Ford. It's hard to explain."

"So what about my father?"

"Well—early this morning, up on that highway, a snow plow operator, a Mr. Mendez saw an injured man limping down the shoulder of the road. The spot is about six miles down from the wreck of that '59 Ford. The area is remote without any cabins nearby. Like I said before, over all these years, others have witnessed the old car, however, this is the first time anyone reported seeing a person up on that mountain highway. Mendez was at the right spot at the right time. Anyway, the injured man stopped, stared at Mendez, and reached out both hands begging for help. Mendez stopped his plow and peered down to grab his radio. When he looked back out at the road, the man was gone. He called in for help. A CHP officer and a curious sheriff deputy responded. They searched the steep embankment directly below where Mendez saw the hurt man. Fifty feet down in a crevice hidden by large boulders, they found your father. On that Christmas long ago, he must have walked all those miles in that blizzard in the pitch dark. As I stated earlier, he desperately wanted to get home for Christmas. The officers concluded, since he was injured and tired, he must have slipped off the road and crawled in between the rocks where he most likely froze to death and has been entombed ever since."

"You're telling me that, all those years ago—my father died?"

"Yes. I'm sorry, Mrs. Vale. Searchers found only his remains. Fifty years ago, he either died from his injuries or froze to death. None of those searching at the time figured he could have walked so many miles in that snowstorm."

"But how could that snowplow operator see him standing on the road?"

"That, Mrs. Vale—I can't explain. Something else. Tucked under his coat zipped up tight, they found a present with your name on it. A gift, wrapped in silver foil with a big red bow. It's crazy, but it looks like it was just wrapped yesterday. The coverage of boulders, your father's heavy jacket, and the thick shopping bag protected it against the elements and animals all these years. Just a minute, I'll get it out of my patrol car."

"Mom, what's the matter? Why is a police officer here?"

"Oh, Karen. They found my father. He didn't abandon me; he died all those years ago—and he had my present."

"Here you go, Mrs. Vale. Again, my sympathies for your loss. My department will contact you this week to arrange for your father's remains. If you or your mother have any further questions you can contact me at this number."

"Thank you, Officer Dixon. Goodbye. Oh, and Merry Christmas!"

"Merry Christmas, Mrs. Vale, to you and your family."

"Come on mom, open it!"

"Okay, Karen! Get Becky and let's gather around the Christmas tree!"

Natalie sat in a rocking chair with Brian sitting in a lounge chair next to her. Karen and Becky, one on each side, knelt beside Natalie.

With childlike wonderment, Natalie peered down at the

present in her lap, and exclaimed, "Oh, such a beautiful present!" She carefully removed the red bow and unwrapped the silver foil with the intention of saving them." When she saw the gift inside she exclaimed, "Ohhh! Oh, my goodness! This can't be happening!" Tears streamed down her cheeks. Karen handed her a few tissues from a box nearby.

"I—I don't believe it," Natalie whispered, dabbing her tears. She held up the unwrapped present and spun it around showing Brian and the girls. With great joy and delight, she burst out, "It's a *Chatty Cathy*! When I was in first grade, all the little girls had one—except me. My dad promised me I'd get one from Santa. When I didn't get the doll and my mother told me my dad was Santa, I was furious. When he didn't show up to see me, I hurt so bad, I hated him. I thought he didn't love me."

"Mom, I'm sorry you hurt so bad, and for so many years, but what's so wonderful about a *Chatty Cathy*?"

Natalie removed the doll from its box and gave the box to her husband. The doll sat in her lap. It looked perfect and beautiful. Natalie found the ring on the doll's back and said, "You pull this ring and she talks. Let's see if she still works." Trembling, Natalie gently pulled the small ring on the string.

In a young girl's voice, *Chatty Cathy* sang out, "I love you, Natti-bug!"

Curse of Kubrik

"Who is it?"

"Adrik, it is Batsakis. Please, let me in."

"Yes, yes, dear brother, come in before you catch a chill. Why are you here at this late hour and on such a cold night? What is wrong?"

"Nothing is wrong—nothing now."

"What do you mean—nothing now?"

"I want to assure you that all I have done is undone and all that would be will be."

"You have done something?"

"Yes and no. All I am trying to say is that I, Batsakis Itzak, and my son, Yervant, indeed everyone, including you and your wife, we are who we were and forever destined to be."

"Me and my wife? What are you talking about? Tell me."

"I will tell you, but first, to be sure—you do not remember?"

"Remember? Remember what?"

"I was here. Here at your home an hour ago."

"No, Batsakis. No, you were not. Have you been tipping a jug of old Yakov's wine?"

"No, no, certainly not, but I *was* here. Did I not knock on your door?"

"No, you did not."

"Did you not let me in?"

"No, I did not."

"Did soldiers not surround your house and arrest me?"

"Soldiers! Oh, my! Soldiers? No. After Kiska and I ate bread and borscht, we sat by the fire. I read a book while she talked on the telephone with her sister Sasha."

"My dear brother, when I arrived here an hour ago, you were drunk, and I am very sad to say that Kiska had left you—but how is your dear wife now?"

"Drunk? Kiska gone? You are crazy! She is fine, though she has gone to bed, as I was ready to. I had just put the cat out when I heard your knock."

"Then, you are sure I was not here an hour ago?"

"Yes, Batsakis, I'm certain. I have not seen you for six months."

"Good, good, sorry to startle you. Since all is back to the way it was, let us sit by the fire in those rickety rockers of yours and I will tell you an amazing story."

"Yes, yes, tell me as we share a jug of old Yakov's wine. I will get the wine. You take off your coat, hat, and gloves, hang them up, and please, throw a log on the fire. Are Minka and my dear nephew, Yervant okay?"

"Yes, oh yes, they are fine. I phoned them that I was coming to see you."

"Good, good. If you are fine, they are fine, and Kiska and I are fine, then I will not worry. Here, hold the glasses while I pour the wine. Let me say, I am glad to see you little brother. Now sit, warm yourself, and tell me what happened."

"Where to begin? First—again, I assure you that all what was, is."

"Ahhh, well then, you need not fear a Siberian prison."

"Yes, oh yes, I fear it. Even worse, I fear I will be shot and then buried in a shallow grave beneath the snow. In fact—I nearly was."

"Batsakis, what—what did you do?"

"Adrik, I did something risky. Therefore, you must swear to secrecy. You cannot even tell Kiska."

"Adriiik! I hear talking. Who visits our home?"

"Kiska, my dear, it is Batsakis. We are drinking wine and having one of our, as you call them, 'boring discussions.' Please, go back to sleep."

"Okay, okay, but in the morning, I cook big breakfast!"

"Thank you, my dear wife. Thank you. Good night."

"Sorry to wake Kiska. I will speak softer."

"Not to worry, Batsakis, she will fall back to sleep and snore so horribly that you will need to speak louder. My brother, I swear, I will keep all secret. Please, continue."

"Okay. An hour ago, I did seek refuge at your home. You opened the door for me and I, Batsakis Itzak dashed into your home a handsome man! I was no longer grotesque and my little boy, my Yervant, no longer suffered the same unsightly curse as I. He too was good looking. And Adrik, he could walk again!"

"Now, now, Batsakis, you are insane or you are joking."

"Listen to me Adrik, I am sane and I am serious. What I did was very, very foolish, yet I did what I did because I could not bear to watch my son suffer. I had to change me to change him, thus ending all the teasing, hence erasing that awful day when bullies chased my poor boy into the street where he was hit by a car."

"Indeed, a very, very sad day."

"I had to prevent his broken spine and paralyzed legs. I had to, for it was *my* ghastly appearance that caused my son's agony. Tell me how ugly I am—to justify what I did."

"No."

"Say, 'Batsakis, you are the ugliest man in the world.'"

"No!"

"Say it!"

"No, I will not! But yes, yes you were born with uh,

different features, features, um, people may find, let's say, um, disagreeable."

"Disagreeable! Oh, Adrik, you are so kind. I am hideous! I have suffered since grade school when devilish children called me that—that hurtful name."

"Batsakis, calling you that—that name was not fair and I assure you, you do not look like a—I am afraid to say it, for you loathe it."

"Yes, I hate it. The school kids, they saw, they laughed, and they made up a fitting name. Indeed, I look exactly like one."

"Please, Batsakis, sit back down before you spill your wine."

"No, I cannot sit. Look at me! My complexion is darker than most of our countrymen and I have this long, thin face with this large, curved nose. I am ugly!"

"No, you are not so ugly. Borya, the mechanic—he is much uglier than you."

"Only that mole, big, black, and hairy in the middle of his forehead makes Borya uglier than I. Even so, I am still grotesque with these dark beady eyes in these deep sockets under this ridge of black, bushy eyebrows. They not only make me look ugly, but angry; however, I am only angry when my son is incessantly teased."

"No, no, you are not that ugly. Think of Slavik. Now, he is ugly."

"Who?"

"Slavik the woodcutter—he is much uglier than you. Is he not?"

"Yes, yes, I have met poor Slavik. Although he is ugly, he used to be handsome until his chain saw hit him in the face. Even so, he has a beautiful head of hair, unlike me. I am bald from front to back with this ring of frizzy black hair making my head appear as an egg in a vulture's nest."

"Really, Batsakis, you are not so ... ."

"I most certainly am with this—this skinny neck on these

drooping shoulders on top of this broomstick body. I am cursed. I look hideous. My son is cursed. He looks like me."

"Oh, Batsakis, looks are only skin deep. I, with all my good looks, am a simple farmer. I have no prestigious job and no children. I have only my loving wife, this small house, this little plot of land, my tiny garden, and a few chickens, goats, and cows. That is it; however, you—you are a brilliant scientist and the most esteemed in your field. You have a nice home with nice things and you are blessed with a family's love."

"Yes, yes, very blessed and yes, very brilliant—nevertheless, I am repulsive. As a child, I hid. I read books. I studied and expanded my genius, and yet everyday I endured horrendous mockery. You know this. We grew up together. Adrik, I cannot, ohhh, how it hurts me, I cannot watch my son, the spitting image of me, suffer such agony. It is pitiful. It is deplorable. It is inexcusable. My pain is his pain and his pain is my pain. Unfortunately, the torment is much greater for Yervant, the poor lad, is not only ugly like me, but is stuck in a wheelchair and cannot escape his tormentors. And now, now that he is thirteen, add pimples and a squeaky voice to his misery."

"Batsakis, he will grow out of puberty and mature into a fine young man."

"Yes, but he will only grow uglier as his head becomes bald, his eyes sink into their sockets, and his nose stretches to its full length and curls. Nearly everyday, when I return home from work, Minka sobs, 'Batsakis, our son came home from school crying again.' I ask her, 'Again, he cries? Have not the children grown tired of teasing him?' 'No,' she says, 'it is worse, now they throw garbage at him and call him *that* horrible name.' My precious Minka knows not to say it, but it is mine; it is his; it is Buzzard."

"Oh, Batsakis, please, sit down, relax, and let me pour you more wine."

"Okay, I will sit, and yes, more wine. Thank you. I detest

being called Buzzard and now those mean spirited children call Yervant, Buzzard too."

"It is true savagery. So Batsakis, tell me—what did you do?"

"I did what I did—to break the Curse of Kubrik."

"Again, the Curse of Kubrik! Why must you obsess over that so-called curse of yours when you have so many blessings? Blessings like your wife and son."

"Yes, I am very fortunate to have Minka, poor, sweet girl, homely and dull, but what a devoted, hardworking woman I found, and dare I say—yes, yes, I will say it; she is very pleasing and I am a lucky man to have her affection. To me, Minka, though she is short and round, as wide as tall, and wears too much make-up to hide her flaws, she is very beautiful to me and to her, I am handsome."

"Yes, a great catch, indeed. Excuse me, I hear the cat. Please, continue while I let it in."

"And my Yervant, a good boy, very intelligent, earning top marks in all his classes. Someday, he will be a remarkable scientist far greater than I."

"Yes, a very smart boy."

"And you Adrik, you are a blessing. We are only half-brothers, yet we are as close as any brothers."

"Indeed, and our mother, Yalenka—God rest her soul—loved you very much."

"Yes, and I loved her though she married my father, Kubrik, a terribly ugly man, who—damn him!—looked exactly like a buzzard!"

"Batsakis, Kubrik, God rest his soul as well, was a good and decent man. Do not forget that after my father Viktor died in the war, Kubrik rescued mother and me from deplorable poverty."

"Yes, he did, nevertheless, he was ugly—ugly like a buzzard. I blame him! It is his fault! He caused my affliction and consequently my son's misfortune."

"That is ridiculous. Please remember that mother loved him

for his kindness. He even adopted me. Where do you think your intelligence came from? Do not forget that at the time of his death he was the top engineer at the plant. So, tell me now. What, Batsakis? What did you do?"

"I could not bear to watch young Yervant suffer as I did and still do, so I ignored ethics, broke laws, and risked changing the world as it is and forever will be. I changed my father, which changed me, which changed my son. All for Yervant!"

"Changed your father? Changed Kubrik? Impossible!"

"No! Not impossible!"

"Adriiik! Are you coming to bed?"

"In a little while, Kiska. Go back to sleep! How, Batsakis? How did you change your father?"

"I will speak softly as not to disturb your wife and I will tell you."

"Tell me. I am waiting."

"Okay, as the chief physicist at the government facility outside the city ... ."

"Yes, yes."

"I have been working tirelessly on a project that you, in fact the entire world would not believe is possible, but I swear to you—is possible."

"I am listening."

"Earlier tonight, did you not see the meteor that streaked over the city?"

"No. Yes! Or did I imagine it? That is odd. It is hard to say. I seem to recall that my frightened animals made such terrible noise that I rushed outside and saw something shooting across the heavens. Yes, Kiska saw it too. It was so bright; we could see the four corners of our farm. It disappeared and we could see a million stars. It reappeared over the city and then vanished. We waited a few minutes, but it did not reappear so we hurried out of the cold and back into the house."

"You and Kiska did indeed see it and I saw it too. I was working alone after hours at my laboratory and entering data on my computer when I was consumed with such devastating grief over my son's pain, my wife's pain over his pain, and my pain over their pain that I quit working. I stood and paced about the room as my sorrow transformed into rage and I cursed my father, Kubrik. Damn him! Damn him and his ghastly genetics! He bequeathed his ugly to me and I bestowed it to Yervant. As I despise Kubrik, Yervant despises me."

"Batsakis, your son does not despise you."

"Yes, Adrik, he has told me many times. In tears, he has told me, 'I hate you,' and I asked him, 'Why son? Why do you hate your father who loves you?' and he sobs, 'because I am ugly, ugly like you!' His words devastate me. So earlier tonight at my lab and immediately after my angry outburst cursing Kubrik, I resolved and then plotted to use my genius along with all of the technology provided me to exact a change. The lineage of 'Buzzard' began with Kubrik, so I, Batsakis would change him to change me to change Yervant."

"Batsakis, that is so—so—absurd!"

"Yes, I know, I know that *now*. Rage and grief drove me insane. At that time, my decision seemed like the right thing for a loving father to do. I was so obsessed with the Curse of Kubrik that nothing nor no one could have changed my mind. What happened next—I discovered later—was not just a coincidence. At that very moment when I made my resolution to change Kubrik, I felt a strange tingling and a driving impulse to run outside. I raced out the backdoor of my laboratory, peered up at the night sky, and saw the blazing meteor. To my horror, it hurled directly at me."

"At you?"

"Yes. I was soon to be its site of impact. I ran toward the woods, glancing over my shoulder. The meteor disappeared so I stopped. While catching my breath, it reappeared now even closer. I saw that the object was not engulfed in fire, but enveloped in a glowing field of energy. Fearing certain death,

I again made a dash for the woods when it vanished a second time and did not reappear. Adrik, the meteorite—it was *not* a random chunk of iron plummeting out of the heavens. I saw it—it was, well—it was a spacecraft."

"A spacecraft?—Unbelievable."

"Yes, a spacecraft, more specifically, a timecraft. A capsule rocketing backward and forward through time."

"A timecraft?—Inconceivable."

"Yes, a timecraft, but I was perplexed."

"And Batsakis—so am I."

"You see, I recognized the timecraft as the very one that I engineered and was in the middle of constructing, yet my incomplete craft was still on its launchpad back in the laboratory. It was not ready for time travel."

"Batsakis, I believe that there could be some sort of spacecraft, but time travel? Impossible!"

"Adrik, traveling through time *is* possible."

"No, no, it is not! It is old Yakov's wine soaking into your cranium."

"It is not the wine! Time travel is possible; however, it is much, much too complex to explain to you."

"Am I so dumb?"

"No, not at all. It is just that it is extremely complicated."

"Batsakis, please explain it to me, though speak fast and be brief."

"Okay, Adrik. I will try. You see, just as transplanting hearts and creating clones was once deemed impossible, but is now possible, time travel too will someday be a common reality by utilizing a technology called *Molecular Manipulation*: a process which reduces all *seen* matter: metal, wood, stone, plastic, everything, including flesh and bone down to its atomic core, down to *unseen* energy."

"*Seen* matter to *unseen* energy? Look how high I raise my eyebrows in doubt."

"Adrik, lower your eyebrows and listen to me. To make it simple, time is like a river of flowing energy. My timecraft and its occupant become pure energy, merge with this time-stream of flowing energy, and like a motorboat racing downstream, they surpass the speed of the current, thus, arriving in the future. The greater the timecraft's velocity, the further into the future it can go."

"And why? Why must we go to the future?"

"Because governments and private industry desire to see the future outcome of their present day decisions. If a decision produces positive results; return to the present and leave it alone. If a negative result occurs, return and make a different decision. The world will be a better place."

"Though, I know you to be a genius and I hate to offend you—you are sounding like a madman."

"Adrik, please hear me. The timecraft you saw, that which your memory of is now slipping from your consciousness, it appeared and disappeared because it journeyed back from the future. I know this because it takes greater energy to travel backward in time against its ever-advancing current compared to traveling with its flow to the future. This enigma stumped me for many years until I conceived what I named the *Salmon Theory*."

"My brother, are we now discussing food?"

"No, not at all! Stay with me. Salmon swim upstream by leaping up and out of the current, therefore, to go backward in time to the past or return to the present from the future, the timecraft, rather than fighting time's streaming current of energy, needed to leap up and out of it."

"Batsakis, I respect your intellect, but fish? Leaping fish!"

"Yes, leaping fish! After the craft vanished out of the night sky, I hurried back to my laboratory. My timecraft: the shape of an acorn, polished titanium, and built tall enough to accommodate a person sitting in a chair, remained on its launchpad, however, the unfinished craft, was now to my amazement, finished, hot and glowing amidst a cloud of steam."

"Hot and glowing, because it had just leapt—leapt like a fish out of water—through time?"

"Yes. Yes! My mind reeled. I pondered, how could this be? Who piloted the craft? Where in time did it go? And why? Before I could begin to deduce any answers, I clutched my head in excruciating pain, stumbled back against my desk, and dropped to my knees as thousands of foreign thoughts dumped into my mind. I visualized people I knew, but never met, and saw familiar places I had never visited. I had memories never experienced and feelings never felt. My emotions boiled, reacting to each occurrence, flashing past my mind's eye. Strange images kept pouring in and just when I thought my head would explode, my timecraft shuddered. I stood up, rolled my office chair between me and my craft, and then watched as the seamless door of the craft slid open."

"And?"

"A man sat in the pilot's seat."

"A man? Who?"

"I did not recognize him. He stumbled out of the craft, peered down at his fingers and feet, then felt his face and patted his body."

"Why?"

"To make sure of course that he was all there. He shuffled a small step toward me, nearly fell, yet regained his balance, and took another step. He was tall and handsome with black wavy hair, perfect teeth, a distinguished nose, and dazzling green eyes; eyes wild with panic."

"So what did he do?"

"He lunged at me, shoved the chair across the room, and grabbed the lapels on my lab coat. He shook me violently, yanked me face to face, and yelled, 'Batsakis, it is I! Who was you! Who is me!'"

"Adriiik, I am trying to sleep!"

"Sorry Kiska! So sorry to wake you! So Batsakis, he was you and you were he?"

"Yes. Then he screamed, 'My dear, ugly me, you have changed your father! You broke the Curse of Kubrik! Soon, you as you will vanish and only you as I will remain!'"

"Adriiik, no more shouting! Okay?"

"Okay, Kiska, we will be quiet. So, Batsakis, you broke the Curse of Kubrik?"

"Yes, Adrik—apparently, I did. The shouting, handsome stranger was me and I was he, no longer ugly, no longer a Buzzard. I beamed with jubilance, when suddenly, a volley of thoughts struck me as his thoughts merged with mine. My knees buckled, yet he still held me up by my coat lapels, and since his thoughts were mine and mine were his and because we were now two as one and each as two, I knew all that I had done and how all came to be."

"Batsakis, if you were not my brother, I would not believe any of this. I must have bread with my wine to settle my stomach. Would you like bread too?"

"Yes, please. And Adrik, I know my story sounds fantastic."

"Yes, it most certainly does; nevertheless, please go on."

"It all began earlier this evening, immediately after I made that time altering, life changing—and now I know foolhardy—resolution to switch my father Kubrik. My decision set me on a course. Over the next two years, my team and I worked long hours with speed and determination. We completed the timecraft."

"Two years from now—in the future?"

"Yes. I brazenly and secretly tested the craft on myself. I traveled to the past, to that very year, to that very day, to that very moment, that our mother, Yalenka had told us about so many times. I left my timecraft hidden in the woods and walked not far to the missile plant where I knew she would be. I touched nothing and talked to no one. I waited but a minute, when I saw her coming out of the factory gates. I was there; there at that crucial moment when she met Kubrick. I watched her cross the street, slip on the ice, and fall. "

"Batsakis, you saw mother? Let me think—she would have been only, um, twenty-four at the time she met Kubrik."

"You are correct. She was lovely with her long dark hair and her bright green eyes; her sunny smile and cheerful radiance nearly melted the snow about us. It was strange, for I was practically old enough to be my mother's father."

"Strange indeed!"

"I have missed mother so terribly since she has passed, that my first impulse was to run and hug her, however, I did not want to frighten her; plus, I had a mission to fulfill. So, I stood outside the gates and watched her. She stepped on a slick patch of ice and fell hard. I winced, yet resisted helping her. I glanced around and noticed that only two other people had seen her mishap. There was a good-looking, well-to-do man strolling to his fancy car and my father Kubrik, Prince Ugly, Mr. Buzzard, climbing on his rusty, old bicycle. I stood not far from both men. Kubrik was as ugly as the other man was handsome, not to mention that Kubrik was just as ugly when he was young as when he was old. His long hooked nose, sunken eyes, bushy eyebrows, baldhead ringed with frizzy hair, and his skinny frame reinforced my objective. Then, since he was as ugly as I, I felt pity for him. I considered forgoing my plan and returning to the future to my laboratory when a few burly workers leaving the plant called out to him, 'See you tomorrow, Buzzard!' He ignored them, dropped his bike, and took a step to help mother; however, I, upon hearing that horrible name, did what I did."

"Batsakis, what? What on Earth did you do?"

"As the rich man and Kubrik both reacted to help mother, I, effecting my scheme, simply stepped in front of Kubrik. He shifted to his right; so did I. He moved to his left; so did I.

He looked at me strangely and why not? It was as though he was peering into a mirror, except I, his ugly son appeared to him as his ugly father. He said to me, 'Please, move away! I must help the woman who has slipped on the ice.' I stepped aside, but by then, the rich, handsome man had rescued mother and was walking her to his car. The way they gazed into each other's eyes, it was obvious that they were smitten with each other. Kubrik, the ugliest man on Earth had lost his opportunity to show our mother, the most beautiful woman on Earth, his great kindness which would have permitted her to see past his unsightly appearance and allow her to fall in love with him and eventually marry him."

"If not Kubrik, then who? Who assisted mother?"

"Jurg! Jurg Nevsky came to her rescue!"

"The son of Ivan Nevsky, the wealthy man who owned the missile plant?"

"Yes, yes, that Jurg. Rich *and* handsome!"

"No, no, not that Jurg! He was a drunkard, a lady's man, and a brawler."

"Yes, unfortunately, that Jurg. At the time, I did not know those dreadful things about him."

"Batsakis, this story of yours, it is crazy! Oh my, I need more wine or maybe I have had too much. No, I think not enough. I am having another glass and I will fill yours as well. So then what happened?"

"Well—I hastened back to the woods feeling satisfied about obstructing Kubrik, thus switching fathers, hence, changing my fate along with the fate of Yervant. I climbed back into my craft and rocketed into the future, arriving ten years beyond the present time of today. My intent: to witness the outcome of Kubrik's undoing, behold who I had become, and check up on Minka and Yervant. During the quick trip, for traveling forward with the time-stream is faster than backward, I began an excruciating transformation as my face and my body altered into a new me. It was as though I was made of rubber, stretching and swelling only to snap back into a new look. All the while, my current state of mind experienced a collision of foreign thoughts and feelings. I had new memories, recollections of Jurg as my father; nevertheless, I was sad. You and mother were sad. Living without the compassion of Kubrik and living with the alcoholic violence of Jurg was horrible."

"Batsakis, I can imagine. I remember frightening stories about him."

"Well, I arrived in the future, five years beyond this night and I again hid my craft in the woods. I hiked a short distance into town toward my house, but instinctively headed in a different direction. I wound up at a small apartment on the edge of town near the train tracks. Heaviness fell upon me and I felt a yearning to provide a better life for my family. Finding the door locked, I pulled my house key from my pants pocket, tried it, and unlocked the door. I chuckled. Even my keys had changed during my transformation. I entered the apartment and noticed myself in the entryway mirror. I was as handsome as Jurg and as beautiful as mother. I beamed with satisfaction, turned, and saw a gorgeous woman standing across the room. I knew her to be my wife. What a lucky man I am, I thought, to have and to hold such a ravishing creature. I, knowing how fabulous I was and oozing with undeniable charm, smiled at her. She placed her hands on her hips, began tapping a foot, and as her angelic face contorted into shadows of rage, she snatched up an empty bottle of vodka and threw it at me. It soared past my head and smashed into the mirror behind me. Clearly drunk, for she could barely stand, she yelled, slurring her words, 'Batsakis, I hate you! I have never loved you! Any minute now, Yervant is coming home from school. Tell the brat, I am leaving you and him forever.'"

"My brother, what of Minka?"

"My sweet Minka was not in my life. I, being so handsome

had married a beautiful woman, albeit an alcoholic witch, horrible wife, and dreadful mother. All the years of matrimonial misery came crashing in on me like a load of bricks."

"And what of Yervant?"

"Yervant strolled through the door. Adrik, he was handsome and he could walk again! Bullies would no longer tease him, chase him, or throw garbage at him. That awful day when the car hit him never happened. My scheme, at least for Yervant, had worked. No one would ever call him Buzzard again. I laughed with joy, yet only for a moment when more memories of my new life caught up with me. I recalled that my stunning young son scored lowest in his class at school. Not only was he *not* brilliant, he detested science and preferred modeling. Even worse, he hated girls and fancied boys. The lineage of Itzak, I mean Nevsky, would cease with him. He would not become a great scientist like me. Then it hit me, even I, Batsakis Nevsky was not a brilliant scientist. My stern grandfather, Ivan, had fired my good-for-nothing father, Jurg, and disowned him as a son. When I began working at the plant, he started me at the bottom to teach me a work ethic that my father had never learned. I was but one of many poor mechanics at his factory. Since I was magnificently good-looking and no longer resembled a buzzard, I did not have to hide, thus I did not study, therefore, I never excelled. I realized that my life had turned out all wrong. I had made a huge miscalculation. I panicked, ran out the door, and back to my craft. I climbed inside and strapped myself in my seat. I flipped switches, pushed buttons, and pulled levers. It leapt like a salmon up and out of the time stream back to tonight when you and Kiska saw the flashing meteor which of course was my timecraft."

"What are you talking about? A meteor?"

"So now, now you do not remember seeing it? A bright light across the sky?"

"No. No, I do not."

"Time has caught up and has totally erased the event. It happened; then again—it did not happen. Our lives are truly back to the way they were."

"I don't understand it all. You returned to the laboratory?"

"Yes, where I climbed out of the timecraft and encountered ugly me, a poor pathetic creature hiding behind a desk chair. I felt dizzy and disoriented from my journeys through time. My life as Batsakis Itzak was fading fast. Memories of Minka and Yervant grew dim. Then I, Batsakis Nevsky grabbed Batsakis Itzak by his lab coat and said, 'Batsakis, it is I! Who was you! Who is me! My dear, ugly me, you have changed your father! You broke the Curse of Kubrik! Soon, you as you will vanish and only you as I will remain!'"

"No Batsakis Itzak? Only Batsakis Nevsky?"

"Correct. The timeline of Itzak diminished while that of Nevsky expanded. Both of us understood that my decision had turned out extremely bad. He as I and I as he wished that I had never broke the Curse of Kubrik. He, Nevsky, said to me, Itzak, 'It won't be long now that my life, the life of Batsakis Nevsky will erase your life. As handsome as I may be, I do not have the genius to fly this craft or even think of how to undo this mess. Please climb aboard the craft, go back in time, and allow the fate of Kubrik and mother to unfold without interference.'"

"And did you?"

"No. I could not. I, Batsakis Itzak was merely a vapor. My timecraft and laboratory too. Then, like a popped soap bubble, I, Batsakis Itzak disappeared. Instantaneously my perception changed to see the world only through Nevsky's eyes. Since I was mostly he and not me, I felt ignorant and did not know what to do. Fixing this calamity required brains not brawn and I was predominantly brawn. I had no clue as to a solution. Then, I heard a commotion outside the back door of the lab and peered out to see soldiers scrambling out of their vehicles and heading for my door."

"Soldiers!"

"Yes, soldiers! They too had seen the meteor, which was my craft and had tracked it to my lab. Unsure of what they might find, they carried guns. I panicked, grabbed my car keys, and ran down the maze of corridors out the front door. I dove into my car and raced here to your farm to see you, Adrik. The commander of the small troop saw me speed away. He and five soldiers followed in pursuit. I arrived at your home and pounded on your door. You yelled, 'Go away!' I knocked again, glanced down the road, and saw the soldiers coming. Adrik, you opened your door and in this new altered world, you were alone and falling down drunk. You were crying because Kiska had left you. You had learned from Jurg how to drink vodka and mistreat your wife."

"Me—Adrik Itzak? Never would I harm my beloved Kiska."

"You did and she was gone. And Adrik, Jurg never adopted you. You kept your father's name. You were Adrik Kovanoff."

"Never adopted? Adrik Kovanoff?"

"The soldiers surrounded your house. Their commander demanded I give myself up."

"Did you?"

"Not at first. I only surrendered when he threatened to arrest you too. They seized me and drove me back to my laboratory at the government facility. Of course, my laboratory was an empty room without my timecraft, computers, and equipment. All hope was lost. I could never change back to my ugly self, living the life I knew and missed."

"All had vanished?"

"No, Adrik. Not vanished. In the world of Batsakis Nevsky—the world of Batsakis Itzak never existed."

"Ahhh, yes, I understand."

"Two soldiers held my arms as two pointed their weapons at me. The other soldier shined a powerful flashlight in my face. After the commander removed his long, leather overcoat

and his hat, a stylish, furry *ushanka*, he turned to me and said
… .'"

"He wore a *ushanka*? That reminds me, I need a new
ushanka. My cat shredded mine."

"Listen to me, Adrik. He turned to me and in a chilling,
restrained voice as though holding back surging rage, he said,
'My name is Colonel Volkov. Who are you?' I am getting goose
bumps remembering how eerie he sounded. I peered at him,
thinking how peculiar he looked. This man was short in stature,
in his late thirties, and wore a well-fitted uniform exhibiting his
excellent physical condition. He also wore, as is customary, the
black leather boots of the *Spetsnaz* Special Forces. As I said
before, he had an odd-looking appearance; a taut, geometrical
face displaying a triangular nose, square chin, right-angled
cheeks, and a rectangular brow. His ashen skin bore a distinct
contrast to his dark, linear eyebrows and the blackness of his
short, calculated haircut. Strange too, he had ice-blue eyes as if
made of glass. He so terrified me, my legs buckled."

"Batsakis, he does sound frightening."

"The soldiers jerked me up. He asked again, this time
sharply, 'Who are you?' I answered, 'My name was Batsakis
Itzak. Now, I am Batsakis Nevsky.' He said, 'So you use an
alias! You are a liar!' 'No,' I said. 'Absolutely not. I was a
scientist here at the facility. I worked on a top-secret project,
developing a timecraft for traveling back to the past and into
the future. You witnessed my craft re-entering this timeline,
which is now an altered timeline. It appeared, disappeared, and
reappeared as a fiery meteor. Though by now, you probably
won't remember seeing it.' He smirked, and then snapped, 'I
do not recall a meteor, and obviously there is no laboratory
here. I have clearance for all classified projects. Where is this
timecraft? There is not one. Time travel is impossible! You must
be insane!' I stammered, 'Please. I—I am not crazy. It is a—a
long story. I traveled back in time to change my father to change

me to change my son. I succeeded which changed me and my life. I now work as a mechanic at the missile plant.' He replied, 'So—you are *not* a liar and you are *not* insane. I completely understand now.' I said, 'Thank you.' He said, 'If you work at the missile plant, then—you must be a spy!'"

"You, Batsakis, a spy?"

"Yes, Adrik, a spy! He ordered his men to take me outside and shoot me. Then, to drag my body into the woods and bury it in a shallow grave under the snow. The soldiers obeyed immediately, forced me outside, and slammed me up against a concrete wall. I shivered uncontrollably from the cold and fear. The soldiers marched out twenty paces and then lined up in front of me. Three dropped to one knee while two stood behind them as all pointed their rifles at me. Colonel Volkov, standing aside, shouted, 'Ready! Aim!' Suddenly, before he yelled, 'Fire,' a thought hit me like a hot bullet to the brain; most likely the very last thought of Batsakis Buzzard Itzak; a life saving, time changing revelation just before my life, my memories, and my consciousness disappeared forever."

"Dear brother, tell me, what was this remarkable thought?"

"You see, Adrik—I made a decision of firm resolve. I drew in what was surely my last breath and spoke my determination boldly with confidence and conviction. I proclaimed, 'I will *never* go back in time to change my father Kubrik!'"

"Good, good, my brother, you came to your senses, nevertheless—the soldiers shot you. Are you now still bleeding?"

"No, I am fine. On the command, 'Fire!' I saw a flashing grin crack across Volkov's stoic face and heard a cannonade of gunfire. Before the bullets struck me, all before me vanished; Colonel Volkov, the soldiers, their rifles, the bullets—gone. I found myself sitting in my chair at my desk in my laboratory."

"All disappeared? Where did it go?"

"Adrik, dear brother, it never existed. Nothing in the timeline of Batsakis Nevsky ever happened. Due to my decision, my firm resolve, my last second change of mind—I never traveled back in time, therefore, all related events never occurred. I did not thwart Kubrik. Jurg never met and married mother. He never became my father. Hence, no Batsakis Nevsky. I never married that witch of a wife and never fathered that spoiled brat. Adrik, you were not a mean drunk and you never hurt Kiska."

"What a relief!"

"I stood up from my desk and peered at my reflection in the shiny titanium of my incomplete craft. There I was, ugly Batsakis Itzak, Buzzard junior, son of Kubrik, Buzzard senior. I thought of my father Kubrik and recalled his kindness and compassion. I remembered as a child how I wept when I was teased. He consoled me, buying me books to read. I read volumes on chemistry, mathematics, and physics. With his encouragement, I focused on science rather than how ugly I was. As mother looked past his hideous appearance and into his big heart, so did I. I broke the Curse of Kubrik not because I changed my father, but because I renounced my desire to change my father. Alas—Yervant is still in a wheelchair, we remain ugly, and our nickname will forever be Buzzard, but I am who I am and he is who he is. We are special in our own ways. I have peace. Life is good. So you see Adrik, nothing is wrong—nothing now and I want to assure you that all I have done is undone and all that would be, will be, and I, Batsakis Itzak, and my son Yervant, indeed everyone, we are all who we were and forever destined to be."

"Incredible story, Batsakis! Shall I open another jug of old Yakov's wine?"

"Thank you, but no, dear brother. It is late and I must go home."

"Adriiik! Are you coming to bed?"

"Yes, my dear, Kiska, I am coming to bed."

ROASTED SEAGULL

Sunburned and near death from starvation, millionaire Langley Upwood, listless, eyes closed, and breathing shallow, lay on his back on the sparkling white sand in the scant shade of two palm trees. The surf roared, seagulls squawked, the air smelled of seaweed, and the tropical sun blazed high in a cloudless sky.

Marooned on the mile-long crest of coral reef somewhere far off the coast of Chile, Tarleton Cayne and Webley Marsh, Langley's long time fishing buddies and fellow castaways, both wealthy in their own right, stood over their friend and peered down at him. He looked gaunt with sunken eyes, dry, cracked lips, and blistered, peeling skin. They didn't look much better. The three pals, all in their mid forties wore sun-bleached Hawaiian shirts, tattered Bermuda shorts, ragged designer sandals and the rumpled hair and scraggly beard of a man marooned. Tarleton, tall and athletic with rigid features, wavy gray hair, and a commanding voice, still possessed a meager strength, while soft-spoken Langley, the smallest and thinnest of the three, blighted with freckles and balding red hair, suffered the worst. Talkative, optimistic, Webley, short and chunky with shaggy, surfer-blonde hair, who began their misadventure with much more body fat than the other two, held up the best.

Stranded on the atoll for five weeks with minimal food, all three men were two-thirds of their normal body weight, terribly weak, and riddled with abdominal pain. If not for the passing storms, they would have mercifully died from thirst. Langley stirred and moaned in misery.

"Poor Langley," muttered Webley. "Hang in there, Lang. You'll get through this."

"No, he won't," spat Tarleton. "Sorry Lang, ol' buddy, if you can hear me, but you're not going to make it and frankly, neither are we."

"Ah, come on Tarl, sure he will, and so will we. We'll have to hang in there, just like we did back in college, helping each other with tests and term papers. How about when our first marriages fell apart? Us three amigos shared an apartment and supported each other. Then there was our failed partnership? We survived that too. We made it then. We'll make it now. We'll survive because he has you and me, you have him and me, and I have you and him. We have a bond, a bond of friendship and memor... ."

"None of us," growled Tarleton, annoyed with Webley's incessant babble, "will make it off this God-forsaken island. So Web, shut-up, okay, just shut up!"

Webley clamed up and at the very instant he did, both men out of the corner of their bleary eyes spotted a reddish rock crab the size of a man's hand crawling out of the white foamy surf. Their shrunken stomachs cramped as they licked their dry lips. Tarleton blinked, thinking he saw a scampering bologna sandwich. Webley had the crazed notion it was a crawling cheeseburger. Simultaneously, they lunged into action, staggering and stumbling, falling to their hands and knees, crawling side by side, kicking up sand, with Webley chattering, "We've got the crab, Tarl! We've got it! It's time to eat, Tarl! Time to eat!" With the crab nearly a bite and a chew away, they dove, stretching with a desperate grab, when in an abrupt blur of gray and white feathers, a screeching seagull swooped down and snatched it up.

Tarleton, on his stomach and breathing heavily, gripped two fistfuls of wet sand and yelled, "No good, damned seagulls! Every time there's food, they gobble it up!"

Webley, exhausted, lying with his face in the sand, mumbled, "Rotten, damned seagulls." He waited a few seconds, lifted his head up, spit sand out of his mouth, and asked, "So Tarl, do you want to check the tide-pools again?"

"Hell no!" snapped Tarleton. "You know those greedy gulls have cleaned them out too."

"How about," suggested Webley, propped up on his elbows, "we try the lagoon again?"

"For Heaven's sake, Web, the last time we swam out and tried to grab a fish, the sharks nearly ate *us*. We're doomed. Lang will die, then me, and then you fat-man."

"Fat-man? Ouch, Tarl, that cuts deep," admitted Webley, "really, really deep." Though skinnier now due to starvation, he still felt the pain of the ridicule he had heard during his entire life. He hung his head, but then thought of a comeback, looked Tarleton square in the face, and retorted, "The funny thing is, you guys always poked fun at my rolls of blubber, but it looks like this time, thanks to my blubber, I'll have the last laugh."

"Shut-up, Web! Please, just shut-up!"

"Okay, Tarl, for now, since I don't like the thought of me being alone here. I mean, who would I talk to?"

"Web, shut up, already!"

"Okay. All right. Okay."

As both emaciated men struggled to their knees and rested for a moment, brushing off the sand, they peered out at the blue-green sea. They searched, hoping as always to see a ship, but as always, there was no ship to see.

Tarleton, exasperated, stared down at the sand, his face drawn with despair.

Webley noticed and said, "Hey Tarl, like when you were kidding me about being chubby, I was just joking too. None of us will die. We'll all get off this island. Soon, very soon. I can feel it; a ship will rescue us. I know it will. We'll see our families again. We'll have fun again. We'll even go fishing again. You wait. We will. It'll happen. I know, it'll hap... ."

"Web—"

"Yes, Tarl."

"You know."

"Yeah, I know, shut up, but I'm just trying to keep our spirits up."

With great effort, they stood and tramped in the sand back to Langley, where they turned and noticed another frothy wave had deposited on the beach a turtle the size of a salad plate. Before a thought could move their feeble limbs into action, a seagull, bigger than the others, swooped down, snatched the turtle up by a leg, and flew off toward the cliffs.

Like a hundred times before, Tarleton shook a fist at the gull and screamed, "No good, damned seagulls."

Webley dropped to his knees and whined, nearly sobbing, "Rotten, damned seagulls," as Langley, still flat on his back, mumbled, "Lousy, damned seagulls."

"Web," said Tarleton, biting his fist out of frustration, "I've got an idea. Let's follow that gull. When it's pecking at that turtle, we'll throw seashells at it, kill it, and butcher it with your pocketknife. You still have your knife, don't you?"

"Yeah, of course. I've had this knife," he patted the right pocket of his shorts, "since my tenth birthday. It's always in my pocket. Do you still have your lighter?"

"Yes, in my pocket. Too bad the cigarettes got all sea-soaked. What I'd give for a smoke right now."

"You don't want to smoke, Tarl, those things will kill you."

"Right, Web, you mean before I starve to death or keel over from the heat."

"Well, yeah, but still, it's …."

"Okay, whatever," growled Tarleton, "so after we kill that gull, we'll find some driftwood, start a fire, roast that big, fat, sea-turkey, and eat it."

"That, sounds like a great idea, and we'll work together, and we'll … ."

"Yeah, yeah, yeah," interrupted Tarleton, "let's go!"

Both men, with mighty hope spurring a measly might, shuffled a step to leave when Langley groaned, "Where're you guys going?"

"To the cliffs," proclaimed Tarleton.

"To hunt gull!" bellowed Webley.

Tarleton and Webley, weak and hobbling, yet riled with hungry determination, headed toward the cliffs. They hiked across the islet through sparse vegetation, the ground rising with every tortured step, and arrived at the craggy cliffs sixty-feet above the pounding surf.

When Tarleton and Webley charged off to hunt seagull, Langley crawled over to one of the palm trees, sat up, and leaned his back against it. The effort sapped nearly all his remaining strength. Though his body was stranded in hunger and heat, his mind drifted back to where their fishing trip began, back to La Serena, Chile; a magnificent city with beautiful beaches, pure air, and an ancient culture. He thought of how he and his friends along with their new wives had dined, drank, and danced through the first four days of their vacation. Now, hungry and delirious, he envisioned a scrumptious *completo*, a Chilean hot dog loaded with mayo, tomatoes, onions, pickles, and sauerkraut. He weakly lifted his hand, opened his mouth, and chewed as if he was stuffing the steamy dog, bite by bite into his mouth. Next, his mind materialized a plate of *congrio frito*, deep-fried conger eel, and *empanada de pino,* a turnover filled with diced meat, onions, olives, and raisins. He groaned, "Ohhh," as if he had just taken a bite of eel and, "Oooh," as if he had just nibbled on the turnover. He pursed his lips as if sipping hot *carbonada* soup with diced beef and vegetables, followed by a pretend sip of *carmenère*, an earthy red wine, and sighed, "Ahhh." Lastly, he bit into a make-believe *alfajor*; a chocolate pastry filled with caramel-like *manjar* and moaned, "Mmmm." Without ever ingesting any real food, he smiled, rubbing his distended stomach, feeling full and satisfied. Then, he recalled the last day of their vacation, the day before they had to return to San Diego. Despite dark clouds gathering on the horizon, the three men had chartered a fishing boat, the *Tortuga de Mar,* the Sea Turtle, and sailed for the open sea. Their wives planned to shop until noon, eat an authentic Chilean lunch, and shop until dinner. Out on the ocean, the men drank *Cerveza Cristal*, smoked *Cohiba*s, and filled the boat's live well with Chilean sea bass. At sunset, while sailing back to La Serena, the threatening storm suddenly and violently came upon them, blowing the *Tortuga* off course and further out to sea. The storm raged throughout the night. The three men donned life jackets and lashed themselves together. Just before dawn, the boat listed to portside, rolled, and capsized, tossing the men into rolling seas. They watched with their heads bobbing above the whitecaps, as the *Tortuga* vanished, sinking to the bottom of the sea, dragging with it, Captain Macario Mendez, a cheerful, middle-aged man. The storm blew over and the three men floated in calm seas most of that day. If one man's strength gave out, the other two held his head above the water. Just before nightfall, they spotted land. Terrified, waterlogged, and cold, nevertheless excited, lucky and grateful, they washed up on the shore of the God-forsaken atoll.

Now, after thirty-five days of starving, Langley, leaning against the palm tree, felt a stomach cramp, opened his eyes, and glanced up at the sun peeking through the palm fronds. Mindful again that he and his friends were stranded and starving, he wept.

At the sea cliffs, Tarleton and Webley inched up to the precipice. A mischievous sea wind blew at their backs trying to shove them off. They leaned over, peered down the cliff's sheer face, and spied the plump seagull on a huge slab of rock just above the reach of the rolling surf.

The gull had dropped the turtle on the rock, cracking its shell, and was pecking at its soft innards. Tarleton, a pitcher back in high school, picked up a smooth, round seashell, loosened up his shoulder, wound up, and pitched the shell at the gull. It missed, soaring only inches above the gull's head. The bird kept pecking the turtle as Webley bent down and picked up a thick shell. He eased up to the brink of the sixty-foot drop, so close, his left sandal jutted out over the edge, and locked his focus on the bird. Just like back when he played catcher for Tarleton on the high school baseball team and he used to rattle batters, he chattered, "Okay, birdie, birdie. I got you now. You're an easy target; you stay still birdie, birdie; that's it; good birdie; I'm winding up; oh yeah, birdie, you're going to die!" He flung his shell, missing too and not even close. Tragically, the momentum of his throw, compounded by his weakness and nudged by the wind, caused him to lose his balance, lurch forward, and plummet off the ledge.

Tarleton, a few feet away, reached out to catch Webley, but missed as Webley reached out to grab Tarleton, but too late.

Webley yelled, "Tarrrrrleton," all the way down, landing on the rock with a smack and a thud. He lay flat on his back with his legs and arms in the formation of an X.

The startled bird snatched up its turtle-tart, flew to the next rock, and resumed pecking at it.

"Oh my God!" gasped Tarleton. "Webley!" he cried out above the thundering surf, "Webley! Are you okay?"

Webley didn't answer.

Tarleton yelled again, "Webley! Webley!"

No answer.

Trembling and faint, he cautiously climbed down, losing his grip twice and nearly crashing to his death. Once on the rock, bent with his hands on his knees, catching his breath, he stared down at Webley and the blood streaming out of Webley's cracked skull.

He wailed, "No, no, nooo, Webley, you can't die. We need you. You've always kept us going. You're the one cheering us on through all our struggles. We need you, man, we need you." He knelt and checked his friend's pulse. Webley was dead.

Driven by anger, raging hunger, and revenge, Tarleton snatched up a baseball-size piece of sharp coral and now, much closer to his feathered target, he wound up, focused on the fat gull as if it was Webley's high school catcher's mitt, and hurled the rock with all of his might.

With sunset a wink away, Langley, sitting against the palm tree, no longer wept, but still in an insipid daze, heard scrambling footsteps and heavy breathing. With blurry eyes, he saw Tarleton approaching on the beach from the long and arduous way from the cliffs.

"Tarl," moaned Langley, "did you get that lousy gull?"

"Yeah, Lang, I did," proclaimed Tarleton, out of breath, while placing the bloody carcass on a palm frond on the ground.

Langley glanced down the beach and asked Tarleton, "How come you came down the beach and where's Webley? I know he's slow, but I don't even see him."

"I'm sorry, Lang," said Tarleton, his face drenched in despair and his bottom lip trembling, "it's very difficult to tell you this, but our good friend, Webley, poor, poor, Webley is—well—he stood too close to the cliff's edge and when he threw a shell at that no good, damned gull, he lost his balance, fell off the cliff, and landed on that flat rock at the bottom. I climbed down, nearly falling too, and found him all broken up with his skull cracked open. So, Lang—Webley's dead."

"Oh my God! Webley's dead?"

"Yeah—Webley's dead. I still can't believe it, but our dear friend is dead. Yet, knowing that you and I, still alive, needed food, I got closer to that stupid gull, took aim, you know like when I was pitching back in high school, and I fired a baseball sized piece of coral at it. Like a strike across the plate, I nailed it. Nailed it good. I heard a wave crash behind me and when I spun around, I saw it wash up over Webley's battered body, and he was gone; gone, I tell you; swallowed by the sea."

"Poor, Webley," murmured Langley, shaking his head. "How sad, dead and gone; swallowed by the sea; fish bait; how horrible."

"Yeah," agreed Tarleton, "sad and horrible."

"But I thought the surf didn't reach that rock," stated Langley.

"It did today, Lang. It did, I tell you, but even though I was bawling over Webley's death all the way back here, I plucked and gutted that damn gull on the way and then washed it in the surf. Now, I'm going to cook it, and pretty soon, we're gonna have roasted seagull." He hastily gathered dried palm fronds and driftwood, stacked them, and with his lighter, started a fire, then skewered the butchered bird with a thick stick and dangled it over the flames.

Langley, lost in grief over Webley's death, snapped out of it when he smelled the roasting seagull. It smelled like fatty pork frying in a pan and after a few whiffs, his senses came to life inciting his ravenous hunger.

The sun sunk below the watery horizon immersing all hues of red and orange in sapphire blue. In the glow of the crackling fire, Tarleton, with a crazed look from a contortion of hunger and grief, rotated the skewered meat, cooking all sides of it. After waiting, drooling, he removed the charred bird from the fire, set it on a large piece of driftwood, and carved off a succulent piece with Webley's pocketknife.

Langley noticed Webley's knife and asked, "So Tarl, how'd you get Webley's pocketknife?"

Tarleton didn't respond immediately, but stared down at the slice of gull meat. He licked his lips, shrugged his shoulders, popped the morsel in his mouth, chewed slowly at first, then hastily, and then swallowed. He carved off another piece, popped it in his mouth, and while chewing, cut off another slice, stuck the hot meat with the point of the knife, walked over to Langley, and said, "Here you go Lang, roasted, *Seagull a la Tarl.*"

Langley reached up, pulled the steamy meat off the knife, and said, "Thanks buddy," then took a bite, and chewed. It was hot and meaty, and although a little gamey, it wasn't bad, tasting more like veal rather than pork or chicken. As the nourishment began to take hold, Langley sat up straight and inquired again, "So, Tarl, how'd you end up with Webley's pocketknife?"

Langley waited as Tarleton chewed his mouth full of gull, swallowed, and replied, "Of course, I took it from him—you know, when I checked his body. He wouldn't need it and we did—for our survival. He would have wanted us to have it."

"Yes, he would have," agreed Langley. "He was a good friend. I wished he could have dined with us on this wonderful *Seagull a la Tarl.*"

"Me too."

"I already miss his never ending chatter."

"Yeah, sure—uh—me too. I never thought I would, but I do, now that he's gone."

The two castaways dined on the roasted seagull, drank from their store of rainwater, and for the first time since arriving on the remote islet, slept with full bellies.

The next morning as the sun peeked over the blue-green horizon, Langley sat up, burped, rubbed his eyes, searched the sea, spotted a cargo ship, and yelled, "Tarl, wake up! A ship! I see a ship!"

Tarleton sprang to his feet, rubbed the sand out of his eyes, blinked, squinted, and spotted the ship too. He raced over to the fire, found that it still had fiery orange embers, tossed dry palm fronds on it, and hollered, "Stoke the fire, Lang! Stoke it!"

Langley crawled over to the fire and fanned the embers until the fronds began smoking. Tarleton dashed to the edge of the surf and waved his arms, jumping, yelling, and pleading to be noticed. A sailor on deck, spotting the smoke and the castaways, hailed the ship's Captain.

One year later, on the anniversary of their rescue, after obtaining the location of the atoll from the rescue ship's log, and after Langley and a reluctant Tarleton chartered a much bigger boat, the *Ballena Azul,* the Blue Whale, and after repeatedly checking the weather reports, they made a return trip, planning to pay homage to Webley, their life long friend, by placing a small granite marker on the cliff where he had perished.

The boat anchored in the lagoon. The two men, wearing Ray-Ban sunglasses and dressed in colorful Hawaiian shirts, fashionable Bermuda shorts, and new leather sandals climbed into a lifeboat and rowed to shore. Langley carried Webley's pocketknife in his pant's pocket and cradled in his arm, his favorite twelve-gage shotgun, the same weapon he used to win his gun club's recent trap shoot tournament. They beached the lifeboat, strolled across the sand into the shade of the two palms, and stared down at the remnants of their last fire. The surf roared, seagulls squawked, the air smelled of rotting seaweed, and the tropical sun blazed high in a cloudless sky. There was a moment of silence as both reflected on their past hardships stranded on the atoll and the loss of Webley.

"Tarl," said Langley with resolve, "Let's do this. You gather palm fronds and driftwood, start a fire, and find a skewer. I'll shoot us a gull."

"Lang, are you sure?" questioned Tarleton. "Are you sure you want to shoot a gull? Let's just pay our respects to Webley and place his marker right here where we slept next to the fire."

"Yes, I'm certain; I want to shoot a gull. I want to re-live our experience. It was so cleansing and revealing. It taught me what is truly important in this world. Tarl, my life has changed. I now value my family and friends more than anything. I've learned how precious life is. Also, I still think the cliff is the best place for Webley's marker." He spun, strutted out a few yards, deftly lifted his shotgun, took aim at a soaring gull, and with mastered skill, blasted the bird out of the sky. It squawked, plummeted to Earth in a shower of feathers, and landed in front of him just out of reach of the surf.

"Good thing," hollered Tarleton above the booming surf, "that this time, we didn't have to depend on a shell, my pitching arm, and a lucky throw."

Langley picked up the dead bird and returned to the shade of the palms. He propped his gun up against the trunk of one palm, then sat and leaned back against the trunk of the other, opened Webley's pocketknife, and began plucking feathers and removing shot.

"Are you really going to eat seagull again?" inquired Tarleton.

"Yes, as a matter of fact," said Langley, "I'm going to eat seagull again."

"It just seems so horribly savage," said Tarleton, "especially since we have beer and *el lomito* sandwiches back on the boat. Come on Lang, please, let's hurry and do our Webley thing, and then get back to La Serena."

"My *la serena,* my peace, my paradise, is right here and right now," asserted Langley. "I feel a tranquility about it all. It's the right thing to do."

Tarleton knew his friend's stubborn resolve, so to get it over with and get gone, he gathered palm fronds and driftwood, started a fire, and found a stick for a skewer. Langley finished preparing the bird, stood, skewered the bird with the stick, and dangled it over the blazing fire. He breathed in a long sniff of the cooking bird. When it was done, he placed it on the same piece of driftwood that Tarleton had used the last time, walked out to the surf, cleaned Webley's pocketknife, and returned. He sliced off a piece and said, "Here you go Tarl, roasted *Seagull a la Lang*."

"No," refused Tarleton, "I don't want any."

"You don't have to eat any," said Langley as he placed the slice in his mouth. With one chew, he realized that the taste was odd. Strange like before, but strange, different. He took another bite and chewed it slowly savoring the taste. Contemplating, he breathed deeply, letting the flavor saturate his pallet. He swallowed and shot a look at Tarleton.

Tarleton had watched Langley during the entire bite, chew, and swallow, but now, looked down at the sand, kicked a small seashell with his big toe sticking out of his sandal, and muttered, "So Lang … uh … not as tasty as the gull, you and I ate, huh?"

"No, in fact," declared Langley, "this roasted seagull tastes completely different. It's no comparison at all to that bird we ate when we were marooned here." He flicked the meat off Webley's pocketknife into the sand, sliced off another piece, chewed it, and swallowed, coming to the same conclusion. He snapped shut the pocketknife, stuffed it in his pocket, and said, "If this is what seagull tastes like, then ….," he whirled around, spied the sparse path that led between the palms, and bolted, making a beeline toward the rocky cliffs.

"No, Langley. Stop!" Tarleton cried out. "Please, the cliffs are dangerous. Let's just go back to *La Serena*."

Langley ignored him and stayed his course. The sun blazed, a warm breeze picked up, and gulls cried out overhead.

Again, Tarleton called out, "Stop! Lang, please stop! It's too dangerous. Don't forget what happened to Webley."

Langley kept marching up the path as Tarleton followed, catching up, and staying right on his heels. Langley hastened to the edge of the cliffs, inched up to the brink, and peered down its sheer face. Tarleton stood next to him. Both men breathed heavily with sweat beading on their brows.

Langley gasped, not believing what he saw and screamed, "Tarleton! How—my word man, how could you?"

"Well—Lang," Tarleton began as he pulled a pack of cigarettes out of his shirt pocket, tapped one out, cupped it with his hands, lit it, and took a drag, "we were starving to death and it was our only hope. My throw, well—I missed that damn, no-good gull. So you see, our dear friend, Webley, saved our lives."

Aghast, Langley peered down again at the fist of a rock jutting above the hungry surf. Now, knowing the truth about the roasted seagull, he gagged. On the rock lay the crab infested, sunbaked remains of one-legged Webley.

STEWART AND MUNGO

Mungo barked, barked, barked. No howls; no woofs; just three loud yaps followed by two seconds of silence while the mongrel sucked in another breath to again bark, bark, bark.

Generally, most dogs howl in concert with the siren of an ambulance or fire truck, understandably so, and normally, all dogs bark when a meter checker or a UPS driver stops by the house, to be expected, and usually, a majority of dogs bark along with other barking dogs and certainly, all dogs bark at a cat strutting along the top fence rail; however, this demon dog, this irksome, neurotic beast barked a relentless, consistent loudness of decibels at all the aforementioned, plus—plus—it barked at chirping birds, roaring aircraft, and laughing children. It barked at the moon in all phases and if a moonless night, it barked at the stars, and if no stars, it barked at the pitch dark. Sunrise, high noon, and sunset, it yapped. It yapped at sunshine, raindrops, and hailstones. It yapped at stormy claps of thunder, yet, the startled dog yelped first before it barked at thunder as if the universe had swatted it on its hindquarters with a rolled up newspaper. While munching on crunchy dog food, it barked with nuggets dribbling out of its mouth. While lifting a leg to pee it barked, starting and stopping the stream three times. When squatting, it yapped as though with every yap someone lifted the handle on an ice cream machine stacking three layers of pooh with a little tapered curl at the end. While asleep, it barked, dreaming a dog's dream of chasing rabbits across a grassy meadow. Sunday through Saturday, workdays, and holidays it bark, bark, barked, barking in every corner of its barren backyard so that each neighbor suffered an equal share of the yapabaloo. Yet, finally—at that treasured moment when there were no cats or other dogs, no meter checkers or delivery drivers, and nothing but a hushed breeze fanning between twilight and sunset—it yapped then too.

How, my word, how, could such a loud and annoying sound emit from such a small creature? Though scrawny with a Chihuahua body, bony short legs, and a curlicue tail, this russet-colored, short-haired canine had a Staffordshire bullterrier head, a heavy, bony cube of a skull strapped with strong jowl muscles, bulging black eyes, and a mouthful of sharp teeth so that this mutant animal's hulking head outweighed its small disproportionate body causing its twiglet hind legs, when walking, to bounce up and down off the ground then float in the air for a few seconds until they touched the ground again, all the while, the lightweight haunches struggling to keep the heavy-headed dog from crashing face first in the dirt. Fortunately, its bullterrier sized puppy-makers, bouncing, swinging, and tangling nearly as long as its short legs counterbalanced, just barely, the dog from head to tail to keep it from doing so.

Who can truly blame this odd, bigheaded, little dog for its endless assault on silence? It was psycho only because its owner was psycho. Right? Shouldn't the dog's owner train the dog not to bark? Swat it with a newspaper and enroll it in obedience school? Isn't it the duty of the dog's master to make certain his pet isn't annoying all of his neighbors, all the damn day, and all the damn night to where they can't eat, sleep, or watch TV, or if, lets say, for example, one of his neighbors is an author, who can't write, because he can't think, due to the never ending yapathon?

Absolutely, it's the owner's responsibility to train his dog not to take a log-stacking dump on the floor, not to squirt on the sofa, not to dry hump a visitor's leg, and not to gobble cat crap or lap up its own vomit. Definitely, it's the owner's task to make sure the dog doesn't rub its itchy anus on the throw rug, not to bite the hand offering a dog treat, and not to bark intrusively, intolerably, and incessantly. Other neighbors trained their dogs not to bark which was an ongoing task since it seemed as though maestro-mutt Mungo lived only to conduct a neighborhood symphony of barking dogs.

Nevertheless, Mungo's owner, Stewart Skoff, ignorant, inconsiderate Stewart Skoff did not train his disruptive pet. He ignored it, except to feed it dry dog food, scraps of fast food, and fill its algae-rimmed, plastic bowl with water. He never affectionately petted the pathetic pooch between the ears or lovingly rubbed its fur all the way back to its haunches giving it a few 'good boy' pats. Nor did he ever toss the bored and lonely dog a ball or a stick for a spirited game of fetch. The dog had no clue what a Frisbee was, the joy of catching it midair and the satisfaction of secretly chewing it to shreds. Stewart never considered exercise in any way, shape, or form for himself or his dog, so he and his furry companion never went for a walk in the park. Furthermore, unfortunate Mungo never experienced a dog's greatest thrill of sticking its head out a car window, feeling the rush of wind flapping back its ears, and smelling the odiferous blast of a thousand different smells, nor did it experience a dog's second greatest thrill of sniffing another dog's doggy-doo butt. Poor, Mungo. Poor ugly, unloved Mungo.

If you follow a homely kid home from school, someone homely will open the door for him. If you follow home a short, obese, slovenly youngster with pasty white skin who wears glasses and whose hair is thick, black, and alarming, someone short, obese, and slovenly with pasty white skin who wears glasses and whose hair is thick, black, and alarming will open the door for him. And if you follow home a child who is unaware, uncaring, and unkind, someone unaware, uncaring, and unkind will open the door for him.

When Stewart, an only child, was growing up, his parents Stanley and Wanda, and he, all three, were short, obese, slovenly, and wore glasses. His parents looked so much alike; one would think they were siblings. Their hair-dos were hair-don'ts, thick, black, and alarming. Wanda's hair frizzed out like a Poso Creek tumbleweed in July and could only be pinned down to the back of her head with an extra heavy-duty banana clip. Stanley's alarming hair was combed out in a tight white man fro, round and rigid as a crash helmet.

Stanley and Wanda didn't work, but subsisted on welfare. They stayed home, Stanley sitting in his lounge chair and watching baseball non-stop while Wanda laid on the couch and read raunchy romance novels. The only time they left the house was to collect their government check, walk to the liquor store for cigarettes and beer, or take their '73 olive-green Ford Pinto to the Super-Wal-Mart for everything else. So most of the time they were home when young Stewart returned home from school; even so, they never opened the door for him.

His parents never had a thought regarding the feelings of their son or for that matter, for the feelings of anyone else, so why should Stewart, their pathetic offspring have any consideration for others? Isn't it a parent's responsibility to train up a child? Most certainly. Shouldn't a mom and dad help their kid be the best he can be? Always. So is it the parent's fault when a kid turns out bad? Mostly, but not entirely. Stewart should have strived to better himself; he could have cared about his exasperated neighbors and trained Mungo not to bark. Indeed, he could have been kind to poor ugly, unloved Mungo.

Stewart Skoff, forty-five-years-old, Stewart Skoff, the

barking dog ignorer and neighbor pisser-offer was still overweight with pasty white skin and still slovenly, wearing loose and wrinkled clothes. He wore 1970s style tortoise-shell, big-framed glasses overshadowing most of his face and his dark unruly hair he mashed to the right with a left side part looking like a deep hatchet chop. He sported a scraggly beard and mustache, both black and kinky looking like the hairy armpits of a Turkish woman. For sure, he was ugly; however, there are people much uglier, much more slovenly, and much more undesirable than he, and yet, they seemed to find someone to love and to love them back. For proof, go to Wal-Mart. It's bizarrely romantic how weird people find each other and happily shop together there. Stewart Skoff, thoughtless, self-centered Stewart Skoff didn't have anybody to happily shop with at Wal-Mart. With both his parents dead from the ravages of diabetes, he lived alone with Mungo in the heart of Oildale, the 'life is, getting high and then you die' area of North East Bakersfield, California.

At the center of Oildale there were more liquor stores and bars, more DUIs, more meth labs and more gangs, more gun shops, more domestic violence in the fashion of wives being slapped and husbands being shot, more police and ambulance sirens, more broken-down cars parked on unmowed lawns, more chop shops, more stray dogs and feral cats, more cigarette butts littering the ground, gutters, and sidewalks, and more mullet haircuts on both men and women and small boys than any other U.S. city per capita, which all totaled up to fueling the economy of Kern County by adding more police stations, hiring more dog catchers, building larger prisons, and constructing bigger hospitals with drug, alcohol, and domestic rehab programs; however, with all of that fiscal growth there seemed to be a shortage of dentists with so many Oil Daleyons missing so many teeth.

Stewart rented a small decaying house, diarrhea brown with dark brown trim. It was one street over from the dirt ditch bank running along Norris Road. One cold and rainy day an unwanted, cuteless puppy, scared and hungry found his way from that ditch bank into Stewart's backyard through a gap in the front-yard, fence boards. Stewart, watching baseball on TV, saw the wet and shivering pup whimpering at his sliding glass back door. Since Stewart couldn't finish his third bacon-cheeseburger and second large box of onion rings, he tossed it on the ground for the dog to eat. The mutt swallowed the scraps without chewing and stayed. As Stewart continued to feed the mongrel, it grew to where the gap in the fence became too small for its great big head. Only its snarling snout and teeth could stick out the gap.

Stewart, like his father watched baseball every minute of his free time. He read and memorized the stats of every player so he could rattle them off to unsuspecting people waiting in the same line as he at the Wal-Mart checkout. He always wanted to play baseball, but he never learned to throw, catch, or bat. There you have it, he kept scores and stats.

Baseball is American, it's fun, it's nostalgic, and it's loved, yet how boring, how ridiculous, and how unprofitable to spend one's short life on such triviality, memorizing the stats of the players, unless one's job is a sportscaster or one sells baseball memorabilia. Speaking of memorabilia, Stewart, of course, collected baseball cards and his oldest and favorite card was one signed by Van Lingle Mungo, a pitcher for the Brooklyn Dodgers during the 1930s. Hence, the dog's name, Mungo.

Since graduating from North High, Stewart had worked for Roy's Small Appliance Repair located on North Chester where he repaired toasters, blenders, microwaves, radio alarm clocks, and because Roy's was in Oildale, he still repaired VCRs, cassette tape players, and more than just a few 8-track stereos. Roy, a short, wrinkled, and baldheaded eighty-two-year-old man always wearing a T-shirt and blue denim overalls sat at the front counter and dealt friendly enough with the customers, the money, and the business side of the business while Stewart, fixing appliances, sat begrudgingly at a wooden workbench in the small warehouse amongst shelves of electronic parts in grimy cardboard boxes.

On one side of Roy's shop sat Christopher's Diner known for their super-sized, chicken-fried steaks smothered in sausage gravy and on the other side of Roy's sat Trout's Nightclub, Oildale's last honky-tonk bar, known for brawls between bikers and cowboys and where oversized or undersized, half-dressed, painted face gals with big teeth or no teeth, old or older, go to meet up and dance with drunken, drugged-out Dalyon men.

On a warm, breezy night in April, at the start of baseball season, Stewart's incensed neighbors, angry over Mungo's incessant barking, met at Mike and Tanya's home across the street from Stewart's. Mike, an in-shape, square cut, clean shaven, flat-topped, forty-five-year-old veteran of Desert Storm who currently worked at a gun range and his wife, Tanya a soft spoken, skinny, make-up smeared waitress who worked at the Highlander bar and grill opened the door and invited in Jane, a thirty-one-year-old bookkeeper and single mom, short with a pear-shaped body, brushed out weedy hair, style-less clothes, yet wearing in-style frame-less eyeglasses on her number-counting face. Divorced with three small kids, she lived on the east side of Stewart's house. Next through Mike and Tanya's door strolled Joshua and Tiffany, a good-looking twenties couple living behind Stewart. Oddly matched, he stood barely five-feet-five while she towered nearly six. Both worked at CVS, the neighborhood drug store. Next entered Gladys, an eighty-one-year-old, silver-haired widow hunched over from the weight of a hard life who lived in the lower half of a two-story apartment building to the west of Stewart's house. Following her was David, a thirty-four-year-old carpet salesman and part time author working on his debut sci-fi novel while living in the upper apartment. His uncoordinated movements, quirky personality, and strange looks complete with alien thin body, long neck, and perfect egg-shaped shiny bald head led one to believe he visited Earth from his novel's distant planet Davidus. Unfortunately, for David, who needed quietude to access his cosmic imagination, his elevated apartment absorbed the worst of Mungo's racket.

As all of them spewed their frustrations concerning Stewart and Mungo, their tempers flared and their voices rose, carrying out the open windows to Stewart's fence gap where Mungo's raised ears picked up every word, prompting him to bark ever louder which drove the neighbor's voices ever louder to that of a mob carrying pitchforks and torches.

With all of them sitting in Mike's living room, Jane griped, "About two weeks ago, I wrote a note to Stewart and slipped it under his doormat. Here, I made a copy. I'll read it to you, *Dear Stewart, I am a single mom raising three little children two, four, and six.*"

Mike interrupted, "Jane, I can't hear you because of Mungo's barking. Will you read a little louder? Thanks."

Jane said, "Sure," and speaking louder, read, "*because of your dog barking all the time, I can't get my children to go to sleep at night or keep them asleep, and during the day when my mother is babysitting, she can't read or watch TV because of all the noise. My mom and me are both suffering from migraine headaches. Please, can you keep your dog quiet? Sincerely, Jane.*'

Joshua, commented, raising his voice over the top of Mungo's barking, "Well, that seemed nice enough!"

Jane added, maintaining her volume, "Yes, I thought so, but what really irked me was, a little later, when I had to go to the store and while I was loading my kids in the car, I saw Stewart on his front porch. He bent over and picked up the note that I had slipped under his doormat. He glanced at it, wadded it up while walking over to his fence, and pitched it over to Mungo. I heard the dog growling and snarling, ripping it to shreds."

Mike spoke loudly over the yapping, "That's not right! What a son of a … ."

Tanya, Mike's wife interrupted, "Now Mike, don't lose your temper."

Gladys chimed in, "Stewart's a horrible man! The other day, down at the grocery store, I went into the uni-sex restroom, you know the one by the in-store pharmacy, and while I was sitting there on that cold toilet seat, someone slammed into the door and rattled the doorknob like a serial killer. It scared me so bad, I thought my pacemaker would short out. Then, while I'm trying to empty my bothersome bladder and not but a few seconds later, the doorknob rattled again even louder this time. So I hurried with my business, quickly washed my hands, and opened the door to have Stewart, yes, Stewart rush in, bump into me, and nearly shut the door on me knocking me down. Can you believe it? A man his size, pushing around a little, old woman like me! The man never said, 'Excuse me' or 'I'm sorry.'"

Mike snapped, "I'm gonna beat the hell out of him!"

Tanya said, "Now, Mike, don't get all worked up. You just can't beat him up and not go back to jail."

"Something else he did," Gladys added, "my church friends, Alice and Ruth were out canvasing the neighborhood and inviting people to our Sunday services. They stopped at Stewart's house. He opened the door and yelled at them, 'What do you want. You're interrupting the game!' They invited him to visit our church and gave him a pamphlet. He snatched it out of their hands, wadded it up, threw it at their feet, and slammed the door. I've never heard of such a hardened heart against the Lord. I fear for that man's soul."

David, the author, in a Da-vidian monotone voice, remarked, "Stewart is just plain rude. I saw him driving the other day in that smoggy junker of his. He had every motorist and a few pedestrians flipping him off. He's a slug on the freeway and a moron on city streets. He made a left turn and then a right without ever using his turn signal. I followed him up the freeway on-ramp where he tried to merge at 40 mph with traffic speeding at 70. An eighteen-wheeler nearly crushed me to death. And then—then there's that mongrel of his. Ugh! I can't write with that crazy dog's incessant barking. I can't hear my inner voice at all. I find myself typing *yap yap yap, yap yap yap* across the page. We've got to do something about Stewart and Mungo!"

Joshua said, "I've got one for you. A few weeks ago, Mungo was barking so loud, Tiffany and I peered over the fence to see why he was barking. The crazy dog was at the sliding glass door barking *at* Stewart while he just sat in his lounge chair and watched baseball. He ignored the dog. I called information, got Stewart's number, and called him. I could hear his phone ringing in-between Mungo's barks and I even saw Stewart pick up his phone and hang it up without answering it. I called him twice more and on the third time, he snatched up the phone and yelled, 'What do you want?' I replied, 'Stewart, it's your neighbors Joshua and Tiffany behind you.' Again, he snapped at me, 'What do you want?' His attitude irritated the hell out of me, so I said, 'Stewart, your barking dog is driving my wife and I crazy! Can you please quiet it down?' He said, 'I don't hear anything,' so I asked him, 'How could you not hear your loud and annoying dog? We can't even hear our TV.' He replied, 'Well, I can hear my TV.' At that remark, I lost my cool and yelled, 'Listen, Stewart, you jerk, just shut your damn dog up!' Do you want to know what he did? He hung up on me and resumed watching baseball."

Tiffany added, "I saw him at the grocery store too. I was coming down the cereal isle and he was coming up it when he stopped to read the ingredient label on a box. He blocked the entire aisle with his shopping cart and was totally unaware that I was patiently waiting to get past. I waited for a few seconds hoping that he would move on his own, but he didn't, so I cleared my throat and asked as sweetly as I could, 'Stewart, excuse me," which he ignored me, prompting me to say more clearly, 'Excuse me. I need to get by,' upon which he had no reply of, 'Oh, pardon me for blocking the aisle.' However, he didn't say anything or even acknowledge me as a neighbor. He huffed and moved his cart. Then—then at the check out stand, where he was a couple people in front of me in line, I smelled the most god-awful odor. So did the other line standers scrunching up their faces. Then it hit me and I knew that Stewart, gross Stewart had ripped a silent stinky in public. It was so bad the smell made all of us gag. I swear, we held our breath until he grabbed his bags and left."

Mike grumbled, "What an inconsiderate bastard!"

Tanya looked at him as if she was about to say something to calm him down, but Mike kept discharging his words, "Listen to this. Last Saturday night when Tanya and me were trying to have a nice romantic night at home that damn dog started barking to where she got a headache. Didn't you, Tanya"

"Yes, I did, baby. My head started poundin' durin' the lunch rush at the Highlander and Mungo's barkin' made it ten times worse."

Mike continued, "She had to go lie down without takin' care of her man, if you know what I mean. I told her, I'd deal with that lousy mutt, so I stomped over to Stewart's and pounded on his door. Stewart took his sweet time comin' to the door, which pissed me off even worse. He opened the door, glanced at me, then stared back at the TV blarin' the baseball game. That beast of his was goin' crazy barkin' and snarlin' up against the slidin' glass door. I yelled, 'Listen, Stewart, you pudgy little puke. Dammit, look at me!' He looked at me and I told him, 'all of us neighbors have had enough of your barkin' dog. I love dogs and baseball, but I'm startin' to hate them both.' He pops off to me, 'Listen Mike, why don't you just go back home and clean your army guns while dreaming about those few glory days back in Desert Storm.' I about kicked his sorry ass right then and there, but I just told him, 'Shut up Stewart! What would you know about sacrificin' your life for your country? You can't even be a good neighbor.' He muttered that he was missing his game and slammed the door in my face. I'll tell you what, my fellow frustrated neighbors, if dogs, when they die, go to a Pet Heaven or Hell, that devil dog will go to Pet Hell and certainly, Stewart's goin' to Hell. I'll say this; I'm about ready to shoot that f'n dog!"

Tiffany exclaimed, "You can't shoot Mungo! You'll go to prison for as long as for murdering a person—maybe longer."

Tanya added, "That's right, hon and the police will take away your guns."

Mike growled not saying a word.

Jane said, "I have an idea. It might sound crazy, but, maybe, if we do something nice for Stewart, he'll work with us about quieting Mungo."

Gladys agreed, "Sure, we could 'kill him with kindness'."

Joshua added, "There's a saying, 'You catch more flies with honey than vinegar'."

David said, "How about if we all pitch in and buy Stewart a big batch of barbeque ribs and then Mungo can have the bones. Maybe if we treat them to a super nice dinner, he'll shut his dog up for us."

They all agreed except for Mike that the 'kindness' idea and the dinner were worth a try.

Mike interrupted their majority caucus and chimed, "I think we ought to all pitch in and throw him a blanket party."

Gladys asked, "What's a blanket party?"

Tanya just shook her head, knowing what Mike was about to say.

Mike answered, "A blanket party is where we all pitch in and buy Stewart a really soft and cozy blanket. Then, one night, we all take it over to him and when he opens the door we quickly toss the blanket over his head so he can't see who we are, and then, we kick him with our boots on and beat the hell out of him with garden tools. Once we've had enough and we're all feelin' better, we'll take off and he ain't the wiser to who beat the snot out of him."

The stunned women were in shock over his proposal and didn't say a word.

David said, "Mike, that's a fun idea to think about for a moment, but how about, like I suggested, we all pitch in and buy Stewart a barbeque dinner and then Mungo can have the bones. If we're nice to them, maybe Stewart will be nice to us and quiet his dog."

Mike surrendered, saying, "I doubt it will do any good, but we could try it. If he doesn't put a muzzle on his dog, then we'll crack down on him with every thing we got. Okay, everybody, pitch in five bucks. I'll pick him up a plate of barbeque ribs and the fixin's on my way home from work tomorrow night. Both of us usually get home about six. I'll take it over to him and tell him it's from all of us as a gesture toward peace. Then, I'll ask him to work with us about shuttin' up his damn dog."

None of the neighbors could have foreseen the outcome of their gesture.

The next evening, Mike stopped by *Champion Barbeque* and picked up a large order of baby back ribs, rice and beans, seasoned fries, honey corn bread, and a hunk of chocolate chip brownie. He watched out his front window and wondered why Stewart wasn't home. Stewart was working overtime trying to catch up on appliance repairs. When Mike saw Stewart arrive home around 7:30, he grabbed the bag of food, walked across the street, and caught Stewart before he went inside.

Mike hollered out, "Hey, Stewart! Stewart! The neighbors and I are tryin' to be nice to you, so we bought you dinner."

Mungo barked ferociously, snarled, and kicked up dust behind the fence.

Stewart, blank faced, just stared back at Mike.

Mike handed him the bag filled with Styrofoam boxes full of food.

Stewart reached out a pudgy hand without stepping any closer and snatched it out of Mike's hand. A fissure of a smile cracked in the right corner of Stewart's mouth or maybe his mouth flinched from saliva like a Pavlovian dog. Mungo smelled the food and yapped sounding like a hungry pack of wild dogs from Borneo.

Mike had to yell above the barking and though his words had an edgy crust reflecting his desire to pound Stewart into the ground and take Mungo out to play on the highway, he said as nicely as he could, "Enjoy it Stewart and give the bones to Mungo. Us neighbors are just askin' you to quiet your barkin' dog. Will you help us out here?"

Stewart, without saying a word, turned, hurried into the house, and locked the door behind him.

Mike stomped back home and yelled at Tanya, "That ungrateful bastard grabbed the bag without even a 'thank you'! I knew we should have thrown him a blanket party!"

Stewart reheated the freebie food in the microwave, plopped down into his lounge chair, and placed the hearty meal in front of him on his folding TV tray. Mungo was now at the back sliding glass door barking at Stewart. Stewart turned on the baseball game featuring his favorite team, the Dodgers, who were playing the Braves, and began eagerly devouring his ribs smothered in barbeque sauce in-between shoving fries in his mouth. He hastily ate six of the eight ribs and most of the beans and rice as Mungo barked insanely pressing his wet nose against the sliding glass door and with every bark blasting it with a steamy hot breath.

Finally at the height of the dog's yapulence, Stewart clambered out of his chair, shuffled across his living room all the while never taking his eyes off the game, and tossed the bones to Mungo wagging his curlicue tail so hard that his entire hindquarters wrenched back and forth like a slinky toy. Crazed, eager Mungo wolfed down the first three ribs barely cracking and chewing them at all. As always, he excitedly barked a yap of joy in-between each gobble, downing two more ribs. When gulping down the last rib bone, the dog barked with such delight that the bone wielding a sharp edge lodged deep in his throat. As terrified Mungo gagged and choked, his barking ceased for the first time in a long, long time.

Meanwhile, while Mungo was choking to death on the patio, Stewart bit off the end gristle of a rib at the same time a Dodger player hit a grand slam homerun causing Stewart to gasp, thus lodging the gristle in his windpipe. Horrified, eyes bulging, and gripping his throat with both hands, he choked. He tried a self Heimlich maneuver pounding a fist into his chest then searched for his cell phone, which had fallen behind the cushion in his chair. As he turned blue, he fell out of his chair and crawled on his hands and knees into the kitchen, pulled himself up the counter, and snatched the phone hanging on the wall. He dialed 9-1-1 and still choking, said, "Gaaack, uuuggh, aaahhh," then dropped the phone and fell back to the floor.

While Stewart choked inside, rolling on the linoleum, Mungo choked outside, rolling on the cement patio. Both, at the same moment, choked, choked, choked to death.

While Jane was reading her children a bedtime story and David was writing an alien bedtime story and Joshua and Tiffany were hot and heavy making a bedtime story and Gladys was fast asleep dreaming a bedtime story, and Mike and Tanya were smoking cigarettes after finishing a bedtime story—they noticed that Mungo had stopped barking.

Jane stopped reading, David stopped typing, Gladys stopped sleeping, Joshua and Tiffany stopped making love, and gun range Mike and Tanya inhaled on their cigarettes, exhaled, and looked at each other with surprise.

There was silence————however, not total silence. Never heard before in the neighborhood due to the racket Mungo made was a crying baby, a husband and wife arguing, and a sixteen-year-old aspiring rock star practicing his electric guitar.

Jane smiled at her kids, Joshua and Tiffany grinned face to face, Gladys giggled and petted her cat, David laughed, lifting his hands toward Heaven, and Mike chuckled as he, and his wife took a celebratory drag on their cigarettes. Their kindness had worked. Mungo had stopped barking.

Though Mungo had stopped barking and the neighbors could go peacefully and happily about their daily lives, the story of Stewart and Mungo doesn't end here.

Mungo lay dead on his back, his stiffening short legs in the air with his unwagging curlicue tail between them. His big dog puppy-makers hung lifeless to his left as his limp red tongue hung to the right dangling out of his ferocious mouth suspended in a silent bark. Gone, was the wild glint in his black bulging eyes.

At the moment of Mungo's death, his ghostly spirit sprang up and out of his body, darted across the cement patio, leapt, soaring through the sliding glass door, and bounded over to Stewart's spirit standing next to and staring down at his own dead body; his face contorted in a choke, eyes open, mouth gaping, and a huge red barbeque stain on his *Roy's Appliance Repair* work shirt, not to mention his zipper had been down all day. Nothing mattered. He was dead. No more baseball. No chocolate chip brownie. As always, he ignored Mungo panting with a happy dog grin and a wagging tail.

Suddenly, a blinding white light appeared above where the ceiling would be. Both stared up into it and blinked at its brightness. The light began to swirl, spinning counterclockwise. Stewart swallowed hard, for he instinctively knew that this light had come from a source of love and standing there spiritually naked, he knew that in his heart he had not lived a life of love. Surprisingly, Mungo, gazing up at the light, wagged his tail and didn't growl, snarl, or bark.

With tremendous suction, the spinning light drew them up out of the temporal physical plane and into a spiritual realm of forever. Nude, chubby, hairy Stewart and his odd, little, big-headed dog, tumbling, flailing, whooshed through the long tunnel of light to land right-side up on their feet with only a mere shake and shudder to regain their balance.

Stewart glanced around as Mungo sniffed about. They stood at the start of a humble dirt road. Not far behind them was a precipice with a sheer drop into hazy blue firmament. Stewart looked down at Mungo. The dogs' furry coat shined. Stewart, no longer needing or wearing glasses, glanced down at himself to find that he wore a loose white robe made of cotton. It was clean without any barbeque stains and it had no open zipper. On his feet were sandals of new leather.

On both sides of the road colorful wild flowers mingled with bright green grass. The sun shone bright, but wasn't hot. A breeze blew, but wasn't cold. Mungo ran, leapt, and sniffed, but didn't bark. Everything felt perfect; however, Stewart, whose spirit was unaware, uncaring, and unkind didn't smile, for he knew, knew in his heart, that he had never believed in a place like this.

Out of a tiny spurt of light near them, a blue parakeet arrived, tumbling in the air. It righted itself and fluttered away from them. It flew above the road to disappear up and over the hill in front of them. Another burst of light and a fluffy white cat with a pink pug nose appeared. It pranced, rubbing itself in a figure eight between Stewart legs and then casually walked over to Mungo where the two animals touched noses. Mungo didn't bark, but licked the cat's face. The cat meowed, and then darted up the road. From a people-sized splatter of light, an old man dressed in a white gown appeared, glanced around, and said "'Ello, 'ello" in a British accent, then said, "Cheerio," and marched promptly up the hill.

Stewart and Mungo followed the old man who was looking younger with every step until he soon out distanced them. As Stewart hiked, he felt ten years younger, light on his feet with a snap in his step. Mungo had the energy of a puppy.

Arriving at the top of the hill, Stewart gazed out and gasped. Before him lay a sunlit valley, a wonderland of green meadows, glistening streams, and beautiful gardens of lush trees and bright flowers. Beyond the breathtaking valley, a vast city of pillars, domes, steeples and towers all made of polished stone inlaid with precious jewels sat amongst and on top of the hills and mountains set before a golden sky. Stewart never imagined that something so beautiful could ever exist. Seeing the splendor of paradise his shameful spirit wanted to burst out singing, but didn't. His eyes followed the dirt road, which continued from the top of the hill down through the gardens, across streams, and around grassy hills leading to the city in the sky. Nearby, to his right the valley nestled up against a glinting sea with gentle rolling waves breaking on a sandy shore. To his left the flourishing valley rolled all the way to an orange-tinted horizon. Not far down the road and at the bottom of the hill stood a colossal gate glimmering in the sunlight.

Stewart, with Mungo by his side, took a step down the hill toward the gate when an excited young boy tore past them and down the hill. Mungo chased after the lad who stopped running, bent down, and with both hands rubbed Mungo from ears to tail. He finished with a loving pat on the dog's haunches and said, "You're a good dog!" Mungo wagged his tail and ran back to Stewart. Stewart glanced down at him, but did not pet him, not learning a lesson from the youngster.

They continued their journey down to the glorious gate, the only entrance to the garden. It stood twelve-feet-tall with a solid gold frame and thick vertical golden rods. Stewart gazed up and read the gleaming words *Pet Heaven* engraved across the top of the frame. There was no latch or knob to open the gate so Stewart wondered when and how it would open. Mungo stuck his snout between two golden rods then sniffed and snorted as he used to do between the fence boards back home. Stewart strolled to the right of the gate to go around it and encountered an invisible force that stopped him. He marched around to the left of the gate, yet banged into another unseen wall. He heard a faint rumbling sound and felt a vibration beneath his feet, when suddenly, the road under Mungo collapsed. The frightened dog floated in midair between the sunshine of paradise and a rapidly widening abyss beneath him. Stewart jumped backward away from its expanding edge. Mungo whined. Lightning streaked across the darkness of the deep pit. Thunder boomed. Mungo yelped. The doomed dog tried to run, but couldn't, captured by the tug of the abyss. With fearful eyes staring at Stewart, who was backing farther away from the precarious edge of the pit, poor, ugly, unloved Mungo surrendered to his fate and stopped struggling. The darkness and lightning bolts beneath the dog began to spin and he descended nearly out of sight into the black void, when, all of a sudden, the abyss spit him up and out as the gap in the ground slammed shut beneath him. Mungo landed hard, rolled a few times across the dirt road, and then jumped to his feet still shiny as before. The gate sprang open and in a blessed turn of eternal fate, the good-hearted pet entered *Pet Heaven*. Stewart followed, terrified he would encounter the same scrutiny somewhere down the road.

Walking in the garden, Stewart saw pets of all kinds. There were pet birds: bright colored parakeets, parrots, finches, lovebirds, and cockatoos. They flew through the pure air and roosted in leafy trees. Not one bird, not even a parrot pecked at any other bird. They chirped, cawed, tweeted, whistled, and sang in perfect harmony.

On the ground, mice, rats, gerbils, hamsters, and guinea

pigs scurried about free and happy. None of the small fur balls climbed on top, scratched, or nibbled on another.

He heard the pleasant purring of happy cats. Stewart never liked cats or really any pets because he hated the responsibility of caring for them; nevertheless, here in paradise he did appreciate the soothing sound of the contented felines. There were all types of cats: tubby, thin, furry, fluffy, and hairless. There were kittens, toms, and tabbies. There were cats of all colors, patches, and stripes. Some had long tails while others had short tails and some didn't have a tail at all. Most of the cats had amber colored eyes, though some had green while others had blue and then there were persnickety cats that refused to look at him. The felines sat high and low in trees and on rocks and watched with fascination the birds and rodents; nevertheless, not one cat attacked the small creatures.

Dogs of every species were everywhere; big dogs and small dogs, tall and short, furry and furless, long legs and short, and with tails and no tails. He did notice that there were very few Rottweilers, Pit bulls and Dobermans; also, surprisingly, not very many Chihuahuas. Dogs slept in the sunshine or in the shade. Cats snuggled up next to the dogs while mice cuddled up with the cats. Dogs not sleeping sniffed around with wagging tails.

Mungo bounded into the meadow. He frolicked in the grass, rolled in the flowers, and sniffed every dog's butt in his path. A furry white rabbit popped up out of a hole in the ground and hopped, racing across the meadow. Happy dogs, including Mungo chased it until the rabbit dropped into a hole to disappear. Mungo then raced over to a sparkling stream where he splashed in the water, laid on his belly, and lapped up the stream's coolness. After that, he ran straight for the shoreline where he romped in the sand and splashed in the surging tide of a glinting sea.

Stewart left the path, walked a short distance toward the beach, and called out, "Mungo! Mungo!"

The dog stopped splashing in the rolling surf and stared at Stewart for a moment, then wagged his tail, barked three times, and raced off down the beach.

Stewart felt sad to see him go and felt remorse for not treating Mungo better, then again, he thought, the mutt was really just a stray. He strolled back to the path and resumed his journey toward the heavenly city.

A middle-aged woman in a white garment walked briskly past him. Stewart followed her, but she soon outdistanced him. He walked over an ancient stone bridge above a slow moving stream of clear water. He stopped and peered down over its wall and saw along the banks frogs and toads, turtles and tortoises, salamanders and geckos, and even a few twelve-inch alligators. Good, he thought, there weren't any snakes. Remembering back to when he was in second grade and he had two pet goldfish one named Joe and the other Lou, he searched the water for goldfish, but didn't see any, prompting him to mutter, "So goldfish really do just vanish down the toilet."

It began to rain, a fresh, cool rain. He cupped his hands and caught enough drops for a long drink. It tasted sweet and more refreshing than anything he had ever tasted. Then, something like thick white snowflakes began to fall from the sky. As soon as it floated to the ground, all the animals ate heartedly. He reached out a hand, caught a few hearty flakes, and tasted them. They were crunchy and sweet, and a little salty. He caught a few more and gobbled them down, feeling revitalized. After all the animals ate their fill, whatever remained on the ground seeped into the soil to nourish the plants.

He left the bridge, continued down the road, and before long arrived at a beautiful gate, standing twenty-feet-tall, gleaming white with the luster of polished pearls. Just beyond the gate, the magnificent city made of stone sparkled of gold, silver, diamonds, and gems. Gleeful music of people singing and playing instruments carried on a breeze. He waited uncertain and fearful in front of the gate wondering when it would open to let him in. He saw his reflection in the shine of the glowing white gate and hung his head knowing he had neither faith nor love. His *god* had been himself, his religion baseball, his church his living room, his congregation were pitchers, baseman, and fielders, his pew his lounge chair, and his altar his TV. He had done nothing worthwhile with his life and had left the world a worse place.

Suddenly, beneath him and to his horror, the ground opened up to a deep and dark abyss. Again, the lightning struck, the thunder bellowed, and the darkness swirled pulling him down. A blinding light filled his eyes flooding his thoughts and he heard a booming voice say, "Stewart Skoff, you never knew *Me*. A thimble full of love, and faith the size of a seed, would have saved you; however, you have neither. Away with you!"

The darkness beneath him spun faster and faster sucking him down farther and farther. Paralyzed, he couldn't move while it drew him down to where he plummeted away from paradise, away from the light, and far from eternal bliss. Above him, the ground closed, shutting out the last spot of sunlight.

In less than a minute, he landed on his feet on a treacherous road with sheer drop-offs on either side. Darkness surrounded him except for a fiery red-orange glow that provided just enough light to see. Behind him, black firmament. Straining his eyes, he saw before him an enormous iron gate, twenty-feet-tall. A rusty-pitted hunk of iron with the words *People Hell* scorched into it with fire. He shuffled to the gate, put his face up to it, and peered between two bars. Before him lay a dry land with vortexes of dust snaking across the torrid landscape. Beyond this, a dark and dull city sat between mountains of erupting fire set against eternal night. Cries of suffering and torment pierced the arid air.

Trembling, he backed away from the gate to await his

horrible fate. He waited, sobbing, not from a contrite heart but from regret that he would spend eternity in this horrible place. He cried out, "Please, show me mercy," knowing full well, he had never been merciful, when the ground beneath him opened up to a pitch-black abyss. Without warning and nowhere to go, again, he floated above it and again, there were lightning and thunder, and the abyss swirled and snatched him down. For another time, he fell, screaming in horror, flailing his arms and legs. He wondered, a flash of fear, what could be worse than People Hell?

He landed on his feet on a craggy road chiseled out of rock. Behind him, blackness. Before him, a fiery red-orange glow. The air smelled of animal excrement and so thick, it tasted of it too. He squinted, strained his eyes, and saw before him another iron gate, rusted, pitted, and covered in teeth marks. He stepped warily up to it to stand a few feet in front of it. Laboring to see, he saw something rushing toward him. He heard a great snarling and gnashing of teeth and the rumbling of stampeding animals charging toward him. The horde drew close and he saw angry, growling Dobermans, Rottweiler's, Pit bulls, and yappy Chihuahuas, all with their teeth bared and the nap of their necks up. Running along side the vicious dogs were huge hissing cats, some with one ear, some with patchy fur, yet all with sharp claws. He heard squeaking and beneath the dogs and cats scurried diseased rats covered in sores. Flying above the dogs, the cats, and the rats were squawking pissed-off parrots snapping their sharp beaks. The multitude of devilish pets arrived at the gate snarling, growling, and baring their teeth amidst hissing, squeaking, and squawking.

Stewart, trembling, covered his ears and closed his eyes, awaiting his fate. The gates creaked. He gasped. They creaked again and slowly swung open. He opened his eyes and glanced above the teeth, claws, fur, and red devilish eyes to read the words scorched across the top of the gate—*Pet Hell*.

Hack, cough, and deep breath. Stewart awoke. Still sprawled out on the kitchen floor, he peered up at the two blurry paramedics standing over him. They loaded him on a stretcher and slid him in an ambulance. On the way to the hospital, they explained to him that 9-1-1 had traced his call and they responded. He was lucky; they were on a dinner break at a restaurant close by. They arrived at his house, busted through the front door, and found him on the floor in the kitchen. He looked dead. They checked his throat, found a piece of meat lodged in it, removed the obstruction, and performed CPR. Thinking he was dead and beyond resuscitation, they were surprised when he took a breath and opened his eyes.

With a hoarse voice, Stewart asked, "What about my dog, Mungo?"

"So sorry," one of the paramedics said, "but we couldn't help the dog."

After staying over night at the hospital for observation, Stewart was back home. He had the SPCA, for a small fee, pick up the body of Mungo. Stewart wept, feeling remorse for not treating Mungo like a loving pet; however, the thought of Mungo running in the sunshine on a heavenly beach made him smile.

Maybe while Stewart was passed out on the floor there was a lack of oxygen to his brain or maybe he remembered his quick trip to Pet Hell. Regardless of the reason, Stewart changed.

He became aware of those around him and treated them considerately. He said, "Hello," to the surprised neighbors and even added, "Have a wonderful day." At the grocery store, he pushed his cart over so that other people with carts could pass. On the road, he drove the speed limit and used turn signals.

On a day with bountiful sunshine, Stewart, while at work at Roy's, met a gal by the name of Tammy, a manicurist at Reba's Salon of Beauty where they specialized in beehives and bouffants. She stopped by Roy's Appliance Repair to have her cassette player repaired.

She was frumpy, but no frumpier than Stewart. She dressed slovenly, but no more than he did. Her black hair was as frizzy and alarming as his, her eyeglasses were just as out of style, and her skin was just as pasty white. One might think they were siblings of sort. She enjoyed watching baseball games and though she didn't quite enjoy them as much as Stewart, she was okay with his big league obsession. Their greatest difference was, unlike Stewart, she had always been caring and kind. Both were horribly lonely.

When Tammy returned to pickup her repaired cassette player, Stewart said, "The repair is free," and then sheepishly asked her, "will you go out with me?"

Not having been asked out on a date before, she asked, "Really?"

He replied, "Yes. Uhhh, really."

She said, "Okay," and on that Friday night they went to Zorba's on north Chester. The historic burger joint served breakfast, lunch, and dinner, and boasted a menu of foodstuffs fried in, *100% vegetable oil. No cholesterol!* A sign on a half sheet of copy paper, handwritten in capital letters with a black Magic Marker, and Scotch taped to their soda machine read, 'DO NOT FILL CUPS WITH SODA IF YOU DID NOT PURCHASE. SHERIFFS WILL BE CALLED. PETTY THEFT CHARGES.

Stewart ordered a quarter pound burger stacked with pastrami, and then layered with melted Swiss cheese, pickles, and mustard along with a large basket of chili fries. Tammy ordered the charbroiled chicken sandwich and fried zucchini. Both drank *purchased* sodas so without fear and a clear conscience, they could refill them without being arrested on petty theft charges by the sheriffs. They chatted a few minutes about their boring lives in between big bites and chewing, and then afterwards went back to his place to watch a game. During the first at-bat, two balls, two strikes, she said sweetly, "Just so you know Stewart, my favorite movie, *The Notebook* is playing on HBO." Stewart wisely changed channels.

From that time on, they spent most of their free time together. Over the next few months, their friendship blossomed into romance and then into a deep endearing love for one another.

Stewart never felt such happiness; yet, he still missed Mungo. He talked with Tammy and they decided that they both wanted a dog.

On a fresh spring day, they drove down to the SPCA shelter and right away spotted a puppy. The little brown mutt was a bit furrier than Mungo and though different with its tail long and straight, its head and body proportionate to one another, and its ears down and snout out, it was still just as ugly as Mungo. Perfect.

Stewart adopted the dog and named him Mickey after the Yankee's Mickey Mantle. Every Saturday he took Mickey for a ride in the car with the windows down and then to the dog park where Mickey happy and drooling chased a Frisbee and sniffed dog butts.

Up's Last Smile

I'm old; so old. Can't dive no more. Bouncin' on a springboard jumbles up my innards; rattles my bones too. Can still get a laugh though; clownin' around's simple; leapin' into the water's easy, but swimmin'—swimmin' ain't so easy; got no strength in my arms and legs; can't doggy paddle neither; sink straight to the bottom. Seein's how I can't bounce, dive, or swim no more, I'm just gonna plop down in this chair by the swimmin' pool here at our cozy little Orange Grove Manor, yep—I'll sip my sweet tea, warm my achin' bones in all this Florida sunshine, and tell you—if you don't mind listenin' to an ol' timer like me—about my best friend, Up, and his last smile. It was a mouth stretchin', teeth gleamin', eyes twinklin', and face beamin' happy, heavenly smile that caught me by surprise, sure did—seein's' how I thought he was dead.

Now, before I tell you about Up's last smile, I got to jabber on a bit about what led up to that smile, but first, let me introduce myself. William 'Splash' Mackleberry is my name. Could've been called, Billy, Willy, or Mac, however, ol' Up nicknamed me 'Splash' my first day workin' out a clown divin' act for the Fabrizio Circus. It was a small travelin' circus made up of just four attractions. It was hard times back then; a time when men wore fedora hats and the world was on the brink of a god-awful war. I was very lucky to find work; odd job as it was; clown divin' into a swimmin' pool; hardly paid anything, yet, I got fed three hot meals a day and had a warm place to sleep every night. Yep. Only needed one set of clothes until somethin' wore out, and then, I'd buy what I needed: pair of socks, drawers, shirt, hat, or whatever. I got the circus job 'cause I was a bit chubby, naw, I was fat, and since I was short, I was round, so ever' time I hit the water, instead of *splish*: where a few spectators get wet, I made a splash: *all* spectators get wet, 'cause my heft like a big boulder would hit the water and drag that splash down, to where it would double-whammy up for a colossal crowd soakin'.

Right there, that first day, while ol' Up was standin' there by the pool and all drippin' wet from my splash, he said, 'That was a heck-of-a splash, 'Splash!'

I always just called him 'Up,' right after he blurted out, 'Hi, my name is Udell Uppenheimer,' and I replied, 'Nice to meet ya, Up.' From then on, for thirty years, we were the *Up and Splash Show.*

Circus posters screamin' 'Fabrizio Circus' were tacked up all around every next town we were headin' to. Couldn't miss 'em. Ever'body seen 'em. Adults and kids gawkin at 'em; all wearin' beamin' fun smiles as if they were already sittin' in the grandstands.

Smack dab in the middle of those posters, a roarin' Bengal tiger with pointy teeth and sharp claws leapt out at you; of course, there weren't no tiger in our circus; it was just an attention grabber.

In the top left corner of that poster, under the caption, *The Tallest and The Smallest* was Juju the elephant, a gigantic gray and wrinkled beast with his ears back as if he'd stampede right off the poster. Behind the behemoth's massive head rode Juju's trainer, Shakti the Punjabi, a dark skinned man wearin' a white robe and turban, and perched up on Juju's curled trunk, just a few feet above the ground, stood itty-bitty, four-foot tall, Miss

Jellybean, a pretty gal, hair as black as night and sea-green eyes shimmerin' like a tropical cove. In her baby-sized arms, she held a tiny white-faced capuchin monkey named Pookaka. Back then, most people had never seen up-close an elephant, a foreigner in a turban, a monkey, or a squat-sized woman. People filled the circus tent to see 'em.

Juggles was printed across the top right corner of that poster right above our jugglin' clown, Juggles, jugglin' five balls: green, blue, red, orange, and yellow. He looked hilarious with that big red smile on his painted white face, those high surprised eyebrows, that red crabapple nose and his stiff blue hair stickin' out the sides of his shiny baldhead. And boy did he look ridiculous wearin' those red saggy-baggy pants, a tight yellow T-shirt, blue suspenders, and big green oversized sneakers. People laughed just lookin' at him. Funny thing, though he made people laugh, Sammy, that's his real name, was the saddest man I ever knew. Lost his wife to drunk driver 'fore she could bear a child. The poor man never recovered; still missed her ever'day of his sad life. Clownin' and jugglin' made him forget about her. However, I gotta tell ya this. Once he washed off his make-up and put away his jugglin' gear, there'd be that forlorn face, so long and twisted up, you'd think he was about to cry. And he did, more than not. Sad. So sad.

Now, down in the left bottom corner of the poster was the *Flying Fabrizios*, Pito and his sister Vivi; her somersaultin' in mid-air with him swingin' upside down on his trapeze and stretchin' out to catch her. Pito wore a sparklin' red leotard and Vivi dressed in a glimmerin' gold one. Pito was a handsome feller; looked odd though; big chest, with pecs as big as beer kegs, big arms too; had to be, to catch Vivi, but his legs; his legs were skinny; and his feet tiny, though his legs were strong enough to hold him hangin' upside down while snatchin' her out of mid-air.

Vivi sure was a pretty gal, petite with short brown hair

styled in a man's short comb and part; she didn't want a ponytail gettin' in the way of Pito's view to catch her. However, don't get me wrong, she was all woman with shapely curves, and I can say this about that, she might have had muscles, nevertheless, she had the softest skin I ever touched. And to gaze into her eyes was to peer into a clear blue sky on a Sunday afternoon. I adored that little acrobat. We were married for fifty-two years until dreaded cancer took her from me. Three years it took to take her. Tough times. I don't like to talk about it.

Though, I will say this about that. She had no fear facin' cancer, and no fear, non at all, as she flipped, twisted, twirled, and soared through the air trustin' her brother with her very life. They've got a sad story though. I wasn't there to witness the tragedy, but when Pito and Vivi were but teenagers, they performed in a family act with their father, Favorico, and mother LaPatrina. Durin' a performance, one of the cables broke that held up the trapeze. Both Favorico and LaPatrina toppled to the hard ground, both missin' the safety net. Neither parent survived. After such heartbreak, you'd think Pito and Vivi would never ever soar on the flyin' trapeze again; however, they carried on the act and kept their family's circus alive.

Okay, now the zany part. Down in the right hand bottom corner of that poster was the headin' *Up and Splash* with ol' Up and me both ridin' on our old yellow bicycle soarin' off the high board above a swimmin' pool, which was just barely wide enough and deep enough to dive in without breakin' our necks. Both our faces were all twisted up in a funny scared to death kind of way. Up, skinny as a broom handle, is doin' the peddlin' while wearin' his yellow with red polka dotted swim trunks as I'm balancin' on the handlebars while sportin' my too-tight, red and white striped, old-fashioned, one piece, swimsuit where my jelly-belly flopped out the front and my butter-butt bounced out the back. My flattop was blonde back then, while Up's straight, shoulder length hair was black and parted down the middle. To round out our clown look we both wore oversized rubber feet. Neither one of us wore clown makeup 'cause it'd only wash off in the pool, besides we were funny enough lookin' without it; me, with my pink porky face, bulgin' blue eyes, and thickset limbs and Up lookin' like a stork with his curved beak of nose, beady brown eyes, long neck, and pencil thin arms and legs.

We sure got the laughs! For our openin' act, ol' Up nervous and tremblin' tiptoed out to the end of the low divin' board and sat on its edge with his legs danglin'. He'd stretch his huge rubber big toe down, down, down to test the temperature of the water, start to touch it, and then jerk that big, big toe up while curlin' into a ball of fright. The crowd laughed, 'specially the kids. After a few times of nearly touchin' the water and curlin' up, he'd finally stretch, stretch, stretch and just barely touch that water with the tip of his toe, then spring to his feet, huggin' himself, shiverin', and shakin' that springboard for added effect, and then scream, 'Oooooooh! That water's cold!' Then, he'd stomp down off the divin' board as if he was leavin'. That's when I'd step up, point to the end of the board, and yell, "Get out there! We got a show to do!" He'd waggle his head and say, 'No!' I'd say it again and he'd waggle and say, 'No' again and I'd say it again and with his lip tremblin' for all to see, he'd inch out to the end of the board, put his hands on his hips, lean over, and stare down at the water thinkin' about it. That's when I'd look at the crowd, point a wavin' finger at his butt, and then race down the board to push him off. Of course—just before I shoved him in, he'd squat down on the board to touch the water and *zooom*, I'd soar right over top of him. Splash! I'd be in the water. I'd swim like crazy, jump out of the water, and while shiverin', I'd holler, 'Oooooooh! That water's cold!' Man, would kids laugh! Then, like a dog shakin' after a bath, I'd begin wigglin' my head all the way down to stickin' out my butt and shakin' shakin' shakin' like that same wet dog waggin' it tail. Right after that, I'd chase Up all around the pool and up into the stands all the way back to the low board where he'd start bouncin'. Bounce, bounce, bouncin' so high, thrustin' his hands up in the air, then down to his side gainin' height, goin' up, and up, and up, to where he was so high in the stratosphere, I feared he'd bump his head on blue sky. The higher he bounced, the louder the crowd murmured, 'His legs are gonna snap,' and 'that boards gonna break.' I waited, timin' my move, rockin' backward and forward, then I rushed and lunged at him, missed, flew underneath him to splat belly flop in the pool again as he soared up and up and over to land gracefully on the high board where he continued bouncin' while stickin' his thumb to his nose and singin' out to me, 'Naa na naa na naaa naaaa!' Then, with the greatest of ease, he bounced once last thrust up and out over the water, posed on a propped up elbow like a movie star layin' on the beach, then maneuvered into a granny dive with his prayin' hands under his chin and his buttocks stickin' out to slip through the water with only a *splish*.

We had more acts that wowed the crowd. One, was both of us jumpin' off the high board holdin' a big umbrella that instantly folded up droppin' us into the drink and another was the rodeo dive where Up rode my back as if I was a wild bronc. We performed a difficult dive where, at the same time, I dove backwards, him forward, and in mid air, I grabbed his ankles and he grabbed mine, and once we bent at our waists, we had a flyin' box dive. Our grand finale was the two of us on that old yellow bicycle; Up peddlin'; me on the handlebars. We'd drag that bike with us up to the high board, climb on it, ride toward the end of the board where Up would slam on the brakes, and shoot me off the handlebars into the air flailin' face first into the water. I'd climb back up and he'd whine, 'I'm sorrrrrrrrry! I'll never do that again!' I'd believe him and then—he'd do it again. I'd scramble back up, yellin' at him, "Don't you daaaaare doooo that again!" and then we'd soar off the board wavin' and yellin' to the audience, "Goooooooooodbyyyyye!" all the way down to make a big splash in the water. We did three shows a day; a lot of fun smiles.

Last week, when old Up died, there was nothin' ailin' him except for just that, he was old. Hold on. I'm eighty-nine, makin' me old and Up was six years older than me, makin' him ancient. He was tellin' everybody long before he passed away at ninety-five, that he was 'a hunnerd-years-old'. Of course, everyone agreed—close enough. More times than not, he'd add on to this slight exaggeration of age with his concocted theory on how to live to be a 'hunnerd.' He'd start out in that low idlin' voice of his revvin' up to where he'd cough, then throttlin' down to where he'd choke, then adjustin' his air intake back up to a rumble again as if he'd learned to speak ridin' in an old-timey Model T Ford. I can hear him as if he's still with us. Usin' lots of 'Yeps' and 'Nopes', coughs and chokes, he'd say, 'I'm a hunnerd years old! Yep. And I'll tell you how to live to be a hunnerd. It ain't hard. Nope. Here's what you gotta do. If you got a bad cough, say, 'Not yet.' Yep, say it out loud, 'NOT YET!' (Cough! Cough! Deep breath). (Ahem). If you can't see, can't hear, and can't remember anything, nope, just remember one thing—say, 'Not yet.' Yep. If you're so tired, so sad, or so lonely you want to die, force yourself, say it by god, say it, 'Not yet.' (Gag! Choke! Deep breath). (Ahem). Now, this is a tough one, yep, no matter how much pain—stingin', throbbin' pain; pain that makes you feel like your nerves are inside out, you got to cry out, 'Not yet!' Harder than that—every time you think of joinin' your sweetheart on the other side, say, 'Sweetie—not yet. Nope, I'm sorry, but not yet.' And, (Ahem), if that Grim Reaper is glarin' at you from the foot of your deathbed, you just glare right back and yell, 'Hell no, Grim Reaper! Not yet!' Yep, just keep sayin', 'Not yet,' and go about your bus'ness until you can't say it, nope, or even think it, nope, then, yep, dive in head first or feet first. As for me, I ain't ready, nope, and yep, I'm still sayin' it—'Not yet!'

Over the years, I heard Up say 'not yet' a hundred times. I recall him sayin' it while he was havin' a heart attack, durin' that bout with pneumonia, and after he broke a hip fallin' down a step, but that moment before he died, he didn't say, not yet. You see, I was with Up when he died. Was it luck or fate that I was there? Naw, neither, he waited for me; waited so I could see his last smile. Our job was makin' fun; our job was makin' smiles. Us, our audience—wearin' face stretchin' fun smiles. I'd seen Up smile a bazillion fun smiles and I'll say this, his last smile was diff'rent—much more than a fun smile. I'm finally gettin' to it now; to tell you about Up's last smile.

It was late afternoon the day he died. I had driven up from Tampa to Gibsonton where he lived in a small old home in a quiet neighborhood. All the way over there, dang drivers kept honkin' at me. I don't know why. Why, maybe I drive a bit slow and swerve a bit, but that ain't no cause to be rude. His house was simple. We might have been almost, somewhat, barely famous at one time, but you know, we never made a lot of money divin' for the circus and after the circus quit us, we did odd jobs to make ends meet.

Anyway, his caregiver, Carmen, a young Cuban woman greeted me at the door. She said with a heavy Spanish accent, 'Señor Up, he's been napping for two days.'

Concerned, I asked, 'Is he still breathin'?'

She replied, 'Sí.'

I stepped into the house, walked through his livin' room, and down the hallway past hundreds of circus photos and posters hangin' on the wall. There was old pictures of Up and me doin' all kind of funny stunts divin' into the water. There was the other circus performers doin' their acts too. Then, there were photos of all of us just laughin' and havin' a good time travelin together and the many sights we saw. More than any other photographs are those of ol' Up and his wife Miss Jellybean. Even though they were married for fifty-five years, and her real name was

Crystal, all of us still called her Miss Jellybean. Just like Vivi and me, Up and Miss Jellybean never had any children. Don't know why. Both of us couples tried. It weren't meant to be.

All of us kept busy after the circus went out of business. We performed at charity fund raisers until all of us got too old. Pookaka the little monkey died first of old age, lyin' there in his baby crib as if he was asleep. Up and Miss Jellybean had kept him as a pet after the circus closed. You'd think he'd be trouble, but he'd been a good little monkey sittin' on the couch in his little diapers while eatin' his fruit and nuts and boy, believe it or not, that little guy loved cartoons.

Juggles passed next in his late forties. I think from a broken heart or maybe from all that drinkin' he did. Next Juju died, and within a year so did Shakti. Both of their hearts just gave out. Pito married a gymnast named Sonja from Cleveland and they moved back to Europe where he performed with her on a super high trapeze until durin' a matinee show, his legs gave out and he dropped 'em both. She landed in the safety net. He missed it and died. Sonja, bein' much older than me, is most likely gone now too.

Then, my sweet Vivi, the love of my life, died. The cancer took her slow then finished her fast. I've never been the same without her, but I get through each day, mostly 'cause I had Up and he had me and we had our memories of the circus, our friends, and our gals.

I must say after Miss Jellybean, poor, little, pint-sized woman passed of a heart attack, Up's fun smile vanished.

Anyway, I made it down the hallway and past all of the photos, and then stepped into Up's bedroom. The curtains were open and the window too; nice breeze blowin' in; bright sunlight. He still had the same old Chester drawers and mirror that he had when he bought the house forty years before, the same bed with the brass headboard, the same night stand with lamp and phone, the same armoire with a small TV, and next to the bed, the same worn out chair for sittin' and puttin' on socks and shoes. He lay on his back with his eyes closed. He still slept on his side of the queen bed as though Miss Jellybean still slept beside him. His head rested on a big white pillow. A blue bedspread atop a white sheet covered him up to his waist. His hands lay across his chest and they were interlocked with his fingers. He looked peaceful. Naw, he looked dead; no color in his face. All he needed was to be holdin' a tulip. I chuckled, not because he looked like he was already strummin' a golden harp, but because he wore his funny pajamas buttoned up snug under his chin. Yeah, he wore them crazy red pjs with printed pictures of steamy hot *Pop-Tarts*. I'd seen 'em before. He wore 'em—'cause he knew I was comin'. He loved those pjs; thought he'd get a laugh. He did. I laughed. He loved *Pop-Tarts* too, the cherry frosted ones with candy sprinkles; ate 'em every mornin'. Weird thing is, he didn't like 'em toasted golden-brown; he liked them with their edges burnt black and so hot you had to yank 'em out of the toaster usin' tongs. A *Pop-Tarts* bathrobe hung on a hook on the closet door. Man, oh man, that ol' Up was one crazy clown.

Lyin' there, Up looked older than when I had seen him the week before. His age spots were a bit darker and instead of five white hairs on his bald head, there were only two. I sat on the chair-for-puttin'-on-shoes next to him. I wanted him to wake up and show me he was still alive.

I called out, 'Up. Hey, Up! It's Splash!' He didn't respond. I leaned in close and peered at him. He looked like he was already headin' to a skeleton's slumber party. I was wonderin' too, if he had had the chance to say, 'Not yet' before he slipped into this deep sleep. Then, all of a sudden, why—he sucked in a deep breath, snapped open his eyes, jerked his head off the pillow, and sprang up straight at the waist with his hands still clasped on his chest. Startled, I lurched back in the chair as he stared past me at the sunlight streamin' in the window. I'd swear he was spring loaded. He stared for a few seconds and like the sun risin' after a dark night, he smiled; like I said before, an ear-to-ear, teeth gleamin', eyes twinklin', face glowin', happiest heavenly smile I'd ever seen. What a smile! His eyes looked bluer and glimmered more than a sparklin', sunlit pool of water.

I asked him, 'Up, what do you see?' No reply, he just kept smilin' and his smile grew bigger, stretchin' out from ear to ear.

I asked, 'Up, who you lookin' at?' Still no reply.

Over the next half-a-minute, his smile beamed brighter, his face turned pinker, and he twinkled happier than a youngster eyeballin' his first bicycle on Christmas, he glowed gladder than a bride hearin' the man she loves say, 'I do', and he gleamed grander than grandparents greetin' a newborn grandbaby. Mind you, while he was doin' all that smilin', he said not one word; made not one sound—until he giggled, that's right, giggled—as if someone had tickled him, then—still sportin' that smile, he closed his eyes, dropped back down on his pillow, drew in a deep breath, exhaled with a happy sigh, and died.

I waited, my mouth open, my eyes poppin' surprised by it all. He never took another breath; that one had been his last. Last smile too and what a smile! Though he was gone, his face was still smilin'; still smilin' when they took him away; still smilin' at his viewin', and still smilin' for the service too—and I'll bet, out there in that cemetery—he's still smilin'.

Now, just so you know, he didn't have to say nothin' to me to explain that last big smile. 'Cause I knew why. The reason I knew? I'd seen him smile twinklin', gleamin', and glowin' like that once before; a long time ago; that first smile and the last smile—the same. I knew why the first time so I knew why the last time.

One night a long time ago, I think we were in a little town outside of Columbus. We had just finished our last show of the day. We had showered and dressed and were sittin' in the canteen tent eatin' our supper when I said, 'Hey, Up, tell me again how you got hooked up with the circus.'

He finished chewin' a mouth full of pork chop, wiped his chin with his sleeve, and dove right into tellin' his story.

Again with lots of yeps and nopes, he said, 'It was on a hot summer afternoon, yep, on a Sunday, my stepfather was angry at me because at church while the preacher was preachin' I was lookin' at a *Dick Tracy* comic book, yep. I plum forgot I was at church and started whistlin' *Jimmie Crack Corn*. Yep. The preacher stopped preachin' and called out from the pulpit, 'Mr. Harden,' that was my mean ol' stepfather, 'please stop that delinquent boy of yours from whistlin'.' Well, it embarrassed my stepfather so badly, yep, that in the car on the way home, he reached over into the back seat and backhanded me three times. Yep, yep, yep. That upset my mama, so they got in a big fight. Once home, she whipped me good. Yep, real good. I told her, 'I'm runnin' away from home to join the circus. It's not far down the tracks. Nope.' My mama told me without sheddin' a tear, 'As long as they feed you, clothe you, and you have a warm and dry place to sleep—then go.' I did, yep. Right then, yep. I packed a few of my things in a pillowcase and left right out my bedroom window. I never looked back. Nope. I walked the tracks for about three hours when I saw the bright blue and green stripes of the Fabrizio's big top. I ran the rest of the way. Yep. I snuck around to the back of the tent and peered through a hole made by other kids from all the other towns. Yep, yep. I'd never seen nothin' like what I seen peepin' through the hole in that circus tent. I'm tellin' you, while hearin' a never-endin' drum roll, yep, yep, yep, I saw for the first time in my life, this gigantic gray elephant, flappin' its huge ears while standin' on its massive hind legs, and trumpetin' loudly while stretchin' its python-like trunk upward to the top of the tent. And there standin', balancin' up on that mammoth's thick trunk was a dark-skinned man wearin' a silky white turban and dressed in blue pyjamas outfitted with a bright red cape. Now, this peculiar fellow sported a white beard, a beard so long, it forked to make two braided cords long enough to wrap multiple times around his waist to come back together in a perfect square knot at his belly. The showy foreigner gripped with one hand the upraised trunk of the blarin' beast while his other hand thrust into the air triumphantly. I remember, the crowd applauded like crazy and as they grew louder, so did the drumroll and I saw more. Yep! Two men wearin' sparklin' red tights and an itty-bitty girl in glimmerin' purple leotards ran, sprang, and somersaulted into the ring where the two men landed on their feet, cupped their four hands together, stooped down, scooped her up, so that now she stood in their hands and in one fluid motion, slingshotted the tiny girl into the air. Yep. In a blur of purple, she soared and somersaulted high onto the foreign man's shoulders, landin' like a dove on a fence without knockin' off his turban. He steadied her for a second and then both of 'em thrust their hands into the air triumphantly. The crowd went wild! I couldn't believe my eyes. The band played louder and faster. Then—of all the crazy things as if the elephant and its stretchin' trunk and the foreign man and the sparklin' tiny girl weren't enough, nope, a small monkey, a hairy, smiley-faced little simian dressed in yellow pyjamas and wearin' also a silky white turban and also clutchin' in its furry little fist a monkey-sized purple parasol, scrambled out into the ring where he leapt into the acrobatic men's interlockin' hands and believe it or not, they launched that monkey into the air to land on top of the little girl's shoulders. She steadied the monkey as it climbed up her arm and into her cupped hand. The foreigner steadied her and both thrust their hands into the air. Then, by golly, that little smilin' monkey popped open that parasol and thrust *it* into the air. What a sight to see, the standin' elephant, its trunk, the man, the girl, and the monkey with the parasol, all stretching toward the top of that big top. When the applause and the band was so loud that it couldn't get any louder, the drum roll stopped, the symbol crashed, and the circus band blasted—Ta-Daaa! I stood peepin' and a gawkin' and I couldn't take my eyes off that little girl. Nope. Her beauty, her smile, her nimbleness, her happy-go-lucky life captured me and I did everything I could do for that circus so I could be her love. That's why I joined the circus and that's how I met the sweet love of my life, Miss Jellybean.'

While he told the story, his face was lit up as if he was in the center ring with all the spotlights. On that day when Up died, he peered into the sunlight and no doubt saw Pito and Vivi, Juggles, Shakti, Juju the elephant with Pookaka the monkey sittin' on the beast's trunk, and of course the love of his life, itty-bitty Miss Jellybean beckonin' him home. She was the twinkle in his eyes and the reason for that last incredible smile.

Up and me were like brothers. I miss him. I long for my Vivi and I miss, Miss Jellybean, Juggles, Pito, Vivi, and Shakti, Juju, and Pookaka too. They were my family. Up and me outlived 'em all. Everywhere I look, I see a circus. People doin' amazin' things. People havin' fun. I look for smiles; fun smiles. Wherever I go and whomever I meet, I hope to make people smile. Life, to me, is a circus. Pretty darn entertainin'. I'm the last one of my circus of friends, and yes, I miss 'em dearly, but I ain't ready to join 'em—so as ol' Up taught me—I'm still sayin', 'Not yet.'

NAKED IN THE FOREST

Feel awful. Eyelids heavy. Must open eyes. Caught a glimpse. I'm outside. It's dark. A faint orange light above. Everything's blurry. Where am I? So weak. Bad headache. I hear laughter. Who are they? Where are they? What happened to me? Can't think. Wait. I know! I know what happened. I'm wasted! Totally wasted! Where was I? Who was I with? How much did I drink? Ugh! Can't remember. Hurts to try. So sleepy. Must close eyes.

Fell asleep again. How long have I been out? Hey, where's my wristwatch? Need to wake up. Open your eyes! Come on! Keep them open! Still dark with that orange glow. It's moved across the sky. Is it the moon? Where are the stars? Ohhh, what a horrible headache. Hard to breathe. I can see my breath. The air is cold. The ground is cold. I'm cold. For god's sake—I'm naked!

Where are my clothes? Where are my phone and keys? Who took them? And why? I remember laughter. Who were they? Are they still here? Got to sit up. Feel exhausted. Skin tingling. Hands and feet numb. Arms trembling. Crawl to that tree. A tree? Yes! A pine tree! Think, man! What happened? Mouth is dry. Headache. Body hurts all over. Stomach is churning. This is the worst hangover ever! I've never partied this hard before to wake up so sick. Stand up! Dizzy. Use the tree. Get on your feet. Good! You're doing it! Legs rubbery. Hold on to the tree. Grip the bark. Strange. Bark is smooth. Pull yourself up. You're standing! Now, look around. Yes! There's another pine tree, and another, and a granite boulder. Everything looks creepy in this orange light. I'm chilled, it's difficult to breathe, and there are pine trees. I know where I am! I'm somewhere in the mountains—at a high altitude. I'm—I'm lost and—and—naked in the forest!

Something is glistening. A patch of snow, orange tinted snow between two boulders. Snow? I'm definitely at a high altitude. What's the name of the mountains where I go hunting and fishing? Think! The—the—Sierra's. Yes! Remembered something. I'm in the Sierra's. Need to move. Keep warm. Hike out of here. Legs wobbly. One step at a time. Out of breath. Bare feet. Pine needles. I need my shoes. Where are my shoes? So thirsty. The snow, it's frozen. It's ice. Can't break it. Odd, the ice isn't that cold.

I don't like this place. Something isn't right. I want to leave. Need my clothes and shoes. Need to call for help. Can't. Phone gone. Don't panic. Think! Think, man! Try to remember. What happened?—Ugh! Can't remember! Feel drugged. Groggy. I'm in danger. I could die. I don't want to die! Yell for help.

"Help! Help! Somebody! Anybody! Help me!"

Listen—Nothing. Yell again.

"Help! Is anyone out there? I heard you laugh! I know you're out there. Please! Help me!"

No answer. I'm alone—for now. They might come back. Calm down. Breathe slowly. Don't pass out. Sit on that granite rock. Regain your strength. This rock—it's smooth. And it's cold! Where the heck are my clothes? Okay, I've watched those survival series on TV. Take inventory. I'm still in one piece. No blood. No pain. No injuries. Just this brutal hangover. Take a few deep breaths. Exhale slowly. Seek shelter, clothing, food, and water. Find a way to make fire.

Listen. What's that sound? Running water? A creek? It's in front of me. Sounds nearby. I'm so thirsty. Move in the direction of the sound. Watch out. The ground slopes. Be careful. Don't fall. Water is louder. It's just past those two trees. It's a creek. It's flowing. Water looks orange reflecting that weird orange moonlight. Squat down. Be careful. Rocks are slippery. Cup your hands. Hope the water isn't contaminated. Drink.

"Aaahhh!"

Drink again.

"Aaahhh!"

Wet. Cold. Tastes good. Tastes different. High minerals. Slow down. Don't drink too much too fast. Slap water on face. That should wake me up. Wait a second. The stubble on my face—feels like three days growth. Have I been unconscious for three days?

Sit down. Rest. Then, simply walk out of here. I'm young, strong, and healthy, I'll keep walking until I find help. Maybe a ranger or a hunter. They will take me home. Home? Where is home? Can't remember. Try something else. Who am I? What's my name? Come on! Try to remember. My name—is— is—ohhh—why can't I remember? I've partied hard enough to forget what I did the night before, but never, ever, forgot my name and never felt this sick before. Drink more water. Feeling better. Rehydrating. Trembling subsiding. Strength returning. Headache not as bad. My name is——is——Come on! Think! Talk out loud. It will help you remember.

"My name is—Jacob! That's it! Jacob—uhhh——Freeman. Yes! Jacob Michael Freeman!"

Great! Remembered my name! Okay, now—where do I live? Picture it. See the road. A two-lane country road. Wildflowers. An irrigation canal on one side. Peach orchard on the other. Right turn. Long dirt driveway. White house. Big porch. I remember!

"I live with my folks! What are their names? Mike and—

and—Laura. I have two younger brothers, Aaron and Cody. I help dad with the farming. We have five hundred acres of peaches, plums, and apricots."

Okay, good. Memory is flowing now. I'm on a roll. Where's the farm?

"Dang-it, where's the farm located? Sanger—Sanger, California. 4365 North Riverbank Ave. That's it! I'm Jacob Freeman, I'm twenty-three, and I live with my parents on a farm in Sanger, California!"

Will I ever see my family again? Hardworking dad. Chatty mom. Annoying little brothers. I hope so. I miss them already. Don't get teary eyed now. Stay strong. Think. What happened three days ago? And how did I end up in the woods? It's coming to me.

"I was at a party. That's it. Harvest celebration. Out in the sticks in——in a big green barn! In the middle of an almond orchard! Weston's place!

Who's Weston? Oh yeah, my best friend since first grade. We study Ag together at Fresno State. Crazy, crazy guy.

"Weston's parents were out of town. There were lots of college students at the party. Some I knew. Others I didn't. There were kegs of beer, bottles of Jack Daniels, Popov, and Cuervo. Pot smoke. Loud country music. Laughing, singing, and dancing."

What happened? What in the heck—happened? Think, man. Come on think. Let your mind go. Don't force it.

"Let's see. The party got wild. Two stuck-up rodeo queens in tight jeans had a hair pulling fight. Two buffed out guys in bulging T-shirts had a shoving match. Three rowdy dudes pushed a big gal the size of a one-ton pickup into the swimming pool behind Weston's house. There was loud splashing and high pitch screaming.

It's all coming back to me now.

I did a little two-stepping. Didn't smoke pot. Never do.

Drank a few beers and a couple shots of tequila. If that's all? Why do I feel so horrible? What happened next? Oh, yeah, I met a super cute country gal. Raised on a farm. Long blond hair. Bright blue eyes. What was her name? Come on, what was her name? Megan, Mendy, Morgan? Ugh—can't recall. Need to though. Got our first date next Friday night. That I do remember. Oh yeah, that's right—her ex-boyfriend got butt-hurt because I asked her out. They had just broken up a couple of days before. He's easy to recall. He was so dang short. Shaped like an egg. He wore that huge cowboy hat and that enormous brass belt buckle. Rodeo roping champion. He was drunk and stoned, stumbling around. Surprised he didn't fall down. He had two goofy sidekicks with him. One had a face like a pack mule while the other resembled a rooster, stick skinny with a beak nose and red hair combed high. All three shoved me around while squat buckle-boy threatened to 'Kick my saddle-crack,' if I took her out."

What did I say? It was good. Come on. Oh, yeah.

"I told him, 'It was up to her whether I take her out, not a Wild West Weeble under a ten-gallon hat.' He fisted-up and took a swing. I blocked it, and then quick punched him in the face. His hat flew off. Landed in the dirt. That really made him mad. He came at me for more. We both fisted up and as we circled each other, something happened."

It stopped the fight. Think! Something strange. What was it? Yes! I remember. How could I forget?

"That meteor flashed across the sky. Both of us lowered our knuckles and gawked up at it. So bright, everyone outside stared up at it. It looked so close. Streaked all the way to the ground. We all thought it was cool. Then, when the excitement stopped over the meteor, both our fists sprang back up. Weston stepped in and said he'd call the sheriff if, 'Big Hat, Mule, and Rooster' didn't leave. The cowboy hollered at me, 'Come Hell or high water, I'll get you for tryin' to steal my girlfriend! I promise you. I'll get you real good!' He glared at me, lit a cigarette, took a long drag, exhaled, flicked the cigarette at me, and then turned and shuffled off in his little cowboy boots. I laughed at him. Wild West Weeble. Just before he climbed in his pick up, he pointed a finger at me and barked, 'Watch your back partner!' Then, the three troublemakers revved up their muddy pick up trucks and sped off down the road."

Feels good to remember. I don't feel so crazy. Lay back. Clasp hands behind head. Strangest night sky I ever seen. No stars. There must be a cloud cover. What makes the moon glow orange? Why orange? Probably a lunar eclipse. Yeah, that's what it is. What else happened after the cowboy and his sidekicks left the party? Keep talking out loud, it's working.

"Around—what time was it? Let's see, it was—pushing 2 a.m. when the party broke up, so, I told Weston goodbye. He stood there with a big silly grin and an arm slung around that Tundra chick in wet hair, runny make-up, dripping clothes, and wrapped in a Shamu-sized beach towel. Man, oh operate, what a big woman. I was okay to drive. Party buzz had worn off. Plus, I never drive buzzed."

So why do I feel so bad? It doesn't make sense.

"I jumped in my red pick-up and drove toward home."

Okay. So what happened next? Come on. Remember. I've got it.

"Glanced in the rearview mirror. Headlights showed up out of nowhere. Had to be the cowboy and his barnyard buddies. They followed me turn for turn, and then disappeared. I had to take a big leak so I pulled off the road into our north apricot orchard. Parked between two rows of trees. Turned off the headlights and the truck. Climbed out and shut the door. All was quiet except for a few crickets and me watering the weeds. I stood in the dark looking up at the half moon and the stars. The stars were bright. I kept staring at the sky. Thought I'd see another meteor. The cool air felt good. Lights lit up the other side of the orchard. Bright white lights and a few red. I zipped up my jeans, took a few steps closer, stooped, and peered between the tree trunks. The lights looked like the headlamps of two pick-ups and the red taillights of another. It had to be that stumpy, fireplug cowboy and his half-witted dipsticks from the party. They were drunk and stupid enough to cause trouble."

Okay. Something bad happened. What was it?

"I grabbed my cell phone to call dad. I heard footsteps behind me. Before I could turn around, there was a sharp pain inside my head. That terrible, god-awful pain. I dropped to my knees and blacked out."

What happened to me? Can't remember anymore. Did I die? Am I a ghost and don't know it? Nahhh, I think that wildcat cowboy and his two coyotes got me real good. Real funny. When I get out of these mountains, I'll not only take out his girlfriend, I'll hunt him down and sic Right and Left, my two knuckle hounds on him!"

My stomach just growled. Good sign. Feeling hungry. Must find food. I must survive here wherever here is. Listen. Voices! I hear voices. Two voices. No, three. They're up by that pine tree. Move closer. Be quiet. Stay low. Listen. Strange. They're not speaking English. Not Spanish, French, or Italian. Doesn't sound like German, Arabic, or Russian. Maybe, it's Chinese. No. It's not Chinese. Never heard this language in a movie. What country am I in? Listen. Be careful. The voices. It's quiet. They're gone. Where'd they go? Who were they? Those three crazy pranksters from the party? What were they doing? Go back to the tree. Be careful. Watch out for them. They kidnapped me. What more are they capable of? What's that on the ground? Same place I was lying. My god! It's a body. Don't move too fast. Legs still wobbly. It's—it's a woman. She's—she's naked! Is she dead? Reach down. Check her pulse. There's a heartbeat. She's unconscious. She must have been at the same party. I don't remember seeing her there. Did someone spike the booze? Did she overdose on something? Do I know her? Get a closer look. Her face is beautiful. She looks Hispanic. Her skin is dark. Long black hair. Hope those drunken thugs didn't hurt her. Try and wake her. Don't scare her. Speak softly.

"Hello. Are you okay?" *She's stirring. Eyelids fluttering.* "Hello. Wake up. Are you okay?" *Her eyes—they're opening. They're brown. She's frightened. She's trying to speak.*

"¿Donde estoy?" (Where am I?)

"I'm sorry. I don't understand."

"¿Donde estoy? ¿Que ha pasado?" (Where am I? What happened?)

Sounds like Spanish. "I'm sorry. I only speak a little Español. Poquito. Farm workers from Mexico taught me a few words. I'm Jacob. Me llamo Jacob. What's your name? Cómo se llama? Maria? Carmen? Rosa?"

"No sé mi nombre. Brrrrr. Tengo frio." (I don't know my name. Brrrrr. I'm cold)

She's shivering. I must find our clothes. Oh, nooo! She sees we're naked.

"Ahhh! Estoy desnuda! Ahhh! Estás desnudo! No me hagas daño!" (Ahhh! I'm naked! You're naked! Don't hurt me!)

She's afraid. My goods are hanging out. Cover up with your hands. Back away. She's trying to cover herself. Calm her down. "I won't hurt you. I don't know what happened or why we're here. I don't know where our clothes are or why we're naked. You need to sit up. Against that tree. Go ahead. Try and sit up. You need water. I'll bring you water. You know; aqua. It will rehydrate you and take away the hangover." *Show her. Act out everything. Use sign language. Put your hand to your mouth like your drinking. Walk your fingers in the palm of your hand. Oh, no, my package is showing again. Why does it have to be so cold?* "Okay, stay here, I'll bring you water and be right back."

"No, no me abandone!" (No, don't leave me!)
That word sounds like abandon. "Okay, I won't go. I'll take you. Let me help you stand up. I won't hurt you. Good. You're doing great." *She's holding her head and her stomach.* "Are you sick?" *Rub stomach and groan.*
 "Ohhh. Tengo náuseas. Siento un terrible dolor de cabeza." (Ohhh. I feel nauseous. I have a terrible headache.)
 "Nauseous and headache? You need water. Come with me. I'll help you. Be careful. Walk slowly." *Who is she? Why is she here? Why are we here? She's weak. Help her. Hold her up. Watch out where I put my hands.* "Here it is. Cool fresh water. Okay, please drink. Wash your face too." *Show her. Splash water on your face.* "It'll help wake you up. You'll feel better. Let's sit down here and rest. Do you speak any English?"
 "Hablo un poco de inglés." (I speak a little English.)
 "Poco. A little. What is your name?" *Point at her.* "And where do you live?" *Wave your arms around.*
 "Mi nombre es—es—Alita! Alita Pri—Prieto!"
 "Alita. That's a nice name. Where are you from?"
 "San—Santiago del—Es—Estero."
 "Is that in Mexico?"
 "No, es—es—Argentina."
 Argentina? What is she doing here with me in the Sierra Mountains? Wave arms in the air again. "You are in the Sierra Nevada Mountains. California. United States. ¿Comprende?"
 "Sí, Sierra Nevada Montañas, California, América."
 "Do you feel better? Es bueno?"
 "Sí. Me siento mucho mejor." (Yes. I feel much better.)
 "Pero tengo miedo." (But, I'm scared.)
 Oh no, she's crying. "Alita. Don't cry. We'll be okay. Can you stand? Now, can you walk? Let's go see where we are. Please, hold my hand and walk with me."
 "¿Dónde vamos?" (Where are we going?)
 "I'm sorry, I don't understand."

177

"¿Por qué la luna esta anaranjada?" (Why is the moon so orange?)

Luna. Anaranjada. Moon and orange. "I wish I knew why the moon was orange. But I don't. Please, hold my hand. I'll take care of you. Follow me. Let's find a way home. Casa."

"Sí. Casa."

Okay, walk up the hill past the granite rocks, past the ice, and past the third pine tree. Keep walking. Wish the moon were brighter. "Alita, please, watch your step. Be careful." *All I can see is more trees and rocks. Wonder where we are in the Sierra's. I've fished and hunted many times in these mountains. I've got to find a landmark. Maybe a road or a trail. A river or a waterfall. How long will it take to hike out of here?* "Alita. Wait. What is this? A wall? A manmade wall? In the forest? I can't tell in this orange light, but I think it's green. It's at least ten-feet tall. We must be at a power station for a dam." *Think. What dam could it be? Millerton Lake? No. It's in the foothills. Shasta Lake? Maybe. Shaver Lake? Most likely. It has the pine trees and the altitude. What's this wall made of? Cement? No. What is it? Can't tell. It's too smooth to grip, too high to climb, and there aren't any trees close enough to help us over it. I wonder where it leads? I know one direction leads down to the stream. The other way up this slope.* "Alita. Shhh. Quiet. Do you hear that? There are voices up there. Let's see who they are." *Campers? Hunters? Our kidnappers?* "We'll follow the wall going up. Be quiet and hold my hand."

"Nooo. Tengo miedo." (Nooo. I'm afraid.)

"Please. Come with me." *We're getting closer to where the voices are. They're louder. Oh, nooo. This can't be. This wall connects to another wall. We have a wall on one side and a wall behind us. The voices, they're coming from behind those two big pine trees in front of this back wall. Whisper.* "Alita, shhhh, don't make any noise. I see them. Three of them. What are they doing? Can't make out who they are." *I don't see a tent or a campfire. No lanterns. No trucks. No cowboy hat. No shiny belt buckle. Hey, where'd they go?*

"Alita, do you see them?"

"No. Han desaparecido." (No. They are gone.)

"Come on. Let's take a closer look. Keep an eye out for them. They disappeared through the wall somehow." *I don't see or feel any way out. This is making me angry. Let them know you're angry.* "Hey! Where are we? Tell me! Why are we here? You sick bastards give us back our clothes! I want my watch, my cell phone, and my keys! Give them to me now!" *Nothing. No response.* "Look, Alita, on the ground. By that tree. They left something. What is that? It's a tray with something on it. There's a container too. I smell food."

"Mmm, tengo mucha hambre!" (Mmm, I'm very hungry.)

"Alita, stop. Let me try the food first." *The food—it's hamburgers and French fries. This fry tastes like a fry, but the texture is different. It's rubbery. This hamburger tastes strange too. The bread is stale and the meat has no flavor. Just a bun and a burger?* "Hey, you cheapskates! Where are the lettuce, tomato, onions, and pickles? Where's the special sauce?" *Wonder what's in this container? It tastes like Coke or is it Pepsi? It's Coke. Less sugar. It's fizzless Coke. Why couldn't it be Dr. Pepper? I think the food is safe to eat.* "Okay, Alita, let's eat."

"Eeew, esto sabe malo!" (Eeew, this taste bad.)

Why would they feed us burgers and fries? And soda pop. "Hey! Whoever is out there! Listen to me! Who are you people? If it's stumpy and his posse from the party, I'll kick the back of your Wranglers so hard the label will end up in the front!" *No answer. Oh no, I've scared Alita.* "Alita, it's okay. Everything will be all right." *This poor girl. So far from home. She's so innocent. I must keep her safe. How old she is.* "Alita, how old are you? I'm twenty-three. Vi-en—ti-tres."

"Tengo dieciocho años." (I am eighteen-years-old.)

Dieciocho. I think that's eighteen. "Alita, how did you—?" *Point at her.* "Come to be here?" *Point at the ground.*

"Todo es borroso." (Everything is blurry). "Es difícil de recordar." (It is difficult to remember). "Estoy recordando." (It is coming to me). "Vivo con mi madre y mi padre en un rancho de pollo grande." (I live with my mother and father on a big chicken ranch.) "Lejos de la ciudad." (Far away from the city.)

Madre, padre, rancho, pollos. Mother, father, ranch, chicken. Grande is big. Lejos is far and ciudad means city. "I understand. I can pick up some of what you're saying."

"Era tarde. Estaba dormido." (It was late. I was asleep.) "Oí los pollos. Tenían miedo." (I heard the chickens. They were afraid.)

"I don't understand, except, late at night and something about chickens."

"Salí de la cama. Me fui afuera." ((I got out of bed. I went outside). "Mi padre estaba afuera también." (My father was outside too.) "Mi padre se fue por un lado y yo me por el otro." (My father went one way and I went the other.) "Había luces brillantes en el campo." (There were bright lights in the field.) "Los hombres vinieron a robar nuestros pollos." (Men had come to steal our chickens.)

"Alita, I only understand a little of what you're saying." *Ugh! Why didn't I pay more attention in Spanish class!* "Okay, you and your father, chickens, and you saw something bright. Men tried to take your chickens."

"Sentí un terrible dolor de cabeza. Me desmaye." (I felt a horrible headache. I passed out.)

"You had a bad headache and you passed out. Just like what happened to me."

"Los hombres me secuestraron. (They kidnapped me.) "Sé que ellos hicieron cosas horribles a me." (I know they did horrible things to me.)

"Men took you and they did horrible things to you. I'm so sorry Alita. Please, don't cry. We'll be okay. We'll find a way home. When we do, we'll call the police and they'll punish all these bad people. For now, we need to hang in there. Did you have enough to eat and drink?" *Keep doing hand signals. It's helping.*

"Sí. Gracias."

"Good." *Okay. Now that we have eaten, we need to move on.* "Let's follow this wall. Watch your step. Hold my hand so you don't fall."

Look for something to make clothes. Dang. Can't catch a break. Huge boulders in the way. Must hike around them. What's that? Between the two boulders. A cave? Step inside. Explore. Be cautious. Not very big, but big enough to shelter the two of us. We'll come back to it if we need to. For now, keep moving. Must find our way out. Around the boulders and back up to the wall. Follow the wall. I wonder how far it goes? Not very far!

"You've got to be kidding me! This walls turns into another wall. We have three walls!" *No way over this wall. A wall on each side and behind us. Walk down the slope. It's our stream. The water flows under the wall, but it's not deep enough for us to swim under the wall. Must cross the stream. Only way to go. Keep moving. I hope there's not another wall.*

"El agua esta fria." (This water is cold.)

"Alita—is that another wall?" *Four walls! Walls all around us.* "This can't be. What is going on here?" *This joke has got to stop. Whoever is behind this is carrying it much too far. To Hell with that cowboy's girlfriend. I give up. I'm breaking my date with her. He can have her.* "Alita, there is no way out. We're trapped."

"Estamos atrapados. Estamos muertos!" (We are trapped. We are dead.)

"Muertos? Dead? No, Alita. We'll live and we'll find a way out of here." *Alita, look around, it's becoming brighter. The sun—it's coming up. The sky. Look at the sky. It's bright orange."*

"El cielo esta anaranjado!" (The sky is very orange).

The moon was faint and orange because it was behind orange clouds. I have never seen daybreak so beautiful. So many hues of red, orange, and yellow. I can see the stream. I can see the mountainside, the boulders, and pine trees. Weird. In this light, everything has an orange tint. "Up there, Alita, can you see it? There's our cave." *Oh my god. I can see the walls. All around us—walls! No gates or doors. No way out. Don't panic! Shout!* "Let us out of here! Please, I beg you! Let us out of here!"

No answer. Our forest is about half the size of a football field. The stream runs lengthwise along the bottom of the slope. There's no way out. I'll find a way out. The air, it's getting warm. It feels good. "Alita, let's go back to the cave where we can rest and figure all this out." *Okay, back across the stream. Need to find a way to haul up water. Need to stay warm. Build a fire and make clothes. Up along the wall, back to the boulders and the cave. At least we have shelter, food, and water. We have each other. I'm glad Alita is with me. I hope she likes me.* "Look, Alita, the sun's coming up. From up here in our cave, I can see it rising over the front wall. Look—at the top of the wall. There's some sort of a guardrail." *Odd. The sun, it's—it's orange! It's smaller and not as bright as usual. It's got to be that lunar eclipse making everything orange. Things don't look right. I hear voices. Many voices. Same strange language.*

"Mira! En la parte superior de la pared. Veo gente!" (Look! At the top of the wall. I see people).

"Look, there must be twenty of them and they're looking at us." *They're silhouettes against the orange sun. Hard to see them. They see us and are pointing at us. Step out of the cave into the light. Cry out for help.* "Help! Please, help us!"

"Ayuda! Necesitamos ayuda!" (Help! We need help!)

What's that hissing and snorting? Is that laughter? They're laughing at us. Just like before. The light is increasing. Looks like families. There are taller people like fathers, little shorter ones like mothers, and there are smaller ones of every size. The small ones are throwing something into our forest. What is this? A French fry? They're throwing French fries! That's crazy! Why are they throwing French fries? The sun is getting brighter. I can see more clearly now. Wait! What? What the heck!

"Alita, come close to me. Let me hold you. Look, the people, they're different than us. Much different than us!" *Where are they from?*

"Quienes son? Que son?" (Who are they? What are they?)

My god, where are we? Their skin, it's—it's red and it's—it's shiny. All of them—they have big black eyes and barely a nose. Holes for ears. When they laugh, they have big teeth. Not one of them has hair. Each one has a head and a body, two arms and two legs, but they're not—not—human. For God's sake! They're not human!

"Son muy feos. Tengo miedo." (They are very ugly. I'm afraid.) "Quiero irme a casa. Por favor, llevame a casa." (I want to go home. Please, take me home.)

"Please Alita, don't cry. You'll be okay. I'll take care of you. Yo prometo." (I promise.)

Hold on. I've seen these beings before. I'm remembering. After the party. In the orchard. It wasn't a jealous, pissed off cowboy and his sidekicks who jumped me. It was these same creatures who are gawking at us now. They drugged me. I woke up not knowing where I was. Equipment above me. Hoses, gauges, and lights. I saw them. Those eyes! All those big black eyes set against that glossy red skin. Looking. Staring. Wide mouths and big teeth. Smiling. Laughing. They paralyzed me. They took samples of my hair, skin, saliva, blood, urine, and feces. They examined me for three days and then they dumped me in this forest—a fake forest. Not a man made but alien made forest. The trees, the boulders, and the pine needles; nothing is real. The nasty burger, fries, and soda; all alien made. We're not in the Sierra Mountains. We're not in Argentina. My God! We're not even on Earth. We're exhibits from Earth.

"Alita—we're aliens in an alien zoo."

CELEBRATE 80

Two weeks before his eightieth birthday, Arthur Artesian received an email. It was on a summer afternoon, hot and climbing hotter without the slightest chance of a breeze when his miniature computer strapped to his wrist vibrated in the middle of his great-grandpa golf swing. As he stood hovering over and staring down at the dimpled white ball on the grassy thirteenth-tee of the Kings River Country Club, the pulsating interruption caught him at the precise moment of ending his back swing and beginning his down stroke, causing him to severely hook his golf ball, soaring it between two majestic oak trees to splash into the cold albeit leisurely flowing Kings River. Aggravated, he groaned and then read the email he had been expecting.

Dear Mr. Artesian,

On July 12th, you will be eighty-years-old! Happy birthday! No cost government health care has provided for all your health concerns and has enabled you to live a happy and fruitful life. Congratulations! You have lived to the golden age of eighty! All of us at Celebrate 80 wish to celebrate this momentous occasion with you. We have scheduled your birthday celebration for Thursday, July 12th, 2097 from 10:00 to 11:30 a.m. at Joyful Hall, Celebrate 80 Center, Kingsburg, California. Invite all

your family and friends (limit 100 guests) and have a glorious
celebration. From all of us who wish you a happy 80th birthday!
   Sincerely,
   The caring people at,
   Celebrate 80

With his birthday celebration on his mind and not golf, he
finished his game four strokes over his best score, a best score
which really wasn't anything to brag about since he had taken
up the game only two years before; keeping in mind, he was
two weeks away from eighty-years-old without the strength
and stamina of a younger man; even so, while he sorely felt
the bothersome aches and pains of stiff joints and suffered
the embarrassment and inconvenience of lactose intolerance
abounding with public flatulence, he was remarkably healthy
aside from sporting free healthcare, laser-signaled hearing-aids
and electronic, smart-focus eyeglasses. For pushing eighty, he
still had a full head of silver hair parted down the left side,
combed over to the right, and squared up in the back with
the front swooped high and backward by a comb stroke. His
sprightly blue eyes were set amongst a sundry of smile lines
and a mirror still revealed the remnants of a handsome man
behind the wrinkles and skin spots of old age. Six-foot in height
lent itself to him being lanky and playing golf six hours a week
helped him keep in shape while also meeting the healthcare
minimum requirement for exercise, and he followed explicitly
all of the healthcare regulations. Brushing and flossing three
times a day with regenerative growth toothpaste, laser dental
floss, and smart toothbrush made his teeth movie star white.
Drinking coenzyme CoQ10 twice a day kept his heart beating
strong. No cost government healthcare and abiding by its strict
laws set forth for nutrition, exercise, meditation, and sleep
helped Arthur reach eighty years old comfortable, active, and
healthy.

In compliance to the *Senior Citizens Employment Act of 2035*, he had worked until the age of seventy-five and then retired from his forty-eight years as a professor of United World Government at nearby Reedley College. Since his wife Elsa, an English Literature teacher at Kingsburg high school had passed away from breast cancer two years earlier, he played golf twice a week while the rest of his time he spent puttering around his house cleaning, repairing, and painting, preparing the home to sell. He and Elsa had lived in their home their fifty-six years of marriage and had raised their son, Change, a very popular name back when the boy was born, who was now fifty-five living with his family in Sacramento and their daughter Hope, also a common name back then, fifty-three living with her family up in Fresno. Elsa had been a five-foot-three excited, talkative, bundle of love with glimmering hazel eyes and a smile for everyone. Her countenance along with her stunning black hair and Spanish complexion led him to fall in love with her. Their son, Change, tall and lanky like his father, but with his mother's complexion and eyes, and his wife Mai had two daughters in their late twenties with the oldest girl married with one child making Arthur a great-grandfather. Hope, short like her mother, but resembling Arthur, had sandy colored hair and blue eyes. She had a teenage son and daughter. Elsa and Arthur had desired another child, but could never afford the exorbitant fee to add a third child to the no cost healthcare package covering only two. With Arthur living alone, it was time to sell the unnecessary four-bedroom, two-bath home.

Two weeks of hot triple-digit days passed quickly and July 12th, the day of Arthur's eightieth birthday celebration arrived. After a fitful night's sleep, feeling restless about his birthday party, he arose at six a.m. rather than at his regular routine of rising at seven, climbing out of his pod bed, an egg shaped crib which as a no cost benefit of the healthcare system created a surrounding atmosphere while he slept by means of an embedded computer system with the ability to sense his comfort level and then adjust the lighting, temperature, rate of air flow, level of oxygen, and soothing sounds for the most relaxing sleep possible. Still wearing his free of charge healthcare issued *Sleep Right* blue and white striped pajamas which automatically heated and massaged his achy joints while he slept, and after stepping into his *Walk Right* slippers perfectly formed to his feet to add support to his drooping arches, he opened his front door as he did every morning to check the weather first-hand. The humid pre-dawn air was thick in his lungs and the damp coolness felt on his face would quickly disappear in the rising heat of the day. He peered out at the silent neighborhood, still dark though there was a creamy orange glow above the Sierra Mountains on the eastern horizon. A few homes had lights on. As always, he looked up and smiled compliantly at the top of the sector light pole across the street. The forty-foot-tall aluminum pole was wide enough and with a mirror polish so that it would be impossible for a person to shimmy up the pole to vandalize the black polyurethane bubble concealing an ever-watching camera; one of the world government's all seeing eyes voted in place to 'protect citizens from crime'. He accepted his lack of privacy in exchange for the absence of crime.

He shut the door and went into his kitchen to make breakfast. The sun sprang up as quickly as lighting an antique gas stove and began heating up the day's forecast toward 108 degrees. World weather reports had called the heat wave *global warming*, but as long as Arthur could remember, Central Valley temperatures had always been hovering above a hundred during the summer months of June, July, and August.

Rays of sunlight streamed into the kitchen through opened solar panels. Two morning doves, roosting in the Japanese maple tree outside his kitchen window, cooed an overture for daybreak. He made a healthcare approved breakfast: a steaming, gluten-free, ready-to-eat *Quinoaffle*, a waffle made from quinoa (keen-wah) flour. He smothered it with *It's Not Butter* and *More Maple* imitation maple agave syrup and then placed three links of *Soysage* in his solar speed oven and then added them to his plate. He set the plate on the table and next to it a glass of orange *Vita-Drink* along with a piping hot cup of *Yerba Mate*. Before he ate, he swallowed his handful of healthcare issued vitamins and minerals, another necessity for all who wished to remain on government healthcare.

While eating his breakfast, drinking his orange drink, and sipping his hot-drink, he glanced at the morning news on the computer hologram built into the kitchen table. To protect the rights and spirits of trees to grow skyward without the threat or pain of a laser saw, news organizations had stopped printing news on paper way back in 2020. A few years later, the government out-lawed the use of paper, in fact, the only paper used at all was toilet paper and somehow, it was recycled to make more toilet paper.

Finished with his waffle and now nibbling on his last link of soysage, he read, as he did every morning over the last few years, the listing of local *Celebrate 80* celebrants for that day. Of course, he saw his name at the top of the alphabetical list and noticed too, the names of a few high school classmates who like himself had never moved away from their small town of Kingsburg. He then scrolled down the page to the obituaries and read each name slowly, letting the name rest in peace upon his memory for a few seconds. At the end of the list, he felt relieved there hadn't been a name of anybody he knew. He finished his breakfast, washed the plate and the silverware, the glass, the cup, and the pan, and then put them all away. He made the bed, showered, shaved, combed his hair, brushed his teeth, and dressed in his favorite navy-blue *smart-suit*, a snug fitting integral shirt and pants with automated climate control inside, heating and cooling his body to the optimal healthy and comfortable temperature, meanwhile, capturing the energy of his body movements which in turn was used to re-charge his wrist pc or any other small electronic device. He had worn the suit to his wife's funeral. He thought about Elsa. As the years passed, her hair had turned gray and her skin had wrinkled; nevertheless, her compelling smile and twinkling eyes always reflected her joy for life. Even at the worst of her illness, traveling to the government's vast *Good Health Center* in Fresno to receive her harsh and frightening treatments, she continued to love, smile, and twinkle. She had been the only gal for him since high school and their marriage had been fulfilling for both. The pangs of missing her caused him to grimace. On the verge of tears, he hung his head in silence. With the advanced medicine of this time, how could cancer steal away his sweetheart? She followed the protocol and fought a good fight; nevertheless, the merciless ravages of her disease stole her away.

He composed himself, thinking, he was glad she passed on before him, because the thought of him dying first and leaving her alone to celebrate her eightieth birthday without him would have caused him heart-wrenching sorrow. Ready to leave the house, he checked all of the rooms and made certain everything was in order. As he stepped outside into the auto-dock, he pushed a home app button on his wrist pc locking up the house and then unplugged his sky-blue *Airpure,* a small, two-seater vehicle equipped with an emissions free generator powered by nuclear thorium lasers. One gram of thorium replaced 7,500 gallons of gasoline: the vile, emissions spewing, planet destroyer. Most of the world population drove these affordable and efficient thorium cars, subsidized by the government to assure clean air and protect the fragile ozone layer, thus thwarting the continuous threat of global warming. He slid into the car, programmed his GPS destination into the car's computer, turned the volume up a little on his favorite compilation of oldies but goodies 2050's music, and then backed the vehicle out of the car dock and down the driveway. Instantly, a *TCWS (Theft and Collision Witness Satellite)* homed in and began electronically tracking the vehicle's identification code implanted on the roof of his car. Government satellites tracked every car, truck, bus, boat, ship, train, and airplane.

He glanced over at the *River Realty* sign stuck in his perfect *Gro-green* biosynthetic lawn. A smaller "Sold" sign hung in front of and blocked most of the realtor's chubby face showing his potbelly stretching out his dark purple energy suit with its red racing stripe. Obviously, the overweight realtor broke all the food consumption laws, so healthcare officers were sure to crack down on him soon.

Arthur drove slowly through his neighborhood. How wonderful to have such little crime. With all the watchful eyes of the nicknamed *I-U* cameras and with all the mandatory *wrist-snitches*, the tag for the small wrist computers with GPS, anyone committing even the smallest infraction would find it impossible to get away with it.

The strictest requirement for receiving free healthcare was that a recipient had to wear the wrist device at all times—if not, a citizen was labeled a 'terrorist' and served a ten year sentence of hard labor on an *Ecology Tour* to Nigeria, Afghanistan, or Antarctica. The waterproof wrist-snitch, always strapped on the wrists of world citizens, not only informed the government of a citizen's location, but also, of all vital signs. The *Body Mass Index Law of 2034* ruled that it was an Earth crime to be more than ten points over the calculation of body weight compared to height. The government whisked away citizens judged obese to *Exercise and Diet Camps (E&D Camps)* for a 'vacation of health'.

Beginning in kindergarten, government schools taught children math, English, science, and the subject *my healthcare*. Students knew all about *Celebrate 80* and what a glorious occasion it was to celebrate one's eightieth birthday. Kids memorized slogans like: *Don't be over weighty; live to be eighty! Eighty for you; eighty for me; eighty for all! Be a humanitarian; praise the octogenarian! Eight zero; be a hero!* The preschoolers learned songs such as, *Super Greaty is Eighty* and *Not Afraidy of Eighty.*

Teachers taught that the *Good Life Foundation*, funded by the *Affordable Care Act* signed into law on March 23rd, 2010, operated *Celebrate 80* and had access to the vast database provided by the *United World Government.* They knew every celebrant's date of birth, health status, and health history, and due to the *Census Ruling of 2020*, the government mandated that the tiny chip of the wrist computers be imbedded at birth into the left wrist bone of each citizen. At first, many world citizens rebelled against the mandate, but the heavily armed world military quickly convinced them to comply.

The *Terrorist Enactment of 2025* made certain that the government's *World Security Division* could scrutinize all emails and internet activity. By analyzing social websites, the government could seemingly read minds. If a citizen was perceived to be a threat to themselves or society, government soldiers called *Peace Guards* were at their door and then whisked them off for an Ecology Tour. The small devices performed all that the old desktop personal computers did including lightning fast access to the internet and social media. With a tap of a tip of a finger on the larger touch screen projected on the wrist above the device all identity and banking information could be accessed and transmitted to buy food and clothes and make a mortgage payment. Stores didn't except hard cash anymore. Collectors and museums owned the only money the government had not destroyed.

The twenty-second century, the year 2100 was only a few years away. As always, winters in the Central Valley fogged up and the summers heated up. People slept, awoke, and went to work. There were solid families and broken families.

There were good kids and wayward kids. There were joyful occasions: weddings, birthdays, anniversaries, and there were also tragic events: divorces, bankruptcies, and funerals. Medicine had made tremendous strides enabling a majority of the world population to reach eighty-years-old healthy and whole. Obesity was nearly non-existent. Space travel, perfected since the first passenger rockets began launching citizens into space in 2018 transformed the way people viewed the world. Extravagant spaceships rocketing from strato-launch aircraft shuttled space-tourists into outer space for vacations at orbiting hotels. From a zero gravity viewpoint, the world appeared smaller. Governments, armies, currencies, and languages merged into one as people embraced the world not as separate countries and cultures, but as one human race inhabiting the tiny planet Earth. Peace abounded. The massive ranks of the world army squashed any resistance whether religious or political.

Arthur shuttled his humming little thorium car down Main Street, Kingsburg past small shops and restaurants, places he had frequented over a lifetime. Some foods such as pizza, chili verde, and orange chicken tasted the same but with less salt, no gluten, and very little unsaturated fat. He merged his vehicle onto the highway 99 eight rails *Autodriver,* a federal magnetic rail system conserving energy and producing zero emissions. His car connected to the magnetized rail with a slight shutter as his onboard computer confirmed attachment displaying a red light and three audio beeps allowing him to relax for a few minutes until three exits later the GPS system sounded a loud alarm, flashed a bright green light, and disengaged his car sending it freewheeling down an asphalt off ramp where he immediately regained control of it. The quiet car purred past vineyards of Thompson seedless grapes and orchards of peaches, apricots, and plums. He recalled back when he was a child how there was much more farmland; however, that was long before the

People's Progressive Party had campaigned and won the vote that the tiny red-legged green frogs in the Delta should have more than their share of water instead of the farmers growing food.

He rounded a bend in the road flanked by orange California poppies. Next, he came to a green hill swathed in yellow daisies and spied off in the distance, against the delicate blue sky, the three white steeples of the Celebrate 80 facility. Amidst the colorful countryside, the steeples looked out of place like three pieces of chalk in a box of Crayons. He had visited the facility many times to celebrate the eightieth birthdays of others. In addition, he had attended the two facilities in Fresno, the one in Reedley, and the one in Visalia. The Celebrate 80 center at Kingsburg was like all the other Celebrate 80 facilities around the globe. Every city had one or many based on population. Los Angeles had seventy-five facilities; Mexico City over a hundred. The world government built the state of the art centers especially for commemorating eightieth birthdays, which celebrated the great accomplishments of medicine and worldwide healthcare. The pristine buildings stood outside the cities in the calming countryside, in the relaxing woods, at a soothing beach, next to a calming river, amongst comforting rolling hills, or a breathtaking mountain view. Foreign to and without embracing their natural surroundings, the modern, stark-white structures, angular in design and simple in form with their three telltale sky-scraping steeples appeared to be places of worship; however, long standing laws separating church and government prohibited them from displaying crosses or any other religious symbol.

As he drove along, Arthur again thought of Elsa and how their young family used to picnic on the bank of the Kings River. She'd read an E-book while he helped the kids fish for trout. The memories made him smile. Of course, now, the government protected all waterways, mandating the Kings River off limits to people who might disturb the natural habitat of the black and yellow-striped petaltail dragonfly.

The winding country road led to a narrow lane lined with oak trees. An entrance sign made of bright brass in connected cursive letters read, *WelcomeToCelebrate80*. After two curves in the road, the lane ended at the parking lot beneath the soaring steeples. He parked his car in the shade of an elm tree and then climbed out to stroll down a river rock pathway amidst green shrubs, crape myrtle, crabapple, and maple trees. The bright and broiling sun made perfect shadows of branches and leaves on the walkway. Flowers bloomed in beds beneath the trees. Birds chirped, hummingbirds zipped, butterflies fluttered, bees buzzed, and honeysuckle scented the air.

In front of the straightforward entrance, a bronze water fountain stood in the middle of an asphalt circular driveway. The fountain depicted two life-size elderly people, a man and a woman facing each other, clothed in energy suits and holding their open hands in the air. Their upward gazing faces displayed their praise to the United World Government for providing a no cost healthcare system and eighty years of a healthy, worry free life. Clear bubbling water, sparkling with sunlight trickled out of their fingertips down to awash and anoint their bodies in symbolic well-being.

Two cathedral-sized clear glass windows adorned the front of the building from the ground up to the base of the steeples. Looking up, the steeples became lost in the blazing sun. A shiny brass *Celebrate 80* sign hung above the windows. Automatic glass doors slid open and he stepped into the foyer. He glanced up and compliantly smiled at an *I-U* security camera in the corner of the room. Like most government facilities constructed in the vein of financial conservation, the walls were painted eggshell white and the floor made of Earth tone cement. Framed watercolor paintings of Celebrate 80 facilities from around the globe hung on the walls.

An Earth-African woman and an Earth-Hispanic man both fit and dressed alike in satin dark-blue body suits stood at the front door and greeted people coming in. They both sang out in perfect synchronization, sounding like one voice, "Welcome to Celebrate 80!" Both glanced at Arthur and said, "Happy Birthday, Arthur Artesian!"

This Celebrate 80 facility could accommodate three separate birthday parties celebrating at the same time with each celebration lasting one-and-a-half hours followed by clean up crews working a half an hour followed by the next three celebrations, the next three, the next three, the next three, and the next three, starting at 8:00 a.m. and wrapping up the last cleanup at 8:00 p.m. Open for business for twelve hours, it celebrated eighteen eightieth birthdays all day every day including Whatdoyouwant Day (December 25th), New Years Day, United World Day (24th of July), and Obamaramadan; however, eightieth birthdays reserved on these holidays cost an exorbitant extra fee.

Three celebration rooms named Happy Hall, Cheerful Hall, and Joyful Hall were connected to the lobby. Each entrance had white double doors. The name and a holographic image of the next celebrator for that particular hall at that specific time floated to the side of the doors.

The three-dimensional image of Heather Draper, an attractive middle-aged woman hovered outside the double doors to Happy Hall. Clearly, this representation of her was not of her at eighty-years-old, but of her in her late forties. A thin woman with a bony facial structure, she wore gobs of make-up in a feeble attempt to hide her mid-life wrinkles. Bright and colorful as a spring bouquet, she modeled rosy cheeks, a pointy, up-turned buttercup nose, narrow, glossy, red hibiscus lips, stemy, plucked eyebrows, and large, leaf-green eyes bordered by violet eye-liner, periwinkle eye-shadow, and long black eyelashes. The *Dental Care Act of 2028* assured that she smiled with perfect gleaming teeth. Her dirt-brown hair was out of style in a swirly up-do from over three decades ago. She wore a morning glory blue top presenting modest cleavage, see-through high heal shoes parading yellow daisy toenails, and a clover-green mini skirt, a nostalgic fashion from the twentieth century.

Arthur stared at her image for a moment wondering, wherever she was, if she felt celebratory. He didn't feel celebratory. He felt eighty. He looked eighty. He was here for his eightieth birthday celebration. This time it wasn't his father or mother, who both lived to see eighty. It wasn't a colleague, a neighbor, or an old classmate. It was he, Arthur Artesian who was eighty. The days of his youth, gone. His career, done. The years of his marriage and raising children, over. His life was what it was. No more. No less. When he was young with spirit and vitality, why didn't he do more? He had a lifetime to pursue his dreams, arise to a calling, and leave a personal imprint where the memory of Arthur Artesian would last more than a season. Like most, he had worked hard and loved the best he could as each fleeting day passed. Now, it was his turn to celebrate eighty at Celebrate 80.

He heard the humming of a vehicle in the circular driveway outside. He turned away from Heather's hologram and looked out the glass windows to see a pastel-green Airpure van with *Oak Creek Living Center* on its side panel. A short, yet muscle-bound Earth-Asian woman and a lean, sinewy Earth-Caucasian woman, both wearing white energy suits jumped out, slid open the side door of the van, and actuated a power driven lift to gently lower an ancient looking woman in a white mobility chair. Her frail body tilted to her right and sunk into the chair with her head cocked sideways nearly resting on her right shoulder while the right side of her face drooped with a glistening glob of dribble in the corner of her mouth. Like a wilted bouquet of flowers finally taken out of the vase, her thin gray hair sagged to her shoulders in a few loose curls while her gaunt face frozen in a pose of anguish appeared flesh tone compacted with medium-toned foundation topped with a perky pink blush on her high cheekbones, yet her boney arms, hands, and gnarly fingers were a pale, bluish tint. Sunlight lit up her predominant green eyes enhanced by shiny lavender eye shadow with thick black eyeliner and mascara. A tight purple-pastel body suit stretched over her like skin over a skeleton. Pink slip-on shoes covered her bare feet.

The Earth-Asian woman activated the mobility chair with the remote app in her wrist pc, transporting the old woman sitting in it up to the entrance while the Earth-Caucasian woman drove the van around to the picturesque parking lot.

As soon as the huge glass doors of the foyer slid open, the pungent scent of the old woman's perfume invaded the lobby.

The greeters sang out, "Welcome to Celebrate 80. Happy Birthday, Heather Draper!"

She warbled, "Thank you," with a contorted one-sided smile using only the functioning muscles in the left side of her face.

Heather had spent the last ten years of her life in a government nursing home after suffering a debilitating stroke compounded by the onset of Alzheimer's. Friends and family consumed by their busy lives forgot about her. Her husband, Jack had died thirteen years earlier after waiting three years for a 'too late' heart transplant. After her husband's passing, she lived alone until her stroke forced her into a nursing home.

Her daughter Jessica, sixty-years-old, lived with her life-partner three-and-a-half hours away in San Francisco and only visited her mother two times a year, on Whatdoyouwant Day and on Mother's Day. Her mother didn't remember her, so why attend her eightieth birthday?

Heather's impaired mind couldn't recall anyone or anything from day to day. She couldn't hold a conversation and didn't do anything but sleep, eat, drool, and turn over in bed to have her pull-ups changed. She had worked since she was twenty-five until she was sixty-eight at the perfume and make-up counter at the Shangri-La department store located just off the 99 Autodriver between Kingsburg and Fresno. Shangri-La was one of the few independent corporations still in business after the world government's bailout and take-over of Wal-Mart changing its name to World-Mart.

She was once a beautiful woman embodying the glamour of her products, applying face and body moisturizers, creams, and wrinkle removers, with her pooky lips glistening with colors of pinks and reds and her shamrock eyes transforming from turquoise to deep blue depending on her eye shadow. She spent her life, coaching women to look their best. Now, on her eightieth birthday, a young aide from the nursing home had helped her look her best.

As the robust attendant shuttled Heather past Arthur and through the white double doors into Happy Hall, Heather with her stroke contorted face smiled up at him as her desperate sorrow formed as black mascara tears.

Arthur's anxiety intensified as his celebratory enthusiasm dwindled. He turned and took a few steps down the foyer to Cheerful Hall, where he stopped in front of the full image of a hardened elderly man wearing an orange body suit. The man looked menacing. Even though it was a hologram, Arthur took a step back away from him. The man sneered full of contempt with clenched teeth and a furrowed brow as accomplices. He had a two-day stubble of a beard and his oily gray hair, buzzed on the sides and long on the top looked loosely swept back by his hand. The floating placard read Charles Killick.

Arthur heard the squealing brakes of a large vehicle outside. He spun around, took a few steps back toward the lobby, and peered again out the window. He saw a desert-tan Airpure minibus with tinted and barred windows slam to a quick halt in front of the entrance. *California State Prison Corcoran* was painted on its side panel. Two buffed Earth-Hispanic men in brown correctional guard energy suits leapt out and unlocked the back door. They dragged out and jerked to the ground an elderly short man wearing wrist and ankle shackles, dressed in a bright orange bodysuit, white socks, and black slip-on shoes. Flanking him, they shoved him along through the entrance. A third guard driving the minibus moved the vehicle out of the driveway.

The scruffy convict had cut off the sleeves of his bodysuit at the shoulders and wore the zipper in the front opened down to his sternum showing off his taught pectoral muscles from doing bench presses for more than four decades. Prison tattoos ran down both sides of his neck, over his shoulders, and onto his arms. A colorful tattoo across his chest leapt out his suit. Though eighty, he had the muscular physique of a twenty-five-year-old triathlete, looking absurdly fit benefiting from healthy meals, daily exercise, and incredible prison health care including dental and eye coverage, which was far superior than that provided to law-abiding citizens.

Charles Killick had been incarcerated for forty-six years after a conviction of robbing and murdering a seventeen-year-old clerk at an Airpure power plug-in station. At the time of the crime, cash-money was still around. The take $115.00, barely enough to buy a carton of milk, a dozen eggs, and a loaf of bread. The community, outraged over the loss of this young man, the star player for their high school computer gaming team, pressed prosecutors for the death penalty; however, a week before his sentencing, the government pronounced capital punishment inhumane and outlawed it. He received a sentence of life in prison without the possibility of parole. After the first few years of adapting to his six by eight foot cell, he lived comfortably. He had his bed, toilet, a wrist pc, and a small bookshelf. A photo of his ex-wife, who had divorced him forty-three years earlier, still hung on the wall. His only child, a son, and the rest of his family members had long stopped visiting him.

Shuffling past Arthur and through the double doors into Cheerful Hall, Charles Killick snapped his head around, glared at Arthur, and burst out in maniacal laughter.

Arthur simply muttered, "Have a happy birthday." He then turned and walked to Joyful Hall reserved for his celebration. His hologram was of him and his family. Taken three years before his wife died, the image captured the smiling faces of he and his wife, their son and daughter and their spouses, four grandchildren, and great-granddaughter.

Arthur stepped through the double doors into the birthday room. He glanced up and smiled at an *I-U* security camera in the corner of the room. His seventy-eight year-old brother and his family of two sons, their wives, and grandchildren were already there. Four elderly couples from his First United Church of Earth greeted him. There were three retired professors, two men and a woman from the good ol' teaching days at the college. His brother-in-law, his wife, and their two daughters attended. Everyone smiled, excited for Arthur who had reached the glorious age of eighty years old.

Arthur's son, Change and his wife, their children, and their three-year-old grandchild strolled in through the double doors behind Arthur. Arthur scooped up his great granddaughter, Elsie and gave her a big hug and a loud smooch on her cheek. She giggled and gave him a wet kiss on his cheek. He handed her over to her mother as Arthur's daughter, Hope and her husband came in, followed by their teenage son and daughter. All embraced warmly. As Arthur moved around the room greeting people, they congratulated him with all the glee that all the years of schooling had taught them, singing out, "Hail to the World Government! Health care for all!" "Eight zero, he's a hero." "Be a humanitarian; praise the octogenarian!"

Elsie burbled her practiced rhyme, "Don't be over weighty, live to be eighty!"

On a small stage at the other end of the room opposite the

entry doors stood a table and chairs to seat five people. Arthur walked up the two steps and sat in the middle chair. His son sat to his right and his daughter sat to his left. Everyone else sat in brown fold-up chairs around tables of six. The tables had white paper tablecloths for easy removal and discarding. The solar and wind powered air conditioner blew out cold air, making the room too cold. Framed watercolor prints of Celebrate 80 facilities hung on the clean, eggshell white walls. Behind the small stage, floor to ceiling windows looked out at the serenity of the gently flowing Kings River.

Change picked up a cordless microphone lying on the table. He stood, cleared his throat, and exclaimed, "What a glorious day this is! My father's eightieth birthday. Eight zero, he's a hero! Let's have a round of applause for him—thank you. My Dad is truly a wonderful man." He looked down with adoration at his father sitting next to him. "Thanks Dad for always being there for me. Thanks for teaching me how to throw, catch, and bat. I will always remember the fun we had fishing in the river and the laughs we had when I was teaching *you* how to golf. Thanks for helping me buy my first Airpure and for not punishing me when I slammed it into the back of yours. I loved our trips to New Texas to visit family and how we sang oldies all the way there and back. I appreciate all the love and attention you give your grandchildren and great-granddaughter. You and mom, and oh, how we miss her, gave us a wonderful life growing up. I am grateful that you are my father. I love you dad. Happy Eightieth."

Arthur replied somberly, with tears of love welling in his eyes, "Your welcome son. I love you too."

Change handed the microphone over to his sister Hope. She stood up, looked out at the smiling people, drew in a deep breath, wiped a forming tear from her eye, reached down, snatched up her father's hand, and while looking at him, said, "Daddy, I love you so much. You are an amazing father. I appreciate the way you always held my hand when I was kid. I felt so safe around you. Thank-you for the dance lessons. Thank you for waiting up for me when I was a silly teenager. You always listened to me when I chattered or sobbed about my arguments with my girlfriends and break ups with boyfriends. You always encouraged me saying that the right man would come along and not to settle. I waited and I have Alan, the greatest husband in the world." She glanced out at her husband, smiled at him, and then focused her gaze back on her father.

Arthur silently beamed up at her.

"Another thing daddy," continued Hope, "thanks for all your patience teaching me how to engage and disengage from the Autodriver. I know it was scary."

Arthur, thinking about it now, chuckled.

"And Dad, you are the greatest grandfather and great grandfather any kid could have. It's remarkable how you can take wailing children and get them to giggle. Your life is a testament to what it is for a man to love and cherish his family. Again, thank you daddy. I love you. Happy Eightieth."

She passed the microphone down to the relatives and friends, and one by one, they told and retold stories about Arthur and the experiences they shared with him during his eighty years of life.

Last to speak was his toddler great granddaughter, Elsie. Shyly, with a little rock and twist of her body, she whispered, barely audible, saying, "Pawpaw, I love you." Everyone smiled at the cutie pie. Arthur adjusted his hearing aids and asked the tot to say it again. She did, a little louder, saying, "Pawpaw, I love you." Arthur's heart swelled with gladness. Elsie's mother handed the microphone back over to Arthur.

Arthur stood, peered out at his loved ones, smiled sheepishly, and said, "I want to thank all of you for coming, especially my cousin Barry, his wife Michelle, and their children Eric and Nancy for traveling all the way from the East Coast state of New Clinton. In addition, I want to thank cousin George and his wife Barbara for their rocket trip in from our bordering country of New Texas." He removed his eyeglasses and gently cleaned them with his napkin, and then continued, "Thanks to our free healthcare system, I made it to eighty. Amazing. Like most everyone, I've lived through some tough times, especially those years when Elsa was sick and going through treatment. Thank you for all the support during that time and after her passing. All of you helped me through the toughest time of my life. It's a miracle I lived to see eighty. Drafted and trained as a hover-jet pilot, I survived the Second Korean War. Many valiant men died and I had many close calls. I never thought I would make it back home to my Elsa. The Ebola virus nearly did me in during the pandemic of 2036. I wanted to die, but didn't. The toll of that virus changed this world. I thought we were all done for during the Jewish-Muslim World War of 2039 and the Hamas Takeover of 2044. We, as a world lived through those fearful times. Thanks to every sort of preventative medicine and living by the strict guidelines, here I stand as a testament to our incredible health care system. I have a few signs of old age, but I feel just as good as did thirty years ago. I am a blessed man to have a life filled with the love of a special woman, my wife Elsa." Arthur, overcome with emotion, removed his eyeglasses, rubbed his eyes, and then put the eyeglasses back on. He continued, "Moreover, to have such remarkable children, grandchildren, and a little great granddaughter; all of you fill my heart with joy. Like kids are taught in our schools, I'm eight-zero, so I guess according to the lessons, I'm a hero. I don't feel like one. I just feel like a man who has been blessed with terrific health and a wonderful family along with great friends. I love all of you. Thanks for coming to my celebration. Let's eat."

For lunch, a catering company served roasted free-range chicken on top of a bed of quinoa with a side of steamed broccoli. After lunch, they brought out a sugar free, gluten free, chocolate birthday cake with an eight and a zero candle.

Hope lit the two candles as all sang, "Happy eighty to you. Happy eighty to you. Happy eighty, dear Arthur, happy eighty to you!"

Arthur blew out the candles, swept back his full head of silver hair, and again, thanked everyone. They all ate cake. Little Elsie looked adorable with icing smeared on her face.

Arthur glanced up at the electronic clock hanging above the entry doors. His one-and-a half-hour allotted birthday time had ticked away. He knew the greeters would come any minute, followed by the clean-up crew. He stood, hugged his son and daughter, and then made his way around the room to shake hands and embrace the others.

His brother noticed the anguish on Arthur's face, leaned in close, and whispered, "It does no Earthly good, dear brother, to be sad or afraid. There is nothing you can do. Soldier up. March out that door. Show your children how to do it. Show your family how to do it. Show your friends how to do it. Show me, your little brother who will be celebrating eighty in two years, how to do it."

Like Arthur did when they were youngsters, he rubbed his brother's now nearly bald head. He turned and once again said to everyone, "Thank you," and, "I love you." A chorus rang out, "We love you, Arthur! Happy eightieth!" Then Hope and Change added to it, "We love you dad!" Hope held a handkerchief up to her nose. Change rubbed his tearing eyes.

Arthur quickly turned away from his family and friends and toward the two double doors. He swept back his silver hair again, and while welling up with the bravery he had leaned on during the war, holding his head high, and without shedding a tear, he strode out of the room.

Two very fit and stocky greeters on their way in met him outside the doors. He saw Heather Draper in her mobility chair and Charles Killick still in shackles coming down the hall accompanied by two greeters each. The three celebrants and the six burly greeters all went down the hallway and through two automatic opening and closing doors. The heavy doors squealed and clanked locking behind them. The narrow hallway led to three small rooms, much smaller than the celebration rooms. Two greeters wheeled Heather Draper in the first room while two greeters continued on to push Charles Killick in the second. The doors locked behind them. Heather stayed in her wheelchair and sobbed. The convict yelled profanities at the greeters as he violently thrashed around the room.

Arthur strolled into the third room. The door shut and clicked locking him in. A tan colored luxurious lounge chair sat in the middle of the room and in front of it, two windows from floor to ceiling looked out at the lazy Kings River. *'What a wonderful journey!'* in shiny brass letters hung above the windows. He sat in the chair, the most comfortable chair he had ever sat in with the cushion form-fitting to his body, then pulled up the foot rest and leaned back. He breathed in deeply and exhaled slowly while gazing out the windows at the serene view.

Eighty years had zoomed by so fast. He recalled voting for the Celebrate Eighty law back in the fall of 2038. Why had he voted for such an absurd law? Easy answer. He was twenty-five, politically progressive, and proud of it. Besides, eighty was a long way off. How could he imagine himself ever being eighty? Who would ever assume to live that long? Plus, he had a small family and was struggling to support them, so he had voted, yes, and made the deal. At the time, with so many suffering from the Ebola virus, the promise of a lifetime of no cost healthcare sounded incredible. The global campaign convinced the citizens of the world that it was patriotic. That it was an honorable, loving, thing to do. 'Serve humanity! Save humanity!' Health care for all, simply could not afford the soaring costs of medical care for anyone over eighty. Every man or woman turning eighty could make a difference. He wondered now, if it wasn't the world government who released the Ebola virus on an unsuspecting world. The Celebrate 80 law passed quickly with very little opposition.

Schools taught naïve children around the world to celebrate eighty. Be happy. Clap your hands. Sing songs. Rejoice for your grandfather and your grandmother. Then cheer for your father and mother. Then you yourself celebrate, for it is written in the obscure by-laws, *'everyone must rejoice'*—or vanish without the pomp and circumstance, without the celebration. No *Ecology Tour*; no *Exercise and Diet Camp*; just gone. Repeatedly, the government persuaded the people of the world. From birth to death, it was driven into the minds of every human being. Everyone benefited from it, yet everyone who voted for it was to blame for deciding his or her own fate; his or her end. They voted, yes, for something now; paying the cost later—if, still around.

He wished he could leave his children more of his assets, but the *Celebrate 80 Tax Act* of 2056 demanded that 50% of all remaining assets revert back to the government. A citizen couldn't fight the law. It was expected. It was excepted. At sixteen, a person received a driver license; at twenty-one, the consent to drink alcohol and smoke marijuana; at twenty-five, the legal age to get married, at seventy-five, the permission to stop working, at eighty, Celebrate 80.

So here he was, Arthur Artesian, celebrating eighty at Celebrate 80. How many octogenarians had sat in the chair before him? Were Heather Draper and Charles Killick as comfortable as he was? It seemed humane for poor, decrepit Heather. Put her out of her misery. After all, suffering cats and dogs received better treatment than people. Poor animals shouldn't suffer. Why should humans? For Charles, justice would finally be served. Eye for an eye; death for a death. The law should have executed him forty years ago.

There was no way of escape. No time remaining for worry or fear. With the thick door locked and sealed, just relax and gaze out the window at the tranquil river. His swirling thoughts faded into a mental fog or was it because of an invisible vapor seeping into the room to calm him? Outside, blinding sunlight glinted off the flowing water. Dragonflies zipped about, hovered, and flitted away. A fish jumped and splashed. A mocking bird landed on a branch just outside the window, stared at him, and squawked like a crow. Was it mocking him, since he was healthy with a life full of love?

A lifetime of Celebrate 80 lessons had prepared him for this moment. He could hear the voices of schoolchildren singing Celebrate 80 songs. All the hype and the propaganda percolated in his thoughts. Yes, it was his turn to sacrifice. It was his turn to be a hero. He had lived his life. It had been mostly good. He felt peace now. No pain at all. Soothing music began to play. A breezy flow of air laced with the sweet scent of garden flowers brushed across his face. He breathed in deeply, feeling euphoric. He smiled; a silly, carefree smile. Mingling with the floral scent, two invisible gasses seeped into the room. Tasteless and odorless, they filled his airways and coursed through his veins. He whispered the name of his wife, "Elsa." His eyes lids fluttered, followed quickly by unconsciousness. Within the next minute, euthanized by the World Government to reduce the ever-increasing costs of no cost healthcare, the strong heart of Arthur Artesian peacefully and efficiently stopped beating.

Only minutes later, three insignificant wisps of vapor, barely visible against the delicate blue sky, simultaneously puffed out of each of the three white steeples.

Thou Shalt be Mine

The deed done, the horror over, young Adora Louray, lying sprawled out on her back, snapped open her eyes and clutched her throat, gasping for air. Sir Botwolf's thunderous threat, "Adora, thou shalt be mine," still rang in her ears. Discovering her neck intact and her breathing normal, she lowered her hands, sat up, and nervously glanced around, finding herself alone on a hill of lush green grass; no Sir Botwolf in sight. A nearby doe and fawn grazing on clover raised their heads, stared at her for a moment, and resumed feeding. Adora climbed to her feet and looking down, was surprised that she wore new leather sandals and a graceful white gown sewn of silk and fitting perfectly. The unpretentious dress had an open neck, just barely covered her shoulders, was modest in the front, snug around her waist, and flowed down to her ankles. She touched her skin on her forearm and it felt softer than after a bath of olive oil and chamomile. Gazing out from the hill, she marveled at the beds of colorful flowers quivering from a whispering breeze and at the ancient trees flaunting their thriving foliage. Two furry, reddish squirrels chased each other around the trunk of a pine tree as a shiny blue butterfly, larger than she had ever seen, fluttered toward her, and then soared up and over her head. In the distance, a rook-like minaret towered above the tallest trees. At the bottom of the knoll, large marble statues of two men and two women each mounted on a mighty horse stood around a stone fountain, its pool of burbling water glinting like diamonds. Cheerful bird songs and a delightful floral scent filled the air while the golden sun, resting in an everlasting sunrise cast hues of flaxen light across the garden. She breathed in deeply and feeling safe now—now, forever in the King's garden, she exhaled with a long sigh of relief, whispering, "Sir Botwolf— thou cannot harmeth me now—not in my King's garden."

The deed done, his fury spent, Sir Botwolf Ziegenhorn the Fifth suddenly found himself perched above a deep chasm, lying on a tiny and perilous volcanic ledge. Red faced and out of breath from bellowing his tempestuous last words, "Adora, thou shalt be mine," he stood, grabbed his chest and finding no dagger wound, flashed a pithy grin, nevertheless, becoming mindful that he stood trapped on a deadly drop-off, his face contorted into terror while hurling himself backward against the black pumice wall. He glanced up and trembled as a forked lightning bolt ripped through the shroud of darkness followed immediately by a deafening clap of thunder. Breathing raggedly, every breath scorching his lungs and filling his mouth with the pungent taste of sulfur, he cautiously leaned outward, keeping his hands stretched behind him clinging to crags in the wall. Straining his neck, his face broiling and pouring of sweat, he peered down into the eerie orange glow, gasped at what he saw, and again backed up against the pyroclastic wall.

One hundred feet down coursed a blazing yellow and orange river of bubbling lava emitting gaseous steam, vapors, and smoke swirling and snaking about as tornadoes. With watery, stinging eyes, he stared through the smoke, ash, and gloom, and beheld a multitude of poor wretches like he, trapped on precarious ledges like his. People of all races, men and women, tall and short, thin and thick, young and old, lay, knelt, or paced on their small ledge. He saw that they all dressed in sackcloth robes, prompting him to grumble, "How unfashionable! To all dress alike, the same as I." Some sobbed, bereaving a cherished life, while others wailed, bearing regrets. A few begged for mercy, folding together their hands, though most cursed, brandishing fists of anger. Many curled up suffering silently, yet more stood screaming hysterically. A menacing lava bubble, swelling with captured fumes floated up toward his shelf. Watching it growing big and bigger, his dark eyes opened wide and wider while his terrified face turned grim and grimmer as the smoldering orb exploded, blasting red-hot globs of fiery death. One shooting gob of lava knocked a haggard man off a ledge directly below Sir Botwolf's. Encompassed in fire, the plummeting soul shrieked all the way down to obliteration in the cremating lava. Sir Botwolf recoiled in terror, laid down, and curled up into a ball, covering his face with his hands as a mass of molten rock struck his arm, ignited his sackcloth robe, and instantly burned through, blistering his skin. Screeching in pain, he jumped up and patted out the fire, but not before it had also lit like a fuse his long pointy beard burning up to scorch his chin. His sore eyes, irritated from the heat and reflecting the firelight, darted about. Seeing only the pathetic souls of the shrieking damned and thinking that there may perhaps be an all-powerful, all-knowing, and all-pervading presence watching him, he shouted in an indignant voice, "Wherest am I?", then coughed violently, choking on nauseous fumes as his words eked out just beyond his ledge where intense heat devoured them without an answer. Again, he yelled, "Wherest am I?" Then, demanding all the louder, "and wherest are my fine garments: my brushed wool breeches, my belt with gold buckle, my silk stockings, my leather boots, my scarlet surcoat, and my peacock feathered, velvet hat?" Each word instantly asphyxiated short of a reply, inciting him to bellow, "It doth not matter wherest I am or howest I am clothed! Death, shalt not stoppeth me! As I vowed, Adora—thou shalt be mine!"

Adora stepped off the grass and onto a seven-foot-wide pathway of flat steppingstones of the same size and seven-sided shape. Following the path down the slope, she paused at the fountain. It was of simple design: round, spanning twenty feet with a retaining wall of flat stones stacked around its circumference seven high to waist tall. Green leaves, colorful blossoms, and the gilded sky reflected on its surface. Runoff from the distant snow-capped mountains quietly bubbled up at the fountain's center and then poured out an overhanging spout into a peppled catch that disappeared underground. She leaned over and gazed at her reflection on the faintly rippling water. Her waist-length, golden-brown hair gleamed like the autumn foliage of a maple tree bursting with sunshine while her eyes shone greener than a sapling's first leaves of spring. Her supple lips were pink like honeysuckle berries in winter and her flawless skin looked as delicate as a white rose in summertime. Neither older nor younger, she still looked nineteen. She rubbed a finger over a spot on her forehead where as a child an olive branch had scratched her leaving a small scar; to her wonder, the scar had disappeared. Even her neck had no hint of injury. Joy tickled her spirit rousing a smile. She looked away from her happy reflection and seeing a gold chalice sitting on the structure's stone rim, she picked it up, held it under the fountain's spout, filled the shiny cup with water, and drank of it. It tasted crisp and clean, washing her spirit of all trepidation. While sipping from the cup, she stopped and perused one of the four statues arranged around the fountain. She moved her hand slowly over its surface, feeling the glassy smoothness of the marble. In awe, she stood for a moment in front of each of the life-size statues: two handsome

men and two beautiful women; all heroic, stalwart, portraying
a solemn face of justice, wearing flowing, shoulder-length hair,
and streaming garments. Each wielded a raised double-edge
sword and rode a mighty horse; one horse posed galloping,
another rearing up, another hurdling, and the fourth steadfast.
Chiseled on the pedestal of each statue were the words,
Protector of Everlasting Peace. After admiring each statue
and finishing her water, she placed the chalice back where she
had found it, and then continued on the walkway, meandering
by beds of flowers and around shrubs and trees. An enchanting
tree of broad red leaves offered its plump purple fruit low and
next to the path. She reached up, picked one the size of her
fist, tasted it, and smiled, relishing its sweetness. She ate it,
feeling invigorated. Next to the fruit tree, a flourishing hedge
of hand-size pink blossoms flashing bright yellow pistil and
stamen captured her attention. She picked a flower, smelled of
its heavenly scent, and slipped it in her hair behind her left ear.
Following the path around an enormous pine tree, its trunk
spanning the length of two oxen nose to tail, she arrived at the
stone minaret buttressing a staircase spiraling up its outer wall.
Holding up her gown, she quickly and rhythmically ascended
to the top of the slender lofty tower to a landing enclosed by
a crown-like parapet. Higher than the tallest tree, she gazed
out at a panoramic view of the kingdom. Beyond the greenery
and bright colors of the garden, orchards, vineyards, and crops
of every variety grew in a fertile valley. Past the farmland,
great herds of animals grazed on verdant hills. Farther than
the rolling hilltops lay a thick forest of pines and above its
tree line arose snowcapped mountains. A misty waterfall
cascaded midway down the tallest peak, forming a spillway
into a sparkling river. The surging river wound back through
the green hills, branching off into three streams: one running
through the garden, another gushing across the farmland, and
the other flowing to a magnificent palatial city replete with

domes, spires, pillars, towers, and steeples as far as she could see. The flaxen light tinted the cobblestone streets gold. On the other side of the river flowing through the garden lay a vast courtyard and at its heart, a huge silver fountain, its great pool of spring water shimmering in the sunlight. Smiling people, all youthful, moved about happily sweeping the streets, polishing the fountain, bringing in crops, preparing the food, and cooking at the fires. How exciting to see both sets of her loving grandparents again, for surely they must all be there, and how fun to know them as young not old. She lingered at the top of the tower enjoying the glory of the kingdom. Closing her eyes, feeling the sun's warmth on her face and a breeze brushing back strands of her hair, she remembered her dearest Errondo and murmured, "Errondo, my love, I pray thee wounds heal and that thee liveth a full and happy life. Though, I am not with thee, I shall not forget thee."

The deed done, his death imminent, Errondo Tortoro lay on his back in another kingdom far away from Adora and the divine garden. Between the rows of olive trees he lay, his blood ebbing out of his fatal wounds with every beat of his heart. His mother, sobbing into her hands, knelt beside him. He looked to his left past his grieving mother at the corpse of Sir Botwolf, a dagger buried deep in his heart; the fatal wound still oozing red blood thick with lust. To the right, lay Adora, her throat slashed and her lifeless body encircled by a bloody pool of innocence. He blinked the tears from his eyes and gazed up into the bright and blue heavens. A cloud drifted. A buzzard circled. An olive leaf floated to the ground. Weak, his lips trembling, he spoke as if his abounding love would carry his words beyond the blue hydrangea sky, past the white camellia clouds, and into the marigold heavens where Adora resided in a realm of eternal days. "Adora, my dearest," he stretched out his hand and touched her limp fingers, "didst thou hearest Sir Botwolf before thou didst die? He cometh for thee; cometh to steal away thy virtue. I say unto thee, fear not, for soon, I shalt be where thou art. I pray—I shall not be too late."

Pacing on his small ledge above the flames of eternal death, Sir Botwolf brushed back his long, oily, black hair from sticking to his face and gawked all about. Above him, the shifting darkness of the smoke and ash filled sky crept and crawled amidst slithering flashes of lightning. Booming thundercracks hurt his ears. His eyes stinging, he witnessed a black churning vortex of smoke arise and obscure a shrieking woman who knelt at the edge of her shelf. The searing whirlwind consumed her, feeding on her condemnation, then passed as another tormented soul arrived, shrieking insanely.

Sir Botwolf stopped pacing, knelt on his knees at the edge of his shelf, and cried out, "Thirst tormenteth me; hunger torturest me; my skin stingeth, my eyes burneth, and each breath scaldeth my chest. Be it not a horrific, dreadful place, a terrible predicament, and an agonizing eternity?" He stretched both hands up and out toward the vast hopelessness and shouted, "Where, oh King, is Thy forgiveness?"

Souls shrieked, lava hissed, and whirlwinds whirred.

"I heareth not Thy answer," he growled, then stood and roared, "therefore, I shall escape my scorching plight in this fiery abyss and findeth a drink of water. More importantly, I shall seeketh and findeth Adora; then, I, Sir Botwolf Ziegenhorn the Fifth shall partaketh of her sweet virtue."

For a moment, forgetting his dilemma on the ledge, the scorching heat of the chasm, and the shrieking voices of the damned, he closed his eyes and envisioned Adora, her long, golden-brown hair, soft and lustrous like corn silk cascading down to her waist. He moaned, imagining her hair brushing across his face, then sighed, thinking of gazing into her alluring eyes, and then shuddered, dreaming of gently kissing her soft lips. Breathing heavily, he visualized her bare curvaceous body prancing about for him. He opened his eyes and beginning with a low groan quickly increasing in volume, he roared, "Ohhh, Adora! How I acheth for thy nakedness! My loins hummeth like a hive of honeybees! Such a sweet and innocent girl thou art: so young and oh so curious, never knowing a man. Ohhh, the things I would doeth to thee to pleaseth me!"

The more he fantasized about her, the greater his lust swelled. Trembling, his legs weak and wobbling, he dropped to his knees, raising his face and fists to the smoke shrouded sky and shouted as though wherever she was, she might hear him, "Why, oh why, Adora, didst thou stick thy pointy little nose in the air and turn thy back to me—me the only son and heir of my father Lord Botwolf Ziegenhorn the Fourth? Yea, though I was twice thy age, I was handsome and wealthy. Thou didst deny me the pleasure of thy beauty, hence, thou provoketh my fury and thus, I loathe thee! Even so, my heart still yearns for thee. If I am hither, then thou must be hither—as I knoweth thee died. Thou must be somewhere on this side. Soon, I shalt findeth thee and then, Adora, thou shalt be mine!"

Death had not slayed his obsessive desires for Adora. Determined to embrace her and driven to satisfy his depravity, he faced the canyon's black porous surface. Peering up, he reached and found a crag, placed his hand in it, then found another notch, kicked off his sandals, and put a foot in it, pulling himself up. Each grip, searing, each step, sizzling, the hot rock face blistered his hands and feet. Though the agony and the heavy burden of his transgressions slowed him down, his lust spurred him on. Another grip, another step, hand then foot, right then left, unrelenting, he steadily climbed. Experiencing unbearable heat, torrential sweat, and blistering breaths, driven by his aberrant attraction for Adora's beauty and heedless of eternal death lapping up at him with its snaking tongues of steam, smoke, and fire, he slowly climbed and climbed, then climbed up under the ledge of another condemned man.

Above the noise of hissing steam escaping from fissures, the pops of exploding lava bubbles, the howls of whirlwinds, and the shrieks of the damned, Sir Botwolf heard the man just above him, a contrite man who had been wailing for a very long time, crying out in a hoarse voice, "Why, ohhh, why did I do it? Why, ohhh, why did I do it? Why, ohhh, why did I do it?"

Sir Botwolf reached up, clamped his hands on the rim of the man's ledge, and peeked over to see a short, middle-aged man with a forlorn face, freakishly elongated from endless lamentation. The man looked down, saw Sir Botwolf's hands clutching his ledge, and stomped on them while yelling hysterically, "No, no, no! Off my ledge thou usurper! Off my ledge! To the lava with thee!"

Sir Botwolf swiftly pulled himself up and over, sustaining a few punches and kicks to the top of his head, nevertheless successfully fending off the man guarding his tiny piece of property. Then, void of any concern for the grieving man's final fate and since there was not enough room for two on the shelf, Sir Botwolf, towering a head taller than him, simply punched the man in his sad, droopy face, grabbed him by both scrawny shoulders, spun him around swapping places, then, lacking conscience and without mercy pitched him with his groveling pleas over the edge. The flailing, falling man screamed all the way down to where just above the fiery molten river, he burst into flames, hitting the lava with an incinerating *thurp* followed by a steamy *fssst*.

All of the ill-fated on ledges near the violent scene witnessed Sir Botwolf hurl the man off, so when he, after a brief rest began climbing again, they hugged their walls, allowing him to pass without a fight.

With fierce whirlwinds clobbering him, raging flames flaring up at him, and with harsh smoke and ash in his eyes and mouth, and after numerous times of nearly losing his grip and plummeting to an everlasting death, Sir Botwolf, driven by uncontrollable thoughts of Adora, compelled by his pomposity, and with tremendous determination and agility, finally reached the rim of the chasm, carefully crawled on his belly over onto solid ground, and stood as the first damned soul in all eternity to escape out of the dark, raging, pit. Standing there in his sooty sackcloth robe and charred hands and feet, he rubbed his sore eyes, spit the grit out of his mouth, swept back his grimy hair, and then peered down at the fiery underworld cloaked in woe and at the countless souls, suffering, unforgiven souls, bereft of faith and devoid of hope, sobbing and screaming on infinite ledges. He laughed loudly at them and their woeful plight, and his maniacal laughter echoed amidst their despairing screams. The horde, who heard him, stopped screaming, stared up at him for a few eerie seconds, and then resumed shrieking ever louder. He looked beyond the damned and saw the glowing river of lava flowing out of the erupting volcano into the chaotic canyon and its channel of fire coursing through a languishing landscape to a starless black horizon. In the opposite direction, he saw, illuminated by the golden sunrise, distant snowcapped mountains, a dense forest, green hills, and the spires, domes, and steeples of a palatial city—all surrounded by a formidable rock wall.

"Indeed," he spoke aloud, "Adora, wouldest thou be abiding thither? For thy beauty and innocence could only resideth in paradise. Yea, I believeth, that thou art thither. No lofty wall can thwarteth me. I shall goest where thou art and then, Adora, Adora, ohhh, my sweet Adora—thou shalt be mine."

Nevertheless, between him standing at the brink of damnation and his consummation of his conquest of Adora, there lay a baked, lifeless land of steaming fissures and smoldering cinder cones. A loud explosion rocked the volcano shaking the ground violently and nearly tossed him back into the chasm.

He shook both fists in the smutty air toward the far off paradise and yelled, "Thou shalt not, oh King, pitch me back into Thy pit of misery!" He then shuffled back a few steps away from the precipice, the desiccated soil crunching like flakes of old parchment under his bare feet. Droplets fell upon his head. Rain? Blessed rain! He eagerly held out his cupped hands to catch of it and drink, to find it only a downpour of ash. Undeterred, he started running and when he tired, he ran faster, repeating, "Adora, Adora, Adora," sporadically in rhythm with three slaps of his feet, all the while building momentum thinking of her tempting body and enticing scent fueling his lust, driving his desire, propelling him closer to his carnal conquest. Though dehydrated, famished, and fatigued, he kept a fast pace through the steam, smoke, and ash, all the while the hot skin on his face, hands, and feet bubbled and blackened to resemble the ancient volcanic rock around him.

Adora, still up in the tower, saw a host of people just beginning to gather in the courtyard for the daily feast with the King. Festive food and drink lay upon countless wooden tables. Melodic notes of harps and flutes and the joyful chatter of jubilant people arose in the pure air and her spirit celebrated a new peace. She looked for the pathway to join them and saw that not far away, the stepping stones lead through a flowery meadow to a high arcing stone bridge crossing over the river from the garden to the palace grounds. Before descending the staircase to make her way to the King's feast, she sauntered over to the other side of the parapet to look upon the scenery in the opposite direction of the heavenly kingdom. Gazing out, she frowned, seeing not far from the tower, a rock wall four times the height of the tallest man, separating the King's garden from a barren land. Beyond this forsaken wasteland and in the ash-filled sky above it billowed the black smoke of a volcano spewing fiery lava down its slopes to a spillway disappearing into a chasm leading to a horizon of unending midnight. She shuddered, saying, "Sir Botwolf, thee and thy demon that dwellest in thy soul must surely abideth in that vile land, where thee, oh wicked man shalt suffer misery for eternity, while I, and someday my beloved Errondo, shalt abideth forever in paradise."

Errondo now counted three buzzards circling ever lower in the sky above him. He no longer felt the pain of his wounds or any feelings in his hands and feet. With labored breaths, weak, and faint, he cried out, "My Creator, I do not want to live without Adora. Please, I beggeth Thee, taketh me now!"

Just ahead of Sir Botwolf, past the final cinder cone, a large one, stood the rock wall, and just beyond the wall, grew a garden, and above the trees, loomed a stone minaret, and at the top of that lofty tower—he stopped and stared, gasping, gawking, nostrils flaring, eyes burning, while his heart pounded like the beating drums of a primordial tribe—he saw a beautiful woman dressed in white, stroll up to the parapet and gaze out. He leapt behind the heap of black pumice and peered up at her. She had not seen him: a dark sooty figure in a dark sooty land. He raked his parched and swollen tongue across his blistered lips, and barely able to speak, moaned, "Ooooh, I spy thee, Adora. Soon, thou shalt be mine."

While Adora scowled, peering out at the disgusting land, Sir Botwolf had slyly snuck, crept, and crawled, reaching the perimeter wall of the King's garden. Hand then foot, right then left, he scaled the rocky wall as he had done climbing out of the chasm. Reaching the top of the wall, he pressed up against it and cautiously peeked over. Through red squinting eyes, for the perfect brightness of the garden hurt them, he peered up at Adora in the tower and uttered, "Lovelyyy. The moment is nigh when I shall taste thy sweet lips and embrace thy divine body."

A lone raincloud drifted in front of the eternal sunrise casting an ill-omened shadow over the garden. Adora peered up at the gray cloud and watched it passing before the sun. So did the King with furrowed brow. She had not a care, yet unbeknownst to her, a grim creature, Sir Botwolf climbed over the wall, dangled for a second, and then dropped to his feet to hide in a thick hedge of bushes inside the garden.

Peering out of the leaves, leering up at her, Sir Botwolf knew that soon, his voracious lust would devour Adora's pure and pleasing splendor, causing him to groan accompanied by a crackling wide grin, making little ashen flakes of cooked skin chip off his face and sprinkle to the ground. He muttered a praise, "Thank you my lord, thank you for such a heavenly creature as Adora," believing that the god of his licentiousness had presented her to him, for him to have and to hold, to caress, to kiss, to fondle, to gratify himself, intertwining their bodies in carnal ecstasy until the end of all time. He heard the gurgling water of a fountain. His swollen tongue felt like an apricot, so he excitedly snuck through the flowers, crawled under shrubs, and crept around trees, quickly finding the soul-quenching spring. Out of Adora's sight, he hastily dunked his head under the sparkling water and gulped down his fill. His scorched tongue only tasted sulfur. He spied the gold chalice and had a mind to steal it, but only after he had his satisfaction with Adora. After quenching his thirst, he stepped into the pool to cool his scorched feet. He then dove in, swam to the other side, and climbed out, his hot skin steaming with guilt. He paused, taking a quick look at each statue, wondered about them, and then hurried down the path, grabbing on the run a plump purple fruit from a red-leafed tree. Though the fruit was sweet, it too tasted sulfuric. He devoured it as its purple juice dripped off his bristly, burnt chin. Feeling alive again, skin cooled, thirst quenched, and hunger abated, he continued down the path and slinked around a huge pine tree.

The cloud moved on and golden light reigned again in the garden prompting Adora to close her eyes, sense the warmth upon her face, and breathe in the peacefulness. The pink and yellow flower blew out of her hair and floated down to alight on the ground next to Sir Botwolf, lurking, scheming at the side of the tower. He snatched up the bloom, sniffed it, sniffed it again, and sniffed it once more, swelling his lust. Joyful bells rang out from the palace declaring the start of the feast. Hearkening the bells, Sir Botwolf, quivering, cackling, and slobbering with anticipation, dashed up the staircase.

When the happy ringing of the bells stopped, the festive music played once again. Adora hummed along with the melody while dancing a few steps to a jig her mother had taught her, and then strolled across the landing to leave the tower. Listening to the music, she did not hear the pattering footsteps of Sir Botwolf coming up the stairwell.

Errondo, lying in the olive grove and very close to death, heard the galloping hoof beats of a horse followed by the booming voice of Sir Botwolf's father, Lord Botwolf Ziegenhorn the Fourth, known as Lord Fourth. Lord Fourth saw the group of olive pickers standing about and roared, "Why are ye not picking olives? What hath happened?"

Lord Fourth, wearing a white wool shirt with a ruffled collar, brown sheepskin pants, a plain black belt, and worn black leather boots, sat high and rigid upon his chestnut colored steed. He was a stout man of fifty-eight years with gray hair high-combed, then flowing, spiraling down to his shoulders in curly locks like the mane of an old lion. His skin was predictably tan and weathered from working hard everyday in the sun and rain to assure his riches. He wore his shirt unbuttoned halfway down to display his thicket of curly gray chest hair, though kept his full gray beard and thick eyebrows neatly clipped. He quickly dismounted and seeing the gory scene with Botwolf lying with a dagger buried in his chest, moaned, "Botwolf! Oh, Botwolf, my son! Thou art dead!" Then exclaimed, "Poor Adora. Thou art dead too!" Then stated, "Errondo, I seeth thy breath, art thee alive?"

"Yea," whispered Errondo, "I am alive, my lord."

Lord Fourth, his teary eyes flashing with anger, marched back to his horse, drew his longsword sheathed to the saddle, and stomped back to Errondo. He grabbed Errondo's mother by an arm and flung her away from her dying son, then put the sharp point of the sword to Errondo's chest, and demanded, "Tell me Errondo! Tell me, what hath happened?"

Before Sir Botwolf Ziegenhorn the Fifth found himself roasting in a volcanic abyss, thus, becoming a charred soul in a sooty sackcloth, he was a very strong man, handsome as he was strong, charming as he was handsome, and wealthier along with his father than any other land owner in the kingdom, yet, his strength, good looks, charm, and riches were trifling compared to his ever-swelling lust, for he thought the kingdom his playground and all the ladies his toys.

Though people feared him, they envied him. When Sir Botwolf rode through the village in his opulent carriage pulled by two pristine horses or when he sauntered through the daily market in his elegant clothes, the peasants and the potentates alike would blather to one another under their breath, saying ... .

"Gaze thine eyes upon Sir Botwolf and seeth how tall and handsome he is; his sprightly skin is unblemished by the sun and his spotless hands and polished nails doth not showeth toil."

"Ahh, and what a smile! Such colossal, perfect teeth! Yea, are they not carved from ivory?"

"I dareth thee, stealeth a glance into his gray eyes and telleth me if thou doest seest a forthcoming storm!"

"I thinketh, I shall grow a beard like his, so black, so long, and so pointy. I bethinketh, he bethinketh, he is Shakespeare!"

"That hair, ohhh, that magnificent hair! How long his hairdresser must toil to fashion such shiny, spiraling ringlets to cascade and then coileth like serpents upon his shoulders. Oh and how his hairdresser must labor to dye it black as coal and then coax it to soareth higher than the highest hat on a tall man's head."

"I envieth Sir Botwolf and all his wealth. I especially wish for his fashionable clothes, so colorful, bright, and made of silk and velvet."

"Stay thee out of his way. Be not a fool to provoke his wrath, for he carrieth knives and swords, and is practiced in them."

"Yea, and hideth thy sister, wife, and mother from his eyes, for if one of them igniteth his desire, he shalt taketh her from thee!"

"Ahhh, to be invited to his masquerades at his mansion amidst the olives. The palace, the garden, the fountains, the music, the dancing, the wine, and a marvelous feast; how wonderful to have it all!"

"Sir Botwolf doth indeed have it all; nevertheless, he always desireth more and receiveth more of all he desireth from his father, Lord Fourth."

Sir Botwolf's father, Lord Botwolf, Ziegenhorn the Fourth, addressed as Lord Fourth told the story many times about his son's stubborn persistence, saying, chuckling, "My son doth not knoweth the meaning of 'no'. He wilt continue asking, begging, or demanding until his tongue bleedeth and he hath his way. I recalleth when the lad was but four-years-of-age, he had eaten his lemon tart and desireth mine, threatening, "Father, giveth me thy tart or I shall burneth my hand with the candle.' I replied, 'Nay, thou shalt not haveth my tart,' and I took a bite. So my young Botwolf snatched up the candle and slowly poureth the hot wax upon the back of his hand and doing so while staring at me with a stone face, he doth not blinketh nor sheddeth a tear. I ignored him as I tooketh another bite of my tart until he picketh up a larger candle and dumpeth the hot wax upon the purring cat coiled in his lap. The cat hissed and scurried away to hideth under my bedchamber's chiffonier. Again, I sayeth to the boy, 'Nay, thou shalt not haveth my tart.' So the indomitable lad tooketh another candle, an even larger one, that he grippeth with two hands, and holdeth it above his baby brother asleep in a crib next to the table. Young Botwolf glareth at me, waiting, watching me, and then ever so slowly tippeth the candle to where a single drop of hot wax falleth onto the forehead of my precious infant Favorel, burning him and waking him frightened and crying. Indeed—I gaveth Botwolf my lemon tart."

Before Adora Louray found herself basking in paradise, she had little of nothing, working hard all day every day with her mother, Lovisa, her father, Happlio, and her thirteen-year-old sister, Purita in the olive groves of Lord Fourth. They earned enough wages to rent from Lord Fourth a small worker's cottage on a tiny plot of land on the far side of his vast estate. They lived in the picker's hamlet of Fourhills amongst other cottages built across four rolling hills of the same elevation forming a square. Down in the gullies between the hills lay two crisscrossing cobblestone streets where stood a stone house of worship just big enough to assure that all the picker families had their own pew. A community water well made of rocks and mortar sat across the lane from the church. On Sunday, the picker's only day of rest, after worship, at the bottom of Onehill and Twohill there convened a marketplace for trading fruits, vegetables, bread, eggs, milk, cheese, goats, chickens, cows and anything else they raised, cooked or crafted. From there, a dirt road with wagon wheel ruts connected the hamlet to the olive orchard leading to Lord Fourth's palace and all the way to the city a half-day carriage ride away. A tiny butcher shop and a store for wares stood between Twohill and Threehill, and a blacksmith shop sat at the base of Threehill and Fourhill. Nestled between the steep sides of Fourhill and Onehill, a tavern beckoned with music, dancing, and greenish ale of fermented hops and olives. Olive trees spanning out in orderly rows as far as the eye could see, surrounded the hamlet of Fourhills. Going west, beyond the olives, grew a dense forest.

The cottages, all owned by Lord Fourth, were built the same: the walls were made of wattle, sticks woven together and daubed with gray mud, the floors made of dried clay, and the thatched roofs steep to accommodate a loft underneath for sleeping. A small window with shutters peered out the front. There was one room and at its center, a fireplace with a clay chimney. Each cottage had a table and enough chairs and straw beds as needed. On one side of the Louray's cottage grew a small vegetable garden and on the other side, they kept in a pen a rooster, two cows, three goats, and four chickens. Wildflowers grew down the gentle sloping hill in the front and up the steep incline in the back. Birds sang all day. Crickets chirped all night. The Louray family had food, shelter, clothing, and most of all, each other. They were content to work the groves and to rest every night in the warmth of their home and family. To barter for other goods, they made cheese from the cow and goat milk.

Adora, nineteen, had a sweet countenance brimming with loving kindness. Her kindheartedness combined with her beauty created a creature so lovely as to steal the breath away from all who gazed upon her. Her skin was baked a creamy olive color from picking olives under the sun and her eyes were greener than the greenest olives she picked. Her long hair awashed in sunlight was golden-brown and her skin was soft and her scent lovely from bathing in olive oil and chamomile. She stitched her own clothes from died wool, fitting her shapely figure perfectly. Her younger sister Purita, twelve-years-old, was a smaller replica of her, although, she was thinner and shorter with a bit of tomboy, catching spiders and climbing trees with the lads of Fourhills. Happlio and Lovisa were very proud of their daughters, though, fearful for them, knowing the lustful ways of Sir Botwolf, they taught their virtuous daughters to stay far away from him and to hide their beauty, which they did, concealing themselves high up in the branches of the olive trees.

On a sun-drenched autumn afternoon, a perfect time for picnicking under the huge shady oak on the white sandy bank of the river, Sir Botwolf, riding his favorite horse, a massive midnight-black steed with red ribbons braided in its mane and tail, galloped down the dirt road cut by a horse drawn wagon to the olive grove nearest the river on the far side of his estate. His flagrant intention was to pluck a young and succulent olive-picking maiden out of an olive tree to pair with his wine and cheese during his riparian outing. Dressed like a mollycoddled prince, he donned purple fanciful knee breeches bound with a black leather belt and gold buckle, lavender silk stockings, shiny black leather boots, a rosy shirt with ruffled sleeves and collar, a scarlet surcoat, and a peacock feathered, red velvet hat, which out from under dangled his black corkscrewing locks trained to coil upon his shoulders like matching serpents under a thicket. He carried a long and sharp dagger with an ivory hilt in a bejeweled sheath on his right hip while a curled deerskin whip and a sheathed longsword hung from his saddle. His stormy gray eyes glinted with eagerness accentuated by a grin of anticipation while his prolonged noble nose soared skyward as his pointy beard aimed down like an arrow to his tight pants. Sitting high upon the horse, straight and proper in the saddle, and having a firm grip on the reins, he trotted past row after perfectly spaced row of olive trees; ancient trees with gnarly trunks, thick twisted branches, and flourishing canopies laden with olives. The first maiden he spied picking olives up in a tree was mostly hidden by foliage, so he called out to her, "Oh, maiden, 'tis I, Sir Botwolf bidding thee, cometh hither from my olive tree!"

"Yea, Sir Botwolf," she replied in a shrill voice, prompting him to wiggle his forefinger in his irritated ear as she continued squealing, "I cometh thither out of thy olive tree."

She lumbered down the ladder until out of the veiling leaves there first appeared a pair of tiny feet in small sandals attached to thin ankles. Having an affection for petite girls, he grinned, but quickly grimaced, seeing next, those ankles supporting thick hambone calves, leading to portly thighs, buttressing enormous protruding buttocks, jiggling, jostling, and vigorously shifting from side to side under her wool skirt like two chubby children playing push and shove under a blanket. Her overhanging waist expanded over her thighs like lumpy gravy boiling out of a pot while her colossal breasts bumped all the way down each extra thick rung of her undoubtedly special-made, reinforced ladder. Standing before him in her full expansiveness, he noticed that the heaviness of her great bosom counterbalanced the weightiness of her grand buttocks. Her face was adorable, but round as a full moon with cheeks of rising dough accompanied by her licking her lips and a pleading look of, *'I art hungry.'* He foresaw rolling about with her on the riverbank where she would surely flatten him, leaving an exact imprint of his body in the sandy bank. Worse, she would undoubtedly guzzle most of the fine wine and gobble nearly all of the aged cheese before he could swirl, sniff, and taste his first sip of wine.

He shook the vision of such ravenous corpulence out of his head and snapped, "Climbeth back up! Resumeth thy work!"

She squeaked, "As thee biddeth, Sir Botwolf."

He kicked his steed and trotted two rows over and three trees down, where he spotted another maiden up in a tree. He commanded, "Cometh hither from my tree! Doeth as I, Sir Botwolf sayeth!"

"Yea, I shall cometh to thee," replied a woman in a husky voice prompting him to swallow hard, wondering if indeed, she was a she or indeed, she was a he.

Long, lanky, and nimble, she swung down out of the tree using branches instead of her ladder to drop square on both feet. Coarse black hair covered her ankles and arms. Black bushy eyebrows in need of a gardener hedged across her forehead while her black hair frizzed out like a parched briar bush. She had the features of a man, a man with small pointy breasts.

"Art thou," asked Sir Botwolf, "a woman? Or, art thou a man?"

"A lady," she replied in a masculine voice while batting her eyes.

He visualized taking her to the river and lying down with her, kissing, embracing, and touching—only to discover that she had lied. Not believing her, he retorted, "Climbeth back up! Resumeth thy work!"

She replied, "As thee biddeth, Sir Botwolf," as she grabbed a limb and pulled herself up into the tree.

Frustrated, he scrutinized the rows of trees, then sulked not seeing any other young maidens around. He pulled the reins to trot away when he stopped, hearing a lovely melodic song drifting amongst the trees. The notes floated into his ears and ignited his desire like a short fuse to a mound of gunpowder. He yanked the reins and pointed his horse toward the sound. His eyes searched the leafy canopies as his elongated nose sniffed the air while he ran his hand down his long waxy beard to rest it firm against his thigh. He listened until his ears directed his head focusing his eyes on a movement in a tree one row over. He kicked his horse over to that tree, spied a singing young maiden high up in the branches, and called out, "Oh, singing maiden, cometh hither from my tree. I wish a word with thee!"

The maiden, startled, abruptly stopped singing and peeked down through the leaves at the man. Though she had never seen

Sir Botwolf up close, she knew it to be him. Though fearful, she summoned her courage, replying curtly, "What word would thou wish to speak to me? I am busy picking thine olives to assure thy wealth to keepeth thee in fine clothes and riding upon a strong steed." She recalled her mother's words she had heard countless times, 'Adora, you and Purita must be leery of Sir Botwolf, the son of Lord Fourth. He is evil and only seekest to satisfy his lust. Hideth from him. If he desireth you, never giveth in to him. I feareth for thee both for if ever his eyes should falleth upon thee and his desire is setteth afire—no one can saveth ye.'

Sir Botwolf, impatient, retorted, "Cometh hither! I commandeth thee!"

"Thee may not speaketh to me with such arrogance," she said, climbing higher in the tree to hide her beauty behind the leaves, "for thee art not my king!" She turned away from him and leaned out to tap a branch, knocking olives to the ground.

He maneuvered his horse under the tree and peered up at her. His eyes like leeches latched on to her smooth shapely ankles, then crawled like spiders up her long legs to focus like a hawk on her sublime buttocks in her tight fitting skirt. He swallowed hard forcing down a lump of slimy lust and remarked, "I hope thy face is as glorious as thy body!" Then, he threatened, "Cometh down now! Or thee shalt lose thy wage!"

Climbing higher up her ladder, she replied, "If so, my loving father and mother will taketh care of me."

Sir Botwolf said with confidence, "Then, they too shall lose their wage!"

Adora knew that if her and her family lost their work harvesting olives for Lord Fourth that they would lose their cottage and that Lord Fourth would warn the other olive growers not to employ them. She wished she were a sparrow hopping to the highest twig on the tallest branch then flying away to hide in a fluffy cloud quietly drifting across the vast blue sky;

however, cornered, feeling like a lamb in a slaughtering chute, she reluctantly climbed down the ladder. Keeping her head down and hiding her face behind her hair, she stood before Sir Botwolf sitting kingly upon his majestic horse and smelling of sickening sweet cologne.

"Brush back thy hair," he commanded, "and looketh up at me!"

Wincing, she did as he bade.

As his eyes beheld her breathtaking beauty: her glorious hair framing her heavenly face, her vivid eyes, her silky skin, her full lips, her ample bosom, her tiny waist, and her shapely hips, the demon dwelling within his soul gasped, then squeezed his brain, tickled his sides, pumped his lungs like a foot organ, and beat his heart like a sacrificial drum.

Sir Botwolf, mesmerized, out of breath, and dizzy, stuttered, "Beauti-ti-ful maiden, what is-is thy name?"

She glanced away, distraught. Unable to hide her beauty, she replied faintly, "My name is Adora."

"How beautiful is thy name," he said. "Adora, Adora, Adora. I like the way it tickles and then rolls off my tongue." He saw sunlit diamonds glinting in her emerald-jeweled eyes and witnessed her sensuous tongue flicker across her full lips leaving a luscious sheen. He focused on her skin and thought, so dark, so smooth, so perfect, and how soft it must be to touch. Captivated, he watched beads of sweat gather, then drip off her brow onto her bosom to trickle down her cleavage. He craved her, prompting him to blurt out, "My dear little olive picker, please cometh out of the hot sun and cooleth down in the river with me where we shall drink costly wine paired with superb cheese and laugh until nightfall."

She turned away while raking olives into a large pail and said plainly, "Nay, I cannot, for I wouldst be beholden to thee."

He nudged his snorting horse closer, forcibly pushing her back. Wearing a smile of shrewd poise, he barked, "Looketh at me! Telleth me who thee turn thy back on! I want to be perfectly certain that thee knoweth with whom thee speaketh. Speaketh my name!"

She jumped at his loud words, turned, glared up at him, and said, "Yea, thou art Sir Botwolf, son of Lord Fourth, for whom my family toileth."

He killed his grin, leaned over, offered her a hand up, and said, "Good, since I am convinced thee knoweth who I am, rideth on my horse with me to the river, drinketh wine with me, bath with me, and lay with me on the soft sandy bank."

"Again, I sayeth, nay, I cannot, for I wouldst be beholden to thee."

"Then, thee shalt dine with me tonight at my palace where we shalt feast on roasted pheasant and quail. I shall ... ."

"Nay, I cannot, for I wouldst be beholden to thee."

"I shall employ musicians and thee and I shall waltz until dawn."

"Nay, I cannot, for I wouldst be beholden to thee."

Sir Botwolf exploded, "No matter how many times you sayeth, 'nay, for I wouldst be beholden to thee,' listen to me— thou shalt be mine!" He jerked the reins of his horse, kicked it, and rode away cursing aloud.

Although his foul fragrance still hung in the air, Adora exhaled a long sigh of relief.

A middle-aged woman, Fortunia, who had been hiding and watching from up in a nearby olive tree, climbed down and hurried over to Adora, asking her, "Adora, dear girl, art thee well?"

Twenty years ago, Fortunia had been the prettiest woman in the olives who after having a child out of wedlock, married, Crulion Tortoro, the meanest man in the olives. She settled for him so that her son had a father and a name. Though the older woman's face was wrinkled from many years in the sun and her hair had streaks of gray and her body had lost its curves, she still retained a splash of beauty in her big brown eyes, absorbing the sunlight while reflecting the soul of whomever she gazed upon for her deep sadness and shame made for an understanding heart.

Adora did not respond to Fortunia immediately, but continued watching Sir Botwolf ride away down the road. When he disappeared over a far away hill, she turned, faced the older woman, and said, "Yea, I am well, now that he is gone. I hope that is the last I seeth of Sir Botwolf. He is not a man—but a demon."

"Thou knoweth his reputation. He shalt return and wilt never cease until he has had his way with you. Do as he biddeth and thy only hope is that once he hath had his merriment, he shalt becometh bored and casteth thee aside. Only, hopeth that thee art not with his child, for then, thee shall forever be spurned by all."

"Nay, never! I shall never giveth in to him. I wouldst rather drowneth myself in the river."

"I praise thy courage; nevertheless, nay shall thy liveth to ever be beholden to another if thee do not pleaseth him. Though thy mother and thy father telleth thee of his wickedness, I shall telleth thee more. When Botwolf was just eleven, he carveth a hole in the bathhouse wall to peepeth in at the naked chambermaids. He threatened them with lies to his father lest they pleasure him. They dideth as he demandeth. During his puberty, his lust snatched his soul and he did unspeakable things, and as a young man Botwolf expected that another man should sacrifice his wife, sister, or daughter or in some cases even his mother if Botwolf so desired her. Wielding bribes, blackmail, bodily harm, and murder—he fulfilleth all his desires."

"Yea," whispered Adora, wide-eyed and trembling, "I heareth many tales of his evil."

"Sir Botwolf," continued Fortunia, "once had a younger brother, Sir Favorel who was kind, hardworking, and a righteous young man. Lord Fourth passed over his eldest son, Botwolf, and chose Favorel to be next in line to lordeth over the olive business. Botwolf was envious of his brother and loathed him. One of the olive pickers, I knoweth whom, but I am sworn never to tell, was gathering mushrooms near the woods when she spied young Botwolf picking poisonous berries. The next day, again whilst gathering mushrooms, she saw the two brothers as they hunteth quail. The boys stoppeth to eat and Botwolf gaveth Favorel a baked tart. Favorel quickly ate it, clutcheth his throat, and falleth to the ground. Botwolf draggeth his brother, sick and paralyzed deep into the woods to a low cliff above a den of vicious wolves with hungry pups. Favorel screamed and begged for mercy, but Botwolf rolled him over the edge, and then fled with nay a glance back. An old chambermaid at the palace telleth me the story that Botwolf told Lord Fourth, 'Dearest Father, wolves hath killed Favorel. I could not saveth him.' Lord Fourth killeth every wolf and burneth the half-eaten body of Favorel. Since that day, Lord Fourth hath always spoiled Botwolf—his only son."

Adora said, "How could a man killeth his brother?"

"Yea," agreed Fortunia, "worse, how could a man killeth his mother? Botwolf's mother, Lady Faine hateth her son's debauchery and forewarneth his soon to be victims of his vile intentions. Botwolf loathed his mother. A palace gardener, again, whom I cannot name, saw mother and son arguing in the rose garden. He overheard her threaten to shippeth him abroad to live with her strict brother when Botwolf in a fit of insane fury grabbeth his mother around her throat and strangled her. Out in the orchard, a few olive pickers hidden amongst the trees saw him hideth his mother's body beneath the clippings, dead limbs, and downed trees, then lighteth a bonfire. He watched it burneth, smiling. The old chambermaid heard Botwolf lie to his father, saying, 'Dearest Father, mother hath grown weary of thy constant work. Whilst thee are away, she hath engageth a young and handsome lover to satisfy her fancies. This morning, she kisseth me on my forehead without shedding a tear and bid me farewell, then departeth in a carriage with her new lover.' Lord Fourth grinned, Botwolf grinned, and that very night, father and son threw a costume ball."

Adora said, "Such evil men. I pray that Sir Botwolf doth not stealeth away my virtue."

"I too pray for thee, for as all knoweth, he stole away my virtue twenty-two years ago and leaveth me with child. I regret that I giveth in to his demands for I wouldst rather have died—until I thinketh of my son. I seeth him not as the son of Sir Botwolf, but so kind and so good is my son, I see him as a gift from Heaven. My son knoweth of his father; however, his father knoweth not of his son."

Without another word, both women returned to picking olives. Adora trembled as she worked. Encountering Sir Botwolf and hearing the stories of his evil filled her mind with horrific visions of a smelly and slobbering Sir Botwolf ravaging her body. Shaking and breathing fearfully, she nearly fainted and fell out of the tree.

As Sir Botwolf rode his horse toward his palace, his every thought of Adora fed his craving for her while the same thoughts stoked his fury.

Adora moved to the next tree, shaking limbs and picking olives, all the while glancing over her shoulder at the far off hill in case Sir Botwolf appeared. Every time she looked and he was not coming, she relaxed more and more until she glanced out to see him galloping back over the hill. Her heart sunk as a feeling of dread drenched her spirit.

Sir Botwolf rode to where he had left Adora, saw Fortunia, trotted over to her, and yelled, "Where is Adora? Tell me now!"

Fortunia kept silent.

"Where—is—she?" he demanded, grabbing from his saddle his coiled whip, unfurling it, and cracking it across Fortunia's face. She cried out in pain, her face bleeding, as he shouted, "You look familiar, what is thy name?"

She stopped crying, glared up at him, and said, "Fortunia."

"Ahhh, yes, Fortunia. I remember thee. Many, many years ago, thee were once a beautiful woman, who if I recall, greatly pleased me, but now," he chortled, "thou have become gray and wrinkled and I seeth that thee have never turned away a meal. I must confess though, you still haveth enchanting eyes. Someday, I may cometh again for thee. For now—where is Adora?"

Fortunia did not answer. Adora, trembling with fear, hid higher amongst the olive branches.

Sir Botwolf yelled, "Adora! I wilst floggeth this old woman, until thee cometh down from thy tree!"

There was no answer from Adora as Fortunia screamed, "Leaveth her alone! She shalt never be beholden to thee!"

He raised his arm and cracked the whip again across Fortunia's face, saying, "I may not want to seeth thee again, for thy face wilst be covered in scars if thou doth not tell me wherest she hideth."

"Stop thy brutality and thy wickedness!" yelled Adora climbing down from her tree as Fortunia, sobbing, collapsed to the ground.

Sir Botwolf saw Adora, kicked his horse, and raced up to her, dismounting from his horse before it halted. He then dropped his whip and grabbed her shoulders shoving her hard up against the tree. Face to face, shaking her violently, he yelled, "Adora, thee igniteth my desire! Yet, thee inciteth my fury!"

Paralyzed with fear, her eyes wide, she stared silently back at him; his wild eyes and furious face appearing devilish shadowed by the rim of his hat.

Seeing her horror, he closed his eyes, drew in a few deep breaths, and cleared his throat, composing himself. He then, opened his eyes, let go of his grip, took a step back, turned, and strolled over to his horse where he reached into a saddlebag and pulled out a small red velvet sack. As Fortunia lay on the ground crying and Adora stood trembling at the tree, he hurried back to Adora. Smiling a toothy grin and smoothly stroking his beard all the way down to the crotch of his tight pants, intentionally doing so to bring attention to the size and shape of his lumpy loins appearing like a dead bunny stuffed in a hunting sack, he said sweetly, "Adora, I have presents for thee. See?" He pulled out a little crystal bottle, wiggled it like a tiny bell in front of her eyes, and said, "It is very expensive perfume." Then, out of the same sack, he drew out a sparkling necklace and waving it in front of her face, said, "And I have jewelry made of precious gemstones for thee, if only thou wouldst embrace me with thy beauty, these gifts shall both be thine."

Adora refused his gifts, stating, "Nay, nay, nay! I cannot, for I wouldst be beholden to thee."

Sir Botwolf exploded, mocking her in her feminine voice, "'I wouldst be beholden to thee! I wouldst be beholden to thee!'" He then roared in fury, which rang out across the grove for all the other workers to hear, "Adora! Thou Shalt Be Mine!"

Birds flew away, butterflies vanished, a snappy breeze swirled through, and the sun hid behind a cloud.

Far across the grove, twenty-year-old, Errondo worked the harvest at the top of a hill. While loading large and heavy pails of olives in a horse drawn wooden wagon, he heard Sir Botwolf's booming threat. His eyes scanned the rolling hills of olive trees and saw a flock of frightened crows take flight. Knowing the reputation of Sir Botwolf and very much aware of Adora's breathtaking beauty, and fearing the worst, he dropped his brimming buckets of olives and ran toward the sound of Sir Botwolf's voice.

Errondo wasn't tall nor short, wasn't extremely handsome nor the least bit ugly, wasn't the most entertaining nor the most boring; he wasn't richer than any other olive worker nor going any further beyond the olive grove than them, and the cottage he lived in with his parents and two younger brothers wasn't different set amidst the same hills of similar cottages amongst the same wildflowers upon Fourhills; furthermore, like every other man working the olives, he had golden skin, dark brown eyes, a sinewy and strong body, wore simple clothes of wool, and dangled his long black hair tied in a ponytail during a day's toil. All in all, he was not much different from any other olive grove worker; however, none of them were as kind, patient, and caring as he. None were more generous than he, none more respectful and hardworking as he, and none, though they all desired Adora as much as he, had her affections as he, for he loved her as she loved him with every breath, thought, and feeling, showing their love for each other with their words, their arms, their lips, their hearts, and their souls.

Sir Botwolf, shaking, barely holding down the steam on his roiling fury, said, offering to Adora, "Sojourn with me to the city and we will … ."

"Nay," she cut him short, "I cannot, for I wouldst be beholden to thee!"

"If thee say, yea, I wilst give thy family many farm animals."

"Nay."

"A magnificent cottage overlooking the kingdom."

"Nay."

"A holiday by the sea?"

"Nay!"

"Please, desireth me," he whined, "enfoldeth me with thy nakedness."

"Sir Botwolf," she snapped, "what might thee thinketh be my answer?"

"I know, I KNOW, I KNOW, what be thy answer! It be, 'nay, for thee cannot be beholden to me!' Hear this, Adora! Thou shall not rejecteth me, Sir Botwolf Ziegenhorn the Fifth, son of Lord Fourth, owner of the largest grove of olives in the entire kingdom. Nothing in this world can stoppeth me for I taketh whom I desire—and my desire dear little girl—is for thee. If thou *not* cometh with me, thy mother and thy father shalt vanish, thy family cottage shalt burn, and thy livestock shalt be slaughtered. Thou knowest I speakest the truth."

Adora replied, "Thou for once hath spake the truth! Indeed, a horrifying threat that it is, even so, I say, nay, never, thee wicked man! I cannot, for I wouldst be beholden to thee!"

At that moment, Adora's younger sister, Purita, shivering, frightened, and hiding, peeked out from behind the twisted trunk of an old olive tree in the row next to them.

Sir Botwolf caught a glimpse of her, snapped his head around, and focused his narrowing eyes upon her. Though her face was contorted in terror, her innocence shone brighter than the sunlight glistening upon her long golden hair, compelling Sir Botwolf to ask, "So who is this tasty young morsel of pleasure?"

Neither sister answered him, so he threw the perfume, jewelry, and red velvet sack to the ground, unsheathed his dagger, stomped a few steps toward Purita, and bellowed, "What is thy name?"

Terrified, Adora's younger sister stammered in her angelic voice, "Pur...Pur...Purita. Adora is...is my sister."

He faced Adora and snarled, "Adora—lay with me! Say that thee wilst, for if thee deny me—I wilst taketh and lie with thy tender little sister, Purita!"

Adora's glowing beauty hid beneath her scowl and with surging rage, forgoing her melodic singing voice, she screamed, "If thou dare touch Purita, I shall waiteth until the darkest hour of the night, then sneaketh into thy palace and into thy bedchamber where I wilt silently stand above thy slumber and when thee taketh a long breath and I heareth a snore, I will draweth my knife and slitteth thy throat."

He clenched his jaws, grinding his teeth, and then growled,

"Slitteth my throat! Slitteth my throat? How dare thee threaten me, when I am the one standing here holding this very sharp knife! Why, oh why doest thee stoketh my anger. Doth thee not knoweth what I wilst do when I do not receiveth my heart's desire?"

She answered, "I knoweth thy evil hath no bounds."

Sir Botwolf started soft and low, "Hither or thither, the place doth not matter," his words increased in volume, "today or tomorrow, the time doth not matter," and then he shouted, "whether thou art willing or thou art not—Adora, thou shalt be mine!"

"Sir Botwolf, in this life," she replied with firm resolve, "thou shalt never possesseth my body nor my heart for I'll wilst never be beholden to thee."

Her words incited in him an uncontrollable rage, turning his stormy eyes cyclonic as his face twisted into a tempest gusting into verbal thunder, "Why! Adora, why? Why cannot thee be beholden to me?"

"I cannot," stated Adora calmly and undeterred, "not only because I loathe thee and see thy charming and handsome elegance as repulsive; and not only because thy vanity makest thee ugly and thy obsessive desires makest thee insane; I cannot be beholden to thee because … ." She stopped speaking, fearful that if she told him why—he would kill her.

"Telleth me! Why cannot thee be beholden to me?"

"Sir Botwolf, I will telleth thee." She drew in a deep breath and let the words slowly tumble out on her exhale, "I cannot be beholden to thee because—I am beholden to another." She then told Purita, "Little sister, get thee back to work," then pointed her petite nose in the air, turned her back on Sir Botwolf, and resumed working.

Still clutching his knife, he grabbed Adora by her shoulders, spun her around, and snarled, "Beholden to another? Beholden to another! It doth not matter to me if thou art beholden to another. I hath found that these 'anothers' are easy to be rid of. Who is this 'another' whom thee art beholden to?"

"It is I," said a manly voice stepping out from behind an olive tree, "Errondo."

Sir Botwolf whipped around and thrust his dagger out ready to fight. Seeing Errondo, he laughed, saying, "Adora, thou art beholden to a poor and soiled picker, when thou couldst have me, the richest and handsomest man in the kingdom?"

"Yea," said Adora, "he is my first love; my only love until I die. We shareth our childhood together on Fourhills and have together toileth in the sun and rain most every day of our lives. He is the first man I hath kissed and wilt be the only man to knoweth the secrets of my body. Soon, we shall marry. So again I sayeth, nay, I cannot go with you, accepteth thy gifts, or lay with you for I am beholden to Errondo; to him only—until the day I shalt die."

Without hesitation, Sir Botwolf faced Adora and took a step closer to her. With his face red and twisted in anger, he shouted, "Until the day thee shalt die? Until the day thee shalt die? Adora, today shalt be the day that thee shalt die!" Without a second thought and without giving Errondo the heroic chance to save her, he swiftly, fluidly raked his dagger's sharp edge across her soft throat, splattering her blood across his scarlet surcoat.

Errondo, Purita, and Fortunia gasped in horror. Other pickers, hiding, peeking from behind trees, gasped.

Adora clutched her throat with both hands as blood gushed between her fingers. She choked, struggled to breathe, and then staggered two steps to where Errondo met her and caught her, gently lowering her to the ground. Fortunia ran to her side, removed her scarf, and tied it around Adora's neck. Purita, casting away all fear of Sir Botwolf, ran to her sister, screaming, "Adora, Adora!"

Sir Botwolf raised his bloody dagger into the air to stab

Errondo in the back. Purita saw him and screamed. Errondo arose, spun, and stopped the dagger's downward thrust by grabbing the wrist of Sir Botwolf's knife wielding hand.

Sir Botwolf, possessing fighting skills with decades of practice had the superior advantage. With his left fist, he punched Errondo twice in the face, then with the same hand, he clutched Errondo's throat, violently shoving him up against the same tree where Adora had just had her throat slashed. Since Errondo's strength lie within his upper chest and biceps from lifting and toting heavy pails of olives and working the levers on the olive oil presses, he grabbed the other wrist of Sir Botwolf and easily yanked it off his throat. Face to face, sweat beading on each man's brow and the sharp knife between them, the two men struggled. Sir Botwolf maneuvered the point of the dagger above Errondo's chest. Errondo's strength kept the knife a few inches away. They clenched their teeth, furrowed their brows, wrenched their faces, and flexed their muscles as Sir Botwolf fought to kill Errondo and Errondo fought for his life.

After a moment of locked strength, Sir Botwolf smirked while letting up on the pressure. His move threw Errondo off balance. Without hesitation, Sir Botwolf dropped the stabbing angle down while leaning his entire body weight on the hilt of the dagger, pushing the knife into Errondo's belly.

Fortunia screamed. Purita shrieked.

Errondo, with eyes wide and mouth gaping, dropped to his knees.

Sir Botwolf pulled him up with one hand gripping his shoulder and the other hand lifting the hilt of the dagger, then yanked out the knife and stabbed him again pushing the knife in deeper. He then jerked the blade out of Errondo's gut, wiped the blood off on Errondo's shirt, and slid it in its sheath.

Errondo again dropped to his knees, peered up at Sir Botwolf, and said, "Fortunia is my mother. Thou art my father. Thou hath killeth thy son."

Sir Botwolf only laughed, saying, "My son? Ha! I killeth just another bastard!"

Errondo crawled on his hands and knees over to lie next to Adora and collapsed on his back. Staring up at the blue sky, he whispered. "I loveth thee Adora with all my heart and I know thee loveth me with all thine heart. After we perish, we shalt embrace in paradise."

Adora, sprawled out on her back, nodded her head while continuing to stare up at the blue sky, though not at the sky above her, but the blue sky above her and Errondo during their spring picnics to a quiet meadow deep in the woods. It was a secluded place of green new grasses splashed with wildflowers far away from the olive grove and even farther away from the picker's plots of Fourhills. A spot so peaceful, she would whisper to Errondo, "Doth thee not heareth a sound?" "Yea," he would whisper, "I heareth a sound," prompting her to say, "And what sound heareth thee, my love?" To which he would lean in, kiss her softly, and say, "Tis the sound of butterfly wings and the beating of my heart." With her lifeblood ebbing away, she thought of the lost life she would have lived with Errondo, in their little worker's cottage with their happy children and of nights by the fire and sleeping next to each other and of all the ways to love another for a lifetime.

Fortunia sobbed, kneeling between them. Purita, wailing hysterically, held the scarf tight around Adora's neck. The fearful workers gathered around, yet kept a safe distance from Sir Botwolf.

Sir Botwolf, proud of his deed, stood smiling over Adora and Errondo. He leaned down, grabbed Purita around her small waist, snatched her up, and carried her screaming and kicking over to his horse. He held her tightly, easily tossed her up to lay across his saddle, and then growled, "Thee are coming with me little girl down to the river where I shall teacheth thee about a man."

Adora's father Happlio and her mother Lovisa along with Fortunia's husband Crulion, Errondo's stepfather arrived at the gruesome scene. They saw Adora and Errondo covered with blood and Purita crying, lying facedown across Sir Botwolf's steed.

Lovisa hurried to Adora as Happlio and Crulion charged Sir Botwolf.

As Sir Botwolf lifted a leg to mount his horse, he heard shuffling feet rushing from behind. He spun, drawing his knife as both men shoved him so hard up against his horse, his peacock feathered, velvet hat flew off his head and fell to the ground. The startled horse bucked, kicking Sir Botwolf in the side knocking him to the ground.

Purita slid off the bolting horse, tumbled to the ground, jumped up, and ran to her mother who was now kneeling and sobbing over Adora. The two enraged fathers dove on top of Sir Botwolf.

Sir Botwolf swiped at them with the dagger. The men held it away. In the struggle, Crulion braced a knee on top of Sir Botwolf's fancy hat, grinding it into the dirt, prompting Sir Botwolf to yell, "Get thee off my costly hat!" driving him to fight with greater ferocity; however, the combined strength of both men shifted the knife around to point down at his wicked heart. During the scuffle, Sir Botwolf's beard became tangled around the hilt of his dagger to where he could not move it far from his chest without great pain to his chin. He resisted, yet their determination moved the knife gradually closer until the sharp point clipped a silver button off his scarlet surcoat, tore through the threads of his rosy ruffled shirt, and then pricked his skin causing a trickling of blood to stain his fanciful clothes. Furthermore, Happlio inadvertently placed one knee square in the crotch of Sir Botwolf crushing it like a sack of freshly picked mushrooms.

Sir Botwolf groaned in agony. Knowing that his own

strength was waning, he moaned, "Ye men are strong and hath greater cause to killeth me. I lost my favorite hat. Ye lost a loved one. My own dagger wilst soon piercest my heart."

Crulion spat, "Yea, and thou shalt burn in Hell!"

Happlio growled, "Yea, and thou shalt ... shalt ... ." Without thinking of something clever to say, he simply repeated Crulion's phrase, "Yea, and thou shalt burn in Hell!"

Of course, the arrogance of Sir Botwolf could not let another, especially two lowly olive pickers take his life, so he not only let go of his resistance, but also, with all his remaining strength pulled the dagger deep into his heart. The full weight of the two surprised men pushed it in all the way to its hilt. Sir Botwolf gasped, his mouth gaping and eyes bulging, then drew in a long painful breath and bellowed, "I vow this!—Adora, thou shalt be mine!" He then took three ragged breaths and died still clutching the hilt of the dagger.

Adora heard his resounding threat, drew in her last breath, closed her eyes, and died.

Lovisa, Purita, and Fortunia wailed. The olive pickers murmured; some wept.

Happlio and Crulion stood up and slowly backed away from the blood soaked corpse of Sir Botwolf. Speechless, they stared down at their hands covered in his blood and dreaded what Lord Fourth would do to them in all his grief, anger, and vengeance.

Errondo, weak from losing blood, lay there under the sun, his life ebbing out of him with every heartbeat. He stretched out his hand to touch Adora's fingers and said, "Adora, my dearest, didst thou hearest Sir Botwolf before thee didst die? He cometh for thee; cometh to stealeth thy virtue. I say unto thee, fear not, for soon, I shalt be where thou art. I pray, I shall not be too late." He grimaced in pain. More buzzards circled ever lower in the sky. Impatient, longing to die, he cried out, "My Creator! I do not want to live without Adora! Please, I beggeth, Thee! Taketh me now!"

Errondo heard the galloping hoof beats of a horse followed by the booming voice of Sir Botwolf's father, Lord Fourth, roaring, "Why are ye not picking olives? What hath happened?" Lord Fourth quickly dismounted and seeing Botwolf lying with a dagger stuck deep in his crimson chest, moaned, "Botwolf! Oh, Botwolf, my son! Thou art dead!" Then exclaimed, "Poor Adora. Thou art dead too!" Then stated, "Errondo, I seeth thy breath. Art thee alive?"

"Yea," whispered Errondo, "I am alive, my lord."

Lord Fourth, his teary eyes flashing with anger, marched back to his horse, drew his longsword sheathed to the saddle, and stomped back to Errondo. He grabbed Errondo's mother by an arm and flung her away from her dying son, and then put the sharp point of the sword to Errondo's chest, and demanded, "Tell me Errondo! Tell me, what hath happened?"

"Thy son," Errondo moaned, "hath killed Adora."

"Yea," spat Lord Fourth, "and then, in thy vengeance, did thee not killeth my son?"

Errondo began to say, 'Nay, I did not killeth thy son', telling Lord Fourth the truth, but then, thinking of Adora's threatened virtue, and concerned for his stepfather, Crulion and Adora's father Happlio, he changed his mind, boldly saying between each laboring breath, "Yea—I killeth—thy son."

Errondo's mother crawled on her knees to the feet of Lord Fourth and pleaded, "Please, my lord, let my son live!"

Crulion and Happlio stepped forward to confess the truth, but were too late, as Lord Fourth snarled, "Then—I too shalt have my revenge," thrusting his gleaming blade into Errondo's heart.

In the King's garden, up in the tower, Adora heard the bells toll and the festive music play again. She hummed along with the bright melody while dancing a few steps to a lively jig her mother had taught her, and then strolled across the landing to leave the tower. Three steps down the staircase, she stopped, startled, her peace and wellbeing shattered, encountering a charred, barefoot man with coal like skin, a soggy short beard, dripping hair, and wearing a wet and sooty sackcloth robe. Since he was taller and two steps down, and she was shorter and two steps up, they faced each other eye to eye. Colliding on the shadowy side of the tower made the encounter more alarming. Frightened, she stumbled back upward a step. Grinning, the hideous man tramped up a step. She backed up two more steps. He, now drooling spittle thick with the smell of sulfur, took two steps up. His bloodshot eyes grew round and twinkled savagely while his mischievous grin widened into a grotesque smile. He grabbed for her. Horrified, she spun and raced across the landing. He pursued, seizing her by her shoulders, twisting her around, and slamming her hard against the parapet wall. She opened her mouth to scream, but he clutched her throat with his blackened hands and squeezed off the sound. Trembling, gasping for air, she peered up into his face. Her heart sank. The beastly man was Sir Botwolf.

Sir Botwolf knew that she knew that he was he. He laughed wryly, and then spoke, "Adora, Adora, Adora. My, my, my, how I like the way thy name rolls off and tickles my tongue. Didst thee thinketh death wouldst keep us apart? Thinketh thee not, for my dear sweet, Adora, as I vowed, thou shalt be mine!"

She struggled, wriggling to free herself and fought, pounding him in his chest with both fists. He chuckled, enjoying his power over her until she punched him squarely under the chin. He reacted to the blow by slamming her against the wall harder than the first time. Dazed, she winced and stopped resisting. He breathed in her sweet scent with a long inhale through his nose, and then exhaled, rolling back his eyes in ecstasy. Leaning in close, gazing into her emerald eyes; bright eyes reflecting his smirking face, he demanded, "Now, a kiss from thee!" His ravenous senses devoured her beauty as he seized her hair with one hand and jerked back her head exposing her luscious lips. Pressing his filthy body up against hers, soiling her white gown, he kissed her against her will, his glistening slobber dripping off their chins.

His lips felt like tree bark and his tongue a rough stone while his breath smelled of stagnant pond water and he reeked of smoldering refuse. Repulsed, gagging, she squirmed and shook her head attempting to avoid his mouth.

Sir Botwolf, moaning and groaning, pulled her hair tighter and kissed her harder, bruising her lips. Then, he let go of her hair, yanking her in closer while his arms, like the coils of an enormous snake, wrapped around her body constricting her breath and movements.

She pleaded, wheezing, "Please, thou hurteth me. I beggeth thee, stop!"

Lost in ecstasy, ignoring her plea, his groping, grabbing, and crushing only increased, as did his groaning, moaning, and slobbering.

She cried out, "Please, I beggeth thee, do not stealeth away my virtue!"

He relaxed his grip, threw back his head, and laughed hysterically, saying, "Please, do not stoppeth thy groveling—it exciteth me!"

As he laughed, she slipped both hands up and out of his grasp, and then raked her fingernails down both sides of his pompous face, peeling off flakes of blackened skin. He released his hold on her, covering his stinging face with both hands as she ducked under his arms and escaped toward the staircase.

Sir Botwolf, furious, trailed a few steps behind her. She raced down the steps around and around the tower. He stumbled, tumbling, rolling, and bouncing down the stairs behind her. She leapt off the last two steps and made a dash toward the bridge leading to the palace. He flew over the last three steps, hitting the ground hard, and then jumped up, chasing a few paces behind her, swiping and stretching out his hands to catch her. They ran across a small meadow covered in clover and tiny pink wildflowers where he snatched her by one of her flailing arms, tackled her to the ground, and then flipped her over on her back.

She screamed, "Help!" followed by a piercing shriek. Deer darted, birds fluttered, and squirrels scurried. All the joyful people on the other side of the river near the palace fountain heard the peace shattering call for help.

The King heard it too.

Errondo awoke in the garden sprawled out on his back. Hearing Adora's shrieking cry for help, he sprang to his feet and raced down the knoll to the fountain and statues. He paused for a moment, listening, confused as to where he was. His senses absorbed his surroundings: the flowers, the trees, the statues, and the fountain with its glimmering water. He knew he was in the King's garden. Looking down, he was surprised he wore new leather sandals, and a white shirt and breeches made of silk and fitting perfectly. He yelled, "Adora! Adora! Wherest art thou?"

Adora fought Sir Botwolf with her all her feminine might. He reared back and slapped her across her face. She started to scream, but he covered her mouth with his dirty hand.

Errondo stood still, listening, waiting for her next scream.

Sir Botwolf, groaning, drooling, removed his hand from her mouth, grabbed the hem of her silken dress, and yanked it hard, ripping it up to her thighs. On his knees, capturing both of her hands by her wrists, he pinned her to the ground, then leaned in close, gawking at her delightful face.

Feeling his hot panting breaths on her stinging red face, she stopped writhing, looked up at his repulsiveness, and cried out, "Please! I beg of thee, do not stealeth my virtue."

A large glistening tear trickled down her cheek. He tilted

even closer to lick the shiny droplet off her cheek and then sighed with a shutter, muttering, "Ooooh, even thy tears exciteth me!"

Adora screamed.

Errondo raced toward the sound, running down the steppingstones, passing a red tree with purple fruit and pink flowers with yellow stamen.

Sir Botwolf burst into a frenzy. With all of his lust boiling and bubbling out of his soul, he muttered, "Thou shalt be mine, thou shalt be mine, ohhh, at last Adora, thou shalt be mine!" He reached down with one hand and ripped open his filthy robe.

Adora, panic-stricken, shattered the air with three loud and long screams.

Errondo heard her screams, rounded the pine tree, saw a meadow between the tower and the trees, and at the center of this meadow, he saw a beastly creature on top of Adora. Running at full speed, he rammed the brute, knocking him off her.

Adora scrambled to her feet ready to flee, but seeing Errondo, she stopped and exclaimed, "Errondo!"

Both men rolled across the grass, then sprung to their feet to face one another.

Errondo growled, "Sir Botwolf!"

Sir Botwolf snarled, "Errondo," then slapped his side groping for his knife that he forgot was far away in a separate realm stuck deep into his chest.

Circling, Sir Botwolf hissed, "So now, Errondo, thee art hither! I wondered how long thy blood wouldst seep. Thou hath stopped me for a moment, but not for eternity." He peered over at Adora and said, "Forever, Adora, my Adora, knowest this, thou shalt be mine! Tomorrow and every day forward, I shalt partake of thy virtue."

With raging fury, Errondo shouted, "Adora, shalt *not*—be thine!" He charged Sir Botwolf, wrestling him to the ground, then climbed on top of him, balled up both fists, and punched him countless times, breaking every bone in Sir Botwolf's face. He then grabbed Sir Botwolf's head and with all of his new found strength, twisted it, snapping the neck, finally silencing him to never again say, 'Adora, thou shalt be mine.'

Errondo stated, "Botwolf, not only a poor olive picker, but a bastard son hath broken thy neck and silenced thee."

Sir Botwolf moaned for a few seconds, closed his eyes, and breathed his last breath. Tranquility returned to the garden of the everlasting sunrise.

Errondo stood as Adora leapt into his arms. He twirled her around with great joy. They gazed into each other's eyes for a long moment while gently touching each other's face hardly believing they were together again.

Adora said, "Errondo, thank thee for saving me. I was saddened by our horrible deaths, but now, I am happy that we are together in the King's garden. Let us turneth away from this grotesque corpse of Sir Botwolf and walketh across the bridge where there be a magnificent palace; a heavenly place filled with jubilant people."

"Yea," said Errondo, "where we shall live in peace and joy for all eternity."

Hand in hand, they took a step to leave, when, from behind them, they heard a throaty, "Adooora! Thou—shalt—be—mine!"

Errondo and Adora spun around and saw Sir Botwolf standing, his face disfigured and swollen with his neck oddly cocked.

Adora muttered, "But, Sir Botwolf, thee—thee art dead!"

Sir Botwolf, grinning, proclaimed, "Only the fire of eternal death can slay my soul and those flames are far, far away. No one, including thy King can stoppeth me! So smile, Adora, my sweet Adora, for thou … ." Sir Botwolf stopped in mid sentence as his face turned serious. He commanded, "Adora, say what I am about to say! Thou shalt speak it!"

Both Adora and Errondo said together, "Nay, never!"

Sir Botwolf's volcanic face cracked into laughter. It then, just as quickly switched to clenched determination as he said, "Since I could say it for eternity, I will! Adora, thou shalt be mine! Thou shalt be mine. Thou—shalt—be—mine!"

Trumpets blared from the palace followed by a thunderous galloping of hoofs crossing the overarching bridge.

Sir Botwolf, Adora, and Errondo spun toward the sound as four riders appeared riding hard and fast. They were the same two men and two women depicted by the statues at the garden fountain; each a Protector of Everlasting Peace. All of them wore silken white garments and each portrayed a solemn face of justice, wielded a doubled-edged sword, and rode a mighty horse.

Immediately, the riders saw a man and woman dressed in white silk and a hideous creature in a sooty sackcloth robe. They easily surrounded Sir Botwolf, cutting off his escape.

A woman rider commanded him, "Lie on thy back!"

One of the men ordered, "Stretch out thy arms and legs!"

Sir Botwolf shouted, "Please, ride away, for I've done nothing wrong!"

Errondo and Adora backed up next to the tower, held each other, and watched.

The Protectors of Peace drew their swords.

The eyes of Sir Botwolf searched wildly for an escape. There was no way past the sharp and gleaming blades of steel. Defeated, he dropped to his knees, laid on his back, and stretched out his arms and legs, all the while groveling, "Pleeease, show me mercy. I am hurting—I was lonely—I was thirsty—It was my father's fault."

Ignoring his pleas, the riders dismounted and quickly shackled him with wrist and leg irons. A thick chain ran through his irons and up to a ring where four longer chains spanned out to latch onto their saddles. The Protectors smiled at Adora and Errondo, then, all at once, rode away dragging Sir Botwolf behind them.

Adora and Errondo ran up to the top of the tower, looked out, and watched them ride along the stone wall toward the mountains where they came upon two magnificent gates as tall as ten men and as lustrous as pearls. The glorious gates opened before them and they rode out of the garden galloping across the desolate land trailing Sir Botwolf bouncing and bumping in their black dust.

The Protectors dragged him to the precipice overlooking the chasm of fire. One of the men, held steady by the team of horses, repelled down the cliff while they also lowered by chain Sir Botwolf, dangling upside-down by his leg shackles. The riders obeyed the King's decree, 'Do not ye pitch him into the fires of eternal death; however, place ye him on a ledge nearest the fires so that he may writhe in agony till the end of time.' The Protector, with sweat upon his creased brow and with his silken clothes wet with perspiration, lowered himself onto a shelf closest to the fire where he took out a stake and a hammer from out of a leather pouch at his side. With great strength, he pounded the stake deep into the chasm wall and then attached a short chain from the stake through the manacles and fetters of Sir Botwolf. As the horses hoisted the Protector up and out of the abyss, Sir Botwolf wailed, begging, "Pleeease, show me mercy. I knew not what I was doing." Of course, just as Sir Botwolf had snubbed all the pleas of his countless victims, the Protectors ignored his.

The Protectors departed from the volcanic hell. Without the excess baggage of a soul laden with transgressions bouncing behind them over fissures and cinder cones, they quickly returned to the King's palace.

Adora and Errondo, smiling, left the tower, walking hand in hand. They felt a new and greater love for each other. Mysteriously adorned in new clothes and with their skin clean and soft, they strolled across the green meadow dotted with tiny pink wildflowers and over the high arcing stone bridge to meet the King and join in his glorious feast.

As it had been throughout eternity, the King's garden of the everlasting sunrise was once again peaceful. Others arrived to find themselves clothed in righteousness and greeted by the glory of eternal bliss.

Sir Botwolf stood chained on his cramped shelf protruding out just over the river of red-hot lava. Raging flames of fire eager to burn on his condemnation flared up and over the ledge. His skin was still charred, his hair still oily, his beard still scorched, his feet still bare, and the backside of his sooty sackcloth as well as the skin on his back were scraped off on his return trip to the fiery hell. Furthermore, his shattered face matched the knuckles on Errondo's fists and his broken neck cocked his head oddly to his left. Breathing raggedly, tasting hot sulfur, he peered out at the perpetual fires and undying, suffering souls, and cried out as he had cried out before, "Thirst tormenteth me; hunger torturest me; my skin stingeth, my eyes burneth, and each breath scaldeth my chest. Be it not a horrific, dreadful place, a terrible predicament, and an agonizing eternity?"

Souls shrieked, lava hissed, and whirlwinds whirred.

In the clamor of it all, he heard a familiar voice, the deep commanding voice of his father, Lord Fourth crying out, "Let me out! Let me out! I do not belongeth here with the damned!"

Sir Botwolf searched the shelves. Seeing his father in sackcloth, standing at the edge of a ledge a short distance away and above him, he shouted, "Father! Father!"

Lord Fourth, hearing his son's voice, peered down and saw Botwolf on a hot ledge down close to the raging fire and bellowed, "Son? Botwolf?"

"Yea, father, it is I! How didst thee cometh to be in this burning place of torment?"

"The olive pickers—all of them—taketh my sword and runneth me through!"

"Why, father? Why?"

"Because, I killeth Errondo!"

"So it was thee, who sent Errondo to paradise!"

"I killeth him. The pickers killeth me. I regret that I am hither and I regret that my sins befell upon thee, my son. I cannot suffer in this hot eternity. I have to end this. I will end this. Goodbye, Botwolf." He stepped off the ledge, burst into fire in flight, and plummeted into the lava, disappearing in a wisp of steam.

Sir Botwolf felt not a pang over his father's eternal death; though, he did feel furious learning that his father, by killing Errondo sooner than not, had spoiled his merriment with Adora. He thought of his own soul, knowing that he was damned to spend eternity hot, thirsty, and alone and that he had no hope of escape and no possibility of leaping to his eternal death. Feeling the ache of unsatisfied lust and the never-ending agony of his eternal fate, he yelled and yelled and yelled until his voice became permanently damaged and his already deformed face stiffened into a contorted expression of a yell. Grotesque and muttering blasphemies, he peered out through the ash, smoke, and warping heat and saw in the distance a ghastly creature rushing toward him, flying just above the hissing, bubbling channel of molten earth. Splashing globs of neither lava nor twirling tornadoes formed of fire, steam, and ash harmed it at all. The imposing beast, blood red in color, had the leathery wings of a mythical dragon, the face and teeth of a roaring lion, the tail of a deadly serpent, the skin of a scaly reptile, and the body, arms, and legs of a muscular man. The fiend flapped its great wings three times and then soared directly at Sir Botwolf to land on his shelf shoving him petrified up against the chasm wall. The beast towered over him and its outstretched wings enveloped him in darkness blocking out the light of the lava's eerie orange glow.

With the luminous eyes of a stalking lion at night, the hideous being spoke, whispering, nearly growling, "Botwolf, I knoweth thee. I am named Asmodeus, demon lord of lust and licentiousness. Since thy birth, I spake to thee in thy sleep."

In darkness under the cloak of its outstretched wings, Sir Botwolf peered up into its glowing eyes and feeling its hot breath searing his face, said, "Yea, I knoweth thy voice, my lord."

Asmodeus continued, "I whispered to thee shameless thoughts and thou didst dwelleth upon them, filling thy heart with wickedness until thy wicked heart beget lust and thy lust beget lies and thy lies beget pride and thy pride ruled as thy worshiped thyself. Thy terrible transgressions hath caused great grief in thy past life; hence, our lord shall bestow upon thee a new form and unbindeth thee from this place of torment. Thou shalt become an unseen shadow that creepeth in the other world, whispering thoughts of immorality and sowing seeds of iniquity into the hearts of men. What say thee?

Sir Botwolf stopped trembling with fear and with a toothy disfigured smile, answered, "If thee giveth thy servant a new form and setteth me free from this place of torment, I shalt, my lord, doeth as thy biddeth."

An honorable king, King Rothgar the Great sat upon his throne in a far away land of mist and bogs. Crowned at twenty-five-years-old, he had now reigned for twenty years, ruling with a fair hand, making his kingdom prosperous and his citizens happy. Tall, strong, and like most kings a bit round from over indulgence, he, unlike a good number of kings, sought wisdom and pursued righteousness in all matters. In his kingdom, he levied reasonable taxes and only spent the revenue on that which created greater prosperity for his people. Since the beginning of his reign, peace prevailed with all the neighboring kingdoms and their commonwealth flourished. He showed immense love to all of his family and great respect to all of his servants: the cooks, gardeners, guards, and chambermaids, especially the young chambermaids, never dwelling upon their fairness with a heart of covetousness; although, being a venerable man, thoughts of their youth and beauty did cross his mind; however, he treated those alluring thoughts as birds flying over head never allowing them to nest in his hair; nevertheless, one night in his bedchamber while asleep in his cozy warm bed, the flames in his fireplace blew out. The King shivered from a cold chill and pulled up his blankets around his neck while next to his bed, hovering quietly over him stood a shadow, an unearthly being from a blistering dry place, leaning in close and whispering into his ear tantalizing thoughts of one of his lovely chambermaids.

The next morning, the King's thoughts of this young maiden and of her beauty and of her purity and of her delightful scent tortured him throughout the day. Every time she wandered into his presence, he could hear his thoughts clearly, whispering, *'Look upon her beauty, her long black hair, and her soft neck. Long to gaze into her sparkling blue eyes, crave to kiss her soft lips, and desire to hold her swaying hips.'*

The King abhorred his errant thoughts of her and battled the temptation to exploit his sovereign power to gratify his selfish desires. That day, he spent much time on his knees praying before the Cross hanging in the castle sanctuary. Again, that night as he slept, the black creature whispered sensuous notions worming into his mind and at that time just before daybreak when one is neither asleep nor awake, the shadowy being with the crooked neck spoke to him again of illicit desires and of gratifying those desires. Upon rising and throughout that day, the incessant whispering spoke of ways and whys and whens the King could and should pursue these murmured depravities, saying, *'Thou art King; wield thy power; take her.'* At first, the King thought these thoughts strange. They sounded like they emanated from a strained voice not his own, though over time, hearing the incessant utterances, he eventually came to believe it was his soul speaking to him. All day, every day, for a month of days, the shadowy creature muttered to the King word paintings of lewdness and debauchery, hissing, '*Thou want to, thou need to, thou shalt.*'

After a season of hearing, thinking, and fantasizing, and on a cold winter night with many fires heating the cold and drafty castle, the honorable King approached the young and beautiful maiden, the girl of his feverish desire, by knocking on her bedchamber door, and said, "Oh, chambermaid … ."

She heard her King, immediately opened her bedchamber door, and said, "Yes, Majesty. How can I serve thee?"

Her beauty and countenance overwhelmed his senses as he asked her, "What is thy name?"

"Amoria," she replied still wondering, yet suspecting the reason the King stood at her door.

"Thy name is lovely. Amoria, Amoria, Amoria. I like the way it tickles and then rolls off my tongue. I dreameth of thee whilst asleep and I thinketh of thee whilst awake. For thee, my heart acheth and for thee, my loins hummeth like a hive of honeybees."

"But Sire," she replied with trepidation and a wavering voice, "I cannot be beholden to thee, for—I am beholden to another." Closing her door a little, she continued, "His name is Philip. He is one of your mightiest soldiers, protecting our Kingdom. We shalt be married in two days on the day of worship."

The King trembled. His gallant spirit wrestled with his iniquitous flesh. He tightly shut his eyes blinding himself to her splendor. His nose exhaled her alluring scent. He heard the raspy, whispering voice within his soul say, *Thou art King! Your subjects are beholden first and foremost to the King!*

He squeezed his head with both hands and shook his head. A

righteous thought swooped in like a hawk on a field mouse and slew the errant notion, saying, *Yea, thy subjects are beholden to thee, but thee, oh King, art beholden first to thy God and then thy wife.*

The King listened to the words of wisdom. He stopped trembling, opened his eyes, and yet, could still see clearly her heavenly splendor, and, yet, also saw the horrified look upon her innocent face. No longer enslaved by his desires, he broke the chains of lust and embraced reason. He stepped back from the girl and with firm resolve and humility, said, "Please, dear child, forgive me for my words. I fell prey to an evil spirit. I regret that I have frightened thee. In a few days, when thou shalt be married, the King and the Queen, after our mid-day meal, invite thee and thine husband to stand before my throne where I shalt bless thy bond of matrimony before thy family and friends."

Amoria said, "My King, I knoweth my beauty and countenance to be enchanting to all men, and I have lived in fear that thee might command me to do things against my will. I have seen thine eyes fixed upon me and have watched thy breaths quicken. I have been beseeching our Lord, asking that thee live as thee always have in an honorable and noble way. I am fortunate and grateful that ye have chosen the path of righteousness. I will accept thy gracious invitation, and will bring my new husband, and invite our families and friends to thy castle. We shall kneel before thy throne as thee, oh great King, blesses our bond of holy matrimony."

The King bid Amoria, "Good night," turned on his heels and strolled through the castle to the bedchamber of his wife, Catherine, the Queen.

Amoria closed her bedchamber door, crawled into her bed, and slept peacefully.

The King smiled as he entered the Queen's room for he had fought a horrendous battle of spirit, mind, and body—and he was triumphant! She sat before a vast mirror brushing out her long dark hair cascading down her back as her white silken night clothes floated to the floor. Her splendor glowed in the candlelight while his love for her swelled in his heart. He strolled up behind her, leaned in, and kissed her on her cheek. Then, while touching her bare shoulder, and breathing in her enticing scent, he whispered in her ear, "My lovely wife, my endearing Queen, my cherished love, tonight and forever, I am yours and thou art mine!"

Additional books by Steven Hagy
Available online and at your local bookseller.

Stop. Look over your shoulder. See the faces. Some embrace faith, courage, and compassion. Others employ desperate means. Those who endure bask in the sunshine. They are the faces in the light.

Thirteen short stories and a novella—action, romance, drama, humor, and suspense.

A riveting page-turner!

Exhilarating and heartwarming!

A literary journey you will always remember!

- Troubled woman suffers mind scream.

- Earthquake victim experiences puzzling events.

- Forsaken skull screams from the grave.

- Unhappy marriage receives eerie second chance.

- Civil engineer sees something odd in the mirror.

- Drunk dialer wishes he had never called.

- Regular guy foresees lottery's lucky numbers.

- Bully terrorizes southern neighborhood.

- Highway fatality keeps ghostly pact.

- Dark and cold demon taunts godly man.

- Winemaker writes love letters from the King's dungeon.

- Strange roadkill terrifies man—and other stories.

Available online and at your local bookseller.

S top. Look over your shoulder. See the faces. Sure, there are a few happy people, rejoicing in their sunshine, but also, there are those hurting souls who are hiding behind their feigned smiles, lost in a fog of pain, woe, and confusion. They are the Faces in the Fog. Nineteen short stories: action, romance, sci-fi, drama, humor, horror, and suspense. Edgy, thrilling, and heartwarming—this book has it all.

- Distraught skydiver contemplates suicide.
- Desperate sushi chef prepares toxic blowfish.
- Grotesque demon taunts godly man.
- Bees terrorize high school football players.
- Love blooms in an enchanted garden.
- Foreign correspondent interviews terrorist.
- Oilrig mechanic finds just a hand.
- All the cell phones ring at once.
- Dying mom makes last wish.
- Obese man discovers his destiny.
- Road rage erupts on clogged freeway.
- Son struggles with his father's death.
- Deaf-mute kid goes missing.
- Expiring old man establishes his life stamp.
- Hypercritical man loses eyesight—and other stories.

Available online and at your local bookseller.

Pirates and clipper ships are the setting for this seafaring story about the turbulent life of sailor Jonathan Bastell Meen. Born the son of a wealthy shipping magnate, Meen sails to exotic ports around the world. When he's not at sea, he lives in an opulent chateau, until evil deeds and catastrophic events rob him of all that he loves. Overcome with debilitating grief, savage jealousy, and rage, he leads a brash mutiny and becomes the captain of the brawny Mendocino. He sinks further into the atrocities of piracy, pillaging ships of the Pacific with his band of cutthroats, until a string of disasters and fateful consequences force him to fight for his own survival.

www.ingramcontent.com/pod-product-compliance
Lightning Source LLC
Chambersburg PA
CBHW060344030726
47497CB00003B/592